The Trophy
TAKER

SARAH FLINT

An Aria Book

First published in the UK in 2017 by Head of Zeus Ltd
This paperback edition published in the UK in 2019 by Head of Zeus Ltd

This is a work of fiction. All characters, organisations,
and events portrayed in this novel are either products of
the author's imagination or are used fictitiously.

9 7 5 3 1 2 4 6 8

A catalogue record for this book is available from
the British Library.

ISBN (PB): 9781788549899
ISBN (E): 9781786690708

Typeset by Silicon Chips

Printed and bound in Great Britain by
CPI Group (UK) Ltd, Croydon CRO 4YY

Head of Zeus Ltd
First Floor East
5–8 Hardwick Street
London EC1R 4RG

WWW.HEADOFZEUS.COM

To all the people I've worked with, whose job it is to deal with all the people I write about.

Prologue

32 years ago

The bride looked beautiful that day. 'Radiant' was how she was described by all who witnessed her slow glide up the aisle on the arm of her proud father. The church was full, each person straining to catch a glimpse of her gown, the smile she wore, the look on her bridegroom's face as he turned to take in the totality of her love for him.

His eyes flicked from one to the other, watching for that moment, that second of pure delight. How he hated it. It was the moment when he knew he had finally lost. It was the split-second reinforcement that he was always the one to be overlooked.

The service had started now. He wanted his love to be the impediment to their marriage but he stayed quiet. He heard the words of the vows as they were spoken, wishing they were being made to him. *Till death do us part.*

She turned towards her new husband and they kissed, their lips sealing his fate. He felt his anger soar. He stared, enraged, as they stayed in their embrace for far too long, her lips now sealing her own fate.

He could feel his heart beating wildly as they pulled apart and smiled into each other's eyes, blissfully unaware of his wrath. They turned and walked down the aisle, hand in hand, alive with happiness, passing all the joyful people on either side, out, out into the bright sunshine of the day.

He fixed his eyes on her as she left, the way her long, blonde hair cascaded down her back. His heart became calm, numb even, and under his breath he muttered to himself.

'You ripped my heart out, Susan. One day I'll have yours.'

1

October 2016

Wind whipped at the top of the trees, sending the upper branches into a frenzy as he drove slowly towards the rear of the graveyard. He stopped, lowering the window with his gloved hand, and breathed in the scent of tiny tornadoes of falling leaves, as they swirled around the edges of the darkened roadway. They smelt wet, musty, earthy; as decaying as the air all around them.

He walked to the rear of the car, grabbed his tool bag and then hoisted her up off the plastic sheeting on to his shoulders, carrying her along the well-worn footway. She was heavier than he had imagined, almost a dead weight.

An ancient lamp post lit his way, its metallic casing rattling harshly, its light wavering and dancing with the breeze. To his left, a row of small blue teddy bears lined the edge of a tiny grave, the words of love on its tombstone starkly illustrating the agony of losing such a young child. Several vases of colourful flowers and toys had blown over, their contents spilling out across the memorial. He saw them and he wanted to restore them to their original positions. The child had done no harm to anyone. It didn't deserve to die, as she did.

The wind was getting stronger. Tree boughs slapped against high stone tombs, a fox skulked out from behind a copse of elms, standing stationary to sniff at the ripples of air as he had done. Cut flowers tumbled along the pathways, mixing with beloved graveside treasures, until they ended up tossed together and thrown into corners. The wind would mask any sound he might make. It was good.

He continued to walk, struggling to keep her unconscious body hefted high. He was nearly there now. The part of the cemetery to which he was headed was shielded by high hedges on all sides, the hustle and bustle of the city held at bay. Here within the sanctuary of the perimeter walls all sound was muted, all sights guarded; it was perfect for privacy. Perfect to give him time with her, time that he never had before, that he had always wanted. He felt her body twitch slightly; maybe she was coming round.

The moon was nearly full, its light bright, intermittently eclipsed by the movement of the clouds as they scudded across the sky, harried by the wind. The path led up a slight hill to his chosen spot. He turned and checked there was no one in sight, stopping momentarily to admire the contours of London's iconic landmarks, silhouetted across his eyeline; a fitting backdrop for the act to come. They were all alone. Through the gap in the hedges and they were there.

He heaved her down off his shoulders and laid her across a smooth horizontal tombstone. Her eyes were closed as if in sleep but her muscles twitched involuntarily; she had yet to properly emerge from her comatose state. Quickly he bound her wrists and ankles, and covered her mouth, watching for any further sign of movement. None came.

He leant over, fanning her beautiful hair out across her shoulders. It felt soft, silky almost, but shorter now than it had been when they'd first met, when he'd fallen in love with her. He followed the neckline of her blouse down towards her breasts, pale in the partial light, catching a hint of her perfume, flowery and delicate, no doubt chosen by her husband. He breathed it in, letting the scent fan his senses, feeling the familiar pangs of jealousy and injustice stir.

His anger awakened, he bent down and opened the bag. His tools were ready, clean, sterile and sharpened in preparation. He took them out one by one, the stiletto blade, the hunting knife, the rib-cutters, and laid them out across the gravestone. He couldn't help smiling to himself. She deserved what she was about to get; every second of pain, every moment, reliving how different it could have been.

A strong gust of wind sent a small branch crashing down next to her. She stirred slightly and opened her eyes, blinking back even the faded light from the sky. She was confused, her brow creased as she struggled to comprehend what was happening. Her head turned towards him and she stared into his face, seeing the familiar features but not understanding as yet why she was there. But did she really recognise him? He didn't know, but he hoped she did because then she might fully appreciate what was to happen.

She tried to shift her body upright but the bindings prevented her easy movement and she was still not yet fully in control of her limbs. She rolled on to her side but he was on to her, his strong, muscular frame pinning her easily back against the tombstone. She tried to struggle but her efforts were futile. He climbed astride her, acknowledging his growing desire. He wanted her. He always had and he always would but she had made her choice and if he couldn't have her, then nor would anyone else.

He could see the fear in her now; real and intense, her eyes full of terror, burning bright like the fires of hell. He took her left hand, running his fingers over hers, through hers, one by one; feeling the softness of her skin and seeing how well-manicured and beautifully painted each nail appeared. Her hands trembled at his touch. Was it passion or fear? He didn't know. He came to her ring finger and saw at once the gold band that symbolised her attachment to another. His heart froze at the sight. His mind was made up.

Picking up the rib-cutters, he slotted the offending finger between the blades and forced them shut. Her finger dropped on to the slab beneath her, blood spurting from her hand. Her mouth moved open and shut with shock but the gag stopped any sound from escaping. She hadn't expected this. She deserved the pain, but he had always loved her and he couldn't be too cruel.

He leant back, his weight pressing her hips to the stone, and spread her jacket open wide, slitting her thin jumper apart with the hunting knife, before carefully unbuttoning her blouse and slipping the blade through the fabric of her bra. Reverently, he peeled the lacy fabric to the sides, taking in his first sight of her breasts; bare flesh, pale and inviting. Her skin was velvety to the touch, fresh and sweet-smelling, gentle against his lips. Her body tensed at the press of his mouth, bucking against his touch. He stopped, his desire immediately waning. She didn't want him now; and she hadn't wanted him then. Her last chance was spent.

He closed his eyes against the sight of her body. He could never have her properly, not the way he would have liked; not if the feeling was not mutual. He had waited this long in the hope she would respond but now her destiny was sealed.

Swivelling round, he picked up the stiletto blade, weaving it slowly across her eyeline. Her pupils followed it, transfixed, as he moved it over her head, her body, her neck and then slowly back down until it was over her heart.

The blade pressed against her skin, the indentation rising and falling with the pressure of the point as her heart beat against it. Her eyes pleaded for mercy, her voice muffled within the binding as she shook her head from side to side, apparently trying to establish an escape route. There was none.

The time had come for her to die. He cared nothing for her fear. She deserved everything she got for her betrayal. Leaning forward, he let his chest rest against the handle of the blade, allowing the metal to pierce her skin. Blood sprang up at the point, pooling around the cut. He lifted his body slightly, excited now at the sight of more blood. She started to wriggle, the desire to live fuelling her last few desperate jerks, but it was too late; far, far too late. The look in her eyes was just as compelling as it had been all those years ago, just as compelling as when he'd found her more recently, but instead of love, they were full of terror.

With a glance at his tools laid out ready for him, he turned and stared emotionlessly at her, before dropping forward again, his body forcing the stiletto blade straight through her heart.

2

DC Charlie Stafford eyed the custody screen with satisfaction. A charge of GBH and robbery was a great result, especially after the four solid months of hard work she'd put into this case. It was also particularly good to see that the Crown Prosecution Service had agreed to her application for the offence charged to be shown as having been racially aggravated. It was a difficult offence to prove but it carried a greater sentence and it was what her unit, the Community Support Unit, was tasked to investigate.

Led by Detective Inspector Geoffrey Hunter, or Hunter as he was better known, the CSU dealt with any cases involving domestic violence or offences targeting persons for their race, faith, sexual orientation or disability. The majority of their work related to domestic incidents, but in the last few years more and more victims of hate crimes were finding the strength to come forward. Taboos were being broken, victims becoming braver. Charlie's unit was therefore becoming increasingly busy, their caseload greater and more varied and their diligence, persistence and hard work noticed by the local Senior Management Team at Lambeth. After their recent success in dealing with a particularly disturbing series of murders, the reputation of their team, and in particular Charlie, was heightened to such an extent that members of the unit, sometimes all of them, were seconded to assist the Murder Investigation Teams. It hadn't been easy though.

The case in front of her now was as close to being a murder as was possible without the victim actually having died. For Charlie it had become almost a personal crusade to identify the perpetrator and get him incarcerated. She stood next to the suspect as the charge was read out.

'On Friday 17th June 2016 at Estreham Road, SW16, you unlawfully and maliciously wounded Mr Moses Sinkler and the offence was racially aggravated within the terms of section 28 of the Crime and Disorder Act 1998. You do not have to say anything, but it may harm your defence if you do not mention now, something which you later rely on in court. Anything you do say may be given in evidence.'

Cornell Miller sniffed, wiped the back of his hand across his face and looked towards the clock, making it obvious he didn't care as the caution was read out. He was thirty-eight years old, solidly built, with over six feet of rippling muscle, having spent his last term of imprisonment working out in the prison gym. He pulled his T-shirt up so that his stomach was exposed, rock hard and toned, and scratched languidly at the light smattering of fair hair that covered his skin, winking towards Charlie as he did so. She ignored him, instead concentrating on the words of the custody sergeant.

'You are further charged that on Friday 17th June 2016 you did rob Mr Moses Sinkler in Estreham Road, SW16. That is contrary to section 8 Theft Act 1968.'

He had nothing to say, he never did, until the time came for his solicitor to ask for bail. This time though even his solicitor's plea was lacklustre. There was no way Cornell Miller would be walking the streets for a good few years if Charlie had anything to do with it. He was scum. Pure unequivocal racist scum and the public, particularly those in the black and Asian communities, needed to be protected from him.

The case had initially been assigned to her office because of the racist element to it. Her boss, Hunter, had given it to her to investigate and tonight was the culmination of all her work. She eyed Miller as he scratched his belly again, thinking about what he had done. She had thought of little else, since reading the details the first time.

It had been 5.15 a.m. when he had struck; 5.15 a.m., when there was hardly a soul on the streets to hear his victim's screams; when there was no one to witness the excessive, unnecessary violence meted out on an unassuming, hard-working Jamaican man, nearing the end of an extended career spent coaching kids to play football. Moses Sinkler had been nipping to the local cashpoint to get twenty quid to give to the missus for some groceries when Cornell Miller had spotted him. Miller was coming down from a crack-cocaine high and needed some more cash to score some heroin before he went to bed, or else he'd never sleep – and he hadn't slept for days.

He'd selected the venue well. It was the perfect place for a quick hit. A quiet backstreet with a remote cash machine, tucked into the rear approach to the local train station, still silent before the first train of the day at half five. He'd waited for the old Jamaican to withdraw his money; waited and watched and hoped that it would be a decent haul. Silently he'd taken a last draw of his cigarette, before grinding it into the ground and following Moses back across the road, stalking him like a predator, before he attacked.

But it was the manner of the assault that had really upset Charlie. A scare would have been all that was needed. Moses Sinkler was not a fighter. At seventy-two, he was too old to exchange blows; he would have done what he was told, handed over the cash, capitulated in the face of a much larger, stronger opponent. Cornell Miller barely said a word; his Stanley knife did all his talking, slicing across Moses' face, neck, shoulders and back, time and time again as the old man screamed out in agony.

Miller's only words to Moses, before snatching the single twenty pound note from his victim's hand were a threat. 'Tell the police and you'll be a dead nigger. I'll be back for you and all your black bastard kids.'

He had then walked nonchalantly from the scene as his victim lay barely conscious in a growing pool of blood. If it hadn't been for an early morning dog walker hearing his cries, Moses Sinkler would most likely have bled to death. Only the fabric of his light summer body warmer had saved the wounds to his skin from being deeper, cutting through larger arteries, causing even greater blood loss. Ninety-eight stitches later and after several weeks in hospital, he had emerged a broken man, his body sewn back together but his confidence mortally wounded. He never returned to work and was too afraid to even leave his house, fearing a sortie from the safety of his home might bring him into contact with his assailant.

Charlie hated the person who had done this to Moses even before she had worked out who it was. The pure evil of the gratuitous and unnecessary violence had sickened her and she had pulled out all the stops to catch the perpetrator. She'd visited Moses many times and watched his struggle back to physical fitness. She only wished she could help his return to full mental strength.

As time had gone on she'd built a stronger and stronger case; Cornell Miller's DNA from a cigarette end found nearby, CCTV putting him heading in the right direction, phone records showing him in the same location, even a jacket with Moses Sinkler's bloodstain on the sleeve, found at his home at the time of her suspect's arrest. Everything to put him at the right place at the right time but, frustratingly, nothing to say it was actually him. Moses had been so traumatised, he'd been unable to pick Miller out in a line-up, even from behind one-way glass. In fact he'd been so distressed it had taken a great deal of persuasion to even get him to the identity parade. When the time came to pick out the suspect who had done this to him, his fear had stopped him looking into the faces of any of the men there. He couldn't do it. He couldn't look at them, and he couldn't pick out his assailant.

Cornell Miller had laughed when told he had not been identified but with the evidence mounting that he'd been close by, he'd not been stupid either. Admitting to his presence at the scene, Miller's defence was that he'd been walking home from a night out and had seen the man lying in a pool of blood and gone over to help, but then realising how serious it was and that he had a criminal record, had panicked and run away in case people thought it was him. But it was him. Every smile, word, expression, movement confirmed to Charlie it was. She had a sixth sense when it came to guilt or innocence and her sixth sense was in overdrive.

Now, as Charlie watched him in the custody office, she knew with even more certainty that he was guilty. She just hoped that when it got to Crown Court the twelve men and women of the jury would listen to their own sixth sense, as well as the evidence, and find him guilty. Cornell Miller, with not a shred of compassion or a pang of conscience, had nearly killed a man for twenty quid. Charlie wanted justice for Moses and that meant putting Miller away for life.

She stared at his back as he swaggered towards his cell in front of her. He was not getting bail and would remain in custody until his trip to see the magistrates the next morning.

'See you in court,' he said, pulling his hand up to his head in a mock salute, before throwing himself down on to his mattress.

'Looking forward to it... and to the verdict.' She stepped back and took hold of the thick metal cell door, swinging it shut with more force than usual so that the heavy thud reverberated along the corridor. 'You'd better get used to that sound. It's all you're going to be hearing for a good long time.'

The man had almost finished now. He looked down at his handiwork and was pleased at the bloody spectacle.

It had taken some time but he had enjoyed every second of it. With each victim he had become more skilled, more able to admire the intricacies of the human body. He liked the precise nature at the beginning of the job, the way each layer that was peeled back revealed more, the way he always finished with a flourish. It fitted him. A man of many emotions, needs, loves, passions; strip one away and another would show. Strip them all away and all that was left was a shell, a cavity that could not be filled.

He packed his tools back in his bag carefully and bent down to collect the souvenirs he had laid to one side in a plastic bag. She was special and he wanted something to remind him of her, but then he always did. He loved to look at his trophies, see how they fared with time, recall each of his victims and the reason he had picked them. They were cool to the touch now and he didn't like it. He started to walk towards his car, feeling the cold of the bag permeating through the plastic gloves he still wore.

With each step he remembered the promise he had made to himself all those years before, as she'd walked away.

Opening the bag he took the larger of his souvenirs out and threw it to one side. His had been tossed away – now it was time for him to do the same to hers.

Charlie couldn't sleep that night.

Sirens screamed all around her, blue lights flashed and the sound of tyres screeching along half-empty roads filled the night. Something was happening. She didn't know what, but she could feel the emotions trembling through the freezing air. Someone, somewhere was breathing their last and it wasn't a peaceful death. Her intuition was at work again.

By the time she had got back to her small rented flat in Clapham, South London, the nightmares were already beginning to take shape. Moses Sinkler was being swallowed up into the darkness, his body writhing in pain, blood spewing out across the concrete. Cornell Miller stood above him, leaning against a wall; a cigarette dangling from his mouth, laughing as he spat at him.

Her current job always followed her home, like a rabid stalker determined to get its pound of flesh. Victims from old and new cases mixed together; visions of bodies in the earth, children, mothers, blood creeping across carpets, roads, clotting in pools, always ending in the same way. Victims like Moses Sinkler, Richard Hubbard, Helena McPherson and Greg Leigh-Matthews would begin to merge into one; spinning round and round, out of reach, down into murky water. Those responsible would stand watching the vortex, laughing, before they all converged together, flailing arms tugging at each other, gasping for breath, trying to get to the surface, swimming and splashing wildly until exhaustion sucked them down into the darkness. Finally she would see Jamie, her little brother, always an arm's length away; so close but yet unable to reach her outstretched fingers, clawing at the water, with bubbles escaping from his nose and mouth as he called out her name. Over and over and over until everything went silent and he was drifting downwards, his eyes closed, his limbs still.

It seemed to be worse if she climbed into her bed, as if to be comfortable was to forget; and she could never forget and was never permitted forgiveness. She plugged in the nightlight and grabbed her iPod, scrolling down to her 'favourites' playlist. Sometimes light and sound helped her to sleep; sometimes nothing did. The job offered counselling these days for dealing with traumatic events but she dared not go. At the age of twenty nine and with nine years' service, she'd already dealt with more horror and tragedy than most people would see in a lifetime. If she began to talk, she feared she would never stop. It was better to remain silent and seal each trauma in a separate compartment in her brain. Some things were better left undisturbed. She could cope with the regular nightmares, but if they penetrated her daytime hours she would be in trouble.

She pulled the duvet off the bed and slumped down on to the huge brown and beige beanbag that took up the corner of her lounge. It had moved with her wherever she lived; too big for most people to entertain in their houses but just the right size for her and Jamie to squeeze into for sleepovers. Like the huge maroon sofa at her mum's house, it was part of their previous life that must always remain, the cement that kept her security intact.

She set the iPod to random and pressed the play button. Every word of every song was imprinted in her memory but she liked the surprise of not knowing which song was next.

'When the Going Gets Tough, the Tough Get Going', sounded out through the earphones, as clearly as when she and her brother had first heard it, on their way out on explorations in the mid 90's. It had pretty much become her anthem after his death, the song that had motivated her to join the police. It was what had kept her going when all she wanted was to have taken his place. It was what made her fight for the likes of Moses Sinkler. The day Charlie ceased to crave justice for the victims would be the day she handed in her warrant card.

She closed her eyes but still she was unsettled. Maybe it had been Cornell Miller's swagger or the knowledge of what he had done. Maybe it was the sirens signalling another victim; of that she was sure. It would only be a few hours before she returned to duty. She felt the darkness blurring from pitch black into a lighter grey; warmer now than before. The music was calming her. Jamie was with her and she was not alone anymore. She settled into partial sleep, knowing instinctively that she would not be able to rest fully while the night's traumas were still ongoing.

Whatever was happening now would be waiting for her in the morning.

3

Cornell Miller lay against the clean white bed sheets, his eyes closed, and chuckled quietly. How easy had that been?

Part one was complete; wait until the early hours of the morning when the cops are tired, then rip your T-shirt into a strip, tie it round your neck moderately tightly, hold your breath and lie still on the floor of your cell. The police gaoler wouldn't know how long you had been there, whether thirty seconds or thirty minutes, and in the ensuing panic you were guaranteed a trip to A&E; just in case. When the A&E happened to be at Kings College Hospital, the local hospital you've attended all your life, well that's just a bonus.

He was now lying in a curtained-off cubicle, wholly satisfied with his treatment so far. Part two was to follow shortly. He needed to get going. The medication the police doctor had given was beginning to wear off. He was craving a proper fix. He twisted his hands in the cuffs, dragging his skin hard against the metal, feeling them digging into the soft skin around his wrists. He half opened his eyes, glancing round at his two police guards. The woman was older, skinny, with sunken cheeks and a pinched expression. She wouldn't have looked out of place in his normal setting, squashed into the corner of a dirty sofa in a crack house. She was eyeing him with a look that said she knew what he was up to, she'd experience of the games they played. He would have to be careful with this one.

On his other side sat a man mountain, thickset, thick-necked, his head shaved to show a snowstorm of scars across his scalp. His sleeves were rolled as high as they could be, his uniform shirt barely fitting over his huge biceps. Several darkly coloured tattoos peeped out from underneath the roll-up. He was easily pigeonholed; definitely more brawn than brain; more Neanderthal than nous. He looked as thick mentally as his carefully honed physique. This was more like it; the kind that would think that just his sheer presence would deter any escape attempts. The kind that would be slow to see what was happening and even slower to take up the chase.

He closed his eyes again and moaned loudly.

The man mountain stood, as if the noise signalled his need to assert himself. He peered out from behind the curtain and beckoned a nurse over. 'When can he be seen, so that we can get out of here?'

His voice was deep and his manner abrupt. The nurse responded accordingly.

'He'll be seen when it's his turn to be seen.'

She turned as if to leave, but just as she was about to walk off, they were joined by a white-coated doctor. He wore a stethoscope around his neck and an expression of irritable impatience on his face. He obviously had a few points on his licence and liked to treat the police in the manner that he felt he'd been treated. He would have kept them waiting usually, as a matter of principle; however, the man mountain was his least favourite type of officer and he wanted him gone. Too thick and stupid to have a mind of his own. He was the sort to give out penalties without any thought for the welfare of the motorist.

Miller groaned out loud again. They both looked towards him and then with a flourish the doctor threw back the curtain and walked in. It was all going beautifully to plan. He let out another moan, this time louder, and rolled his arms in the cuffs. The doctor leant across and lifted his hands up, staring at the red wheals around his wrists.

'Get these cuffs off him while I carry out my examination.'

The policewoman was twitchy. She didn't want him released. Her voice was high and whiny and the doctor easily overruled her.

'I said get them off now or I'll move on. I've plenty of other people to see.'

Miller could hardly keep the grin from appearing on his lips as the doctor spoke. The man was doing his job for him. He lifted his hands and watched gleefully as the man mountain removed them. After all, who would try to escape from such an imposing guard?

He let the doctor check the marks around his neck and wrists, take his blood pressure and pulse, and then he answered what questions he could. It was clear that the doctor was on his side; two against two, an equal match. He was nearly finished now.

The doctor stepped back and started to write his notes up, leaving space for the man mountain to move past him and squeeze over to one side. That only left the skinny policewoman on the other. He could see her hand hovering over her baton. She could read him well; but it didn't matter, her size was the only significant thing. The huge officer was leaning over him now, grasping his nearest hand and placing the hard metal cuff back on. Miller held his breath. The time was right. He felt the man mountain relax slightly as the first cuff was on. He raised his other hand as if to allow the officer his other wrist but as he was about to take hold of it, Miller grabbed the metal restraints with his free hand, lifting both hands up against the man mountain's grip. The officer grunted and lunged forward but Miller was too quick.

Leaping up off the bed, he swung his two hands round, complete with metal cuff, before bringing them down with a crack against the policewoman's upturned face. She staggered back, clutching her nose as blood sprayed across the sheets, her baton crashing down on the floor. She'd been more switched on than her thick colleague; just not quick enough.

He gave her a shove, barging her out of the way and then he had a clear run. The man mountain was trapped behind the doctor, who sprang back to let him through, but the thick hunk was far too slow. He was on his way, navigating through the emergency room and waiting areas towards the exit. Everyone was watching but nobody intervened. Nobody ever did.

He knew the way well. He could hear the man mountain shouting down his radio for assistance but he was wasting his time. By the time any backup arrived, he'd be swallowed up into the local estate, the maze of walkways and concrete landings easily concealing his route from policemen or police dogs.

He slammed out the exit into the darkness of the night. It was just gone 4 a.m.; the air was chilled and the cold slapped him hard across the face. His breath was coming quick and shallow but he didn't need much oxygen; he was running on adrenalin, pumped and psyched up to the maximum. Nothing could stop him. He ran on until the sound of the chasing officer merged into the distance. He'd made it out and he wasn't about to go back inside, whatever that fucking DC Stafford thought. Anyway, she'd have to catch him first.

He thought of their last conversation. The stupid bitch. He'd never plead guilty. Ever. Why would you, when even the smallest cock-up by the prosecution could see you walking? Maybe he should get hold of the snivelling black bastard who'd made the allegation in the first place, Moses Sinkler. A little bit of pressure and a few threats to him and his family and he'd be sure to drop the case. Maybe he should have finished him off properly when he'd had the chance.

He slowed down as he came to a small parade of shops. A charity shop nestled in the middle and several bags of clothing were stacked up by the front door. Quickly he split one of the bags open and found it full of men's clothing. He was in luck. He chose some items; a nearly new T-shirt, a black woollen jumper, a nice thick parka-style jacket, complete with fur-lined hood. It was a little scruffy and a touch on the large side, but who cared, if it was free. The handcuffs were still attached to one wrist; they made a useful weapon but it wouldn't do for them to be spotted.

He pulled the parka sleeve over them. He'd get one of his burglar mates to remove them with a set of bolt croppers later. He'd seen it done before.

He started to walk, watching all the time for any sign of the Old Bill. An alleyway ran along the side of the shops. He slid into it as a police car turned into the road. They hadn't seen him, and anyway, they wouldn't recognise him hidden within his new hooded jacket. But he didn't want to take the chance.

Sitting down on a low wall at the back of the shops, he made a mental list of what he needed. First was money; he had to get some cash to buy his gear. He needed crack and heroin now; the cramps were starting to take a grip of his guts.

Rooting around in a rubbish area, he found an old glass Red Stripe beer bottle. He held it by the neck and smashed it on the brickwork, lifting it up in the dim light of a nearby street lamp. The jagged edges glistened menacingly with the remnants of the beer. He liked its look.

The sky was beginning to lighten on the horizon now, a thin flaky glow just beginning to rise and grow in strength. It was his favourite time of the night on the streets.

He held the broken bottle up to the light again, feeling the adrenalin starting to mount. He liked the idea of the Red Stripe too; it was his calling card.

All he needed now was to find the next victim.

4

'How the hell could he have escaped?' Charlie was incredulous. 'After all the time and effort it took me to get him charged. I don't bloody believe it.'

She'd given up trying to sleep and had eventually got up, slipped on her old trainers and jogged in. Twenty minutes later, after tweaking her right leg in the final sprint, she had been stretching out her calves on the cycle rail at the front of Lambeth HQ when she'd heard the news of Miller's escape from one of the home-going night shift.

She'd taken the stairs two at a time, before bursting into her office and now, at just gone 7 a.m. she was standing in her running gear, sweat prickling on her temples and down the base of her back.

Bet was the only one in their office so far, her own body clock waking her at an ungodly hour every day, whether she wanted to be woken or not. She was normally the first one in; her self-appointed jobs being to get the first hot drinks of the day organised and to read through what had been happening since their last duty, so as to brief everyone on their arrival.

Bet indicated the night duty occurrence book, now highlighted on her computer where all the events of the previous night were logged. Charlie slumped down in front of it, massaging the back of her leg as she stared at the screen. The details made grim reading. She scanned through the circumstances, shaking her head as she noted the removal of the handcuffs.

'Bloody doctors. Unless it's life or death, they shouldn't be allowed to dictate when and how we use handcuffs. They're our prisoners and our responsibility, even when in hospital. Now because they insisted his handcuffs be removed, Miller's disappeared and worse still, he's got another victim to his name.' She squinted at the name of the WPC on the report. 'How is Annie?'

Bet shuffled stiffly across to the kettle, holding the base of her back. After slipping on the stairs recently she'd bruised her coccyx and the ensuing inactivity had resulted in a little weight gain. She was starting to feel all of her fifty-plus years and with Halloween fast approaching she'd commented recently that her usual apple-shaped figure had expanded more to the size of a pumpkin.

'Poor girl, she's got a broken cheekbone and badly bruised right eye, but she'll live. She's cursing herself for not having reacted quickly enough when she had a gut feeling he was going to try something. But… Annie's not the only victim by the sound of things. About an hour ago, uniform were called out to a robbery, not too far from Kings College Hospital. Black female victim slashed across the face with a broken bottle, racially abused and had her handbag stolen.

It fits the description and M.O. of Miller to a T. She's at K.C.H. now.'

'For fuck's sake.' Charlie stood up abruptly. 'And there'll be more. He won't care because now he's been charged he knows he's going back to prison anyway. He's got nothing to lose.' She felt a small bead of sweat trickle down the back of her neck and wiped it away angrily. 'I'm going to jump in the shower while it's still early, Bet, then I'll phone Moses and update him that Miller's on the loose. Hopefully we'll have more idea about the recent attack too. If Hunter's interested, I'll see if he wants me to pop to the hospital and see the latest victim.'

She took the mug of tea that Bet was holding out, almost like a peace offering, and smiled grimly.

'Nothing like hitting the ground running on a Monday morning.'

Fifteen minutes later Charlie was back, with wet hair dripping down the collar of a hastily thrown on tailored black shirt. It fitted a little more snugly these days than she would have liked; testament to the dual motherly influences of Bet and her own mother Meg. She logged on to her computer and read the details of the most recent attack. It certainly had all the hallmarks of another vicious Cornell Miller robbery.

She then typed Miller's name into the search engine of the Police National Computer. His name came up immediately. There weren't too many Cornell Millers thankfully; either in the list or, in her opinion, on the streets. He wasn't, as yet, shown as wanted. She would have to get that done straight away, in case he was stopped further afield. She hoped that by now all the officers in Lambeth would be on the lookout for him; after all, he'd assaulted one of their own, never mind what he'd done to Moses and the latest victim.

Miller's record was long. At the age of thirty-eight, he'd notched up nearly thirty years of arrests and convictions, having started prior to even the ten-year age of responsibility. She didn't bother looking through all his convictions. She already knew them off by heart, having listed them when doing the paperwork for his charge. It had totally depressed her then, and now there were several further violent offences. It was hard to see how the justice system could have dealt so leniently with him. He needed locking up, for everybody's safety.

Scrolling through the record, she printed out the list of previous addresses and associates. Most were probably historic, but they should at least give her a good idea of the areas he might now head towards and was likely to know well, along with old friends and neighbours where he might find refuge. Next, she searched the latest intelligence, noting down the more recent places he'd been seen, stopped or arrested, as well as any mention of dealers or other users whose addresses he might be holed up in. It was doubtful he'd be signing on, knowing that DSS offices would be one of the first places police would look, but if receiving benefits direct to his bank account it was possible he'd use cash dispensers close to where he was staying. She'd contact the DSS later and find out his bank details. If he had any sense though, he would look to his past; just as she was now.

She was still collating the information when Naz and Paul came in together. Charlie turned towards them and couldn't help smiling as Paul held the door wide, giving a flamboyant bow and arm gesture to welcome Naz into the room. Naz walked through, almost regally.

'Now, don't be getting the wrong idea!' Paul said immediately, grinning towards Charlie. 'We're just good friends. Aren't we, Naz?'

Naz raised her eyebrows towards him. 'Well yes, unless you've finally realised that women really are the most physically perfect, emotionally sensitive and highly intelligent gender?' She pulled her jacket off, inadvertently revealing slightly more of her cleavage than usual before laughing and readjusting her top.

Paul made a show of looking horrified and turned away. 'No thanks, I think I'll stick to men.' He walked over to the kettle and touched it, pulling his fingers away quickly at the heat. 'Much hotter.'

They all laughed. Sabira, the last member of the team, came through the door and joined in the laughter even though there was no way she would have known what the rest of them had found so amusing.

Bet pushed Paul away and flicked the switch on the kettle again to make them all a fresh cuppa. Charlie felt some of the irritation from her earlier news slipping away. It was Monday morning. She hated Mondays; Mondays and Wednesdays – but at least they had the whole week ahead of them to get Miller back inside. Everyone would do what they could to help. They were a good team, smaller and more tightly knit than ever these days; the recent revulsion and betrayal they'd all experienced during the course of the previous case having cemented an even closer bond between them. Naz, in particular, had found it hard to re-adjust, having been deceived so totally, but they had all pulled together and were now moving on. If Charlie ever felt the need to let off steam about the horrors or frustrations of what they dealt with on a day-to-day basis, it would be to them, not a job shrink.

Charlie beckoned Naz over. She would be the perfect person to take to the hospital to visit Miller's latest victim, having experienced racial abuse herself in the past. Naz was black, feisty and proud; both of her origins as a second-generation immigrant and how she had risen above them. Her mother and grandmother were her heroines, not only for taking on the racist culture that first pervaded London on their arrival in England, but also for teaching her the importance of work and family. Her two boys were her life, although sometimes the need to get out and socialise eclipsed the monotony of motherhood. That's where her mother and grandmother came in. She wore her heart on her sleeve and was not afraid to stand up and be counted, especially if there was even a hint of racism.

Charlie admired her strength and tenacity greatly, although it seemed incredible to her that this sort of discrimination still occurred. Over the years, even with the influx of migrants of all nationalities into Lambeth, the statistics for racist crimes had remained steady, but since Charlie had joined the unit she had watched as the numbers had increased. Where previously people had lived in harmony, the rise of UKIP and the vote for Brexit had fuelled a surge in racist rhetoric, anger and resentment, which in turn had led to a steep rise in the number of reported offences. Goodness knows how many more went unreported. They were all sure it was the tip of the iceberg.

'Cornell Miller escaped from hospital last night a few hours after he was charged with the GBH and robbery on Moses.'

Naz went to open her mouth. Everybody knew how hard Charlie had worked on that particular case.

Charlie raised her hands to stop her speaking and continued. 'I know. You don't have to say anything. Fucking unbelievable. He assaulted Annie Mitchell, the girl on B shift, in the process, and it seems that he has almost certainly robbed and GBH'd a middle-aged, black woman called Marcia on her way to work this morning. She's still in Kings College Hospital having her face stitched up after the suspect, who matches the description of Miller, slashed her with a broken bottle. The number of stitches she will require is likely to run into dozens apparently. She'll be scarred for life. I was going to pop down to the hospital to see her when she's been sewn up and I was hoping that you'd come with me.'

As she spoke the door was flung open and Hunter strode in. 'Sorry, Charlie, I've just heard what happened with Miller and I know you'll be wanting to follow up the latest attack, but Naz and Sabira will have to go to the hospital for you. I've been called out to a body found and I want you with me. The Murder Investigation Team will be in soon, but they've asked me to get down there straight away to start things off. Hopefully, then we'll be able to assist in their investigation.'

Charlie was immediately curious. Although she desperately wanted to follow up the robbery allegation, who could turn down the chance of dealing with a suspicious death and all the intrigue it entailed? Her investigation was in safe hands with Naz and Sabira. She would catch up with the manhunt on Miller as soon as she was back.

'You've got five minutes to get your stuff together and then we need to get going. The body was found by an early morning jogger. Uniform are with it now and are setting up a crime scene as we speak, but I want to get there and monitor the investigation properly from the start.' He looked her up and down. 'Not too bad for a change, Charlie, though your hair is still soaked.'

'I'll be fine.' She was used to his comments about her appearance. Today's was better than usual. She ran her fingers through her hair. It was still damp and lifeless.

She waited for Hunter to disappear into his office before checking the weather outside the window. It still looked chilly. Quickly, she selected a large, grey woolly hat from a selection of multicoloured hats and caps in the cupboard next to her desk. She pulled it down over her wet hair so that it covered her whole head, grabbed some car keys from the cabinet and threw her work rucksack, containing crime scene equipment, pens and notepads, over her shoulder.

Naz and Sabira were already getting to work on the Miller case. She explained to Naz what she'd already found out, before apologising profusely for leaving her with all her work. Naz didn't mind. None of her team did. It was happily accepted that Charlie was young, single, unattached and enthusiastic and Hunter favoured her to join him. Paul and Sabira had hectic social lives and the others had family commitments outside the job. Given the choice, all except Charlie preferred to do their set hours, unless of course something important came up. Hunter would never change. He was job-pissed and Charlie was definitely following in his footsteps. They were all glad to let her.

Bet took one look at the woolly covering and shook her head. 'Not sure the boss will still think you look OK with that thing on, but hopefully he won't have time to object.'

Charlie shrugged and cocked her head, grinning. 'Oh well, at least he won't have to worry about me catching a chill.'

5

Hunter briefed Charlie as they drove.

'The body is a middle-aged, white female, about five foot three, slim to medium build, with shoulder-length, blonde hair. We don't have a positive ID on her but there is correspondence in her bag which relates to a female by the name of Susan Barton. There are officers going to her address now. The body is in quite a state by the sound of it. She's been mutilated and left out in the open. It's too early to say whether she was killed at the venue or how long she's been there, but it's fairly safe to say that it would have been some time during the night. Given it was Sunday yesterday, the cemetery would have been busy with visitors, probably until it got dark.'

'I thought West Norwood cemetery was closed to the public at night?'

'I thought the same, but apparently the gates have been broken for some time, since a lorry reversed into them.

There's twenty-four-hour access at the moment for cars and pedestrians.'

'So do we think the killer drove or brought her there on foot? It would be handy if he drove, because there's CCTV all the way up Norwood Road. We might be able to get a registration number.' Charlie was immediately optimistic. Although it was still only just gone 8 a.m. on a cold, damp October morning, the disappointment of her earlier news was fast becoming eclipsed by her thoughts of how she would solve this next case. Having said that, she was still scanning the profiles of pedestrians she passed in case she saw Miller. She had a knack of seeing a face in a crowd, even if driving past them at high speed.

They were nearly there now, the blue lights and two-tone sirens assisting their passage through the rush-hour traffic. She navigated the one-way system at Tulse Hill, watching as a train trundled slowly over the low bridge ahead of her, before veering off to the right and up the final half mile of shops and restaurants in Norwood Road. The area of West Norwood was mainly residential; pockets of council estates nestled behind streets crammed with private houses whose value had soared towards the million pound mark. It had several railway stations in close proximity, providing links straight into Central London, and as such, was the choice of many aspiring city workers. Charlie drove straight up through the main shopping street towards the cemetery, glancing up at the numerous cameras positioned all along the route. Hopefully one of these would provide details of whoever had lured their victim to her grave.

The cemetery was set back to the left, where the road split, a large church taking up the central position at the junction. Charlie took the left fork and slowed down as she saw a police van positioned across the entrance. She pulled over towards the huge stone arch and immediately noticed the black metal gate to its right, hanging askew on its hinges. The other gate was open wide. Switching the sirens off, she left the blue light flashing and waved towards the uniformed officers. They waved back and reversed the van to allow access to the outer perimeter of the crime scene.

Slowly, she drove through the arch into the cemetery, any conversation stunted by what they were about to witness. The area the cemetery covered was vast, with small roads spanning the circumference and criss-crossing through the different sections. Half a dozen police vehicles were parked up towards the back of the site, near a small hill at the very rear. Charlie made her way there and parked alongside. Now they were actually there, she was nervous. Although she'd seen blood and gore many times before, she never got used to it; and was determined never to allow the sight to become routine. Every crime generated a host of victims, each of whom was affected in different ways and would have the shock of the crime imprinted in their memories for the rest of their lives. She would never allow herself to forget this truth. She took a deep breath and opened the car door.

The stillness of the site was the first thing that hit her. The winds of the previous few hours had died down completely and the trees stood silent, their night-time battering only apparent in the number of fallen leaves blown into untidy piles. Even in the daylight, the whole area felt eerie. Although surrounded by busy streets, somehow it felt far removed from reality, like going back in time to the age of horse and trap. All was quiet, the nearby traffic a distant and indistinct hum.

Hunter slammed his door and the silence was broken. Charlie felt a slight sense of relief wash over her. She got her rucksack and joined Hunter and together they walked towards a small group of officers standing by the blue and white tape of the inner cordon.

'Morning gents,' Hunter addressed the group.

The uniform Duty Officer stepped forward. 'Morning. Thanks for coming so quick. We have Scenes of Crime on the way, but I'll show you the body first. I'll tell you what we've got so far as we go.'

They donned overshoes and gloves, gave their details to be added to the crime scene log and stepped forward across the tape. A path led them up a hill, then through some thick hedges into a smaller, more secluded area. Only about nine graves were here, positioned side-by-side in three rows. In the centre of the graves, laid out across the central stone, was the body of a woman. Her chest had been torn open, her ribs prised apart and a huge, bloody cavity took the place of where her heart should be.

As if voicing their thoughts, the Duty Officer spoke in hushed tones. 'It appears that her heart has been removed.'

Charlie stared at the hole, mesmerised by the awfulness of the sight. Even after nine years' service she still wondered how one human being could do this to another. Hunter too seemed transfixed momentarily. She eventually dragged her eyes away from the cavity and looked over the rest of the scene. The woman's body had been arranged carefully so that it fitted the stone on which it was laid perfectly, her head at the top of the slab, her feet at the base. Her hair fell neatly on to her shoulders, her eyes closed, as if in sleep and her arms were positioned by her sides. She wore casual outdoor clothing which was intact across the whole of her body except for her torso, where it looked to have been sliced apart in several places with a sharp implement, revealing the remains of her chest.

'We think her name is Susan Barton. There's a driving licence in her bag.' The Duty Officer pointed to a small, black leather handbag laid down at the side of the body. 'I've just heard from the officers I sent to the address shown on the licence and there's no one there to confirm her details.'

'Any sign of a break-in?' Charlie lifted her eyes away from the body.

'No. They've forced entry and there's no one in the house. They've had a cursory look around though and there are plenty of family photos, showing what appears to be a couple with two teenage children, one boy and one girl. The description of the female in the photos fits our victim here. The officers are staying there for the time being. It's quite nearby, if you want to join them after leaving here.'

'Thanks, we will do,' Hunter replied. 'I presume then, if the handbag is still here and she's dressed for outdoors, she was probably out already or left her house to meet someone, as opposed to having been abducted. And if there's no sign of a break-in, we can probably rule out burglary or robbery.'

'I'm not so sure, guv.' Charlie was staring down at the woman, examining every inch of the scene. She pointed to the victim's left hand, laid out, palm open against the slab. A pool of blood spread out from underneath it, dark crimson against the grey of the stone. 'The ring finger is missing. It's been severed from the hand. Maybe the killer was after her jewellery.'

Hunter peered down at the hand and then scanned the area around the grave. Eventually he turned to the Duty Officer. 'Any sign of the missing finger or heart?'

'Not as yet, but obviously we don't want to root around too much.'

'We'll have to keep the whole cemetery as a crime scene then. I'll arrange for a specialised search team to come to search the wider area, as and when the Scene of Crime Officer has examined the inner cordon here. We can't afford not to find either of the missing parts. Is there anything else obvious that the killer has left?'

'No, it doesn't look like it. He or she has been quite meticulous in tidying up. Everything is laid out precisely.'

'Well in that case, we'll go to Susan Barton's address and see if we can establish a definite identification and next of kin. We'll be able to see if our victim here is the woman in the photographs.'

Hunter indicated to Charlie and they all turned to leave, the Duty Officer stepping forward first. A mobile phone started to ring. It wasn't Charlie's and both Hunter and the Duty Officer weren't going for their pockets. Charlie turned back towards the victim. A small light was pulsing out from inside the open handbag. Hunter nodded and she started towards it, reaching carefully into the bag with her gloved hand.

The name Emma was showing on the screen along with the smiling face of a teenage girl. Charlie pressed the receiver switch and put the phone on loudspeaker. Before she could say anything, a young girl's voice sang out, bright and enthusiastic.

'Hi Mum, hope I've caught you before you get stuck in at work. I've got to start a new assignment and I was hoping to pick your brains about it. Can I pop back this evening and have dinner and a chat? I can tell you all about my plan. You'll love it.'

She stopped talking and waited. Charlie was dumbstruck for a few seconds. It was obviously the victim's daughter. How was she going to tell such a young, happy-sounding girl that her mother was laid mutilated in front of her.

'Mum, are you there?' the girl's voice sounded curious.

'Hello, this is DC Charlotte Stafford from Lambeth police.'

'Where's my mum?' the girl's alarm was obvious. 'Is she OK?'

'Are you Emma?'

'Yes. I'm her daughter.'

'Emma, where are you? We need to speak to you.'

The girl was crying now. 'Why, what's happened? Why have you got my mum's phone? Why can't she talk to me?'

'Emma,' Charlie dropped her voice, trying to remain quiet and calm. 'Tell me where you are. I promise I will come straight to you and explain everything.'

'I'm at Roehampton Uni.'

She had no idea what she could say to explain what she was looking at now, but somehow Charlie knew that she would have to find the right words.

'OK, Emma. Go to the office and tell them that the police are on their way to speak to you. We'll be there as soon as we can.'

6

The journey to Roehampton University was solemn. Charlie drove with the blue lights on and sirens blaring, navigating through the traffic on autopilot, her mind going over and over what she could say to the girl. Hunter was with her, but she knew it would be down to her to speak the words that would destroy the world of Susan Barton's daughter; if indeed the body was that of Susan Barton. It did however look increasingly likely. After taking the call, she had compared the photograph on the driving licence with that of the victim and, for Charlie, there was no question they were the same. Identification was really going to be a formality, but the evidential process dictated that it must be done. Viewing the body of a loved one was hard enough in a family home or hospital setting; viewing a body in a mortuary or chapel of rest was infinitely worse, especially when they were there as a result of inhuman violence. She hoped it wouldn't be Emma who would have to perform this task.

They were there within half an hour, pulling into the car park slowly, watched by the growing numbers of students sauntering in for lessons. Charlie could feel a lump in her throat as they headed towards the reception. The door was open and a young girl stood waiting. Her blonde hair swept down her back, with a side parting that allowed a long fringe to fall across her face. She flicked it to one side, as the receptionist escorted them through, and fixed startlingly blue eyes on them. She looked like a younger version of the woman they had left. There was no mistaking who her mother was.

'Emma Barton?' Charlie didn't need to ask but in the absence of a word from the girl, the question broke the silence. The girl stood rooted to the spot, mute.

'Yes,' she said at last. 'What's happened to my mother? Where is she?'

'Take a seat, Emma, and I'll tell you what we know.'

They moved into a small office, with six chairs spaced around a large table. An older woman shuffled in and introduced herself as Emma's tutor. She was in her fifties, with a rounded body and rounded mannerisms; no sharpness in the way she spoke or moved. She looked like a classic, archetypal grandmother, ready to smooth away every trouble. The news Charlie was about to impart, however, would not be smoothed away; ever.

Emma sat on the edge of her seat, her body leaning forward expectantly. There was nothing for it but to start.

'Emma, there is no easy way of saying this. We've just come from West Norwood, where the body of a woman has been found. She had a driving licence with her photo and name on it. The name is Susan Barton.'

The girl let out a scream, muffled with cupped hands over her mouth. The colour drained from her face and her hands started to shake. 'No, no it can't be my mum. I was only talking to her yesterday evening. She was fine. It can't be her. You're mistaken.' She stood up shakily and started to hoist a rucksack up on to her shoulder. 'Mum must have somehow lost her handbag. Maybe this woman, whose body you've found, picked it up?'

Charlie took a step towards her but she backed away, her expression rigid. 'I checked the photo on the driving licence against the lady we found, Emma. They looked the same. I'm really sorry.'

The tutor moved towards the girl and put both arms around her. Emma's body crumpled into hers and they sat down together, Emma now sobbing unashamedly. Charlie waited for the girl's tears to subside a little.

'We do need to make absolutely sure we have the right identification though. Can we take you back to your house to check some of the family photographs? Is there anyone else who lives with your mum?'

'She's on her own at the moment. I'm in digs with a couple of other girls and my brother is at uni in York. My mum and dad split up recently. They weren't getting on, so he moved out. He wants to know what's happening, by the way. I rang him before you got here, to say you were coming.'

'Can we speak to him?'

She nodded and typed into her phone. The name 'dad' blinked on and off. Charlie passed the phone to Hunter to speak. He could better explain what they knew so far and what they needed from him.

Hunter took the phone and moved outside the room. Charlie could hear his deep voice, calm and concise. Emma seemed to calm slightly herself. Maybe the pressure had been removed a little now her father had been informed.

When Hunter came back in, Charlie already knew what had been arranged. They were all to leave the university and return to the family address where Emma's father would meet them.

Emma collected her things together and climbed into the police car. She was on her own now, having thanked her tutor and assured her she would be OK and would be with her father soon.

She sat in the rear of the car, her head resting on the back of the seat. For a moment she closed her eyes as Charlie pulled out into the traffic. As was often the case, now the shock had receded a little she wanted to know everything.

'How did my mother die?'

Hunter turned towards Emma.

'We don't know at the moment. We're doing everything we can to try to find out.'

'Was it an accident?'

'No, it doesn't look to be an accident.'

Emma frowned. 'So, it was deliberate? Are you saying somebody killed her? Or she killed herself?' She leant forward and buried her head in her hands. 'She couldn't have killed herself. She wouldn't have done that to us. However hard she was finding things. She seemed fine when I spoke to her yesterday evening. She wouldn't have killed herself.'

The girl turned towards Hunter, her eyes steely. Charlie was reminded of when she had first told Emma they had found a body; of the way in which Emma had the ability to disregard the evidence in favour of what she herself could accept. For her mother to take her own life was out of the question. Murder, however awful, was clearly more palatable than suicide. She'd seen the same attitude many times before.

'We don't believe that she took her own life, Emma. I'll explain a little more of what we do know when we're with your father.'

Emma nodded and closed her eyes again.

'What time did you speak to her yesterday?' Charlie picked up on what Emma had said, trying to focus her mind away from questions about the cause of death.

'About seven. We chatted for fifteen minutes then I said I'd call back in the morning as soon as I had my assignment agreed by the uni.'

'Do you know what she was doing? I mean, did she say that she was going out or had visitors?'

'As far as I knew she was staying in. She mentioned catching up with some stuff she'd recorded on the TV. I think she even said she was planning an early night in bed. Where was she found?'

Charlie's mind rocketed back to the cemetery. How could they tell this young girl what they had just seen? But at some stage she would have to be told; before the details got divulged and it was all over the papers. For a few seconds she thought of her own mother, Meg. What if it had been her? How would she cope with the knowledge that the last few minutes of her mother's life were likely to have been filled with such terror and pain? She hoped that Susan

Barton had known little of what was happening; that she had been rendered unconscious before the killer had taken his knife to her. However at this moment in time they knew nothing of the circumstances.

'Do you know how she died?' Emma's voice cut through her thoughts.

'Sorry, Emma, we don't know as yet,' Charlie spoke the truth softly. She needed to protect Emma from the gruesome details as long as possible and, in any case, wouldn't attempt to speculate on the exact cause of death until after the post mortem. 'We'll tell you what we can when we get back. We're nearly there now. You said she was finding things hard, a little earlier. In what way?'

'I think she felt guilty about the break-up with my dad. She said that she had been unhappy for quite a while, and that since me and my brother had moved out, they didn't have much in common. She said they'd been leading their own lives for some time.' Emma clearly wanted to talk. 'She's a teacher and has friends in those types of circles that she socialises with. My dad's a car mechanic. I think he embarrasses her a bit when they go out together, although they do still get on. A few months ago my dad agreed to a trial separation and he moved out. They have stayed friends and I think he still has a key to our house and pops in now and again to see her, but he's definitely not happy about the situation. He didn't see it coming and he keeps asking to move back in, but even though she doesn't want him back, she feels guilty about what the break-up has done to him... and to the family. However much she thinks she's done the right thing for herself, she still feels bad.'

'And your father? How has he been?'

She was turning into Chestnut Road, SE27, now. She slowed, searching for the numbers. The road was long and straight with a mixture of large detached and semi-detached houses. A marked police car was parked about halfway down on the left. She headed towards it, pulling up outside a smart, well-kept, red-brick, detached property. A man was standing on the pavement outside next to a uniformed officer.

Emma started to cry as she looked towards the man. 'That's my dad now. Why don't you ask him?'

7

Mickey Barton threw his arms open as Emma got out of the car. She ran to him and he pulled her against his chest, stroking her hair clumsily with huge, blackened hands. He glanced up towards Charlie and Hunter as they walked towards him, his expression unreadable.

Charlie had the distinct impression that he was a man not much prone to public displays of affection. Her immediate assessment was heightened as he ruffled Emma's hair, took her by the shoulders and moved her to one side. It was the sort of action a father would do to a son who had just scored a goal at the Little League football match on a Sunday. It just seemed awkward.

Emma stood next to him as Mickey Barton held out a hand towards Hunter, ignoring Charlie.

'You must be Mr Barton. I'm DI Geoffrey Hunter. We spoke.' Hunter proffered his hand in return and Barton shook it strongly. 'And this is DC Charlotte Stafford. Thank you for seeing us.'

Mickey Barton nodded towards her.

'Alright. You'd better come in, if we're allowed, and tell me what you know.' His voice was gruff but a slight quiver in its tone gave away an attempt to maintain control. He was clearly reining in his emotions.

Hunter nodded. The house had not as yet been designated as a crime scene although it was a possibility at some stage. More essential was the need to firm up the identification of their victim and as both Mickey and Emma appeared to have regular access to the premises it was probable both their DNA profiles and fingerprints would be present anyway. Still, they had to be careful.

'Is there a back door we can use? That way I can leave the front door area undisturbed.'

Mickey leafed through a bunch of keys and nodded again.

'OK, that's good. Please don't touch anything unless I ask. I'd like you to have a cursory look to see if you can tell us if anything obvious is missing or has been moved from its usual place.'

Mickey Barton nodded and set off, walking down the paved driveway towards a side passage which ran between the house and a detached garage. The frontage of the house was smart, with double glazing and lace curtains on every window. The paintwork on the sills and doors looked smooth and freshly painted and the whole house gave the impression of having been well tended and under control. The garden was laid mainly to lawn, with shrubs dotted around the edges at regular intervals. They had been cut back now in readiness for the winter months, their limbs stubby and squat, devoid of the softness bestowed by leaves or flowers. The front door was open to the elements, with only a small tiled overhang to provide shelter to visitors and little chance of providing any forensic evidence that might assist.

The side entrance had a locked metal gate, with a fixed plate above it preventing easy access to the rear. The security seemed good. Barton unlocked the gate and it swung open, clicking on to a catch on the garage wall to prevent it swinging loose. He nodded towards his daughter as they disappeared towards the rear of the house. Emma was to remain with the uniformed officers initially.

Charlie watched him as he strode ahead. He looked to be mid-fifties but with a strong body that belied his age. He was about five foot ten, but his stockiness negated his average height and made him appear much larger than he really was and much more imposing. He had a thick neck, with toned, muscular shoulders and arms, and a full head of blond hair that he kept short and spiky. He was dressed casually in jeans, a heavy navy jumper and a pair of brown DeWalt safety boots.

Charlie peered into the rear garden while they waited for the back door to be opened. It looked wilder than the front, the grass in need of its last mow of autumn, shrubs and small trees in need of pruning back, their boughs still heavy with leaves and the shrivelled remnants of flowers. A buddleia bush blocked her view further to the rear, its long arching branches and ovate leaves having invaded the space across the pathway that ran the length of the garden.

As if on cue Mickey Barton nodded towards it. 'I've been keeping the front garden up for Susan. As you can see she's rather let the rear garden go.'

He spun round again and opened the back door with another key, ushering them straight into the kitchen. Charlie remembered what Emma had told them about her parents having split. Mickey Barton certainly seemed to be treating the house as if he had never left. She stepped into the house and was immediately hit by the aromas of cooking. A newly baked sponge lay on a wire tray on the work surface, covered over with a clean, red and white striped tea towel. Half a jug of fresh coffee sat on the hotplate of a percolator, cool now the machine was off. A table stood to one side with six chairs spaced round it, a bowl containing a variety of apples, pears and bananas, some slightly over-ripe sat in its centre on a white lace doily, and a stack of paperwork, leaflets advertising local fast-food and charity collecting bags, were spread out to one side. Like the rear garden its appearance was a little messy but Charlie immediately loved it. It was a 'lived in' kitchen, the hub of the house, its sole occupant, Susan Barton, the one who breathed her body and soul into it. It was awful that life force was now gone.

Mickey Barton scanned round the room, shaking his head slightly, before turning to face them. 'So, who do you think has done it?'

The question appeared to catch Hunter off guard a little. Barton was certainly direct.

'Mr Barton, I haven't said anybody's done anything yet.'

'You can call me Mickey. But you told me on the phone that a body had been found that you believe may be my wife and that it wasn't an accident or suicide. So that only leaves one thing that it can be; murder. So have you any idea who's killed her?'

'Mr Barton. Mickey. It's far too early to know that. We still have to formally identify her and there will have to be a post-mortem to establish the cause of death.'

'So you don't know how she died?'

'No, not yet.'

Charlie watched the man with curiosity. She couldn't work out what was going on inside his head. He was obviously emotional but was trying to cover up any perceived weakness, showing them he was a macho mechanic. Only girls cry! That sort of thing. But why? Maybe he was just incapable of showing his true feelings; maybe he was trying to find out any possible suspects on whom to get revenge. Maybe it was to cover any involvement he might have? Or maybe, after their recent split, he just didn't care. Or cared too much.

Whatever the case, she couldn't read him yet. And she usually could. She would normally get the measure of a person within minutes of meeting them.

Hunter, too, was obviously being careful what he said. He turned the question round.

'Have you any ideas who might want to cause your wife harm?'

Mickey Barton stretched up and scratched the top of his head with both hands, then looked at his nails, as if checking there was nothing nasty on them. 'No, to be honest I can't. Everybody always seemed to love her. She has lots of friends in lots of places. She works as a teacher in the local Academy and gets on well with her colleagues. Even the kids seemed to like her.'

'Was she married before she met you?'

'No, she was single. Susan Roberts when I first met her, but Susan Barton ever since; the love of my life: and I of hers.'

'So, no previous partners that might be out to get her?'

'None, just me, her and the family.'

'That's nice. Does she have other interests or hobbies?' Charlie asked, wanting to see how he reacted to her.

He continued to look towards Hunter.

'Well, apart from her career, she goes to church and helps out on various committees and women's groups, visiting sick and disabled people in the area. Personally, I don't have much to do with that sort of stuff these days. I used to, when I was younger, but I've grown up.'

'And there's no one at the church or in the various groups she works with that might have any reason to want to hurt Susan?'

Barton appeared to freeze momentarily at the mention of his wife's name, before shaking his head. 'Not that I can think of, but then you do get some pretty weird people in schools and churches. Crack-pots. They don't think the same as the likes of us.' He nodded towards Hunter again. 'Do you know what I mean? You know, us, we just get on with life, go to work to make a living, eat, sleep, watch a bit of footie when we get the chance. Some of that lot at the church or in schools walk around with their heads in the clouds. They think they are above us.'

'You didn't get on well with her friends then?' Charlie was determined to elicit a response. 'Emma mentioned that you'd recently split from your wife.'

Barton closed his eyes momentarily, before turning to face her for the first time, his expression closed. 'It was only temporary. It was an age thing. Lots of women go through it, so I'm told. Kids left home. Nothing to do. I was working on it. She would have changed her mind and had me back. It was just a matter of time. She loved me, but yeah, her friends didn't help. Some of them at the school egged her on, they wanted her to get the key back, but it's my house too. And anyway we would have worked through it. She loved me and I loved her.'

He stopped, his voice breaking slightly, and walked across the kitchen, looking up at a large gold-framed photo on the wall. The photo had obviously been taken at a restaurant on a summer holiday. Mickey stood at the back wearing a white, open-necked, short-sleeved shirt unbuttoned halfway down his chest, exposing a raft of blond, downy hair. One arm was slung territorially round the shoulders of a woman, slim and willowy, with long blonde hair, wearing a lilac, floral, loose-fitting dress. She appeared slightly off balance as if he was pulling her towards him. His other hand rested on the shoulder of a young boy stood in front of him, the spitting image of Barton himself, with blond, tousled hair. Emma was next to the boy, her arm reaching up across her body to hold the hand of the woman in the lilac dress, whose other hand in turn, rested on her shoulder.

'That's us on holiday about eight years ago in Spain. That's Susan. She's a real beauty, isn't she?' He pointed to the woman standing next to him in the photo. Charlie had recognised her instantly anyway. Their victim was definitely the same woman as in the photo, just a little larger and with shorter hair.

She nodded. 'Yes, she looks lovely.'

'And that's Mickey Junior. He's a good boy; he's just been accepted onto the first team, playing football for his uni. He's clever too.' He pointed towards the young girl. 'And you've met Emma of course.'

Mickey was gazing at the picture. Charlie watched him as he did so. He was the man of the house, the provider, the alpha male, and they were all his possessions, the fruits of his labours. How difficult must it have been for him to have his wife say she didn't want him anymore; that she wanted to make a life without him, after everything he'd done? How might he have reacted to her decision, particularly if his efforts to get them back together were not working? But at the same time, he clearly loved them all deeply.

There was a knock at the back door. Charlie went and opened it to find Emma standing on the doorstep.

'Where's my dad?'

'He's here. Come through, we've nearly finished.'

She led Emma through to join them and the girl's eyes immediately fixed on the same photo, filling with tears as they flicked between the image of her mother and herself. She wiped at them with the side of her hand. The family unit was gone, her mother taken from her in the most appalling manner. How would she ever cope with the knowledge of how she had died?

Hunter checked his watch. 'We'll give you some time together for a few minutes, but I'm afraid we'll need to search the house for anything that might help us find out what happened. Just one thing though. Do you know if Susan still wore her wedding or engagement rings? We believe they may have been stolen.'

Emma nodded. 'I think she still wore her wedding ring, but sometimes she took her engagement ring off. I know where she kept it in her bedroom. I came in recently and saw her with it. I'll have a look.'

Charlie followed her as she ran off upstairs. The bedroom, as with the kitchen, was messy; a pile of clothes lay on a chair folded untidily, cupboard drawers left ajar, the duvet lying askew on the pillow. An assortment of face creams, make-up and perfume were scattered across the top of a chest of drawers and the smell of Chanel Coco infused the room. She watched as Emma carefully peeled back some clothing on the shelf of a wardrobe.

'It's not here,' she said, her voice faltering.

They returned to the kitchen and Emma started to cry again.

'She must have been wearing it because I can't see it in her usual place. She said that she wanted me to have it when she... died. Now she's gone, and it's gone too.'

Mickey put his arm around her shoulder and pulled her into his body. Again it looked a little awkward, but at least he seemed to be trying.

'We'll need to be going now.' Hunter drew the conversation to a close. 'Do you have somewhere you can stay for the time being?'

Mickey nodded. 'I've my own flat just around the corner and Emma and Mickey Junior have their own places, but if they don't want to be there, I can have them at mine or we could go somewhere together.'

'I'll also need someone to help with a formal identification.'

'I will,' Mickey said straightaway. 'I should have been here to stop it happening in the first place.'

★

Mickey Barton stepped out of the police car and squared his shoulders. He'd changed his outfit. He liked to look good whatever he was doing, so he'd swapped his dirty work clothes for his smart designer jeans and a navy T-shirt. He was going to wear white but had changed, just in case there was any blood around. A smart jacket and brown brogues completed the look. Appearances were important to him.

He wanted to do things right.

The detective, DC Stafford, led the way towards the mortuary. She was OK, he supposed, but not very smart; scruffy even. The older man was more professionally turned out. He was the boss, which was good, the right way round. He didn't really agree with women bosses. Give her a few years and she'd be leaving to have babies anyway; just as it should be.

He followed her as they entered a reception room and greeted a man in a white gown, like that of a doctor. He was beginning to feel a bit nervous now. Would she look like she had when he last saw her? How was he supposed to react? Would he cry? He'd only ever cried once before and he never wanted to show that weakness again.

DC Stafford was standing with him explaining what would happen but he wasn't really listening. He watched her lips, not hearing the words, his ears ringing and the panic rising. It didn't feel real. Everything was a blur. She was saying something about not touching the body, just looking and saying yes or no, but that was all he could pick out. The doctor person opened the door to a room off the reception. It smelt of disinfectant, but it was a strange smell, not clean but cloying. It clung to his nose and hit the back of his throat. The room was lit with fluorescent lights and was very bright and white. They stepped into the brightness and he could see a metal trolley in the centre of the room. A body lay in the middle of the trolley wrapped in a white cover, with just a gap in it.

The policewoman was speaking again now. She took him by the arm and led him towards the shape. Inside the white cover was a plastic bag with a zip. The zip was undone, letting him see a white face. The white face belonged to Susan, his wife. It looked strange because it was so white; there was no colour in her cheeks. Her eyes were closed; she was expressionless.

He stared at her and said her name.

'Susan. It's my wife Susan Barton.'

The words sounded peculiar coming from his mouth. His voice was as expressionless as her face. Normally when he spoke those words it was to call her, speak to her or about her; normally they were attached to a sentence. But as he peered through the gap, he realised that normality had disappeared. His head was all over the place. Susan had gone for good and he could never reverse what had happened. His life would be so different now and there was no going back. Mickey Junior had lost his mother; Emma too and they had been so close. He thought of how she'd broken down just now, her agony at the missing ring, the one thing that she could hold on to of Susan. Everything had spiralled out of his control. He should have found a better way of handling things. He shouldn't have done what he did. He felt sick.

He took a step backwards and felt the bile in his throat. He'd thought he could do this but the fear was building up in him and making him dizzy. What if they found out what he'd done? The policewoman was steering him backwards out of the door now. He was out of the spotlight at last, into the gloom. He could see the door out into the car park. He didn't want to talk about anything. He wanted to escape from the nightmare and have everything like it was, before she'd cast him aside.

He pulled his arm away from the policewoman's hold and bolted for the door, wanting suddenly to be as far away as possible from Susan and her unseeing eyes, the brightness and the smell of disinfectant.

As the cold, fresh air hit him he bent over and vomited.

8

'They've found her heart,' Paul shouted towards Charlie as she and Hunter walked back into the office. It was late afternoon and she'd already been on duty for well over her normal eight hours but her mind was still processing everything she had seen.

'Really. Where was it?'

'It was a short distance away from the body, thrown over on one side of the path, as if he'd chucked it away as he walked along. The SOCO has bagged it up and it's gone to the mortuary to be reunited with its body.'

'Thanks. Nice way of putting it, Paul.'

'Well it's nice to think she has a heart again.' He chortled to himself.

Bet was still there too. She and Charlie both groaned. Office humour never changed. The more gory the crime; the more corny the comment. He'd obviously been waiting all day to say that.

Hunter shook his head and disappeared into his office.

Charlie turned to Paul. 'You're sick, you know that? Poor woman, we've just had to tell her daughter and ex-husband she's dead.'

'Maybe he's an ex-husband for a reason? The heart thing's weird. A bit personal, don't you think? Maybe it's something she's done? Or he's done?'

She raised her eyebrows and cocked her head. 'Maybe! It's a good theory, but there's nothing to say so at the moment. We'll see though. Who knows?'

Charlie slumped down and pulled her woolly hat off. It had remained glued to her head all day, even in the mortuary, where she thought she really should have removed it. By that stage though she knew, without doubt, her hair would be completely flat and lank. It was. However much she attempted to raise some life into it, the more it clung to her scalp. After a few minutes, she gave up and pulled the hat back on.

Hunter popped his head back round the door.

'Charlie, you can go if you want to now. It's going to be busy tomorrow. I've spoken with the guys in the MIT team and we've been seconded to the enquiry, in particular to assist around any possible domestic issues Susan might have had. Mickey Barton will have to be looked at closer. He had a possible motive and access. It's a strange murder with the heart and finger being removed, like our suspect is making a point.'

'Paul just said exactly the same.'

'I'm not aware of anything, but we'll have to ask around and see if there are any solved or unsolved murder cases or attempts that are similar. We'll also take a look at Susan's background; where she works, her family, the church she goes to and anything else that might be a reason for someone to want her dead.'

'That will keep us busy then. It sounds as if she's got quite an active social life.'

'And the post-mortem is pencilled in for first thing tomorrow morning, so we should have a definitive cause of death then.'

'Poor woman! I hope he didn't cut her heart out while she was still conscious.'

'I hope so too. Oh, and they're gathering as much CCTV as they can. Our team can start going through it, while we're out and about.'

'I'll volunteer for that.' Bet was squeezing herself into a thick coat. She winced as she manoeuvred her arm into a sleeve. 'Bloody back. It's still so painful moving. I'll quite happily sit and go through CCTV footage.' She slipped a weighty handbag over her shoulder and winced again. 'Anyway, you know how nosey I am. I love looking at hidden camera footage. People do the strangest things.'

Charlie laughed. She enjoyed that too, although it did get a little tedious after a while. The funny bits didn't make up for the hours and hours of boredom, unless you were working backwards looking for a suspect. Then it was great. Identifying a suspect and their movements leading up to a crime was heady stuff. It could make or break a case. She got to assist with CCTV footage regularly, being one of only a hundred and forty officers classified as a Super Recogniser in the Met. Picking out the correct face in a crowd and following their progress through the streets was vital work and she enjoyed the challenge. This time though, she was happy for Bet to get the job started. She wanted a more active role.

'Have a good night then,' she waved at Bet. 'And get Dave to give your back a massage.'

Paul held the door open for Bet as she walked past. 'Ooh Bet, you could be in for a wicked night if he does that. A bit of deep heat and all that.' He winked.

Bet let out an amused squeal and cuffed him round the back of his head. 'Go on with you, Paul. The only heat my Dave'll muster is when he boils the kettle to make us both a Horlicks before bedtime. I'll see you all in the morning, bright and early.'

'Me, too. I'm off now.' Hunter was behind Bet.

Paul groaned. 'I don't do early, you know that. And if I have to do early, it certainly won't be bright!' He went over to the coat stand and unravelled his jacket, pulling the sleeves back through from where he'd taken it off in a rush earlier. 'I'm on my way too. I'll see you in the morning, at some point.'

'Will do. Oh, before you go,' Charlie wandered over to Naz's desk to see if there was any paperwork with Cornell Miller's name on it. There were only a few scribbled notes. 'Is Naz back? I want to see how she's got on tracking Miller down.'

'She is still around.' Paul paused briefly. 'I saw her just before you came back in. See ya tomorrow.'

He waved and disappeared, leaving Charlie alone in the main office. Quickly she logged on to her computer and checked on Cornell Miller. He was shown as wanted now for being unlawfully at large, after the escape from custody and also for the assault on Annie Mitchell, the WPC. Naz had obviously been working hard. He wasn't as yet shown as wanted for the new GBH but that wasn't surprising; he would need to be identified by the victim before that could be done and that might take a few days at least.

She looked up the crime report detailing Annie's assault. She had injuries that would be classified as a GBH. Miller had now clocked up over a dozen victims who had suffered life-changing injuries at his hands. He really needed to be locked up for a long time. There were some new additions to the enquiries, but in the main, Naz had spent most of the day circulating him as wanted, overseeing the assault allegation on Annie and visiting the new victim. She hadn't had much time to start searching for Miller himself.

She scrolled down to see the details of the most recent assault just as Naz and Sabira walked in.

Naz had a handful of statements in her hand. She looked tired.

'Hi, Charlie, your murder sounds bad. Any leads as yet?'

'Not yet. We've been like you really; dealing with the victim and her family. Thanks for sorting out the Miller case.'

'No worries. I'll update you now, if you want.' Naz walked across to her desk and sat down.

Sabira busied herself logging back on to the computer. She was always there in the background, quiet, hard-working and determined. Charlie watched her briefly as she typed into the keyboard. She admired her strength. As a young Asian woman she had gone against her parents' wishes in joining the police service. Coming out as a lesbian a few years later brought them even more disappointment. She spoke little about the reaction she'd received, but it couldn't have been easy. Sabira, however, was forging a life, her own life, and nothing was going to curtail her ambitions. Charlie pulled up her seat next to Naz, making a mental note to invite Sabira out for a drink soon.

'So, do you think Miller is responsible for the one that came in this morning?'

'Almost certainly.' Naz leant back in her seat.

'Shit!'

'The victim is a middle-aged black lady called Marcia Gordon. She's ended up with ninety-three stitches, mainly to her face, neck and scalp. One of the cuts has gone through the cornea of her left eye. She could potentially be blinded in that eye for life. They'll be carrying out further ops to try and save the sight in it.'

'Cowardly bastard.'

'Marcia is lovely. She's actually quite philosophical about it. She walks to Kings College Hospital every morning where she works as an orderly and has walked through the same estate almost every day for the last eight years. She knows she would be better off going a different route but she takes the risk because it cuts off such a huge chunk of her journey.'

'She shouldn't have to worry about a risk. People should be safe to walk where they want; especially at that time in the morning.'

'I know, anyway, she said so far she's only been robbed on a couple of occasions in all that time. She thinks that is good! Both of the other times they got her handbag too. To her, it's only property that can be replaced. She doesn't keep much of value in it, nor does she try and hang on to it and fight; and she didn't this time either. She was walking through the estate towards the hospital when the suspect stepped out in front of her. He fits the description of Miller exactly. She offered her bag because she could see he was a crack-head and looked desperate. He had a broken bottle in his hand. He just started slashing at her face with it, over and over again. Oh, Charlie, you should have seen her. Her face was cut to pieces. I took a few instant photos of her injuries to show the immediate aftermath, but I've arranged for an official photographer to come and see her tomorrow.'

Naz pulled out an envelope and spread half a dozen photos across the desk, each one listed as exhibits.

Sabira glanced over as Charlie stared down at them, her eyes not quite believing what she was seeing. 'Sickening aren't they?' Sabira said in almost a whisper.

Charlie stared at the images taken from different angles of Marcia Gordon's profile. Her features were swollen out of all proportion. Rows of stitches zig-zagged across her face and neck; black thread tied as neatly as possible in tiny knots, holding the jagged edges together. A particularly nasty gash worked its way from the side of her scalp, through the corner of her left eye and down across the cheek, almost to her lips.

'Oh my God! How can he do this?'

'And the most disgusting thing is that he didn't have to. Marcia had thrown her bag down almost immediately. He could have picked it up and gone at any time, but he didn't. He kept slashing at her, screaming and calling her a "Black bitch", saying that he didn't just want her bag, he wanted to fuck her up and that she shouldn't be in his country. It was awful. She could have been my old mum. She's lovely.

'Luckily someone heard all the noise and phoned for an ambulance and police. The paramedics got her to Kings really quick. She's lost a hell of a lot of blood but after they patched the worst of it up, she was happy to tell me what had happened. She'll be staying in for a few nights until they can be sure none of the cuts are infected and for a specialist to look at her eye. I was going to take witness albums to the hospital to show her possible suspect photos tomorrow. She got a good look at him and is saying she won't forget his face.'

'I know the feeling. I have nightmares about his face too and I'm sure there are quite a few others who feel the same.'

'I'll make sure his photo is in the album and keep my fingers crossed that she picks him out. Then at least we can get him circulated for this too. At some point when we get him in, we'll get a full ID parade sorted and hope that she picks him out on that as well.'

'Naz, you're a star. I'll try and get the hunt going for him properly as soon as I can, but I know I'm going to be strapped for time tomorrow.'

'Don't worry. I'll carry on as long as you need. I've got a vested interest in the case myself now. I want him convicted of Marcia's assault too, the evil racist bastard.'

'Not to mention the one on Annie Mitchell and Moses Sinkler. Have you had a chance to speak to him yet?'

Naz shook her head. 'Sorry, we've been run off our feet and I thought it would be better coming from you anyway.'

Charlie put her hand up to stop Naz's apologies. Since their first meeting in the hospital a few months before, she'd grown very fond of Moses and was always happy to speak to him. She was not looking forward to this particular conversation, however, as he would be devastated.

'No time like the present. Thanks for everything, Naz.'

She picked up the phone and dialled his number; smiling, despite herself, as the sound of Moses' deep, rich Jamaican accent came on the line.

'Hello, who is it?'

'Hi Moses, it's Charlie. I have some news for you.' She tried to keep her voice as normal as she could. She should be ringing to tell him Miller had been remanded in custody.

'Charlie, my favourite girl. It's good to hear from you. How's it going? You got him banged up for good yet?'

She didn't want to tell him the news. He didn't even like mentioning Miller by name. She didn't have to.

He caught the slight reluctance in her voice, the pause before she spoke. 'Oh no! What's happened?'

She heard the old man cry out as if in pain before he covered the mouthpiece with his hand to try to muffle his sobs. She heard the sound of the back of the chair hitting the wall and the groan as he slumped down on to it and there were no words she could say to stop his anguish.

'He's out, isn't he?'

9

Ben was tying his trainers up when Charlie arrived. She threw her bag down in his lounge and pulled off a couple of outer layers. However cold it was, she always liked to run with little on. Only when it was really icy or snow lay on the ground did she ever cover up, and then only with one thin layer of Lycra. Bare-armed, bare-shouldered, bare-legged; her only concession was a pair of woolly gloves and the woolly hat which was still attached to her head now.

She caught Ben staring towards her. 'Oy, stop it, lover boy. You're not supposed to be eyeing up your coach.'

'I can't help it if my coach is also perfectly formed and gorgeous.'

She laughed, pinching the slight muffin top that protruded over the waistband of her shorts and slapped the top of her thighs. 'Well if you happen to be looking at me through the eyes of a seal, I might be. At the moment I have more blubber than a Mediterranean monk seal waiting for the winter.'

Ben laughed out loud. 'For goodness sake, Charlie, where do you get these ideas from? I've never even heard of a Mediterranean monk seal.'

'That's because there's not many of us left. We're nearly extinct. Apparently we're similar to the more common monk seal but are mainly based in the Mediterranean. I liked the idea because I thought it would be a bit warmer there. David Attenborough was talking about us on TV the other day. Think it must have been that sultry, sad expression, looking up at Sir David from a rock.'

'What are you like? Anyway I thought you didn't like the water?'

'Ah, that's true. I'll have to become a land-based animal.' She tilted her head to one side, looking up at Ben sadly through large watery eyes. She didn't have to pretend. The thought of water always brought back bad memories.

'Maybe a gazelle then? They have big sultry eyes and run like the wind.' Ben's voice brought her back.

She smiled at the idea. 'Hmm, I wish. Right, let's get this over with and then we can sit down with a coffee and a doughnut.'

Once outside she set off at a sprint, before relaxing down to a steady jog, heading towards Brockwell Park, their favourite route. Within a couple of minutes she heard Ben puffing up behind her, his footsteps next to her, solid and reassuring. The evening air was cold and dank and a slight mist was descending across the top of the trees. A murder of crows sat spaced out along the uppermost branches, each bird occupying its own observation point, their black feathers and beady eyes making the park seem sinister and menacing. She always remembered their collective name;

somehow seeing them out tonight seemed appropriate after the day's activities. Charlie pointed at them and Ben looked upwards, grimacing.

'They're called a murder of crows because they look so evil, but they're actually very sociable birds. They just have a bad reputation because they're scavengers.'

As if to prove a point, one of the crows took flight, its black wings flapping noisily in the gloom, landing with a slight commotion next to another. The branch dipped and the two birds nestled close, preening and pecking, before settling amiably together.

'Never judge a book by its cover, eh?' Ben sucked in a large breath of air. 'You might think I look unfit and that you can beat me, but you can't.' He took off at a sprint. Charlie upped her speed too and caught up with him as they were about to leave the park. She clapped him on the back.

'Ben, I don't know what I'd do without you. You bring me back to earth with a thud every day.'

She slowed down to a comfortable jog again and they meandered through a few backstreets to Ben's flat, slowing down to a stop as they reached his front yard.

'Are you coming in tonight?' Ben turned to speak to Charlie as she stood stretching her calves out against the wall next door.

'If you're offering me a long, cold drink I will. We need to talk about our strategy for getting through "Tough Guy".'

They had signed up to an event that was based in Wolverhampton twice a year, in winter and summer, and were in training for the winter event that was held every January. It was an assault course over fields, hills and water, through the thickest mud she'd ever seen. Eight miles of it; including barbed wire to crawl under, hanging electrified strips giving a painful shock if brushed against; lakes and water obstacles that left extremities frozen and lines of burning hay bales to jump through.

It was the sort of thing that Charlie loved, and as part of Ben's rehabilitation, she'd persuaded him to join her. To be fair, as soon as he'd seen the footage of it on the internet he'd been up for it too. It was the part of being in the armed forces that he'd loved; the sport, the physical tests, the team spirit. It had been watching those same team members die, blown literally into bits before him, after stepping on landmines that had brought him to his knees, unable to deal with life, unless through the haze of alcohol. He spoke little of it, except on the odd occasion when the nightmares got too much, but she could see the anguish that remained, only too obvious from the pain and fear in his eyes. Ben was determined to run for 'Help for Heroes'; Charlie was running for the RNLI, both charities close to their hearts.

'I'm offering water, waffles and good conversation.'

'How can I turn you down then? I'd be a fool.'

'You'd be a fool to turn me down whether I was offering you nothing but the skin I was born in.'

She turned and wrapped her arms around him. She'd first chatted to Ben when he was sat, often half-drunk, collecting for charity outside the Imperial War Museum, around the corner from her office. Their friendship had further developed after he'd been beaten and robbed and she'd helped bring the perpetrator to justice. He was such a lovely guy, so gentle and considerate; very quickly both had felt able to confide in each other some of the sadness and guilt from their pasts. For the moment though she was happy to keep him as a friend and to help him conquer his issues and get fit after breaking his leg in a recent fall. She'd see what happened then. Right now, her job was her priority. Love, marriage and kids could come later, if the right person came along. Maybe it was Ben, maybe it wasn't.

'I've got standards, Ben, and I would certainly need more than just your bare skin. A mankini at least.'

'Eugh, not a good thought. Let's stick to water and waffles.'

'Yes, let's.'

They both laughed. Charlie followed Ben through the hallway to his flat and filled them both a pint from the tap. The flat was clean and tidy with no sign of the piles of empty beer cans and ashtrays full of dog ends that had been there on her first visit six months before. He was doing so well. No more booze and the cigarettes had been swapped for vapes. He'd even cut right back on them. The next step would be trying to get him back into employment.

'Looking good in here. Here, get this down you.'

Ben took the pint and downed it in one, placing the empty glass upside down on the top of his head. Charlie laughed and tried to do the same, spluttering and choking when only halfway through it.

'You're hopeless. You'll never make an alcoholic.'

'Maybe you should tell my mum that, Ben. She's convinced that either me or my sisters will take after my stepfather, and I'm sure she thinks it will be me. She checks out the contents of my fridge every time she visits and lectures me on healthy eating.'

'That's parents for you. Anyway it's their job to give us youngsters the benefit of their experience.'

'I don't think any previous experience would have prepared me for today.'

'Bad one?'

'Just a normal day in sunny Lambeth. One murder, one escaped prisoner and several victims of GBH.'

'You wanna tell me about it?'

'No, not really. I'm back straight into it in the morning, early. I might grab a shower here and doss down on your sofa, if you don't mind me keeping you company tonight. It'll save me trekking to mine and I can keep you on the straight and narrow too.'

Ben nodded enthusiastically and went to open his mouth.

Charlie put her fingers to her lips. 'Shush. I know what you're going to say and the answer's still no; though ten out of ten for effort.'

He pouted good-humouredly and shook his head. 'You don't know what you're missing. One day you'll give in to my charms and let me be your knight in shining armour.' He filled the glasses with water again and passed Charlie hers. 'But for now, when we stagger through the finish line at "Tough Guy" in January, freezing cold and they throw a space blanket at me, I'll just be your mate in silver foil.'

Cornell Miller twisted his body on his mate's sofa. Well he wasn't really a mate, more like an old guy who didn't have the sense to say no to him. Cecil was known to everybody, but friends with none. He was in his late sixties, with a thick head of long, grey, greasy hair which hung down his back in wavy locks, joining up with an unkempt beard and moustache if he leant forward. He was thickset and dirty, with wild, staring eyes. Cecil was mad, or at least he gave that impression. He would walk down the road muttering and shouting out loudly and neighbours and pedestrians alike gave him a wide berth. The police gave him an even wider berth. The feeling was mutual; he hated them. At the merest sight of a uniform he would stir from passive aggression to full on rage.

As far as Cornell Miller was concerned, anyone who hated the Old Bill was a friend of his, like Blackz the night-time burglar who had happily removed the handcuff in return for a single rock of crack. The pigs would never come for him at Cecil's, especially not that bitch DC Charlie fucking Stafford. It had been sweet, knowing that she would be doing her nut when she found out he'd escaped. Even fucking sweeter when she found out, as he was sure she would, that he'd robbed that old black bitch on her way to work.

He flicked his lighter and drew on the cigarette hanging at the corner of his mouth, blowing out the smoke into the foetid air. Cecil didn't like opening the windows. He didn't like opening the doors either. He'd only got in himself by buying Cecil some fags, following him home and sweet-talking the madman into the promise of more cigarettes and drugs in return for letting him stay. Now he was in though, Cecil was already counting him as an ally. He was Cecil's friend.

Miller stretched and closed his eyes, sucking in another lungful of nicotine, before expelling it out through his nose. It took away some of the stench. Rubbish lay around the room; piles of discarded food containers and paper bags full of rotting chicken bones coated with the grime of many years. Cecil's place was a shithole, but it was somewhere to sleep out of the cold and it was somewhere he hadn't been before, ever.

He looked around at the clutter and disarray. This was his life. It wasn't great, in fact it was pretty shitty at the moment, but he survived and he was still free to move about and do what he wanted. There was no way he was prepared to give up that freedom yet. He would stay at Cecil's for a few more days and then move on. Keep moving. Keep ahead.

He leant forward and stubbed the cigarette out in an overflowing ashtray. His guts tensed as he moved, sending a spasm through his torso. It was a few hours since they'd last scored and he, for one, needed crack again.

Cecil was sitting opposite, rocking backwards and forwards staring intently at him. He was emitting a low almost sing-song growl as he moved.

'Do you need more gear?' Miller asked.

Cecil nodded.

He checked his watch. It was just gone five thirty in the morning. He got up slowly from the sofa, stretched again and pulled back the sheet that covered the window so that he could see out. It was still dark but from behind the roof of the block opposite a weak light was just visible. The sun was on its way. Before it started to rise properly and cast light on his activities he would be back, hidden inside these walls, secreted within Cecil's dysfunctional life.

'Let me back in, won't you. Or you won't get your white and brown.' He stepped in close to the old man. 'And if you don't open up I'll smash your fucking door down, you understand?'

Cecil nodded and stood up, walking slowly to the door. He opened it and stood to one side.

'I'll be back soon with what we both need.'

He sauntered out and turned one last time towards the old man. He could feel his heart starting to pump at the smell of the fresh, cold air and he couldn't help a grin spreading across his face, ear to ear. That's what he'd do next time. He'd get a fresh bottle, find a new fucking immigrant victim and split them open ear to ear.

10

Today had been busy. He'd been called to deal with work situations and had to behave as if nothing was wrong, that everything was the same as always, or had been. He'd turned up on time for work, showered and fresh, even though he could have slept far, far longer. What sleep he'd managed had been deep and contented, the sleep of the righteous. He'd avenged himself for what she had done to him, an eye for an eye, a tooth for a tooth, a heart for a heart.

It had been a hard day, waiting for work to end. Time had gone so very slowly.

He wasn't returning to his usual house immediately, the one he shared with several others from similar professions, the address that he gave for everything official. Tonight he was going straight to the room he'd recently rented, the bolthole he used only for planning his future activities, the place where he kept his equipment. Tonight he needed to make everything ready for the following Sunday.

It was only a single room, inside a larger shared house, with little more than a small washbasin, a two-ringed gas hob and space for a single bed, fireplace, table and chest of drawers. A small gas fire stood within the fireplace, the only means of heat. When lit, it barely provided sufficient warmth to keep the frost from the windows. A shared toilet and bathroom was situated down the hallway, a luxury he rarely used.

He'd called a cab to get him to work this morning, his own car being hidden under a cover, in the derelict garage at the rear of his rented room. The garage was in a secluded car park, with few other working vehicles, most of the occupants of the house being unemployed, itinerant sorts who hardly had the money to pay the rent and eat, never mind run a vehicle. Once clean it would be usable again.

As his evening cab dropped him round the corner from his room, he congratulated himself on how outwardly normal he had been; when inside, he could scarcely contain himself. Next week he'd be doing it all over again.

Everything needed sorting out before that though. His hand shook as he removed the heavy-duty padlock from the door to his room. His bag was secreted in the chest of drawers, where he'd hidden it after his night's activities. Once open it brought the whole exhilarating scenario back to him. There was blood, her blood on his tools, on the clothing he had been wearing, on the bag, on the container. Carefully he sterilised the tools; each one boiled in a large saucepan of disinfected water for ten full minutes, as clean as in an operating theatre, cleaner probably.

He washed the small orange juice carton out and threw it in the bin. It didn't smell of the drug but then it hadn't at the time either. It was tasteless and odourless and easily concealed within the stronger flavouring. He smiled to himself as he remembered how readily she'd agreed to the walk when he'd turned up on her doorstep out of the blue; to the drive, to discuss plans. How she'd so daintily sipped from the carton until it was all gone, how quickly she'd become unconscious. Her body had never encountered anything like it before. The reaction had been smooth and speedy, spectacular to watch.

The clothes and bag he scrubbed, one at a time, in the hand basin and hung out on the back of the bedstead. He would discard the clothing later, far away, with no obvious signs of blood, just a few rips and tears to put anyone off retrieving them from the rubbish.

The car was next. He prepared what he needed and took it out to the garage, flicking the switch and watching as the meagre light from the single bulb banished some of the darkness. He pulled on a pair of plastic gloves and started setting it back to normal. It needed to be cleansed in order to provide the anonymity that he craved, at least until his mission was complete, if indeed it ever was. He couldn't be caught. Not until he'd eliminated all those on his list that had done him wrong. Then he would disappear, blend back into society. Start a new list if required.

The plastic sheeting was scrubbed and folded neatly back in the boot, the interior vacuumed, the windows washed in disinfectant. He liked everything to be perfect. He took the air freshener hanging from the mirror and resprayed it with the scent he loved the best; the smell of his childhood, the aroma of his life, until it was taken away from him so cruelly, by dirty insinuations and gossip.

He locked the car doors and made his way back to his room, a surge of resentment overwhelming his composure. He had done nothing wrong; nothing, but shown love and compassion for the vulnerable. He had loved, so many times, so many beautiful, pure times, just to have it thrown back in his face, made sordid. He thought of those he'd loved, some were still alive, some had died; all were imprinted in his memory, most were easy to find.

Once his bag was dry he'd pack everything ready. He'd measure out the next few batches of the drug. It was so easy. The internet told him everything he needed to know about the quantities required and practice made perfect. He couldn't wait. Tomorrow he would act as normal, concentrate as normal, communicate as normal. Tomorrow and the next day and for a few days longer he would go to work and return to his usual home to eat and sleep, but in the spare hours of the evening he would come to this room to confirm his plans. He would drive out, check on his intended victims and make his last preparations.

Tonight wasn't over yet though. He still had time to review the documents on his laptop. The name of his next victim was there; along with their current address, their car, where they worked, their associates, hobbies, family. Everything was so readily available for viewing these days, on Google, Facebook, Instagram, Twitter; whole lives displayed for the world to see. It had made his mission so much easier.

He scrolled down to his favourite part of the document; the photos, copied and pasted from the internet. His next victim smiled back at him – little did they know what was coming. The images were all there: holiday snaps, selfies, photos on the train, in the street, eating, drinking with friends, alone, with one particular man. He hated the man even though he knew nothing about him. All he knew was that man had taken his place and for that, he was willing to kill.

He wanted one last look. They looked so happy together, smiling, close, their arms wrapped around each other. He stared down at their faces, recognising the look of love; he'd seen it many times before. They were obviously satisfied and fulfilled, carefree. Their life was so different from his.

His fury was threatening to engulf him again. Now was not the time. He snapped the laptop shut and stood up, pacing round the room angrily. His eyes turned towards the fireplace in the centre of the wall and he stood stock-still, calming immediately.

He cast his sight onto the box on the mantelpiece, between two photos; one of himself at work and the other of his parents, standing together, proudly smiling, both dead now. They had been all the family he had, bittersweet memories. The box was made from gold plate, with rows of coloured jewels that shimmered and shone if touched by the slightest suggestion of light. It had been his since childhood. His parents had given it to him when he'd reached the age of sixteen.

At times when he'd looked at the box he'd hated it. At times he'd wanted to throw it to the ground, to watch as it smashed and splintered into tiny pieces. But he could never do it; it remained like a chain around his neck, a constant memory of his parents and all they had wanted. It had travelled with him throughout his life, his feelings for it waning and flourishing with his life's experience.

At present though, it was loved; much loved and treasured.

He dipped his head and leant forward, flicking the hidden catches and removing the lid. Carefully he reached inside the box, lifting out a strong, Perspex container. The container was clean and clear. He held it up to the light to get a better look at its contents, his heart soaring at the sight. The new addition was floating in the liquid. It looked fresh and new and perfect. It bobbed up and down enticingly. There was plenty of space for more, many more.

He moved the container round in his hands, counting aloud as he relived each addition.

'One, two, three, four.'

He smiled at his latest acquisition; so perfect, the varnish still fresh and bright.

'Five fingers and counting!'

11

Tuesday morning started with a phone call from her mother, Meg.

'Are you still coming over for dinner tonight?'

Her mother phoned her every Tuesday morning to ask her the same thing, and each week she said the same thing in return. 'Yes please, Mum, but I'll let you know how the day is going as to what time I'll be there. Feel free to join me tomorrow morning?'

Every Tuesday morning her mother would respond with a silence that seemed to last longer each week before finally saying, 'OK, love, I'll see you later then.'

Meg would never answer her question and would never come to Jamie's grave with her.

Charlie checked her watch, swallowing back the tears of disappointment and broke into a jog, sprinting the last few hundred yards towards Lambeth HQ. By the time she got there, she had run the frustration out of her system for another week and was ready to face the day, a smile planted on her face, prepared for any new challenge.

Hunter was already in his office, scanning through the day's enquiries. He saw her and beckoned her in.

'We've got the post mortem to go to first thing but after that I want us to get to the academy where Susan Barton worked. See if we can catch some of her colleagues while they're not too tied up with lessons or have their lunch breaks. Bet is going to start on the CCTV and Paul is searching Mickey Barton's history.' He looked her up and down, shaking his head in mock despair, like a weary parent. 'Smarten yourself up while I check in with the MIT team and then we'll head out.'

Charlie grinned and headed straight to the bathroom, dousing herself in perfume and attempting to pull a brush through her hair. Ben's shower was OK but, without her toiletries, she always ended up smelling more of Paco Rabanne than her favourite Ylang Ylang. She had to admit she wasn't the most feminine policewoman at the station; far from it, but she did like to at least try to smell like a girl. She was ready in double quick time, a fact not lost on Hunter as she walked back in, still attempting to smooth out some of the wrinkles in her trousers.

'Quick, but sloppy-looking. You'll have to do. At least you smell nice.' He sniffed the air and shook his head. 'One day…'

Bet laughed. 'Boss, we'll be long gone by the time that *one day* comes around, if it ever does. Mind you, it's Wednesday tomorrow. At least she'll have a pile of fresh laundry done for her by her mum tonight. Isn't that right?'

'Ah yes, thanks Bet.' Charlie's face broke into a wide grin. 'I must remember to bag all my dirty stuff up ready for dinner. There's rather a lot this week. I've been in training with Ben.'

'Your mum must love you,' Hunter scolded, clearly amused.

'You all love me. You know you do. It's like home from home when you come to work. Stroppy teenagers and all that. Though, as you've pointed out I'm more sloppy than stroppy.'

'I don't know about that, but at least you get on with the work, not like my boy. Never gets out of bed. I have to prise him out from under the covers every morning when I'm there and even then he rarely shows before midday.'

'Well there you go then. Be grateful I always turn up and work hard; what's a little dishevelment among friends. Anyway I'm ready when you are, boss.'

Hunter pulled a coat on and started walking. 'Bet, Paul,' he called over to them. 'Let me know if you get anything straight away.' He turned back to Charlie. 'Right, first stop, the mortuary.'

The mortuary was situated next to St Georges Hospital in Tooting. It was a large facility whose staff conducted both coroner's and forensic post mortems, and it was also the regional centre dealing with stillbirths and miscarriages in South London and South East England.

Charlie had been there on many previous occasions before. Post mortems were one of the worst parts of the job for her, having often dealt with the walking, talking person before death, but she did have to admit to being fascinated by the intricate workings of the human body when it was literally laid out before her. She had harboured a desire to join the medical profession prior to joining the police service but would never have got the grades required. If the main pathologist, Dr Reginald 'Reggie' Crane saw her there, he would always take the time to show her exactly what had caused the person's death, if it wasn't obvious.

It didn't take long for them to get there and they were soon parking up and walking towards the building. It was relatively new and featured a few single rooms as well as the main lab where Charlie had often seen up to twelve bodies all laid out ready for examination.

Susan's body had been moved from the main viewing room where Mickey Barton had identified her, to one of the smaller path labs, clinical and sparse, made up mainly of stainless steel slabs, drains and wash areas. She and Hunter donned surgical gowns, hair nets and overshoes and entered the lab, choosing initially to leave their face masks down across their necks.

A detective from the Murder Investigation Team was already there, having spent a couple of hours with the Scene of Crime Officer and pathologist bagging up each item of clothing and taking hair and saliva samples, as well as various other swabs and scrapings. Blood and urine samples had already been taken to be sent off for a toxicology report, testing for alcohol and drugs primarily. A large row of paper evidence bags, tubes and containers were placed across a work area, all neatly written and exhibited by the SOCO and witnessed by the detective.

By the time they entered, Dr Crane was almost ready to start the actual examination.

'Good morning Reggie,' Hunter greeted the pathologist. 'Good to see you again. How's it going?' He nodded towards the SOCO and the detective, DC George Robertson, who Charlie knew of old. She mouthed the word 'OK?' to him and DC Robertson pulled his face mask down, shrugged and grimaced back. They had obtained all the evidence in the way of DNA, fibres and samples. His job was nearly done.

'Good morning, Geoffrey. Charlie, always good to see you too.' Dr Crane went to hold out his bloodied, gloved hand to Hunter, then obviously thought better of it and withdrew the offer. 'Sorry it's always under these circumstances though. Maybe one day we should arrange to meet in a bar rather than over a body. Much more amenable to conversation don't you think.'

Hunter nodded. 'Yes, we should. We'll have to see about it soon.'

Charlie couldn't help smiling to herself. She wondered how exactly a conversation between the two men would go after a few drinks. It would likely turn into a competition between them as to who had dealt with the worst cases, and knowing how competitive they both were, by the end of the night it would be too grisly for human consumption; certainly to be overheard in public. Thankfully, it was unlikely to ever happen; both men were far too busy.

'Right, ladies and gents, are we ready? Let's get started then.'

Dr Crane pulled his face mask into place and moved across to the body, getting his Dictaphone ready as he approached. With a bit of luck, in a few hours they would know exactly what had caused Susan Barton's death, what had led up to it and what happened afterwards. Neither man would be satisfied with anything less.

Charlie looked at Susan Barton, her body naked and exposed on the stainless steel slab. There was no dignity in death, even less when the death came as a result of murder. Every part of her body had to be swabbed, scraped and examined in minute detail, every scrap of self-respect stripped from her. Only if they could find and convict her killer would she and her family be offered any solace, only then would she be allowed dignity and to finally rest in peace. They needed to do this.

'Right, we have a white female, in her early fifties, approximately five feet three inches tall, slim to medium build. On first sight her thoracic area has been opened and her heart removed. Her left ring finger has also been severed. There are a number of contusions and grazes, synonymous with possible ligature marks on her wrists, ankles and mouth, along with some possible blunt trauma injuries.'

'So, she was tied up and taken to the cemetery?' Hunter queried.

'It's too early to say yet. With respect, might I suggest you listen to my observations and allow me to conduct the full examination before asking me questions? I might then be in a position to make statements based on fact, rather than trying to presuppose what has happened.'

Hunter frowned. He didn't like being told what to do, but Dr Crane clearly was the boss in this environment, just as Hunter would be in a police station. He nodded and took a step back; his way of letting the pathologist know he would accede superiority to him, without having to actually apologise.

Dr Crane cleared his throat and continued.

Charlie watched fascinated as he worked his way along every part of Susan Barton's body, from her head downwards, measuring and describing each of the injuries. He also noted several blunt trauma marks on her hip and elbow, possibly from being dropped on to a hard surface. He would finish with the largest wound to her torso and chest cavity.

At times it was hard to bear, particularly when the doctor checked for any signs of sexual assault, but it had to be done and they all knew it. There was no time for squeamishness.

When he got to her left hand, he noted again the absence of the ring finger and bent forward so his face was close.

'Fourth digit on left hand missing. On examination it appears that the skin around the amputation edge is clean cut, rather than jagged. I am of the opinion that the finger has been severed with a sharp implement that has cut through the finger in one motion. There doesn't appear to be any sawing type marks that would indicate it has been removed with, say, a blunt knife or saw blade. Was there much blood?'

Charlie nodded. 'There was a fair bit where the hand was lying.'

'Well, I'll examine the amputation point in more detail when I've finished the main examination but if there was a reasonable amount of blood around the hand, it's fair to assume that the finger was severed while she was still alive. If she were already dead there would only be a small amount of leakage.'

Charlie winced at the thought. Dr Crane looked towards her.

'Although a relatively small part of the body, there are two arteries feeding each finger. If she was alive when it was removed, the blood would continue pumping and it would be excruciatingly painful. All injuries to the hands are particularly painful due to the abundance of sensors on the skin surface.'

He stopped talking as they took in his last words. After a few moments he moved up parallel to the main wound.

'Right, now to the thoracic site. The skin appears to have been cut open quite neatly with a sharp implement and the edges peeled back.'

'Like unwrapping a present.' Charlie was trying to picture it in her head.

Reggie Crane turned his head towards her and smiled. 'Yes, you could say that. Your killer seems to have some knowledge and experience of the human body, although I suppose most people know where the heart is situated. He's marked the area with a large cross and then peeled each flap back to get entry. He or she is well-equipped and well-organised. Ribs one to six on the left hand side have been cut, again quite neatly, by the sternum and pulled back so the thoracic cavity is exposed. If your victim was still alive while this was done, there would have been a huge amount of blood loss. We'll measure how much blood is left in the body when we can and that should determine the answer.'

'There wasn't too much at the scene.'

'Well, in that case, hopefully she was dead when he opened her up. I'll carry out further tests of the organs surrounding the heart and should know further when this is done. I gather the heart was found nearby?'

'Yes, it was.'

'Right, I have it here. Maybe now would be a good time to take a look.'

He moved across and lifted a heart from a separate work surface.

'We've already taken a sample of DNA from it and it matches the victim's. We can safely say it is Susan Barton's heart.'

He bent down over it with a scalpel and moved the outer skin of the organ gently. A hole opened up. Following its path, he turned the heart on to its side and saw an exit hole out from its rear. He indicated to Charlie who leant over to better see. It was fascinating.

'Neat. It appears – and again I will need to do further tests – that your victim was probably killed with a single, sharp, pointed implement which went straight through her heart, puncturing the left ventricle. It would have been quick. With its main muscle taken out, the heart would have stopped beating almost instantaneously. Any blood pumped from the heart before death would have probably remained within the cavity, even when the chest was opened up.'

He placed the heart carefully back on the surface and returned to the body.

'The area where the aorta and pulmonary artery meets the heart appears large and jagged, as if the heart has been ripped out. I'll see if I can find the ends of the blood vessels left in the body and see if they too appear to have been cut or torn. There might still be bits of the pericardium, the protective sac around the heart, attached to the ends of them.'

Reaching down into the bloody cavity, he moved his hand about carefully, trying to locate the surrounding blood vessels.

Charlie continued to stare, transfixed with what the pathologist was doing. She watched as his look of concentration was replaced with a curious frown.

'There appears to be a foreign object in here,' he said quietly. 'It feels hard, like it's made from metal.' He started to lift the item up out of the hole. 'I think we've found one of your missing pieces.'

He placed the item down next to the body and wiped it with some surgical tissue. The band of gold glinted in the fluorescent light.

'Fucking hell,' Hunter mumbled. 'That's got to be Susan's missing wedding ring.'

12

'So, we have a victim who last spoke to her daughter, Emma, at about 7 p.m. and had no other contact with anyone after that time that we know of. She didn't mention she was seeing anybody, or going out, or indeed having anyone to visit.'

'And there were no signs of a break-in at her house.'

'So, how the killer managed to get her from her home to the cemetery is a mystery at the moment.'

Hunter and Charlie were running ideas across the interior of the car as she drove towards Harris Academy. They always did this. Hunter liked to see if she was on the same wavelength as him. Normally they were.

The post mortem over, they now had a good basis on which to work for the cause of death. They had yet to have full reports from Dr Crane on some of the exact details, including the toxicology report, the time of death and the exact sequence of events as far as could be predicted, but they knew pretty much how. They now needed to find who.

'So, did someone entice her out, or did she have a visitor that she voluntarily let in to her home?' Hunter rubbed his hands across his face.

'Or someone with a key?'

'And with a motive?'

They both knew who they were talking about.

'What we all seem to agree on is that it's personal,' Hunter continued. 'Why would a killer do the sort of things to a random stranger that he or she has done to Susan? Bind her, gag her, cut her finger off, rip her heart out, throw it away nearby and then leave the wedding ring where her heart should be. You'd think with that sort of weird shit, it's got to be someone she knows, someone who hates her, for whatever reason.'

'Or someone who loves her? People do weird shit when they can't have what they want.'

'True. The trouble is who? Susan had a wide circle of friends. Even putting Mickey to one side for a moment, there could be any number of suspects. She must have hundreds of friends or associates, and if Mickey Barton does have one thing right, a lot of those in education or religion do have pretty bloody strange beliefs.'

She laughed at his prejudice. Coppers, particularly of his era, were on the whole not particularly religious, rarely university educated and markedly right wing. They dealt with harsh practicalities, rather than allowing their minds to roam into the worlds of spirituality or theology; although this was changing a little with the latest batches of forward-thinking graduates.

'Well, we'll soon see how many unusual people she's worked with. We're at Harris Academy now.'

Hunter checked his watch and chuckled. 'And they'll all be sitting down to their houmous and chickpea salads as we speak.'

Harris Academy, where Susan Barton worked, was situated down the hill from Crystal Palace, the area of which was named after the large, cast-iron and plate-glass structure that had been transported there for the Great Exhibition in the eighteen hundreds. The Victorians had been delighted with the building that shimmered and shone as the sunrays bounced and flickered over the glass. However, after a huge fire had razed the building to the ground, nothing was left to show for the magnificent structure other than its name. Now it was better known for the athletics track and swimming pool that hosted athletes and swimmers from all over the world, and a rather dilapidated dinosaur park.

The school, a large mixed-sex comprehensive school and previously maintained by the local council, was now an academy. It housed over a thousand children from eleven to eighteen years of age and had a reputation for achieving outstanding results. The staff were numerous, eclectic and motivated. On the whole they wanted what was best for their students and worked hard to assist each young person to reach their potential, or at least that was what was said in promotional literature. The actual reality was slightly less glowing, considering the run-down state of the building.

Charlie manoeuvred the police car into a small overcrowded car park at the rear of the main block and they weaved their way towards the reception round several empty bike sheds and a mobile classroom, which had evidently been there for years and lacked any sort of mobility.

The reception was staffed by an elderly man with the stiff, formal bearing of a Victorian gent. She couldn't help thinking that he might have been better suited to the age when The Crystal Palace had been around.

'Can I help you?' He looked up at them curiously over thin, silver-framed glasses.

'We'd like to speak to the headteacher if we may?' Hunter responded formally, much to Charlie's amusement. She wasn't used to him being so polite.

'Have you an appointment?' He didn't wait for a reply. 'If you don't have an appointment the headmaster won't be able to entertain you.' It sounded more like a rejection to a tea party than a refusal to allow a meeting.

Hunter reverted to form, pulled out his warrant card and thrust it towards the man. 'I'm sorry if it's not convenient but it is important. I need to speak to your headteacher about one of his staff.'

'What about my staff?'

The question came from an eccentric-looking man, who had just broken into a jog as he approached the reception. He was in his early sixties, of medium height but portly, with a pot belly, squeezed into a bright mauve waistcoat. His head was bald on top but framed by a valence of long, thin hair that fell on to his shoulders in untidy grey clumps. He was carrying a small trilby hat, which, on stopping, he placed over his bald spot. He reminded Charlie of The Mad Hatter from *Alice in Wonderland*.

Hunter held his warrant card out again and the man squinted at it, before offering him his hand.

'Detective Inspector Hunter, good afternoon! Vincent Atkins, the headteacher. Nice to meet you. You'd better come through. Thank you George.'

He nodded towards the receptionist, who pursed his lips and frowned.

Charlie introduced herself and held her hand out. Vincent Atkins shook hands before taking a few paces forward and ushering them both into a large orderly office, set back from the reception. The whole room was spotlessly clean and tidy, everything in its place. Several gilt-edged photograph frames held images of the headteacher proudly posing in mortar board and gown. He'd clearly continued his education for as long as possible, an academic, whose whole life revolved around academia.

'You said you wanted to speak to me about a member of staff?'

'Yes,' Hunter was taking the lead on this conversation. 'Susan Barton. Did she work here?'

'Yes, she's head of the languages department, but she's not here today and she didn't turn up for work yesterday. I was calling her most of the day. It's very strange. She doesn't normally go absent without first letting me know...' He stopped as the fact that Hunter used a past tense obviously registered. 'Why? What's happened to her?'

Charlie watched as the colour drained from his cheeks. He took his hat off and closed his eyes.

Hunter lowered his voice. 'A body was found in the early hours of Monday morning, which we've now had confirmed as Susan. We believe she was murdered.'

'Oh my God, no, not Susan.' Vincent Atkins sat down heavily on his seat. He looked to be close to tears. 'Why would anyone do that to Susan? She was the sweetest, most friendly, softly-spoken lady you could hope to meet; always looking at the positive. The kids all love her. They will be heartbroken.' He dabbed at his eyes with a cotton handkerchief, similar to the style that Hunter himself used. 'As am I.' He blew his nose hard on the hankie, unconcerned about the noise it made. 'I did wonder what was up when I couldn't get hold of her... And I heard that a body had been found. But I never thought it could be her. Why would it be?' The question hung in the air for what seemed like ages, while he shook his head and frowned.

'Have you any idea who might want to do her harm?'

'No, no idea at all.'

'Are there any of the staff here or students that have had an issue with her? Any bad feelings? Any crushes? Any relationship issues?'

'Students will always have issues with teachers, but aside from a few minor welfare concerns, I'm not aware of Susan having had any problems. And my team all seems to get on pretty well. There's sometimes the odd disagreement, normally about policy or practice, but other than that, no problems that I know of. Will you want to speak to the staff?'

'Yes please, particularly those who worked directly under her leadership. They might be able to shed some light on any issues she may have encountered.'

He leant forward and pressed a button on the desk. 'George, could you see which members of the language department are having their break and ask them to come to my office please.'

A muffled reply but within minutes there was a knock on the door and two members of staff walked in. One was a young woman, with long dark hair, swept up on to the top of her head and held with a white, floral hair grip. She was slim and pretty and wore what appeared to be a black wrap-around designer dress and black low-heeled ankle boots. A sky blue neck scarf, decorated with tiny white flowers was tied loosely around her neck. She looked effortlessly stylish.

Holding the door open for her was an older man, in his late fifties. He was a bear of a man; a few inches off six foot, heavily built, with a head of dark hair that hung over his forehead in an untidy fringe. A full beard and moustache that were verging on untamed graced the lower half of his face and he wore dark-rimmed, rectangular glasses that peeped out from between the masses of hair. A brown tweed suit, matched with a cream cotton shirt and bottle green tie completed his look.

'Come in please, Sophie, Daniel. Thank you for getting here so quickly. This is Detective Inspector Hunter and DC Charlotte Stafford from the Metropolitan Police.' He turned to the two teachers. 'And this is my French teacher, Miss Sophie Pasqual and Latin teacher, Mr Daniel Roberts. Are any of the others available?'

Daniel shook his head. 'Sorry, they're on various other duties but we can pass on a message. What's the problem?'

Vincent Atkins pulled out his handkerchief again, running it through his hands. 'I'll come straight to the point. It's Susan. She's been murdered.'

Sophie let out a gasp. Her expression was one of complete shock and disbelief. 'Oh no, it cannot be true.'

'The officers here have just told me.' Vincent put a hand on her arm. 'They need to speak to us all to see if there is anything we can help with. Anybody that we can think of that might want to hurt her?'

'Of course, of course. But there is nothing I can think of. She was always so nice.'

Charlie looked towards the young woman, her eyes wide and full of tears, and nodded. 'There might be something, anything you remember once you've got over the shock. We'll let you come to terms with the news first and somebody will come back later in the week when you've had time to think, and take your statement.'

The Latin teacher cleared his throat, removed his glasses and gazed towards the headteacher. 'Have you made a statement yet?'

Vincent Atkins shook his head almost imperceptibly. 'No, Daniel, not as yet. I've only just heard the news myself.'

'And, you are all right?' Sophie looked towards him too.

'Yes, yes, I'm fine. Shocked obviously. I've known Susan for many years. She was a valued member of the team.' He turned and smiled towards Charlie and Hunter. It was apparent he wasn't going to elaborate any further.

Charlie looked from one member of staff to the next. There was something strange about their interaction. Some matter that was not being aired openly. Her interest, previously dormant, was now aroused. She was aware that the Latin teacher was watching Vincent Atkins closely. They knew something and she wanted to know what. Moreover, she suspected that Daniel Roberts already knew she had worked this out.

'I can come back later and take statements from them all.'

She looked at Hunter, who appeared slightly bemused by her sudden declaration. She wasn't normally the first to volunteer for the more mundane statement-taking chores. He didn't disagree though.

She turned to the three teachers.

'I'll give you a ring and arrange it for the next day or so. I will need to know as much as you can remember about Susan – when you last saw her, what she might have said, any worries she told you about – so we can start to piece together who might have done this to her.'

Daniel Roberts nodded back at her, his expression warm but still unreadable. Sophie Pasqual pulled out a tissue and dabbed at the corners of her eyes carefully, while Vincent Atkins rubbed his hard with the handkerchief.

There was more to this group than met the eye. Everything was indicating to Charlie that they were keeping a secret and she was determined to find out what it was.

13

'Hunter, Charlie, I think I've got a possible vehicle for the murderer.' The excitement was palpable in Bet's voice over the mobile phone speaker. 'I've shown Paul and we're backtracking now to see if we can get a full registration number. We've only got a partial index at the moment but hopefully we'll have one soon. Are you nearly finished with your enquiries?'

'Yep, we're on our way. You guys have got twenty minutes to get me the suspect's name before we arrive or I'm sending you back out on the beat,' Hunter teased.

'You'd better be quick then. Paul looks like he's just spotted something.'

Hunter ended the call and indicated for Charlie to put her foot down. If they had identified a vehicle, hopefully they would have a suspect, or at least a line of enquiry with previous owners that might lead to the current one. They needed to get the murderer banged up in a cell for life, before he took someone else's. The only slight ray of optimism was that, if it was indeed personal, it was likely to be a one-off. Susan had been targeted for a reason. Hopefully the same set of circumstances that had driven her murderer to kill her wouldn't fit anyone else. But they couldn't take the chance.

Charlie slapped the blue light on top of the car and started the sirens. She waited a few seconds for the motorists all around her to work out where the noise was coming from and then pressed her foot on the accelerator. The London evening rush-hour parted and she shot through the middle. After a few minutes, she passed West Norwood cemetery. The blue and white incident tape indicated that officers were still on the site, no doubt combing every last inch of the place for the missing ring finger and engagement ring. It would probably take a good few more days of intense searching until they were satisfied they hadn't missed either. She was glad it wasn't her. She'd never have the patience, although, just like watching hours of CCTV, it could be the key to solving the case.

They passed through Tulse Hill now and headed towards Brixton. Her mind switched automatically to thoughts of Cornell Miller. Could he be holed up in one of the blocks? Could he be roaming the 'front line' in Brixton, searching for a dealer, or worse still searching for a fresh victim? She made a mental note to check in with Naz and Sabira for any further progress on that investigation. She'd get back to it as soon as she could.

On into the town centre and then left towards Stockwell. A small shrine of flowers and handwritten notes outside Stockwell tube station reminded passers-by of the death of Jean Charles de Menezes, shot by police in the wake of the 7/7 London bombings. It was a shooting that had left a scar on the memory of the community; another victim of the terror that had pervaded the capital that July. And no doubt would again.

They were passing through Vauxhall now, round the one-way system, under the railway arches where the clubs and saunas of Lambeth's gay community were situated. It was quiet at this time; too early for the start of the evening activities, too late for the last of the midday clubbers. A few rainbow flags still hung from lamp posts, thin and tatty remnants of the London Pride festivities.

The Thames came into view as she accelerated along the Albert Embankment, grey and murky in the October shadows. With just over an hour or so before sunset, it was hard to imagine how much darker and gloomier it could get. She shuddered involuntarily at the thought.

And then they were there. She switched the sirens and blue lights off, leaving the flashing headlights on to indicate to the gatekeeper they needed a quick entry. True to form they didn't get one. By the time they had warrant cards checked and the bar was lifted, Charlie could have run round and done it herself. Still, security had to be adhered to. There was no more vaulting barriers and expecting a mild caution. These days disciplinary action would be taken and with all the hassle that involved, even Charlie had to observe protocols, however much it irked her.

Bet and Paul were bent over a bank of computer terminals when they got into the office. Naz and Sabira stood directly behind. The four of them were deep in conversation, pointing at the screen, before waiting for Paul to rewind the DVD, only to stare at the footage again. They didn't even notice Hunter's and Charlie's arrival.

'Can you zoom in on that registration plate?' Bet said, propping her reading glasses further up the bridge of her nose. 'It's got to be that one; same make, model and partial index as before, same single male occupant, right direction and look it's 01.37, so the time fits.'

Naz pushed her head forward, in between Bet and Paul as he adjusted the screen. 'Bingo! Look there it is. LV07JCF. It's got to be the right one. Bloody hell, Bet, Paul, well spotted. That's wicked. The boss'll be made-up.'

'Good evening, team. Glad to see you're all working so well together. What'll I be made-up about then?' Hunter stepped forward, pretending not to know and was immediately propelled towards the group by Naz who had run across to them and taken both he and Charlie by the arms. They leant in as Bet pointed excitedly at the screen.

'I've spent all day scanning what footage we've been sent so far. Lambeth Council have cameras positioned at intervals all along Norwood Road and Norwood High Street and back towards Tulse Hill, Herne Hill and Brixton. It's a bit sketchy further south. Anyway, I concentrated on the cemetery initially. You can see vehicles turn in and come out through the broken gates, though the cameras are at the wrong angle to see registration numbers and with the winds that night they're vibrating about a bit so a lot of the footage is blurry. I started from 7 p.m. because we know that Emma phoned Susan on the home landline then. There were actually quite a few vehicles that came and went throughout the evening; though God knows why anyone would want to be going in there on a windy, dark Sunday night. Anyway, I noted down what I could of the vehicle makes and models and the times they entered and left. Most stayed between fifteen minutes to an hour or so. As it got later fewer cars came and went.'

Bet checked a piece of notepaper in front of her on the desk.

'But then at 23.19 a dark-coloured Vauxhall estate enters. I checked back several times, but it looks to only have one occupant, the driver. Anyway, it stays until 01.34. It's in there for over two hours! Why on Earth would a single person be in a cemetery for two hours at that time of night?'

'Unless he's not alone? Maybe there is another person with him that we can't see,' Charlie voiced her thoughts.

'Exactly what I was thinking too. So I started checking it out more carefully. When the car comes out at 01.34, it turns left onto the one-way system because it has to, but then goes all the way round and heads off north in the direction of Tulse Hill. Paul has helped me track back over its movements after it left. We've looked at all the cameras in Norwood Road but only managed to get a partial index; the film was too grainy and blurred because of the weather conditions. I thought it was still a good lead and that's when I phoned you. I know they can do wonders with partial index numbers these days, especially if we know the make and model of the vehicle. But... while we were waiting for you to come back, Naz and Sabira came in and we've all been viewing the CCTV from around the Tulse Hill one-way system. It's much better lit and the car comes to a stop at the lights for ten seconds at least. Look at what we've just found.'

'I think we heard. You were so engrossed you didn't see us come in, but let's have a look.' Hunter moved closer.

Paul rewound a minute or so of recording and they moved aside to let Hunter and Charlie see better. She watched as a large, dark-coloured estate car came into view, driving slowly around the one-way system, its brake lights illuminated as it eased down the hill and stopped at the red light on the South Circular. The wind had made the footage vibrate with tree boughs swinging in and out of the camera sights, obscuring the view intermittently, but they could still see the stationary vehicle. Paul paused the footage and zoomed in and they could clearly see the registration number LVo7JCF, just as Naz had shouted out.

'That's great work, all of you, but especially you, Bet and Paul. Maybe I won't send you back out on the beat after all. There's only one thing that I'm thinking though. Can we say that the car at the cemetery is definitely this one? If we weren't able to see the registration plate as it entered and left, and then only got a partial index between the graveyard and here, could the defence say that it's not the same car?'

Bet turned to Hunter, a triumphant look on her face. 'Boss, watch this. Press play, Paul.'

He did as he was told and they watched as the traffic lights turned to green and the car pulled slowly away.

Bet pointed excitedly at the screen. 'Look, boss. As it pulls away, the driver takes his foot off the brakes so the brake lights go out. Without them dazzling the view of the light cluster, you can see that the rear nearside light is out. That's the same as the vehicle going in and out of the cemetery and along Norwood Road. Every image we have shows the same defective light. The car leaves the murder scene at 01.34 and after three minutes arrives at Tulse Hill at 01.37, which is spot on too. With all the other details and the timeline as it is, the defence wouldn't have a hope if they tried to argue that. It all fits together perfectly.'

Hunter clapped his hands together enthusiastically. Charlie could see he was fired up. They all were.

'Excellent work, Bet. It looks like we've got our murderer's car bang to rights.' He looked round at his jubilant team before raising his voice slightly. 'Right team! Now we've got our car. We've just got to find who was driving it.'

14

'LV07JCF comes back to a dark blue Vauxhall Vectra 1.8i five-door estate. It's registered and insured to a single male by the name of Oscar Abrahams, date of birth 29/12/1968, who is shown living at 14 Burnet Grove, Camberwell, SE5.'

Charlie scribbled the details down in her pad before entering the male's details into the computer. 'Woah, he's very well known. Shown as an RSO with sixteen previous convictions. I'll have a look at what they are.' She started scrolling down through them.

'Dirty bastard,' Paul muttered. 'I hate registered sex offenders. There's no excuse these days. If you want sex, it's easy to get, without forcing it on others. Just sign up to one of the hundreds of websites and say you're not interested in a relationship, you'll get plenty of offers.'

'Is that how you do it, Paul?'

'It's how everyone's doing it. Ask Naz and Sabira. They've signed up with a few recently.'

'Not that it's doing me any good.' Naz raised her eyebrows. 'All the ones I meet who say they want a relationship, clearly want relationships with fourteen others at the same time.'

'And there're not too many young Asian females out there either who are brave enough to have come out,' Sabira added. 'Most are too frightened of being sent back to India by their parents if they do.'

'I thought things were changing in that respect, Sab,' Bet queried.

'I wish I could say they were, but attitudes are slow to change, especially in the older generation, and my culture is based on respect for the elderly. Younger people are more enlightened, but just too scared. You can meet Asian girls online, but having any sort of relationship is nigh on impossible. Arranged marriages are still the norm and homosexuality still a taboo. Can't you see that from my workload?'

Bet nodded. The majority of Sabira's work was dealing with domestic assaults and offences around 'honour' customs, as well as the increased Islamophobia heightened by the terror attacks in France and the rest of mainland Europe.

'Yes, you are busy. It's a real shame. Let's hope things improve a bit quicker.'

'It can't come quick enough. What about you, Charlie?'

She stopped reading the screen momentarily. 'I haven't time for all that, besides, Ben keeps me busy enough as it is. He's doing well beating the booze and getting fitter. It's not long to go before Tough Guy and, at the rate he's going, he'll be the one waiting for me, rather than the other way round.'

'I thought he was always waiting for you?' Paul said. 'One day you'll either make him the happiest man on Earth or break his heart.'

'Don't say that, Paul. He's such a lovely bloke. Anyway, back to business,' she changed the subject. She didn't want to dwell on what might or might not happen with Ben in the future. 'This Oscar Abrahams guy is a real sicko. Most of his convictions are for sexual assaults on young boys, some as young as five and six, plus two for buggery with victims aged eleven and twelve years. He's been to prison on several occasions; which has probably widened his social circle and made him even worse. He's also got previous for possessing obscene material, some random theft type offences and drugs.'

'So why would he be targeting middle-aged women?'

'I don't know.' Paul had a point. She tried to think of anything remotely credible. 'Maybe it's not all middle-aged women. Maybe it was Susan Barton specifically. She was a teacher and his address is not that far away from the Academy where she worked. Maybe he was conducting some sort of liaison with one of the kids at the school and she'd found out and gone to the headteacher.'

She thought back to the secret that she suspected the three teachers were keeping. 'Maybe there was some sort of connection between him and the Academy that they were trying to hide? There was something going on there.'

'Well, it's an interesting theory, whatever the truth.' Paul pulled a pair of handcuffs out of his drawer and banged them on the table in front of him. 'Hopefully he'll have a chance to explain himself, very shortly.'

'I'll get a photo of him and check the address we've got. If that looks current, we could go and bring him in now.'

Charlie ran the address through various search engines. The voter's register and Police National Computer showed him living at the same address in Camberwell. There was no one else shown as living there and no other obvious risks, such as dangerous dogs.

Hunter walked back through from his office and Charlie filled him in on what they'd established about Abrahams. She knew that he would feel the same as Paul. He'd often said how he hated 'nonces'. There weren't many police officers, or for that matter, members of the public anywhere who didn't.

'Right, give me a few minutes and I'll get a few troops lined up. We'll go and get the dirty bastard straightaway.'

'OK boss. I'll get a quick briefing prepared.'

True to his word, within a matter of minutes the office was buzzing with extra officers. The briefing was short and to the point, with the group huddled round Charlie's workstation listening intently.

The house at 14 Burnet Grove, SE5 was a large Victorian property, split into three converted flats, each flat occupying a floor to itself. Abrahams lived in the first-floor flat. She pulled up an image of the house that she'd found on Google Earth and pointed to the front door to the premises. To its right were three doorbells, so it was probable that a security system was installed to prevent easy entry to the building. Access to the rear garden was open, with no fences or walls to bar their way.

Sabira would go immediately to the rear of the house to watch for any signs of movement, or on entry, for anything discarded by Abrahams. Charlie didn't want to give him the chance to dispose of evidence before they were in and muddy the waters should the case reach court.

Paul would then try to establish definitively if Abrahams was there by pretending to be a pizza delivery man and persuading Abrahams to let him in to speak with him. He was a dab hand at this, having undertaken the same role on many occasions before. He was already in the process of organising himself a high visibility tabard, crash helmet and leaflets from a locker at the back of their office, as well as ordering an actual pizza in case Abrahams called his bluff.

If there was no sign of their suspect or they were unable to confirm his presence, they would wait and watch, while Naz got an out-of-hours warrant from a local Magistrate. She was typing one up in readiness. They couldn't force entry, if Abrahams wasn't there, without one.

If, however, Abrahams was there Paul would hold the communal door to allow the arrest team easier access. On Hunter's order they would queue up behind the building line, before advancing in through the communal door, and heading upstairs to Abrahams' flat. A member of the MIT team would smash through it with an enforcer, or 'big red key' as it was more fondly known, and once breached they would enter, secure and arrest Oscar Abrahams and anyone else in the premises. If Paul wasn't able to hold the communal door, it too would be forced.

All officers were to wear their body armour and carry safety equipment and the two officers first through the door would be armed with tasers, to use if they assessed any threat of violence.

That was it, the whole operation shouldn't last more than a few minutes before they had their suspect arrested, in handcuffs and ready to be processed, hopefully through to charge. They just needed him to be there.

'Any questions?'

Charlie stood back and waited, but there were none.

'Right, I'll show you the latest custody image of Abrahams. He has warning signals of 'violence' and 'drugs' and is a registered sex offender with pre-cons for sex offences against children, predominantly boys. He is also a drug user, so be prepared for needles or any paraphernalia you might find in the flat. And, needless to say, we have to do this correctly if we're not to give the bastard a get-out-of-jail-free card. So please, be professional; even though you might not want to be. You know the score.'

There was a hum of disapproval at her words. They knew the sort of stuff they would be expecting to find. It was not a job that any of them relished.

Quickly, she put Oscar Abrahams' details into the custody imaging icon and watched as his name sprang up; last arrested for possession of indecent images at the end of 2015. Within a moment, Abrahams was staring out of the computer at them from the front and side profiles; thickset, thick-jowled, shaven-headed and with a tattoo of the male gender symbol on both sides of his neck.

Every now and again she'd seen an image that made a chill run down her spine. His was one of them. She clicked on the forward-facing photo and looked at it closely, letting her mind take in the shape of his head, hairline, set of his jaw, the size and shape of his lips, nose and ears, every wrinkle, every nuance. She wouldn't forget him after she'd done this; ever. His eyes were the most startling feature; black, fixed and soulless, devoid of any emotion. He stared straight at the camera, as if challenging anyone to find an ounce of guilt for the offence for which he'd been arrested. She had a look at previous arrest images. His appearance had barely changed from one to the next. Barring a few signs of ageing he was the same now at nearly fifty as he had been at eighteen.

She reminded herself of the last few words she had said, about being professional. Looking at his face now, she felt sick to the core, thinking about what he had done in the past. She would need to concentrate hard to put her words into action, when everything in her head wanted to lock him in a cell with a group of his now adult victims and leave him to their mercy.

She stared back at his image, wondering whether he would show the slightest bit of emotion when told he was to be arrested for the crime they were investigating. Somehow she doubted it.

Within the next hour, they would find out.

15

Camberwell was a forgotten area, squeezed to the east of Lambeth and to the west of Peckham. It sat within the borough of Southwark and housed Camberwell Green Magistrates Court, first stop for all criminals charged in the neighbouring boroughs.

Other than regularly attending the courthouse, Charlie knew only two facts about the area; the first one being that Carter Street police station, now renamed Walworth police station, had had a reputation for treating their customers roughly in the 1970s and 80s. Her mate Bill Morley had often told her about times when suspects arrested on the borders of Lambeth and Lewisham would plead to be taken to Brixton, rather than Carter Street, because they feared a beating. That was in the old days though, when summary justice was meted out regularly and criminals accepted that was the price they paid for getting caught. Things had changed a lot since then and, according to Bill, not all for the better.

The only other thing Charlie knew about Camberwell was that some of her distant relatives had come from the area. One day she'd do some research and see if any of them were likely to have had experience of Carter Street. With the family history she had been made privy to, it was likely they had.

Her mind was idly thinking about this now as their convoy passed Elephant and Castle and travelled along Walworth Road towards Camberwell. They passed Walworth police station, recognisable by its distinctive red-brick walls and blue lantern, like all the old police stations in London, and turned left into East Street. This was home to a daily, bustling market; closed now for the night, its stalls empty and locked up. An array of discarded rotten vegetables and fruit, empty food containers and boxes lay in piles, awaiting the attention of the night cleaners. A few stray dogs sniffed around the debris, looking to hoover up any scraps before the night-time rat population graced the pavements.

A few lefts and rights and they were there. They parked up in the next road along and quietly made their way, with Sabira heading off first to the rear of the premises. Paul donned his crash helmet and prepared to leave. A number of trees would give cover for the line-up of police officers, as they waited for Paul to make his enquiries. Hunter stood back watching from behind. He would be taking the call from Paul and issuing the command to go, or re-bus as the case may be.

Charlie moved to the middle of the line of police officers. She wanted to be one of the first in, after the entry team. Whether arresting Abrahams or not, she needed to know that they had done everything they could to obtain justice for Emma Barton and her brother. Her earpiece crackled into life, just a check that everything was ready and communications were working correctly. Her heart was pumping almost as loud as the radio broadcast. It always did. It was this part of the job that she loved the most.

'There's a light on at the rear in the first-floor flat but I haven't seen any movement as yet. I can also see people in the ground-floor flat.' Sabira's voice was loud and clear.

Paul's voice followed. 'Standby. I'll check the front door.'

There was silence for what seemed like hours, before he addressed Hunter again. 'The front communal door is locked. Boss, do you want me to deploy in my pizza delivery gear now?'

'Yes, please. Give his flat a try. You know what you need to do.'

'All received. Will do.'

'Standby! Everyone in position?'

Charlie moved forward with the line to their allotted spot behind the row of trees at the side of the property and confirmed for the benefit of Hunter and the others they were all in place. Sabira verified she was still in position and was ready. Hunter was at the rear of the line.

She could see her breath fanning out in front of her in the cold autumnal air, her heart beating rapidly. She tried to hold her breath.

'Paul, go ahead now.' Hunter instructed.

Paul moved forward to the front door. He had the crash helmet on, but had pulled the visor up and was holding a large red bag, with its zip open slightly, to show a pizza box. Charlie could just see him, from behind a tree trunk. He pressed the doorbell and she heard a short conversation.

After a few moments a buzzer sounded and Paul pushed the door open, moving forward into the hallway and wedging it ajar. A light came on and he disappeared up the stairs and out of sight. Charlie held her breath waiting as the seconds lengthened. Two minutes later he walked back into view, holding the door wide open in the light from the hallway, his tabard shining eerily.

'To confirm,' Paul's voice piped back up on the radio. 'It's a positive ID. Oscar Abrahams is in his flat and I have the communal door open.'

'All received. Everyone else go, go, go!' Hunter commanded.

The line moved forward, up the steps and into the front door, across the hallway and up, to the first-floor flat. One punch through with the enforcer did the job. The interior door was flimsy and easily gave way. And then they were in, the rapid entry team shouting loudly to disorientate their quarry.

Abrahams was in the back room, lounging on a settee, a can of beer by the side of him and a laptop open on his knees. He snapped it shut as they streamed in, and tried to throw it down under the table to his side. He was too late. The first two officers through the door took hold of each arm and Charlie, who was right behind them, grabbed the computer.

After initially attempting to resist, Abrahams' arms were forced up behind his back and handcuffs prevented any further movement. He relaxed and smiled suddenly towards his captors, a brief twitch of the lips that didn't extend to his cheeks or eyes.

'You are macho, aren't you, boys! Just how I like 'em.'

Charlie watched as the two officers lifted his arms up behind him, the tiny adjustment forcing him on to his toes, calling out in pain, as his shoulders took the brunt.

'Alright officers, you win.' He smiled again as he spoke, his words slurring into a drawl which made his speech difficult to understand.

They released their grip and he slid back down on to his heels.

Charlie looked him up and down. His head glistened with sweat, even though the temperature in the room was cool. His tattoos could be clearly seen, inked in black against the paleness of his neck. He was tall and well-built, but with more fat than muscle. A navy T-shirt barely covered a large beer belly, which hung over the top of grubby, beige cotton slacks, straining to be freed from the tight waistband. His zip was open. He was disgusting.

Hunter nodded towards her so she stepped up to speak.

'Oscar Abrahams, I'm arresting you on suspicion of murder. You do not have to say anything but it may harm your defence if you do not mention, when questioned, something you later rely on in court. Anything you do say may be given in evidence.'

Abrahams didn't flinch, nor did his expression change. It was as if he didn't care what was said to him, or had known what was coming. He stood staring at her, with exactly the same look on his face as in the images she had recorded in her memory. Somehow, seeing him now in person, made them that much more ugly. There was something about the man that was dead. If anyone could do the sort of things that Susan Barton had had done to her, he could.

'Murder, you say?' He appeared nonchalant. 'Yet another police stitch-up. Am I to be told who I am supposed to have murdered?'

'A female called Susan Barton.'

'Really? Is that the best you can do? You should know I don't like women. So, what now?' Even his voice was flat and lifeless.

'You come back to the police station with us.'

'Oh, what a surprise,' he snorted with derision. 'Then you interview me, realise it's a pile of crap, dust me down and bail me out and then after six months you bring me back in to say there's no further action!'

She hated his sarcasm. He was nothing more than a sick paedophile. She didn't like the man and she wasn't going to even attempt to sweeten him up.

'If you think I am going to dust you down and NFA you, you'd better think again. I promise you I will get officers here, who will tear your flat apart to find every little thing of interest to us. So you may as well tell us if there's anything here before we do.'

'Look, officer,' he turned to face her. 'You can try and scare me as much as you want. I've been arrested a dozen or more times and been to prison for seven years, so if you think you're going to find anything incriminating here, you must be more stupid than you look.'

She stepped in so close she could smell the beer on his stinking breath. 'And if you think we're not going to find every single thing we need to get you sent down, then you're more stupid than you look, if that's possible. I promise you that every single one of us here will not stop until we get what we need to bang you up for a lifetime.'

'You can try.'

Abrahams made a point of staring individually at each officer in the room. She knew what most of them would be wishing they could do. She did too.

Hunter didn't wait for Abrahams to get to him. Stepping forward he stretched out his fingers and pushed the man, not hard, but with enough force to make him lose his balance, teetering ungainly before falling backwards on to the settee.

'Sit down and shut your mouth, you sick shit. I can guess what you were doing when we came in and if it's what I think, I'll make sure I, personally, will get you charged.'

Abrahams lay across the cushions, unable to push himself upwards into a sitting position, his arms still pinned behind his back with the metal restraints. His T-shirt rose up, exposing his belly still further as he struggled to move, like a seal, floundering pathetically on pack ice. The fly of his trousers gaped. His eyes flicked up to a large painting on the wall and he smiled lazily. The painting showed a Christ-like figure, surrounded by children, some sitting on his lap, some at his feet, all looking up at the man adoringly.

'What's on the computer?' Hunter indicated the laptop that had been thrown down on their arrival.

Abrahams opened his mouth, as if to remonstrate but then said nothing, instead staring at them both intently.

Charlie picked it up and placed it on the table, opening the lid. It hadn't had time to shut down and was still showing the page he'd been viewing. A video clip was playing, on an endless loop. She heard the voices first before she saw what was on display. The voice was that of a young boy crying as his face was forced forward into the crotch of a grown man. The camera zoomed in for a close-up of the boy's face, his mouth forced open, his eyes wide with pure fear. As Charlie realised, with horror, just what they were all watching, the man took hold of the young boy by his hair, pulled his head forward and grunted loudly one last time.

Oscar Abrahams ignored the Detective Inspector. He was just a bully.

Instead he watched the policewoman. He hadn't liked her when she'd first spoken but now he was watching her with delight. It turned him on, the way her sight was concentrated on his favourite viewing. It was special; a man's expression of love towards a boy. What was wrong with it? The boy was just a little upset because it was all so overwhelming. Little did he know how good it could be with an older man to show him the way? Youngsters were the future; they needed to be moulded, taught. They needed to experience the love between two people. They needed to start young, to learn from the beginning. It was pure and beautiful and it was how all his group of friends felt.

He caught a glimpse of himself in the mirror on the opposite wall and tried to sit up and suck in his stomach. He needed a bit of work, but he was still pretty impressive and manly. Everything a young boy could want. Everything a young boy could aspire to.

The policewoman had snapped the laptop shut again. Her expression had turned from mild curiosity to disgust, almost within seconds. He didn't like it; not one bit. She was like all the others who didn't understand and wanted him to stop. She was looking down on him now, judging him.

A swell of pure anger rippled through his body, burning like a red-hot poker in his brain. His head was pounding. Why wouldn't the police leave him and his friends in peace? Why couldn't they understand he would never stop? Why should he? He didn't want to change and if anyone ever tried to prevent his life continuing as it had, he would be forced to take action.

He glanced at the officers, finishing at the policewoman, DC Stafford. She was a bitch and he hated her for judging him. He wasn't hurting the boy. He never intentionally did. Anyway these days when he did join in, he made sure he hid the evidence. He'd been arrested enough to know the score. Whatever he did would not be discovered. She was a fool to insist they'd find what they wanted.

He turned his eyes towards her and fixed her with a stare, trying to remember her face. One day he might bump into her out on the streets and have the opportunity to put her straight. One day all the judgemental bitches would leave him alone. He thought about what he might do to them. One day.

16

It was early morning when Charlie walked into the churchyard to visit Jamie's grave. The gate creaked behind her as she entered, enclosing her in its silence. She knew the way with her eyes shut. It was dark and the sun was low, only its uppermost edges able to push weakly through the low-lying clouds. A dusting of frost lay on top of the trees and bushes, ice-topped needle grasses growing liberally from the edges of the tombstones. The trees were still. Everywhere was quiet; even the birds sat mutely on high branches, their beaks closed in silent despondency.

As she walked, Charlie gazed around at the piles of dull, fallen leaves. She hated autumn. The green vibrancy of the spring and summer foliage had disappeared and the world seemed bathed in decay. At the sound of the alarm that morning she had so wanted to roll over and fall back to sleep but she couldn't, her guilt forced her up. She had to come, every week, on a Wednesday, whatever the weather and however much she wanted more sleep. She owed it to her brother. Besides, she needed to be there to remind herself of the injustice of his death and to give herself the motivation to fight for every single victim who had ever been let down by the judicial system.

Her mind rewound to the events surrounding his death as it did whenever she entered the graveyard; her and Jamie in a boat with her stepfather Harry and his mate Arthur, both drinking, both unaware of the fast-approaching storm. Then the fear, the panic, the freezing water as the boat went down with no working bilge pump, no flares and just one life jacket given to her as the only girl aboard. Nothing to save her little brother being swallowed into the blackness of the ocean. She would never forget being hauled from the sea alongside Harry, knowing that Jamie was still within its depths, the agony of waiting; waiting for hours and hours before his cold, lifeless body was recovered.

Arthur too drowned that day, his death preventing her and Meg ever receiving the justice they craved for failing to maintain a seaworthy boat and for being drunk when, as the skipper, he should have been alert to the dangers. Harry chose to forget his part in the tragedy; Arthur's demise allowed him to place the blame squarely on his mate's failing.

It had been Charlie who had suffered the most though. It had been she who had wanted the adventure, who had persuaded Jamie to come. Now it was she who was constantly wracked with survivor's guilt.

So every Wednesday without fail, she turned up alone and lonely, her trek also serving to emphasise the gaping hole that still existed between her and her mother, who she was sure blamed her for her brother's death.

Today however seemed worse than usual. The arrest of Oscar Abrahams had been well executed but they hadn't as yet found the car. Cornell Miller was still on the loose. Her mother was still as distant as ever. Even the fact that Ben was on the road to recovery and doing well raised its own issues. A sense of dejection descended on her shoulders like a thick, heavy cloak, which she was powerless to shift. Everything looked dead and everything felt dead.

She stepped forward into the copse where Jamie's gravestone was situated and tenderly ran her finger along the carving of his name. The air was freezing within its sanctuary and the stone, too, felt cold. She slid down and sat on the frozen earth, with her back against it, imagining her brother's cold body underneath her, spiralling downwards into the iciness of his watery grave. She couldn't tear herself away from the image. Normally being in his presence motivated her and stirred her into action, but today nothing helped.

A low buzz and a slight vibration in her trouser pocket roused her from her thoughts. Her work phone was ringing. She checked her watch. It was far too early for normal work calls. Pulling the phone from her pocket, she saw a name illuminated on the screen. It was Moses Sinkler. She pressed the button and put the phone to her ear, recognising immediately the low gravelly voice of her friend.

'Hello, is that Charlie?' His voice was tremulous and she could feel his fear crackling through the line.

'Yes, Moses, it's me. Are you alright?'

'No, not really.' He paused briefly. 'He's been here. He's left a handwritten note threatening to torch the house and that he would laugh as he watched us all fry.'

'OK Moses. I presume you mean Miller? Do you know if he's still there? I'll get help straight away if he is.'

'Yes it's Miller, he even signed his name on it, but I'm pretty sure he's gone. I heard a clatter from the letter box about an hour ago when I was still in bed, but when I heard nothing more I went back to sleep. I've just found the message since getting up, but I don't really want to leave the house to check.'

'Stay where you are. I'm coming but I'll be about an hour. If he comes back in that time, call 999. I'll let the control room know to deal with all calls to your address as urgent. I'll be with you as soon as I can.'

'Thanks Charlie. Be quick.'

She heard the phone click off and stood up, dusting the earth from the seat of her trousers. A sudden gust of wind teased the topmost branches of the trees that surrounded them. She looked up as the breeze rippled across the conifers and noticed suddenly the green of their leaves, contrasting with the bright red of the berries of a holly bush that was competing for light with a large oak, rising majestically behind. There was life thriving all around her after all.

She started to run from the graveyard, knowing instinctively that Jamie was the one who had sent the phone call from Moses, breathing new energy into her and her surroundings. She kissed the end of her fingertips and blew the kiss back towards his gravestone, whispering a word of thanks to her late brother. If Cornell Miller wasn't already on the daily briefings, he soon would be. They would be on his tail every step of the way, until he was banged up for good. She would make sure of that.

★

Moses Sinkler saw Charlie pull up directly outside his house from his vantage point behind the curtains in the front room. He had been sitting there for just on an hour, glued to the spot, watching in case Miller came into sight.

He was so frightened he hardly dared breathe. He watched as the detective slammed the car door shut and strode up the path to the front door before getting up and letting her in.

'Quick, Charlie, come in,' he wanted the door shut as soon as possible. He called to his wife who he could hear moving about in the kitchen. 'Claudette, Charlie's here, can you put the kettle on, love?'

He led the way back to his little front room, casting a glance anxiously towards the window and offered Charlie a seat. From the first time he had set eyes on her she had been his saviour, sometimes sitting for hours dealing with his fears. He was glad she'd come so quickly now. The letter lay on the table, written in a barely legible scrawl on a scrappy piece of paper. He pointed to it and watched as Charlie pulled on blue plastic gloves and threaded it carefully straight into a see-through evidence bag, before reading it.

'You've obviously touched it, Moses. Has Claudette?'

'No, just me. I showed it to Claudette, but she hasn't touched it. It's been there on the table since I read it. I keep coming back and looking at it.' He moved across to join Charlie. 'Look, he's even signed his name.' He pointed to the bottom of the note. There, clearly on display in large, bold letters was the name 'Cornell' with a smiley face drawn after it. 'He's sick in the head, don't you think?'

'Yes, I think you're right but we're on to him, Moses.'

He watched as she spoke. The words were upbeat but her face told a different story.

'We've tried his family addresses, but he's not stupid. He won't go to the obvious ones that we know about. He'll find other places to go, but we'll get him soon.'

'How long do you think it will take?' He could hear the tremble in his own voice.

'That's the trouble, we don't know. We could strike lucky and find him at one of his old haunts; sometimes we'll get information as to where a suspect is and can go straight there. Sometimes we'll catch them in the act of another crime.'

'Has he done another?'

'Yes, we believe so.'

He watched as she picked up the evidence bag and read through the note again.

'So what do you want to do, Moses?' She placed the bag back on the table and sat down.

He followed suit, sitting forward on his favourite chair opposite the TV. All around him were the trappings of his life, photos of his children and grandchildren, mementos of places they'd visited, gifts from friends, family and even the kids he'd coached at football. In the centre of the mantelpiece were images of his parents, standing tall, in black and white print, faded over the years but with the undeniable pride of a generation born into the knowledge that everything they achieved and owned was the result of their own toil.

Claudette shuffled in with a tray holding a steaming mug of tea for each of them and a small plate of Charlie's favoured biscuits. He looked on as she took the cup from his wife and helped herself to three biscuits. This was what his life was about; his wife, his home, his family.

'What can I do?' He knew what the answer would be.

'Well, obviously Miller will also now be wanted for threats to kill, which means we will have greater powers to track him and his phone, but, having said that, at present we don't have a number for him. We'll put the word out to try and get a new number from anywhere we can. We are doing everything else we can to track him down, but sometimes it just comes down to luck. In the meantime there are measures we can take to help you. We can move you to a different address.'

He felt his panic spike at the thought. This was all he'd known for nearly thirty years. His own little fortress against the outside world; until Cornell Miller had attacked and everything had changed. He'd withdrawn into its safety, pulling the drawbridge up as he retreated. Only recently had he dared to leave the place, venturing out locally to buy bits and pieces, gradually feeling the confidence begin to return. Now, every rampart of his castle was under attack again and it scared him to the bone. But at the same time he didn't know if he could leave.

'Or if you don't want to leave here we can have panic alarms fitted so that you can press a button at the slightest suspicion that Miller is nearby and all calls will be treated as urgent. We are also able to get cameras and mikes fitted and I'll see if we can put on extra patrols around your area. I will personally make sure this is done today, if this is what you choose.'

He liked this option better. At least here he knew the place, every nook and cranny where someone could hide, every place that he could secrete a stick or pole to defend himself and his wife. He looked up at his partner of nearly forty years, settling down in her own favourite chair, pushing her long, white hair back over her ears. They both loved this house, this road, their neighbours and everything about the place. How could he drag her away from everything she had known?

His reverie was broken by the sound of Charlie's voice again.

'Obviously the threat is arson which is quite hard to deal with. He could pour something through the letter box or throw something through a window in a matter of seconds; so if you choose to stay you will need to take as many precautions as possible. Board up your letter box or at least have nothing flammable nearby. I can arrange for you to have a couple of fire extinguishers to keep near you at all times. Make sure you have a plan of what to do if he does turn up; have keys to escape routes on hand. If the worst comes to the worst, have an area that you can remain as safe as possible, until fire crews get you out.'

'You think it could come to that?' He was appalled.

'I'm looking at the worst case scenario, Moses, but it is a possibility, if Miller really does have a point to make; however sick and twisted that point is.'

'He might still do that even if we moved out.' His mind was racing now. 'We could be sitting in a strange place and hear that our house has been torched. We could have everything we've worked so hard for destroyed without even having the chance to fight for it. This is our home, where our children were born and raised. We have every right to live here in peace.'

He saw Claudette turn her head towards him and tried to read her thoughts. She trusted him to make the right decision. She always had. Now as he looked at her he saw the merest nod. Her eyes held his and at that moment he could sense her inner strength and knew what she would want him to do.

He stood up and walked to the window, standing with his back to Charlie and Claudette. It was becoming clearer now. He had a choice, even though the choice was an unenviable one: stay and try to save his house if attacked, or leave and possibly come home to a burnt-out shell, their whole life destroyed in the strike of a match. An elderly neighbour hobbled past and waved cheerily towards him with her walking stick, the show of friendship echoing Claudette's thoughts. He felt the pressure lifting from his shoulders. The feeling of helplessness was receding and in its place the first stirring of strength was creeping back into his body. He waved back, his mind made up.

'Charlie, can you arrange all those things for us. We'll make some backup plans like you suggest.'

She got up and came across to join him, patting him on the back gently, before placing her hand on his shoulder. He was so glad she had made the time to come and speak to him, but now he needed to do something himself. It was his turn to take back control. He reached up, placing his hand on top of hers and his confidence soared.

'I'm not going to let this vicious bully drive us out of our home. Cornell Miller is not going to beat us.'

17

Hunter was in his office when Charlie walked in.

'What time do you call this? I've been waiting for you. We need to interview Abrahams and the time is moving on.'

He looked her up and down with an expression that alternated between full-blown professional irritation and a hint of paternal tolerance and amusement. She thought he was going to launch into one of his 'dragged through a hedge backwards' monologues but instead she saw his eyes flick between the desk calendar and his watch. He knew where she always went on a Wednesday.

Still it was nearly ten o'clock and she did have to admit to having a muddy seat to the back of her trousers and some tea stains where the third biscuit she'd dunked at Moses' house had disintegrated in her hands on to the front of her shirt, before rolling down over her bust in a gingery mudslide. No manner of soaking and wiping by Claudette had been able to fully remove the path of the biscuit.

'Sorry, boss. I had a call from Moses Sinkler. Miller had been to his house in the early hours of the morning and left a note threatening to torch it and anyone in it. Naz and I are in the process of setting up special measures to give him as much protection as possible. He didn't want to leave.'

Hunter shook his head. 'Must be a hard decision for Moses. I can't believe Miller's still terrorising that poor man. We wouldn't drop the case now, even if Moses wanted us to. Miller's too much of a threat. Do what you have to, quickly though. We need to get him nicked. I know Naz is taking the lead at the moment. Brief her and then we'll go and speak to Abrahams in...' He checked his watch and raised his eyebrows, 'about fifteen minutes. Oh, and try to smarten yourself up just a little. You look like you need a bib.'

She felt the colour rush to her cheeks, but he was right. She did look a mess. She'd chucked the bag of clean clothes her mum had left by the front door straight into her locker when she'd arrived. As she started making her way towards the locker room, she hoped there'd be a few nicely washed and ironed shirts in it.

The locker door barely closed with the amount crammed into its base. Christ! She needed to sort it out. Her old uniform still hung from the rails, old white shirts now replaced by smart polo shirts in an attempt to bring today's uniform up to date. Her epaulettes sat on the top shelf, with her old shoulder number spelt out in white metal numerals. Since becoming a detective, it still felt strange being referred to by name, not number. She preferred the anonymity of numbers; they felt safer. These days with the popularity of social media, names were too easy to trace.

She pulled the nearest bag out from the bottom of the locker, gave it a quick sniff test that confirmed it was the latest addition and selected a checked shirt. That would have to do, though it looked more outside casual than cutting-edge smart. There were no clean trousers; she'd just have to sit down as often as she could so that no one could see the muddy marks.

Back in the office, she spoke with Naz and Sabira. There was another robbery that looked to be attributed to Miller just coming in, reported a day after it had happened by the hospital after the victim, an illegal immigrant, had eventually staggered in with open wounds from the previous day's attack. By all accounts he had been too afraid to come in at the time for fear of being deported. It had all the hallmarks of Miller; excessive violence and racist abuse for little actual gain. She felt sick at the thought. Naz and Sabira were following up Moses' wishes, making sure all the contingency plans agreed earlier were being actioned.

She herself would phone Moses later to check that everything was in place and he was as prepared as he could be for all eventualities but hopefully it wouldn't come to that.

Bet and Paul were sitting in front of several computer screens at Bet's desk, a pile of DVDs in evidence bags on either side. An array of nibbles lay in front of them, ranging from tortilla crisps and peanuts with a savoury sour cream dip, to Jaffa Cakes, chocolate Minstrels and Skittles, crowned in the centre with a large bag of jam doughnuts.

'Great spot yesterday, you two. What are you doing now? It looks like you're set up for the day.'

Paul looked up as she spoke, a slight chocolate residue from his last Jaffa Cake still at the corner of his lips. 'We are. Bet's got her savoury bits and I have my sweet bits. We have to keep going with the CCTV stuff and try to track the car before and after the murder as far as we can. Hunter is hoping we can plot it coming from, and going in the direction of Abrahams' flat, though I'm not sure how many cameras there are out that way.' He leaned towards the pack of doughnuts and held them out towards her. 'Here you go. We've got a pack of eight, extra jammy, haven't we, Bet?'

'Don't you dare, young lady.' Hunter was marching towards them.

Charlie snatched her hand back quickly, reddening slightly again and the others laughed.

'She looks relatively tidy now. I'm not going to interview a murder suspect and be distracted by a big jammy stain down the front of my colleague's clean shirt. She can't be trusted; at least, not when it comes to food and drink.'

'You've got a point there, boss,' Bet laughed. 'No doughnut for you, Charlie, until you've got an admission.'

'Well, that's an incentive if ever I needed one.'

Hunter had already started walking towards the door. Charlie turned to follow him, lifting her shirt at the back as she walked. Bet burst out laughing. Hunter turned round and she shrugged, pretending not to have seen the big dirty smudge on the seat of Charlie's trousers.

Oscar Abrahams was finishing a consultation with his solicitor when Charlie and Hunter entered the custody office.

The door to his interview room opened as she moved past and she caught a glimpse of the man, leaning back in his seat, with legs splayed out in front of him and hands clasped together at the back of his head as if he didn't have a care in the world. She thought back to the recording of the young boy, crying as he was abused. She remembered the sight of Susan Barton's body ripped apart. Those memories would be the thing that would spur her on to getting an admission.

He turned towards her as she passed and his lips turned up in a smirk but his eyes remained dead. She felt a wave of revulsion roll over her. She had rarely had such a strong instantaneous reaction like it. The man disgusted her. She heard the sound of his solicitor telling Abrahams to stay where he was. Though how anybody could defend someone like him was beyond her.

She stopped to get an idea of whether they were ready to start and waited for the solicitor to leave. A shock of white hair in a ponytail belonging to the tall, debonair figure of the solicitor emerged first from around the edge of the door. His skin was tanned and he wore an expensive-looking navy pinstripe suit, with a cream shirt open at the neck in an obvious attempt to appear less formal. She recognised him immediately as Justin Latchmere, a disgraced barrister with whom she'd had previous, unpleasant dealings.

As he turned, she saw, with amusement, the top of a designer 'Mont Blanc' pen sticking out from the breast pocket of his jacket. He just couldn't help himself; money was patently more important to him than morals.

The door shut behind him and he turned to face her.

'Well I never. How the mighty have fallen. I didn't think I'd see you again in this line of work.'

He fixed her with an imperious expression and held his hand out for her to shake. She declined.

'I may have been down, but I am certainly not out. I have been found not guilty of any criminal behaviour or misconduct, except maybe a little impropriety, and I therefore intend to continue my career within the law profession. I aim to speedily regain my previous position, but for the time being I am quite happy to defend individuals who have had spurious allegations levelled against them by police.'

He turned his back on her and paused before opening the interview room door.

'Now, if you're ready to interview my client, DC Stafford, perhaps you can inform the custody sergeant and we can get on, without any further ado.'

He disappeared back inside, taking care to pull the door shut behind him. He would no doubt be reviewing any advice he might give Abrahams now he knew she and Hunter were conducting the interview.

Preliminaries over; Hunter got straight to business. He was to do the main interview, with Charlie watching Abrahams' body language. There were few people when placed under the pressure of an interview that didn't show signals when lying and few people better equipped than Charlie to pick up on them.

'Where were you on Sunday 2nd October 2016?'

'No comment.'

'Were you alone or with anyone?'

'No comment.'

'Were you at 14 Burnet Grove?'

'No comment.'

'Were you working that night?'

'No comment.'

'Do you have any other addresses you go to? Any family, friends, work colleagues that you stay with?'

'No comment.'

'If you were home, what were you doing?'

'No comment.'

'Were you watching TV, or on the computer, doing social media, perhaps?'

'No comment.'

'Was there anyone who could verify where you were that night?'

Abrahams showed no emotion, in fact he appeared to display only boredom and a total lack of interest in anything Hunter asked. Each time he replied, Charlie watched Justin Latchmere's satisfaction appear to grow. They were getting nowhere. Hunter changed his tack.

'Do you know a woman called Susan Barton?'

'No, I don't.'

She pricked her ears up at an actual answer. Hunter continued his line.

'Are you sure you've never met her?'

'No comment.' He was back to his previous retorts.

'She was a teacher. Are you sure you've never met her in connection with her teaching?'

'No comment.'

'Have you been involved in any extra studies?'

'No comment.'

'Have you any connection with any Harris Academy school?'

'No comment.'

'Particularly the Harris Academy at Crystal Palace?'

'No comment.'

'Do you have any connections with anyone else who works at the school? Or any pupils who went there previously? Or go there now? Or anyone who might know Susan Barton?'

'No comment.'

'How about her church? She was a regular churchgoer. Might you know her from her church?'

'What do you think?' Abrahams grunted with obvious amusement at the question, before turning to see the expression on his solicitor's face. 'Look, officer, I do not know her.'

'She helped out with lots of church meetings and charities. Might you know her from any of them?'

'No comment.'

'So if we find any links with her we will know you're lying?'

'No comment.'

Hunter sat back, flicking through some notes that he had made earlier. He took his time and as the seconds lengthened into minutes, Abrahams started to fidget. Charlie knew exactly what Hunter was doing. He'd been taking it easy, allowing Abrahams to think he had the upper hand, allowing him to make any comments or denials that might be shown to be lies if any further evidence or links came to light. Now he was relaxed the more important questions might catch him off guard. Eventually Hunter leant forward across the desk and stared straight at him.

'Do you own a dark blue Vauxhall Vectra estate registration number LV07JCF?'

'No comment.'

'You're shown as owning one, according to the DVLA. So where is it?'

Abrahams coughed and threw his hand up over his mouth. He looked down at the tabletop between them, his hand still locked in place. Hunter did not avert his stare.

'The car is still registered to you and you have paperwork and keys for it in your flat.'

'They're spare keys.'

'So where is the car?'

'I don't know.'

'Well I suggest that you do know and you tell me where it is pretty damn quick.'

'I-I don't know where it is. Why?' Abrahams was stammering now. He obviously had something to hide.

'Because your car was seen coming from the place that Susan Barton's mutilated body was found. And I believe you were driving it. So, you'd better be able to give me a very good reason as to why it was there, or else I'll be perfectly within my right to suggest you know a lot more about this whole incident than you are letting on.'

For the first time since coming into contact with Abrahams, Charlie saw a flicker of emotion appear on his face, the first sign of panic. His cheeks were losing their previous colour, his mouth gaped and sweat was beading on his forehead.

'I lent it to my friend.'

'What friend?'

'I don't know his name.'

'Don't lie. Why would anyone lend their car to someone whose name they don't even know? What's his phone number?'

'I don't know.'

'So you've lent your car to someone whose name you don't know and who you can't even contact? That's rubbish.'

'I only know him by his online name. We chat on a website. He asked to borrow it. I've lent him stuff before and he's always returned it with no problem. He said he'd bring it back in a few days.'

'When, exactly?'

'I don't know.'

'So what is his online name?'

'I-I can't remember offhand.'

Abrahams was sweating profusely now, the skin on his cheeks and forehead almost white. He turned towards Latchmere with what looked like a plea for a lifeline. He was digging himself a hole with his own words and now he was teetering on the edge.

'My client needs medical attention immediately, officer. I insist that you stop the interview now, in order that he receives it,' Justin Latchmere's voice boomed out. 'Or I will end the interview myself and make a complaint of abuse of process to the custody officer.'

Oscar Abrahams felt sick. His wordless plea for assistance from his solicitor had worked, thankfully, but he couldn't stop now. He had to carry on the act. He folded his head down into his hands on the table in front of him, moaning noisily.

Why did he always do this? He should have taken his solicitor's advice the whole way through and made no comment. He had been too gobby. He was always the same. It was his own words that got him into trouble, every time, and yet again he had said more than he meant to and needed an outer.

He could feel his heart racing. The panic was not shifting. His solicitor and the police officer were still arguing. Their words were blurred and indistinct but he guessed the gist of the conversation. Justin Latchmere seemed like a good bloke. Maybe he was one of them? Maybe he liked children too. Maybe he should subtly enquire at some point.

His solicitor was standing now, his voice still loud, moving towards the door.

As he heard the police officer eventually say that the interview was concluded and heard the buzz of the tape machine being switched off, he smiled to himself and sent a silent prayer of gratitude up into the ether.

18

'The bastards. The absolute bastards. Just when we had him rattled.' Hunter was fuming.

The interview had been concluded and Abrahams seen by a custody nurse, who had decided that he needed time out to recover. It would be some hours before he was sufficiently well enough to be re-interviewed. Latchmere had disappeared too, his expression that of satisfaction with a job well done. Charlie and Hunter firmly believed that if he could hinder justice, he would – and now it was personal. He would be trying to frustrate them both with any investigation they were involved in. Charlie was equally as annoyed.

'It's shit. You had him squirming. He didn't know what to do with himself at the end there. He knows what's going on. He's up to his neck in it.'

'And yet that fucking slimy bastard Latchmere got him his outer. "PACE says the interview must be stopped. PACE says we need to get him medical assistance." Blah

blah blah. Well the Police and Criminal bleedin' Evidence Act shouldn't be their way of getting out of answering questions. It was absolutely obvious Abrahams was playing a game and Latchmere loved it. He was straight on to it. Sometimes I wonder why we fucking bother. Our hands are tied whatever we do. He'll have sorted out his story by the next time we speak to him.'

'Can we interrogate his computer and see if there is any evidence of this so called "friend" on it?'

'I'll bet a million quid there is no other guy. Or certainly not one that he's lent his car to. He knows he's cocked up with the car so he's hidden it and concocted this story.'

'I'm surprised he panicked so much though. It was like he went into shock, sweating, white and clammy. You'd have thought he would have been calmer, especially bearing in mind how he'd been earlier in the interview.'

'Sometimes the body just takes over. Like you say, it was almost like shock. He couldn't help himself.'

It had been an eye-opener to Charlie. She was used to the hidden clues, the involuntary movement of limbs, eyes being averted, the tone of speech altering slightly, but Abrahams' reaction had been significant. Maybe he thought he'd got away with it. There had been no trace of it at his flat or any of the surrounding roads although they had conducted a thorough search. They hadn't made too big a deal of the car when he was arrested, wanting to play down its importance for just this reason. Better to spring it on him now. It made his guilt so much clearer even though his little game had bought him some time. She thought back over the answers he had given.

'So... he knows that his car is the key. Apart from saying he didn't know Susan and a few facetious comments about her lifestyle, he gave nothing away; he didn't explain what he had been doing on the night of Susan's murder and wouldn't give an alibi at all that we could investigate.'

'That's the trouble. If Abrahams is our man, it's a good cover story. He's claimed to have met a fictitious guy through a chat room; no doubt a secret one he's part of with all his other sick little paedo mates. I'm sure if this friend exists, Abrahams will know his real identity, but he's never going to tell us who he is because he knows this bloke could drop him in it if we were to find him and put pressure on him. He also knows how hard it is for police to break into these websites and chat rooms. They're all on the dark web, they're encrypted, and the bastards that share their sick perversions don't use their names, or certainly not in conversation. We'll be lucky if we can get into the site, never mind an IP address or identity, and if we are actually able to, it'll take weeks. We don't have that time. If we can't find that bloody car or prove some sort of connection between Susan Barton and Abrahams, we'll have to let him out on bail.'

'But, boss, if he is telling the truth and really has lent his car out to a paedophile friend, then this male is another suspect. Or they could be jointly involved? And how on earth is Susan connected?'

They carried on walking in silence, both sickened at the thought. They still had a bit more time to hold him without charge, but if they had nothing further he would be released by the weekend. A forensic team were hard at work in

Abrahams' flat, searching for anything; any fingerprint, fibre or scrap of DNA that might link him to Susan Barton. It was unlikely Susan would have been in his flat though and he'd already intimated that they wouldn't find anything. Why would he have said that unless he knew it was clean? He'd learnt from experience not to leave clues. Paedophiles had a reputation for being devious. If they were lucky, they might find something of note on his dirty clothing or even the most recently washed in his chest of drawers but they certainly couldn't go through every item of clothing in his wardrobes and cupboards in the kind of detail required to get a match. It would take forever.

They needed to find the car; and they needed to find it as soon as possible.

School was just finishing for the day when Charlie reached Harris Academy. With any further work stalled on Abrahams she wanted to put to rest her niggle that the headteacher and staff were hiding something.

As she arrived in the car park she was surrounded by a crowd of babbling teenagers, running, walking and strolling from the building in a mix of large groups, smaller cliques and lone students. A young girl, barely more than thirteen, walked past her alone, with shrunken cheeks and vacant eyes, carrying a large, heavy rucksack whose straps dug into her shoulders, pulling her skinny frame off balance. Charlie had the urge to jump out of her car and run to catch up with the girl, who looked as unhappy in the school environment as she had been. Maybe she too had lost someone close or had issues that were just too hard to discuss. How much easier to keep the hurt locked away and stay detached, rather than bring it out into the open and risk ridicule.

The moment passed and the girl was gone and as the number of students began to dwindle Charlie got out of her car. The reception was nearly empty. It was amazing how quickly a school vacated on the ring of a bell. George, the Victorian receptionist, was seated in his usual position. She went towards him and was about to ask if she could speak with the headteacher when Vincent Atkins himself poked his head out from his office.

He caught sight of her and frowned. 'I thought you were going to ring first to make an appointment. I have a meeting now.'

'Don't worry, Mr Atkins. Maybe I can speak to the others first and come back to you at the end if you're free.'

A door swung open behind her and she immediately recognised the voices of Sophie Pasqual and Daniel Roberts, the two language teachers she had spoken with before. Sophie was carrying a large stack of books.

'Ah hello again, Ms Pasqual and Mr Roberts. Maybe one of you would be free now for a quick chat.'

The headteacher's frown deepened. 'Really officer? I would have preferred a little more notice.'

The Latin teacher looked slightly bemused. 'Vincent, I'm quite happy to speak now. I've nothing I need to do that can't be done later. Or would you rather go first, Sophie?'

Ms Pasqual shook her head. 'You go first, Daniel. I have a pile of marking to get through.'

'Well if you're sure that's all right, Daniel, and you have nothing more pressing?' Atkins cocked his head as if querying the teacher's willingness. It seemed to Charlie that he was trying to give his staff members any excuse not to speak.

Daniel Roberts didn't take the hint. Indicating a small interview room off the main reception, he led the way, holding the door open for her, before entering himself. As it swung shut she caught a glimpse of Vincent Atkins standing motionless, still staring towards them.

'Thank you, Mr Roberts, for making the time to speak to me.'

'You can call me Daniel.' His smile was friendly.

'Thanks then, Daniel. Anyway I apologise for not giving you prior notice. I had some space in my diary suddenly and thought I would take the opportunity to catch anyone free before the school is closed. It appears to be a bit of a problem with your headteacher though?'

She put her observation as more of a question, hoping he would take the bait. He did, coming straight to the point.

'Vincent's worried because he and Susan had recently started an affair. He thought the staff were not aware but it's common knowledge. You can't keep that sort of thing a secret for long. Susan mentioned it to one or two of her friends and it soon got out. She was separated from her husband, so it wasn't really an issue for her, but Vincent is still married. That's why Sophie asked him if he was all right the other day and why I queried whether he had spoken with you. We expected him to have mentioned it straight away, but for some reason he hasn't.'

Charlie nodded, understanding now why the headteacher had been so reticent about talking to her. 'How long had the affair been going on?'

'I don't know exactly when it started, but maybe two to three months.'

'Do you think he was happy that news of their affair had got out? Might it have been getting more serious than he was wanting?'

Daniel Roberts frowned, staring straight at her, and ran his fingers through his beard. 'Now there's a thought. Maybe it was going a bit quicker than he had expected. He was trying to keep the affair quiet so that his wife didn't find out, and I know Susan was a very religious person. She spoke about her faith often and I know she regularly attended her local Catholic church. She was involved in lots of good works. I suppose she could have been putting pressure on him to tell his wife. I can't imagine she would have been happy conducting an affair with a married man in secret. Everyone was surprised that the two of them had got together. He must have thought it was his lucky day.'

'She was popular then?'

'Yes, she was. Everyone liked her. She was pretty and fun to be around and had a bubbly personality.'

'Is there anyone you can think of that might have wanted to cause her harm?'

'Not that I can think of. She got on with all the staff and the pupils all loved her. She'd relaxed more recently too, since splitting with her husband, Mickey.'

'You knew him then?'

'I've met him a couple of times. He always had a lot to say for himself, and when he was around, she was quieter than usual. It's funny really; Mickey liked to look good but was all brawn and no brains. Vincent is all brains, with no looks and barely two coins to rub together after losing a load on some dodgy investments. They're total opposites, but then they say opposites attract. A lot of women are attracted to intellectuals, especially at her age.'

'So they got on well, Susan and Vincent?'

'They were always deep in conversation in the staffroom. That's what got people talking, but I think everyone was surprised to learn that they'd begun a relationship.'

'Do you think Mickey knows about the affair?'

'Now I wouldn't have a clue about that. I know they were still quite close, a bit closer than she would have liked actually. She often complained that he still had a key to her house and she wanted it back. I think she suspected he might let himself in sometimes.'

'Did she say anything else about him? Do you think he was the jealous sort?'

'Well I know a few months back, before they split, we were all at a male colleague's retirement party and Mickey got all upset because he thought Susan was talking to the man for too long. He went and put his arm around her shoulders and started interrupting them, as if to assert she was his property. She looked awfully embarrassed and they left shortly afterwards. I felt sorry for her.'

'Could he have been violent towards her, do you think?'

He paused, stroking his beard and closed his eyes briefly. 'Who knows what goes on behind closed doors, but I have to say, I never saw anything.'

Sophie Pasqual was next. She said almost the same as Daniel had. The affair between Vincent Atkins and Susan Barton was a badly kept secret that they all knew about. Vincent had been conducting the liaison without his wife of thirty-five years' knowledge and she was likely to be devastated. He was trying to keep it quiet.

Both Vincent and Mickey appeared to be harbouring strong feelings for Susan Barton still.

By the time Charlie finished taking her statement, it was late and the school was almost empty. Vincent Atkins had not stayed to be interviewed and Daniel Roberts had gone. Only the caretaker was left to usher them out of the premises.

It had been a long day.

As she drove back towards Lambeth HQ she passed the front of West Norwood cemetery. It was a huge area. What if the car turned out to be a red herring? What if their murderer had somehow got Susan into the cemetery on foot, either by coercion or persuasion? What if there were other entrances or exits he might have used to walk her to her death? They couldn't rule it out.

She thought about the murder scene. She thought about Susan Barton's body ripped apart, her missing finger and the wedding ring inserted in place of her heart. It was sick. It was twisted. It was personal.

She pulled over and dialled Hunter's number. They now had two more credible suspects.

19

Mickey Barton was still in bed when they knocked his door down the following morning. The flat was only about a mile from the family house and was small and cramped. Half his life seemed to be crammed into the tiny space with the only single wardrobe in his bedroom bulging with designer clothing. Several rows of polished, shiny shoes and new trainers were spaced out on racks taking up the whole of one wall. Boxes of belongings remained unpacked, their lids opened to allow for the removal and return of necessary items. He clearly had no intention of living there any longer than he had to.

Charlie read out the provisions of the warrant, obtained by the night duty CID, and explained that his flat was to be searched. Paul then told him he was to be arrested on suspicion of the murder of his wife Susan Barton. He said nothing in reply.

She watched as he slumped backwards on to his bed and lifted his hands up to his face. He'd obviously known it was coming. Most partners came under the finger of suspicion when their loved ones were killed; even more so when they were ex-partners. Domestic troubles were still the most common reason for murder in the country and with their recent split so clearly causing them both tensions, he must have been waiting for the bang on the door at any time.

Now it was here and she would soon be interviewing him. They needed to get his side of the story down, under caution so that it could be used evidentially at court if he were to be charged later; when he last saw his wife, his movements before and after her death, the history of his split with her and any ongoing feelings that might have led to violence. With more witnesses claiming that he continued to have access to the family house and could be jealous, added to the fact that Susan appeared to have been abducted by someone she knew, with no forced entry to the marital home, there were ample grounds to suspect his involvement. What they didn't have as yet was the evidence to prove it.

Hunter indicated towards Barton and Paul stepped forward with a set of handcuffs.

'I've only got my boxers on.' He raised his eyebrows towards Charlie before directing his question to Hunter. 'Can I at least get washed and dressed first in private please, before those things get put on me?'

Hunter grunted and waved Paul back again. 'Go with him, Paul, and make sure he behaves.'

Charlie moved away to allow him some space. The boys dealt with the boys and she was happy to leave it that way. Still, the sooner he was in handcuffs the better. She never felt comfortable, especially in the home territory of suspects, until they were put in restraints. Anything could happen.

She watched as Barton strutted across the hallway into the bathroom, with his bare chest puffed out and his hands balled loosely into fists. He was such a poser, obviously quite happy to show off his physique without any inhibitions. Never mind wanting privacy. A second of unease flashed through her. She put it to one side; Paul was right behind him.

She would enjoy interviewing him later. Having to kowtow to a woman would rattle him and when people were rattled they said things they didn't mean to say.

Mickey Barton held tight to his wife's engagement ring. He'd managed to slide his hand under his pillow and take hold of it as he was making a show of getting off the bed. No one had seen the slip of his hand and now he held the ring within the palm of his fist.

He glanced over his shoulder and saw the police officer watching him. He needed him to look away. The officer had seemed a little camp when he'd cautioned him. Maybe he could play on this. He didn't look like the macho type who would totally ignore what he said and take pleasure in his discomfiture.

'Excuse me. Do you mind? I need to take a piss.'

The officer looked embarrassed. He was averting his gaze, glancing away. Mickey bent forward; making a big play of what he was doing, grunting with the effort, making as much noise as possible. He hoped he wouldn't be noticed. The policeman was still looking away. He had to take the risk. He moved the ring in his hand so that he was gripping it with the end of his fingers and lifted the top of the toilet cistern, pushing the ring forward through the gap and listening as it hit the water with a tiny plop.

The policeman hadn't reacted. The idiot hadn't seen what he'd done.

When he got back out from the nick, he could retrieve it. He just hoped it wouldn't be found. He loved that ring. He loved that he himself had chosen it; that he himself had placed it on Susan's finger. He loved what it symbolised. He kept it under his pillow every night, safe in the knowledge that a little part of her was near him.

It was a little part that had also cost him a fortune.

Charlie and Hunter were on their way again.

The first warrant had gone well; one suspect arrested for murder and the flat sealed off ready to be searched. Now they were rolling on to their second. She was not expecting any violence at this one, but they were still going to perform a rapid entry. There was no way she was going to be criticised for allowing a suspect to hide any evidence before he deigned to answer the door. If you lied to police and were suspected of murder, you took whatever treatment you got.

The house was not far away and it took only ten minutes to arrive. As they pulled in, a few houses along from their target venue, she was surprised to see the difference between the two environments Vincent Atkins inhabited. They were total opposites. The rambling house she was now looking at was as far from the almost OCD overtones of his school office as was possible. An overgrown privet hedge sprouted leggy twigs across the footway and the small wooden gate at the entrance was broken; skewed over to one side and propped up between the branches of a magnolia. The front garden was running riot; at best it could be described as an ecological wonderland, at worst, an overgrown jungle through which not even the local tomcat dared to tread. A pebbled footpath led to the front door, the sound of the tiny stones masked by the carpet of fallen leaves.

It fitted Vincent Atkins' appearance far better than his office environment. She wondered why. Perhaps he was just able to keep his work and home life totally compartmentalised. It was strange, but looking at the front garden she now expected the whole interior of the house to be the same; rambling, slightly disorganised but full of well-intentioned choices and designs of grandeur. Before getting stuck into executing this warrant she rang Paul and checked that everything was still running smoothly at the previous one. It was.

Mickey Barton was in the station van and about to be whisked off to a police station. Now they had two suspects for the same offence, he was to be taken to Charing Cross police station as they couldn't risk any cross-contamination with Oscar Abrahams who was still in custody at Brixton. She acknowledged the information and raised her hand to beckon everybody forward.

Very soon they would have three suspects in custody.

It was a nice day and Vincent Atkins was browsing through a magazine in the conservatory with his wife, Molly. She was repotting some houseplants before allowing them to lie dormant for the winter. They would be glad of the bigger pots when spring came. They could spread their roots and thrive. Several pots stood on the top of a large oak bookcase, leafy fronds hanging down over the top couple of shelves. His bookcase was his pride and joy, filled with books on his favourite subjects – history, theology, psychology, and education – with titles ranging from *The Holy Bible*, *On the Origin of the Species* and *The Social Animal* to lighter bite-size books containing educational analysis, historical articles, sermons, and a stack of magazines, well-thumbed and folded to pages of interest.

He slotted the magazine carefully back in its place before selecting a book on the risks to the psychological development of teenagers, if engaged in drug use. He liked to keep himself abreast of the latest theories, even though he left most of the working practices to his staff. It wouldn't hurt though to show off his knowledge during a staff meeting and instruct them on the signs and symptoms to look out for. It elevated him to a higher educational and mental plane.

The October sun was bright and he and Molly had been up early. He rarely slept later than 6.30 anyway, and even though he hadn't had to go into school, he had woken at his usual time. He was to attend a headteachers' conference later and he was pleased. The arrival of the policewoman at the Academy yesterday afternoon had unsettled him. He hadn't wanted to go in to school today in case she turned up, even though he knew he was just delaying the inevitable. If it gave him the weekend though, so be it.

His reverie was shattered by the sound of splintering wood and shouting, as four burly policemen crashed through the front door and ran along the hallway towards them. Molly looked petrified, dropping the plant pot she had been holding in fright. It smashed on the tiled floor, spilling its contents across the conservatory. Two officers took hold of his arms, but he couldn't tear his eyes away from the soil, spread still further in the treads of their boots. No doubt it would be distributed all over his beautiful house, trodden into carpets, sprinkled across the wooden floors, squashed into small gaps and crevices until his house was spoilt.

In that instant he realised that just as his house would be trashed, so too would his life; everything he'd tried to rebuild over the last few years would be as nothing. He would be the subject of gossip, starting at his academy and spreading throughout the education system, his friends and family, his whole career ruined.

The policewoman, DC Stafford, was speaking to him now, telling him he was under arrest on suspicion of the murder of Susan Barton. He looked across at his wife of thirty-five years and knew that he and only he had destroyed her life. She was totally innocent. She was his rock. She had done nothing wrong. As he watched the tears of hurt and bewilderment roll down her face, he regretted, in an instant, everything he had done and said.

20

Friday afternoon was almost upon them. Rather than finishing the week with the euphoria of a job well done, Charlie knew that they were instead finishing the week with a job in progress, several actually.

Cornell Miller was yet to be found. Moses was as prepared as he could be, but there was no guessing what was going through Miller's crack-befuddled brain.

As for progress on Susan Barton's murder case, although they hadn't a charge, they did have three credible suspects – four if you included the yet unidentified friend of Abrahams who was allegedly in possession of his car. All three identified suspects had been arrested and interviewed. All three had made some admissions before pretty much giving no comment interviews, save for denying they had any involvement in Susan Barton's murder.

Abrahams had given no more information, other than admitting to owning the Vauxhall Vectra seen coming and going from the murder scene. Crucially the car was still unaccounted for and they really needed it found.

Mickey Barton had objected to being interviewed by a woman but after being firmly put in his place, had admitted using his keys to enter the family home, but only with the express permission of his wife, who he still loved and wanted to win back. The keys had been removed from his key ring now and the investigation team were in possession of them.

Vincent Atkins had broken down in tears, admitting to his affair with Susan but denying any involvement in her murder. He was sorry he had omitted to tell police about the affair and confessed that he had wanted to keep it a secret from his wife who deserved better. He had then, rather mysteriously, refused to answer any more of their questions.

All three had now been released on bail and all had been refused access to their normal place of abode whilst full searches were progressing. Each had provided a suitable address in which to stay temporarily. While not desirable to have them back out in the public domain, she and Hunter had had no choice but to release them. The law allowed set time limits to question suspects in custody. Abrahams had almost reached his limit, while the other two had now provided some details of their movements and motivations, which could be given in evidence, if they were later linked to the crime by forensics, further CCTV or previously unknown witnesses. With a little longer left on their time clocks, there would be less pressure to charge or release, if they needed to be brought in for a further interview.

It was not ideal but it was the best they could do. Given the fact the murder appeared to be personal, they could only hope that if it was indeed a 'crime of passion', their suspect would have no need to commit further offences. None of them wanted another victim on their conscience.

Oscar Abrahams had no conscience. As he walked out from Brixton police station he yawned, stretched and headed towards the front line to buy some weed. It was only a matter of time before he would be NFA'd, as always. Coppers were useless, they couldn't find a thing, thankfully.

He turned into Coldharbour Lane, glancing across at a bench of drunks in Windrush Square. A woman had fallen from the end of the bench and was flat out across the pavement, her dress caught on the edge of the seat, her underwear exposed. Everyone could see her and she was so pissed she made no attempt to cover herself. He was disgusted.

'Cover yourself up, you dirty bitch,' he barked towards her. She stuck two fingers up at him.

He laughed. He wasn't going to concern himself with old drunks like her; he had other things on his mind. He was more worried about how he was going to get his kicks later when he would be holed up in a hostel with no computer for company. He would have to get talking. There would be others just like him there. There always was. He just had to find them.

Mickey Barton felt small as he looked across at the statues of the four majestic lions that guarded Lord Nelson's column, reaching up into the sky above Trafalgar Square in the heart of London. Once he had been king of his domain, his house his castle, his family his possession; but now because of Susan's betrayal everything was crumbling around him. He knew about her affair with the headteacher but he hadn't told the police he knew. Why give them extra ammunition.

He was on his way to see his son, Mickey Junior. Emma and her brother had been staying with Susan's parents, rather than squeeze into his small flat. Word had got round that he had been arrested for their mother's murder and Emma didn't want to speak to him, at least not for the time being. She was apparently too upset.

Mickey Junior was more open though. He had agreed to see him and hear his side of the story. His son had always been closer to him than Emma. Mickey Junior was a man's man; just the way Mickey was. He was a good lad.

They would meet for a bite to eat and then go their separate ways; Mickey Junior to his grandparents, he to his sister's house, though he was pissed off at being shunted on again. Hopefully, his boy would come to join him there soon. He didn't want him poisoned by Susan's parents. They'd never really liked him anyway.

He glanced back at the busy, chaotic London scene briefly, before diving into the relative calm of the underground station.

The ring thing wouldn't be an issue now, even if the police found it. He'd been thinking about it in the cell. He'd just say Susan had given it to him. No one would ever know otherwise.

Vincent Atkins was losing his mind. He couldn't go back to his house and he didn't know where Molly was. She hadn't answered her phone when he'd tried to contact her from the police station and now he was out, she still wasn't answering it. It was switched off.

He didn't know what he could do to get her back. He had been a fool to betray her. An old fool. He'd read about others who had done the same in the past and had always wondered about their sanity. He'd thought he would never do that to Molly. Not his Molly.

And now she wasn't picking up.

Tonight he would be staying with an old friend that he'd known all his life. As he walked out from Wimbledon police station, he looked up and saw the Centre Court shopping precinct. He'd taken Molly to the tennis once; they'd watched a men's semi-final together and she'd got so excited as it reached its conclusion. That was once, a million years ago, when he had a life.

He could feel the panic rising in his chest again. He'd do anything to keep Molly, anything, he always had.

Cornell Miller had moved on from Cecil's. The guy was just a little bit too crazy for him and he was taking the piss anyway; after each robbery he wanted a bigger share of the spoils and was smoking too much gear. He was a greedy bastard.

They'd left on good terms though. He wasn't stupid. Cecil might have his uses again in the future.

In order to pay for his lodgings, he'd robbed a couple more illegals. The first had dropped everything and run when he saw the broken bottle. There was no way he was going to chase the guy, so he'd picked through several bags, taken what he wanted and disappeared. Still, he'd missed the bloodbath. He always enjoyed that part.

The other black bastard he'd gone to town on. The fucking immigrant hadn't done what he'd been told immediately, he probably didn't speak English. Even if he did, it wouldn't have made a difference. He got what he deserved and now hopefully he'd fuck off back to his own country.

It was like that on the streets. It was war. The weakest fell and the strongest got the spoils, and if you needed gear anything went.

So, it had been time to move on and a couple of days ago, he'd headed south, towards his favoured areas, where very few Old Bill came. He was now by Streatham Common, just around the corner from that old bastard Moses. If it hadn't been for him, he wouldn't be wanted by that bleedin' woman detective. She was always on his case. It had been a right touch having the bastard's address disclosed to his solicitors by accident though. He liked playing games with the stupid old sod, knowing the terror he could invoke. He loved the power it gave him, the thrill of the chase, the adrenalin rush. It excited him.

Tonight he was feeling chilled. He would smoke some brown and enjoy himself before he went out to play.

He unwound the scarf wrapped round the top of the container and unscrewed the cap. The reek of petrol fumes filled the room. He inhaled the stench and felt immediately light-headed. Tonight, when it grew dark he was going to have fun. Tonight, he was going to light up the sky and watch those bastards burn.

21

'Who's for the last scoop? It's not worth me putting it back in the freezer.'

Charlie lunged forward, grabbing one side of the carton of her favourite caramel and toffee ice cream. Beth took hold of the other side and they both screamed with delight as the carton flipped up into the air, landing upside down in the centre of a dirty plate. Not to be deterred by a small amount of gravy and a leftover sprout, she reached out and claimed her prize to further laughter. It was always the same when she got together with her two half-sisters. They reverted to acting like children again, much to their mother's amusement.

'Oh my God, you're not going to eat that now are you?' Meg was wiping the tears from her cheeks. 'I can't believe you girls still fight over every last scrap. You haven't changed since you were kids fighting over...'

'The cherries. We know. Mum, it has to be done,' Lucy joined in the banter. 'The day we stop fighting over the leftovers, will be a sad day.'

'True! Ben, do you do the same with your brother?' Meg started to stack the dishes. Ben cleared his throat and sat up straight at being asked a question.

'No, not really. My dad was military so our mealtimes were very formal. My brother and I had to be on our best behaviour at all times.'

'Oh, that's a shame, Ben.' Beth leant forward and plunged her spoon into the last scoop of Charlie's ice cream, eliciting a rap across her knuckles for her troubles.

'Oy, hands off my last bit of extra sticky toffee. I was saving that.' She held it out, 'For Ben.' She watched as Ben laughed and took the gift, licking the last few drips off the end of her spoon.

She was glad for the chance to change the subject. Ben's childhood had shaped the troubles he now had. Since taking to drink after his return from Afghanistan, his father had effectively disowned his son, and now Ben was on the mend, Charlie had no wish for anyone to remind him of those days. Meg hadn't meant to, but she did have a habit of putting her foot in it.

She scraped the last few dregs of ice cream from her bowl. 'Have I told you about the cherries by the way, Ben? Every summer, when the cherries were in season, Mum used to pick a load from nearby trees and then we'd have them for pudding on a Sunday. As we ate them we'd line the pips up along the edge of the plates, count them and then argue about who had the most. It would drive Mum mad because half the time the pips had come out of the cherries when they were cooked so it was never accurate, but it didn't stop us fighting over them.'

'I always got the least,' Beth stuck out her bottom lip.

'You did not!' Meg cuffed her round the top of her head playfully. 'I was always scrupulously fair. You just thought you did because you were the youngest.'

'I did,' Beth laughed again. 'And I still get beaten to the scraps.'

'Aw, you poor thing,' Charlie stood to help with the dishes. 'You need to toughen up a bit more then and be quicker.'

Ben stood too and they started to clear the table. Friday evenings with the family had always been the most relaxed, though these days it was unusual for them all to be around. Lucy was at uni in London and often stayed for the weekend. Beth hadn't quite decided what path her life was taking her so her Friday evenings usually revolved around the local pubs and clubs with friends. And Charlie was usually stuck at work.

With a slight lull in the action, Charlie had dropped in on Ben for a training run and then decided, on the spur of the moment, to invite him to the family Friday evening get-together and unbelievably everyone else was in.

They all loved Ben; he was always welcome in the family home, though sometimes the expectation that he would eventually become part of the family unit, rather than a best friend, piled extra pressure on her.

Beth and Lucy scraped their chairs back and headed straight for the big maroon family sofa. They still acted very much like teenagers; fed, watered and only thinking of themselves. Charlie was the grown-up sister and, as such, she was expected to do their share of the chores.

Meg had nearly finished clearing up when they got out to the kitchen with the last few bits. She was endlessly organised, tidying as she went. Even after cooking a family meal, Meg's kitchen was cleaner and less cluttered than Charlie's was before she started.

'Thanks Mum,' she walked up behind Meg and gave her a hug. 'That was lovely.' She felt her mother tense slightly. Physical affection didn't come naturally, although she got the sense that her mum always wanted to be hugged. She just didn't know how to deal with it.

'Yes, thank you for having me, Mrs Stafford.' Ben stood to one side stiffly.

'Oh Ben, it's Meg,' she smiled and planted a kiss on his cheek primly, winking at Charlie as she did so. 'How many times do I have to tell you? You're practically family.'

Jason Jennings had no inhibitions about physical affection. JJ, as he liked to be known, was 'in a relationship' but sometimes felt the need to stray. His was a civil partnership but he liked to think of it more as an open relationship; just slightly more open on his side.

Brighton was where JJ lived now. He'd tried various parts of London – Vauxhall and Clapham in the south, then across the water to Camden and Haringey in the north – but no area in London was quite as welcoming as Brighton. No area in London held quite the same social opportunities.

Sometimes when he was bored and Roger was away on business he'd check out Grindr for a quick commitment-free fuck and find up to one hundred like-minded guys, all within a mile radius. He was spoilt for choice. He was sure Roger wouldn't mind. He probably did the same when he was away but still, he didn't want Roger screwing any bloke they got chatting to, under his nose, so to speak and he respected Roger enough not to do that to him either. As long as when they were together, they both remained faithful, everything was fine.

He loved Roger. He had no doubt about that. He loved him with every bone in his body and had willingly become his civil partner a few years back. Now they were legally allowed to marry, they had been considering it. They had been together for as long as he wanted to remember. Roger had literally picked him up and transported him to another life. He was weak but Roger was strong; Roger was his rock and JJ had his lifeline firmly embedded in his partner's strength. He could stray occasionally, but if ever he started to slip too far on the pebbles of infidelity, he would always rein himself back. He'd read that once in one of the cosy, crafty shops in The Lanes in Brighton and it had become his motto.

He was waiting for Roger now. He'd walked down to the Brighton Tavern from their flat in Trafalgar Lane and was standing outside lighting up a Marlboro. It was their local and he knew most of the regulars. There were a few of them braving the weather to smoke and they'd started to chat about where Roger had been on business this time. Everyone knew that he and Roger came as a pair and if one was missing, it was always a topic of conversation. They all looked after each other in his community.

It was cold and his breath fanned out in a cloud of smoke. His hands were frozen and he could twist his commitment ring round and round on his shrunken finger. For some reason he was more excited than usual to see Roger. He had been away far too long this time and sex with strangers was not nearly as fulfilling as with the man you loved.

As if on cue, Roger came into view, walking purposefully along the street towards him. He wore a long coat which he unbuttoned as he got closer. JJ felt his pulse quicken as he saw his partner heading straight for him. He stepped out and Roger wrapped him in his coat, pulling him close to his warm body. They kissed, JJ happy to be held in the security of Roger's arms. It was lonely when he wasn't there and JJ was glad he was back.

Frustratingly, this time was only going to be a brief reunion. Roger had to leave again in just two short days. On Sunday he was staying out overnight in readiness for a conference on Monday. They would have to make the most of the time they had. In fact, as this thought occurred JJ decided they should go straight home. He reached up and whispered in his partner's ear and then, with a wink to his friends, they turned, still in each other's arms, and walked away.

At the sight of their embrace, he felt his guts tighten and his head spin. Although he'd seen the photos of them together at their ceremony, it was still hard to watch in the flesh. He had loved JJ for years, years when the boy had had no one else, years when he had fed him, clothed him and cared for him. He had shared as much of his life with him as was possible. He had shared a bed with him, treated him like a precious jewel and savoured every part of his body. And JJ had repaid him by running away.

Well, now he had found him, in the arms of the other man. He already knew JJ's address; he'd done his research and had confirmed it earlier. JJ lived his life in public now, not hidden away as he had for a few years. They all did.

He turned and walked away, feeling the anger starting to bubble up from within, imagining JJ in the arms of his lover. This time he would not allow him to run away. The rage always concentrated his mind. He thought about the coming hour when he would have JJ's heart literally within the palm of his hand, cool to the touch, just as it had grown cold towards him all those years ago.

He stretched out his fingers, imagining the next addition floating in the liquid, a pristine, perfect trophy to add to the others.

This Sunday he would be waiting and JJ would pay the price for giving his heart to another.

It was still pitch black when her phone buzzed. Night-time at her mum's place in the countryside was so much darker than at her flat in London.

Her sight was blurred and she couldn't focus on the name on the screen. She pressed it to her ear and in an instant recognised Moses' voice whispering hoarsely in the silence.

'Charlie, come quick. He's here now.'

Cornell Miller was in his element. He had shot up an hour ago and was off his head on crack. He was buzzing. The end game was in sight; now he hoped to participate in the action before watching the finale play out in front of him.

He was opposite Moses Sinkler's house smoking a joint; staring straight up at the bedroom in which the old black bastard would be sleeping, probably next to his wizened old bitch of a wife. He'd been sitting there for quite a while watching and thinking. He should have really finished the bastard off back in the summer when he was lying on the ground bleeding like a stuck pig, but somewhere in the back of his mind he'd still wanted to be free. Now he didn't care. He was enjoying the game.

The windows of the house were jet black. The street light was still broken after he'd smashed it a few days earlier when he'd left his note, so not even the residual reflection of the lamp glinted against the glass. In the dark interior, his prey lay sleeping and he would now pay the price for getting the police involved. He would burn in his bed because he had been responsible for making that bitch DC Stafford target him. It was her fault really. She had hounded him and hounded him and wouldn't let things rest. Well, now he would make Moses rest… in peace.

He took another drag on his joint, grinning lazily to himself at his joke and flicked his lighter on and off a few times, watching as the flame danced in the darkness. His bag was at his feet, primed and ready to go, the overpowering stench of petrol fumes escaping from the confines of the plastic as he opened it.

It would all be over soon. A petrol bomb straight through the bedroom window would ignite anything it splashed against; the curtains, the bed, skin, bodies. He would wait for a few minutes, hoping to see them engulfed in flames, smell the pungency of burning flesh, and then he would melt away into the night and be gone.

*

Moses had lain awake for at least an hour. He couldn't sleep knowing that somewhere skulking about in the shadows was Cornell Miller. He hadn't slept properly for days, since seeing the signature on the note; how the man had signed his name in such a brazen manner; the way he had drawn the smiley face afterwards. Miller thought it was all a joke. He didn't care and someone who didn't care was dangerous, *the* most dangerous.

Claudette was sleeping in the spare room at the rear of the house. He couldn't take risks with her safety. She'd objected immediately, but one word from him and she'd known not to argue. For the first time in their married life they were sleeping apart. He needed to be at the front, on the lookout, and he would have it no other way, until the madman was caught.

So, about an hour ago, he had woken. He didn't know what had made him stir, other than a deep sense of foreboding. Looking out of the window carefully from behind the curtain, he had seen the slightest of movements, hardly enough to register, but he'd known it was Miller straightaway.

Charlie had been his first thought. Get Charlie. She'd come. He didn't really want to start pressing panic buttons, not until he was sure. So he'd phoned her and was waiting for her to arrive, and while he waited he watched for anything further. It was only in the last few minutes that he'd seen the tiny glow of a cigarette and now the flicker of fire. He still wasn't sure whether he should bother the police, but he moved across the room to where the panic button was located anyway, fumbling for it in the darkness. Better to be safe than sorry.

The sound of footsteps and a muffled yell caught his attention, before the window came in with a deafening crash and the safety of his world exploded in front of his eyes. As he pushed the button and squeezed himself flat against the wall, he knew he'd left it too late.

'What do you mean you're not there yet?! I thought you would have dealt with the situation by now.'

'We've only just received a call, literally in the last few seconds. Panic alarm activated.'

'But he's been there for nearly an hour.' Charlie couldn't understand what was happening. Why hadn't Moses pressed the button and summoned help when he'd phoned her?

After the call from Moses she'd thrown on some clothes and legged it out of the house, followed closely by Ben, who was still pulling on his jacket and carrying his trainers. He'd been sleeping on the sofa but he must have heard her clattering around in her haste. There was no point even trying to tell him to stay. He was coming, whether she wanted him there or not.

As it happened, she did. He'd have to stay in her car and she'd told him so, but it was good to know she wasn't on her own, even though she was a little nervous at what they might find on arrival.

'We're getting another call now, Charlie,' the operator's voice was clear over the hands-free set. 'Sounds of an explosion, smoke coming from the front, first-floor window.'

'Shit! How far off is your nearest car?'

'It's close. A few minutes at most. And the LFB have been called and are on way.'

'OK. I'm just round the corner now too. Stay on the line and I'll let you know what's happening as soon as I can.'

She put her foot down hard and spun the car left off the main road, catching a glimpse of the flashing blue lights of the London Fire Brigade in her mirror. Thank God they were just behind her. They could deal with the fire; she would go hunting for Miller, just as soon as she knew Moses and Claudette were safe. She just hoped they were, though why the fuck Moses had not pressed the panic button sooner was beyond her.

As they got closer she could see smoke billowing out of the first-floor window but no flames, which was good. She'd been to house fires that had taken hold, where the whole sky had been lit up like a beacon, but this didn't seem to have happened. Maybe Moses had fought it off; but where was he? A small group of elderly neighbours were in the street watching, their voices high-pitched with alarm. She screeched to a halt, scanning the faces, but Moses and Claudette were not amongst them. The fire engine was right behind them, the fire fighters disembarking within seconds and already unfurling the hoses. She ran to the senior officer and shouted that there were two occupants still believed to be inside and then headed for the front door.

Pushing the letter box open, she shone the spotlight from her phone into the hallway, shouting out Moses' name. Two figures were huddled inside, towels held to their mouths.

'Charlie, is that you?' a voice said and for the second time in an hour she recognised his distinctive low drawl. 'Is it safe to come out?'

'Yes, yes. It's me. Come out,' she screamed over the sound of the engines.

The door opened and Moses shuffled out, his arm around Claudette protectively. Apart from looking dishevelled and anxious from the ordeal, they appeared otherwise to be unharmed. Charlie couldn't stop herself throwing her arms around them both. She was so relieved.

'I left it too late, didn't I?' Moses shook his head. 'I didn't think he would actually do anything until I saw him flicking his lighter. I was hoping you'd get to him first before he ran away.'

'I'm so sorry, Moses. I came as quick as I could. I thought you'd have pressed the panic alarm at the same time as you called me. Are you all right?'

'Yes, we're fine. I put the flames out with the extinguishers and sealed up the bedroom and then we came down here to wait by the front door. There was just smoke. I didn't want to come out straightaway in case he was waiting for us.'

'Is anyone else in there?' A fire fighter was striding towards them.

Moses shook his head. 'No, it was just us.'

Charlie put her arm through Claudette's and led her and Moses out to the street as the fire fighters streamed into the house. A row of police cars, fire engines and an ambulance was now lined up, their blue lights all flashing haphazardly. She took the elderly couple over to the waiting ambulance and watched as the crew helped them aboard, wrapping bright red blankets over their night clothes. She saw her colleague Bill Morley speaking to some of the gathered crowd and beckoned him over. They would be safe with him. For now.

*

It had been fucking brilliant throwing the petrol bomb. He couldn't stop himself laughing as he'd launched it at the window. The explosion had been impressive, the way the petrol had ignited in a ball of fire. He'd hoped to hear some squeals of terror, some screams of pain, maybe even see the bastards alight but that hadn't happened. It hadn't been as effective as he'd hoped. Then he'd seen that woman detective again and decided it was time to leave.

Maybe he'd try it again but with a larger bottle next time; or with two or three together through different windows. There were quite a few different ways to skin a cat.

For the moment though he had to sort something out. He strolled around a corner away from the noise and smoke, slipping into the shadows silently and pulling out a Stanley knife from his pocket. There was someone following him.

Ben had disappeared. He'd been animated during the journey up, whooping at times at the speed of her driving. She'd told him to stay in the car on their way but half expected him to be right behind her, watching over everything she did. Now he was nowhere in sight.

She tapped his name into her phone and waited for him to pick up, wondering why he didn't say anything when the line clicked in.

'Where are you, Ben?'

'I'm following a guy,' his voice was quiet and slightly nervy. 'When we arrived I saw him dart away. He stared at you for ages and then left. I don't know if he had anything to do with it but he just looks wrong.'

'What does he look like?'

'Tall, muscular white guy, in his late thirties, quite erratic, likes he's on something.'

As he gave the description, Charlie felt a shiver of fear run down her spine. It was Cornell Miller. It had to be. 'Where are you?' She had to get to him quickly, before it was too late.

'I don't really know. I've been following him for a while now. We're in an estate back in the direction that we came from. Hang on; he's just gone round a corner. When I catch up with him, I'll see if there's a block name.'

'Ben, stay where you are.'

She was already running. She guessed the estate and it wasn't that far. As soon as Ben confirmed the name of the block she'd get some more backup on the way. She could hear shouting from the handset. She started to sprint. Pushing the receiver to her ear, she tried to hear what was happening. She heard Ben cry out but his voice sounded distant, the handset seemingly away from his mouth. It sounded like a fight but she couldn't tell whether the sound came from the phone or through the air.

She ran into the estate, homing in on the noise. Turning a corner, she found Ben lying in a crimson pool, clutching the top of his arm. Blood was pouring from a deep cut and she could see further slash marks to his hands, where he'd apparently tried to fend off his attacker. She rushed to his side and knelt down next to him, glancing up to see the shape of a man disappearing around the end of the block ahead. He turned and stopped for a moment; it was Cornell Miller, she'd never forget his face. She wanted to chase him but she had nothing to fight him with and Ben needed tending. She had to let him go. Miller was laughing as she pushed the phone back up to her ear to summon an ambulance.

'You're too late, DC Stafford. You'll never get me.' He lifted the Stanley knife up, making a play of slashing it through the air and screamed out loud maniacally. 'Next time, it'll be you.'

Hunter met Charlie at the hospital on Saturday morning. She was sitting with Ben waiting for him to finish his treatment. The main laceration was to his upper left arm. This had been cleaned and seventeen stitches now held the wound together. He was waiting for further stitches to be put into the cuts on his hands where he had tried to protect himself, but X-rays had confirmed they were superficial, with no damage to ligaments or tendons. Fortunately his jacket had borne the brunt of the Stanley knife blade. Several neat slashes in the thick cotton fabric now showed where Miller had struck.

'I heard all about what happened. How are you both?'

'Well I'm fine and Ben's been lucky. Quite a few stitches but nothing too serious and nothing permanent, except maybe a few scars.'

'He was the lucky one,' Ben interjected. 'If I hadn't been chatting to Charlie on the phone, I would have been ready for him. He must have heard me speaking and hid round the corner; jumped me as I came into view, but I did manage to get a few well-aimed kicks in, which sent him flying. He didn't dare come back at me after his initial go.'

'Thankfully. He's one of the most violent men I've ever dealt with. It could have been much worse.' Charlie turned to Ben. 'You should have stayed in the car like I told you or at least let me know where you were going!' She felt awful for not having realised.

'He was very brave, Charlie. There're not many coppers that would have even noticed what Ben saw, or gone after Miller on their own, never mind civvies. Anyway it sounds like you had your hands full with Moses.'

Hunter didn't often give praise, certainly not that freely. She looked up and saw him give the most imperceptible of nods, coupled with a look in his eyes that told her to shut up, immediately. For a second she was confused but then she realised what he meant. Scolding Ben like she had would emasculate him and knock his confidence. She hadn't meant to; but for a strong military man like Ben to be told that he should have sat still or checked with her first about following Miller was misplaced and totally insensitive. He had made a decision, and it was a courageous one. He didn't need her permission. Anyone could have done it. It was just a shame he hadn't known quite what he was up against. He had done well in the circumstances.

Hunter was right and in that moment she realised why she respected him so much and loved him. He was her role model, the father she wished she'd had. He just had that intuition to know what needed to be said. Ben had been brave, but it hadn't worked out quite the way he had hoped. He could have stayed at her mum's but instead he had come out into the cold to keep her company. He needed to be told how much it was appreciated, not admonished for failing to tell her where he was going. She gave Ben's knee a squeeze.

'Yes, you're right, boss. I didn't even notice Miller.' She turned to Ben, who was still looking embarrassed and crest-fallen. 'If you hadn't spotted him making off from the scene and followed him, I wouldn't have been able to identify him and we wouldn't have the evidence to pin the arson on him. Moses couldn't say it was definitely him. He couldn't see properly in the darkness. I'm sorry for telling you off. I was just worried. There was so much blood.'

She looked up at Hunter and again saw the tiniest of nods. When she turned back to Ben his face was glowing.

'And Moses? How is he?' She hadn't heard anything further.

'Naz and Sabira have come in and are dealing with him and Claudette. They are both good and unhurt and are making statements. Even the house is pretty well still intact, just a bit of fire and smoke damage to the bedroom and the smashed window. You and Naz had briefed him well on what to do in case of an emergency; it's a shame he didn't put the instructions into practice sooner. Naz has given Moses a gentle telling-off, as only Naz can. Apparently he didn't want to bother police until he was sure. Just you.' Hunter laughed. 'As Lambeth's number one crime-fighting weapon, he thought you'd be able to get Miller single-handedly.'

'I wish I could have lived up to his expectations.' She laughed too but underneath the words, she didn't feel like smiling.

Hunter stood up to leave.

'Thanks for coming in especially, boss. We do appreciate it.'

'No worries. Keep me posted on how you get on. You both did extremely well.'

She heard the words but didn't believe them. She'd certainly tried, especially without the security of having her safety equipment and radio, but in her own mind she'd failed. Moses and Claudette were lucky not to have been burnt alive, Ben was fortunate not to have been seriously injured and, even though she had every justification in the world for staying with Ben and tending to his wounds, she'd chosen to let Cornell Miller go.

22

JJ watched as Roger left for his conference. He was suddenly depressed at being alone again, after such a short reunion. He enjoyed all the time they spent together. They rarely argued and if they did it was short-lived and normally about inconsequential rubbish.

He grabbed his coat and decided to go for a walk. The sea in October was often spectacular and it might lift his mood. You could walk along the seafront for miles and rarely would anyone ever bother you. Tonight was no exception. He walked slowly, breathing in the sea air. It was fresh and cold; the tiny molecules of salty spray whipped up by the wind stung against his cheeks, making them feel moist and grainy. He loved the freedom of Brighton, so different from the estates and concrete of London. He'd done this on many occasions when he wanted to escape. Walked and walked and forgotten. However troubled his mind was, the sea always calmed him. It was constant. It had always been there. However much its mood changed from welcoming tranquillity to wrathful fury, it would still be there the next day and the next, and he liked that. He needed a constant.

He walked for miles, not caring who saw him, not looking for anyone, just walking. Evening became night. The promenade emptied of even the few residents out late with their dogs, the last joggers finishing off their weekend with a burst of energy. He felt as alone as he'd ever felt.

By the time he got back to the central pier it was gone ten. He climbed down on to the stony beach, and walked across the larger stones to where the pebbles lay in mounds, ground down by the constant motion of the waves. The surface shimmered with residual reflections from the glitzy displays and winking lights of the penny arcades on the pier. He sat down on the top of a mound and stared out to sea. Some nights when JJ had been out walking it wasn't even safe to venture on to the beach, nights when roller after roller crashed down, hurling stones at anyone who dared get too close. Tonight was different. The waves were large and indignant, as if they were discontented, rather than furious and raging. They crashed on to the pebbles, sending them spiralling out of reach in front of them, before sucking them back quickly into their grasp.

He stared at the ebb and flow of each wave, watching as it visited and left, the small smooth pebbles scurrying in its wake. As he watched, he noticed one particular stone. It was larger than the others and slightly misshaped so it moved less and was more immune to the force of the water. He concentrated on the stone, marvelling at how steady it stayed, while all around the smaller stones danced to the tune of the waves.

'Are you OK?'

The voice behind him was low and he could hardly hear it over the noise of the shoreline. He turned and saw the shape of a man, silhouetted against the last remaining lights on the promenade.

'I was worried. I thought you might be in danger. I saw you earlier and I thought you looked distracted. You're very close to the waves.'

He stayed sitting still facing out to sea. He didn't really want to talk but the man sounded friendly, concerned even.

'I'll go away if you want me to, as long as you're all right. But if you need someone to talk to...'

The man left the sentence unfinished. There was no pressure, just an offer of help; a genuine moment of concern from a Good Samaritan. In Brighton there were many who knew the high suicide rates among the gay community and the anguish of being different and trying to fit in with a society that wanted everyone to fall within an accepted norm. The man was just being friendly. Who was he to shun this offer?

'Thanks. I'm fine, but I'm happy to talk.' He turned towards the man, who was wrapped up warmly against the cold. Only a small part of his face was visible from within the hooded top pulled tightly over his head, but he was smiling. The man held out his hand and he took hold of it. The man's grip was strong and his skin warm. He suddenly didn't feel alone. The man pulled him upwards until he was standing, continuing to hold his grip even when he was fully upright. JJ didn't attempt to pull away.

'So, do you want me to walk with you?'

JJ looked at his physique, large and athletic with a thick neck and bulky shoulders. He was strong and secure while he was weak, like the little pebbles on the beach. Roger was not there to be his rock, but this man was. He did want to walk with him; his voice sounded warm and friendly and vaguely familiar. He didn't want to be on his own. He wanted to be with someone tonight and he didn't really care who.

He nodded back at the man and they started to walk slowly back towards the promenade.

JJ hadn't changed much after all these years, not like *he* had. He was still thin and wiry, like he had been as a child and his eyes were still haunted. His honey blond hair was thinner now and both ears were pierced, but he was still baby-faced and he still had the appearance of a lost boy. It was that look that had always attracted him.

JJ had only been young when they had met, having run away from a care home into the solace of his arms. It had been easy. The boy craved love and he was readily available to oblige. He had all the time in the world and in his position nobody would ever suspect that he got as much from their relationship as JJ. He had loved JJ with all his heart and with all his body, watching as he changed from a boy to a man and revelling in the way he could mould him whichever way he wished, do with him whatever he desired. Sometimes if his passion made him a bit rough, it didn't matter because it was done with love. JJ was putty in his hands, or so he had thought, so he had been distraught when JJ, the man, had run away. He had searched for him for ages, months and months driving from one place to another, acting on tips only to find he was too late. JJ had moved on. JJ was not there. JJ had found someone. JJ didn't want to see him ever again.

The knowledge had been hard to bear. That's when he had gone travelling, spending time in other countries, moving around poverty-stricken areas where life was cheap and death was a blessing; meeting, loving, killing; moving, meeting, loving, killing; always restless, always searching. That's when his heart had hardened again, after fighting his compulsion for several years. That's when his desire to avenge each heartbreak had reawakened. That's when he'd started the list.

JJ was on his list, after Susan, the next to feel his revenge; second in the refreshed record, which continued to grow with every new romantic disappointment. He fell in love easily.

Finding JJ and walking with him now, he could tell he was still the same vulnerable boy, still the man who craved love. Even though now in his forties he could only think of JJ as a boy. He always would. He took hold of his hand again, but this time all he could feel was the thick gold ring, a symbol of his love for his partner Roger, the metal band punching a freezing spike through his palm.

'Are you on your own tonight?' He knew the answer.

JJ nodded.

'Do you want to come back to my place?'

JJ nodded again.

They were nearly at his car now. It was parked in a backstreet, with his kit in the back and a small vial of liquid measured out ready. It had all gone to plan. JJ could never turn down the chance of attention.

He opened the door and JJ got in, undid his trouser fly and splayed his legs without a word, as quiet as a church mouse. Maybe he did still want him. He climbed in next to his prey, and turned, kissing him roughly, thrusting his hand down against his groin. JJ's eyes remained open, fixed and staring straight out through the windscreen. He barely reacted to his touch, wanting only the physical pleasure; not able to return any of the love he so wanted; the mental and spiritual connection that he desired.

His last hope foundered. JJ was disgusting. He needed to get the job done, fulfil his plan.

'Here, have some G. It'll help you relax and have a good time.'

He squeezed a few millilitres of the odourless liquid into a small bottle of Coke. It was the drug of choice for many in the gay community. Little did his hostage know that there was already enough metallic alloy wheel-cleaner in the bottle to render him unable to fight.

JJ took the bottle, swigging the whole of the contents down. He watched as JJ's eyes first became alive, then fixed and glassy and then closed. He watched as his body started to twitch and spasm, each muscle in his face moving independently as if trying to rip his skin apart. He smiled at the analogy. He'd soon be doing that to JJ himself.

He wasn't going to let him die yet though and not from the drug. Locking the car doors shut, he pulled away slowly, carefully winding through the backstreets, savouring every second of how his plan was unfolding. JJ was his, to do with as he pleased. Before his final moments he wanted JJ to recognise the kindly stranger and then very slowly understand what pain was all about and why he had to die.

*

The Downs cemetery in Bear Road, Brighton, spread out over a huge area, not far from the South Downs, from which its name had derived. The driveway led to the main crematorium with areas of graves stretched as far as the eye could see in all directions, in neat squares with the tombstones upright and the grounds well tended.

He had already scoped out the location, particularly liking the area set aside for war veterans and the Jewish community. His favourite part, however, was the woodland area in the far corner. It was left natural and unkempt and just right for JJ, the wild child.

JJ was conscious now but his body continued to twitch and spasm with the drug's effects. His captive could do little more than lift one foot in front of the other and even this appeared difficult. At present he had complete control of JJ's movements, but it was only a matter of time before he would rouse further, so preparations were in force.

He guided them through a part of the outer wall which had been damaged by a fallen tree and walked slowly towards the woodland. A thick scarf stopped his hostage crying out for help and further ligatures kept his hands and feet bound loosely, allowing some movement but not enough for him to break free and run or fight, should the drug wear off. Anyway, he was more than capable of overpowering his prey. JJ was weak. He always had been.

The sky was heavy and the wind still gusted temperamentally. Only tiny shafts of moonlight were strong enough to break through the cloud cover, so the graveyard seemed shadowy and threatening.

As they walked, the grounds became more disorganised, the neat squares changing to less formal shapes, with tombstones protruding from the earth at disparate angles. He said nothing. JJ was silent too, making no attempt to speak; it was as if he was content to go without question; as if he didn't care that he was being led to his death.

They were nearly there now and he didn't know how he felt. One minute overjoyed to have his lost love with him again; the next hating him for his betrayal and desertion.

He guided JJ along the dirt path towards the small copse of trees at the rear, listening as their footsteps crunched on the frozen soil; imagining the natural earth mixed in with the ashes from the bodies of the dead. He indicated for his hostage to sit and JJ sat down immediately on a tree root, turning his head to stare as he unpacked his bag of tools, laying each implement carefully on a cloth.

He heard a low hum, it was a tune that he knew well, a melody that had stayed with him all his life, that he had sung many, many times. JJ was humming it. It made him want to cry with the pleasure of the memory. He continued to listen, putting lyrics to each line, on the verge of singing out loud. Maybe, just maybe, JJ had recognised him and this was his way of reaching out and asking forgiveness.

He removed the gag that had prevented JJ putting words to the song and waited to hear if he continued. In the silence that followed he yearned to hear the phrases he knew so well.

After a minute the singing started up again, this time with the words almost whispered in tune to the music, JJ nodding his head in time with the beat.

He started to join in, his baritone tones blending well with JJ's tenor, the words forming in his head, even before he opened his mouth. As he did so he pulled the hooded top down from over his head and removed some of his disguise, staring straight at JJ.

'It's you,' JJ stopped singing and frowned. 'I knew you were familiar as soon as you spoke to me, but I didn't realise it was you. You've changed so much. What do you want from me?'

'Drink this,' he ordered, offering JJ another bottle of Coke, laced with G.

JJ took the bottle and swigged from it, without question. It was just like it always had been; him and the boy, doing what he was told. Maybe he would change his mind after all and let him live with him again.

'You ruined my life, you bastard. I hope you rot in hell,' JJ spat suddenly. 'Look what you did to me. You made me like this. I'm dead already. You killed me a long time ago.' He indicated the implements, his eyes focussing on the long, sharp stiletto blade. 'So do what you have to, or fuck off. You can't make my life any worse than you did in the beginning.'

JJ lay down on the cold grass, with his legs straight out and his arms above his head, as far as the bindings would allow. His anger had receded as quickly as it had come, as the G took effect. Fuck, the stuff was good. He didn't care what happened now; in truth he never really had.

He had always known his time would be limited and that he would die young. Roger had saved him from his captor all those years ago, but he had never been able to properly save him from himself. Tears welled up at the thought of his partner, so innately sensitive and forgiving, so content to love him how he was, damaged and debased. He let the tears slip from his eyes, hot against his temples, and allowed them to flow freely, feeling their warmth on his skin, realising he would never see his lover's smiling face again.

He felt his hand being lifted and saw the hatred in the man's eyes, then the most excruciating pain shot through his body. As his hand was released from the man's grip, he raised it above his head and tried to focus. Blood was pumping out from a stump, where his ring finger should have been. It looked strange and made him want to laugh.

He saw the man take hold of the stiletto blade and hold it above his chest. Its point hovered above his heart, but he didn't care anymore. Death held no fear for him. He opened his mouth and started to sing the song again, his voice sounding strangely detached. The man joined in, chanting the words loudly, drowning out his singing. His head started to swim, the voices merging into a discordant clamour.

He started to scream and opened his eyes for one last time, watching in terrified awe as the blade was plunged down into his chest.

23

'We've got a second murder.'

Hunter paced through the door from his office, speaking as he strode. Charlie looked up. They were the words that no detective wanted to hear, especially not on a Monday morning, and even more so when they hadn't a charge for their first murder.

'Forty-two-year-old, white homosexual male in Brighton. Same MO, killed in a graveyard, chest opened and heart ripped out, ring finger missing. His ring could be seen in his chest cavity and has now been removed by the Sussex Scene of Crime Officers for identification.'

'What was his name?' Paul looked shocked. She'd seen him react like this before. He always took it personally when a gay guy was killed or died of an overdose. The LGBT community was a small world and many were known to him or by friends of his.

'Jason Jennings, better known as JJ. His civil partner, Roger Stevenson, has been informed and has confirmed the ring belongs to JJ, but we're still waiting for a formal identification of the body.'

Paul shook his head. 'Can't say I know either of them personally, though probably some of my friends or friends of friends might. I'll listen out for any snippets that might help. Any suspects?'

'None as yet. Roger was away for the night on a business trip and has no idea why JJ should have been found where he was. He was well liked in the community, though Roger is aware that he did stray sometimes. It could be something to do with that; he may have been picked up randomly, although, with the MO of his death being identical to Susan's, we've got to assume it must be linked somehow to her murder.'

'Wow, a middle-aged woman and a forty-two-year-old gay man? I wonder what on Earth the link between them can be.'

Charlie went and gave Paul a quick hug. He was looking as if one of his own family had been killed.

'His partner says that JJ was originally from South London. Maybe there's a link there with any or all of our suspects. Paul and Bet, get on to that. Research as much as you can on Jason Jennings and see if you can find anything, anywhere, that shows he may have been connected to the same school, church or area as Mickey Barton, Atkins or Abrahams. He may even have been one of Abrahams' previous victims. Stranger things have happened. I only need the smallest link to that bastard and I'll happily bring him back in, with his snivelling solicitor. I'd love to see the look on both their faces when I read out a charge.'

Paul brightened up immediately and nodded across to Bet enthusiastically. 'Come on then partner, let's see if we can crack another case for the boss.'

Hunter indicated for Charlie to get ready, before turning to the others. 'Naz and Sabira, are you OK to carry on with the manhunt for Miller? He's racking up more victims every day and we need him caught quickly.'

Naz nodded. 'We're doing our best but we're barely having time to search, in between dealing with each new victim. I'll see if the fugitives unit can assist us with a few extra officers and get the source unit on to it; maybe they've got a few snouts that can sniff him out.'

'Good idea. We need to find him before Ben does.' He winked towards Charlie. 'Oh, and just to let you all know, we're getting a new team member to bring us up to a full complement. Not sure who it will be or when they'll arrive but at least the bosses upstairs have realised at last how stretched we are and are doing something about it. I'll keep you posted as soon as I know. Right, Charlie, let's go!'

The murder scene at Downs cemetery was a carbon copy of the one at West Norwood.

Charlie stared at the bloody sight, comparing murders. Jason Jennings' body was sealed off from public view, laid out flat on the grass, carefully placed with his limbs neatly by his sides. His ring finger on his left hand was missing and his eyes were open, staring straight upwards, dark, static pupils devoid of life. What had he seen in those last few moments before he died? What pain had he gone through in his last few seconds? If only they knew, they'd be able to catch his killer straightaway, but now it was too late. They were back to square one again.

Jennings was only a small man, yet his wrists and mouth

showed clear signs of ligatures having been used. His chest had been opened, his ribs cut cleanly and peeled back and blood had clotted around the open wound where his heart had once been. It was as grisly and disturbing a murder as Susan Barton's.

A small tent had been erected about thirty feet away from his body. A peek inside showed an outlined area where Jennings' heart had been located, apparently tossed to one side as the killer left. It had been removed now in readiness for the post mortem but a small marker showed where it had lain.

Hunter turned to Chief Superintendent Bernie Groves, the Senior Investigating Officer from the Sussex Constabulary who had made the call this morning. 'Thank you for calling us in on this.'

'No worries. We're only a small force and I'm not ashamed to say we could use the help and resources that you have in the Met. I presume you're already some way into the investigation your end? At the moment we have nothing to go on at all. No CCTV, no witnesses, no idea why our victim was here, or how he got here. With it being an outside scene, the forensic opportunities are likely to be sparse, and, like yours, the motive doesn't appear to be robbery; his wallet and phone were still in his pocket. To be honest, we're going to be struggling. His partner was away on business and we have already ruled him out as a suspect. He's got several cast-iron alibis and hotel CCTV that show him booking into a hotel in Luton yesterday evening and staying in the bar drinking until the early hours. There's no way he could have been involved.'

'Can we speak to him?' Hunter asked.

'Yes, of course. He's in a bit of a state, as you would expect, but he seems very willing to help in any way he can.'

'Well, that makes a pleasant change.' Charlie couldn't help saying what was in her head. Maybe it was just London but everybody there seemed so guarded when asked to assist police.

Bernie Groves turned to face her and she immediately wished she hadn't said anything. He was tall, stern and had a distinct military air and although he appeared gracious in his communications with them, she suddenly felt as if she'd upset the sergeant major and was about to be bawled out.

Hunter came to her rescue. 'What DC Stafford here means, is that we have three suspects so far for our murder in London, and none of them are being particularly helpful in allowing us to piece together their movements around the time of our victim's death. In fact they seem to prefer to be extremely economical with the truth.'

'Maybe because they are being treated as suspects and not witnesses?'

'If only that was the case. I could at least understand that, but it's been the lies as much as anything that have caused them to become potential suspects. Let's hope Roger can help us out.'

Roger Stevenson looked as if he'd been crying constantly since the moment a police officer had turned up at the door of his hotel room in Luton and given him the news of his partner's death.

Now staying with a couple of friends back in Brighton, he sat slumped on a leather settee, his head bowed forward.

He got up when Hunter and Charlie walked in and held out his hand to them both. She reciprocated, feeling her own small palm swallowed up immediately within the vastness and strength of his grip.

As small as Jason Jennings had been, so Roger Stevenson was the opposite. He was the Goliath to Jason's David and Charlie could see straightaway how the dynamics of their relationship had worked. She waited while he settled himself back down before she spoke, his bulk filling one space completely and overlapping on to the adjacent cushion.

'Thank you for seeing us. I'm so sorry for your loss.'

'I always knew the day would come sooner rather than later, but thank you for your kind words.'

'Why do you say that?'

His comment was clearly designed to provoke a question. He obviously wanted to talk and, like Bernie Groves had said, he seemed open to telling all he knew. Still, she had to tread carefully. She didn't want to say anything that might offend him or cause him to stop talking freely.

'JJ was a lost soul. I looked after him and he relied totally on me. He always had, from our first day together. I wish I could have stayed with him all the time because I know without me he was vulnerable, but sometimes I had to work away from home. He hated me leaving him but he never said anything because he didn't want to upset me. I also know he met other men when I was gone. Other people told me.'

'And you didn't find that hard?'

'Yes, of course I did, especially at first, but JJ was different. I know he loved me as much as he was capable of loving anyone.' He stopped and cleared his throat, fighting back the tremor in his voice. 'But he was damaged. For him, it was all about physical affection. He needed to be wanted and he thought that he would be liked if he gave other men his body. He didn't care what they did to him. Sometimes when I came back from business trips he would have bruises, sometimes marks where he had obviously been tied up, once or twice he had bite marks. He thought I didn't notice but I always did.'

'And you didn't say anything?'

'What would be the point? JJ was JJ. He would have carried on doing it because he couldn't stop himself. And I loved him for who he was. In fact, in a strange way I loved him more because he was so lost. I wanted to protect him. If I'd said something he would have felt he'd let me down and I didn't want that. I was all he had and he gave me as much of himself as he could. I know he loved me. He would tell me that every day. But there was always a part of him that didn't care about what happened to him. He never really spoke about it, but he'd been like that from the day I first met him.'

'When did you meet him?'

'It was Millennium night. In a club in Soho. He was there by himself, sat in the corner drinking. I thought he looked cute, so we got chatting. He was very drunk and very sad. Something had obviously happened but he wouldn't tell me what. He never has. All I know was that night he ran away from everything and everyone he'd ever known and he never went back. He's stayed with me ever since. He always says I rescued him, but I don't know what or who I rescued him from.'

'So he's never given you a name.'

'No. He only gave the most sketchy details about his past. Said his life began when we met. All I know was that he was in care and was shunted from one care home to another and around various foster parents. He was kicked out of several schools because of his behaviour and arrested a few times. On one occasion a policeman turned up on my doorstep in North London asking after him. He said that JJ had been reported missing. He didn't say who by. JJ told him that he was safe and well and didn't wish to be contacted. As he was an adult, the policeman said that the person who had made the report would just be told he was alive and had left by choice and nothing else but he was terrified afterwards, in case the policeman passed on where he was living. In the end we moved down here and he was much more settled. I don't think he was ever truly happy though. He always said his past would catch up with him one day.'

'So do you think it has?'

'I don't know. I thought initially it was some bloke that had picked him up last night. There are quite a few men around our scene who like sadomasochism and other sick fetishes. I've never gone in for that sort of stuff myself.' He pulled a tissue from his pocket and blew his nose hard on it, looking suddenly stricken. 'I shouldn't have left him. I should have got a job where I didn't have to travel.'

'It's not your fault, Roger. You did the best you could for JJ.'

'Well, I tried to help him but it wasn't good enough, was it? I let him down. I tried to save him. God knows how I tried.' He slumped forward, dropping his head down into his hands and broke down in tears again. 'But maybe I never could.'

24

'Boss, there's every chance that Jason Jennings could be known to our suspects and possibly even Susan Barton. He's originally from the South London area. He could well have crossed paths with all of them. He was quite a handful by the look of it.'

Paul held up a stack of computer printouts. Charlie took the pile and skimmed through the first few pages.

Jason Jennings had been very well known to police. The first time he had come to their notice was as an eleven-year-old when he was found in a filthy house, with no food or warmth and just a dog for company. His father was located later in the nearby pub, pissed and proclaiming that if his lazy bitch of a wife hadn't walked off and left him, none of this would have happened. It turned out that she'd only left him after a thirteenth recorded assault but was so scared that he would find her she'd refused to give a forwarding address. Jason was therefore, through no fault of his own, taken into care.

There followed a huge number of reports detailing times when the boy had run away from foster homes, then care homes, caused damage to his surroundings, assaulted, or threatened to assault his carers and generally been out of control. He had been arrested on numerous occasions for petty crime, mainly for criminal damage, theft, assaults, public order offences and later for possession of drugs and drink-related crimes. The boy had been crying out for help.

Charlie had seen it before and hated the fact that she could do nothing to help. In the first month of her service she had dealt with a young girl, abused and left to fend for herself by drug-addicted parents. Over the following nine years, she'd watched as the girl had been lured into addiction and prostitution, before eventually ending up in a mental hospital. Jason Jennings' childhood and teenage years appeared to have followed the same path.

'Another kid who didn't stand a chance.' She threw the papers back down on Paul's desk and sat down heavily next to him.

'I know. It's criminal. It's no wonder so many of them end up dead or in prisons,' Bet chipped in. 'If I had my way I'd string their parents up. There's no excuse. I've been through a few dodgy partners myself, but whatever happens you don't take it out on the kids.'

'And JJ probably had an even harder time if he was struggling with his sexuality,' Paul added. 'It's difficult enough when you have good parents. God only knows what it must have been like with a father like his.'

'Is his father still around?' Hunter brought their attention back to the job in hand. 'If he is, he needs talking to. He could be a suspect for JJ's murder. Though whether he will have any link to Susan is a different matter. Who knows?'

'I'll take a look, boss.' Paul made a note of the enquiry.

'You said Jennings might be linked to all our other suspects?'

'Nothing firm as yet but he has a lot of history. He moved from one school to another around South London, so it's possible he was at a school that Atkins worked in at some point, or Susan. He may have been taught by her or have been known to her through the schools or possibly the clubs at the church she went to. If he was known to Susan then he could have come into contact with Mickey. Likewise with Abrahams; paedophiles like him used to make a habit of working at care facilities or with vulnerable children whenever they could in those days, so it's very possible that they came into contact with each other. JJ could even be one of his unidentified victims.'

'Good work, you two, but we need definitive links.'

'Easier said than done, boss, but we'll try. There's a mountain of background information on JJ to sift through, especially from his childhood. There must be links, it'll just be a case of finding them.' Paul dipped into a handful of peanuts that Bet had just poured into a bowl. 'He appears to have settled down a little more when he became an adult. From eighteen onwards there's less on the system for him our end.'

'Sussex have given us access to everything they have on him since his move down there with Roger almost sixteen years ago. He's been stopped with lots of different people and come to their notice mostly on the gay scene, but nothing that stands out particularly as yet.'

'Thanks, Bet. So if that was sixteen years ago he must have been around twenty-six years old when he moved there. So find out what calmed him down between eighteen to twenty-six; was there something or someone that influenced the change. Roger Stevenson says that he met JJ in 2000 at a club in Soho and he believed something had recently happened to make him want to run away. See if you can find out who he was around in those years, particularly if he came into contact with any of our suspects during that time. Paul, if you work backwards from that date, and Bet, you work forward, hopefully one of you will find something, anything, to link JJ to one of our suspects and give me an excuse to bring them in again.'

'Any chance we can help too?' Naz piped up from across the office from where she was seated with Sabira, underneath a large 'Wanted' poster of Cornell Miller. 'We're at a bit of a standstill with the Miller case at the moment. Can't do much until we get a bit of livetime information. He's circulated on every relevant database and Sabira even contacted *Crimewatch* yesterday to get him up on the next programme's "Most Wanted" appeals, but that's not for another week.'

'Yes, have a break from Miller for the day. He'll show up soon. He has to. Can you go back through Abrahams' previous convictions and if possible link in with any officers who dealt with his crimes. See if we can get names for all his known victims and faces or descriptions of any of the unknown children from the kiddie porn found in his possession.'

'Will do. I know a few people on the Sapphire and Jigsaw teams. I'll link in with them and see if he's known to them.' Naz pulled her phone out immediately.

'And I've got a mate in one of the new Child Sexual Exploitation Teams. I'll give them a shout.' Sabira jumped up and went to her desk.

'What do you want me to do, boss?' Charlie was excited at the prospect of finding a link now, especially with everyone involved.

'Well, I'll go and try to get updates on how the forensic stuff is doing at the various addresses and if Abrahams' car has pinged up on any ANPR activations. I'll also make sure Bernie Groves has his registration number for his squad in Brighton to look out for.' Hunter started to walk towards his office, stopping as he got to the door to turn back. 'I'd like to take a quick drive back up to Harris Academy with you in a few minutes; see if that old receptionist knows anything and will let us have the records of Atkins' and Susan's previous schools and education. We also need to pay a visit to the church Susan and Mickey attended, while we're down that way.'

Harris Academy was unusually quiet when they pulled up. It was mid-morning and would normally have been buzzing with the sound of hundreds of students moving from one lesson to another but it was as if the whole school were subject to bail conditions, not just the headteacher.

George was sitting upright at his desk when Hunter and Charlie approached. He sat up even straighter when they came into view.

'Mr Atkins is not in today, as I'm sure you are aware. He's on self-certificated sick leave. What can I do for you?'

Hunter dipped his head towards the receptionist. 'We wondered if you could assist us with the record of which schools and educational facilities Mr Atkins has worked or studied at, prior to being appointed as headteacher here. Susan Barton too?'

'I'm not sure I'm at liberty to help. I certainly couldn't allow you into Mr Atkins' office without his express permission.'

Hunter peered at the badge the receptionist was wearing before clearing his throat. It showed George's full name.

'Mr Lincoln. We've already searched the office once, when Mr Atkins was arrested. I'm aware that he had files containing his previous history. We had no need to take them at the time as we knew that Susan worked here and it wasn't therefore relevant. Now, however, we have another dead body, so I would suggest you co-operate with our enquiries because otherwise we might have to think about arresting you for obstructing police in the execution of their duty.'

Charlie stifled a snigger as George Lincoln swallowed hard and propped his glasses back up on the bridge of his nose. There was no way Hunter really would want to be arresting the receptionist and creating even more work than they had already. Technically, if he refused to allow them entry they would have to get a warrant, but if he co-operated with them, it would save them a good few hours of typing and court visits. A little squeeze of the rather stuffy receptionist would save them a lot of time and trouble.

'Well, officer, I really don't know that I can allow you access without at least making contact with Mr Atkins.

I'm sorry. I'm not being awkward on purpose. If you'd just allow me to make a phone call?'

Hunter beckoned towards Charlie. 'Have you got your handcuffs on you, DC Stafford?'

'But, but...'

'What's going on here, George? DI Hunter, DC Stafford, what can I do for you.' Charlie looked up and saw Daniel Roberts striding towards them with Sophie Pasqual trotting along in his wake. They seemed to be joined at the hip. He smiled at her and pushed his hands deep into the pockets of some green corduroy slacks that looked ancient.

'The officers here want access to Vincent's office to look at his CV. I was just saying that I should get his permission first.'

'Well I'm sure that won't be necessary. I doubt he would be particularly bothered, wherever he is, and the police have already been in there once, haven't they? Besides, I'm sure if they were to conduct a few searches on the internet, most of the details would be a matter of public record anyway. George, if there are any problems just say that I gave them permission.'

George Lincoln nodded stiffly and took a key from a drawer next to his desk. 'If you say so,' he said, making a show of passing it to Daniel Roberts rather than Hunter. Charlie stifled a smile again. He was so prim and proper. He really should have lived a hundred years ago.

She turned towards Daniel, who looked as if he'd read her amusement and was himself entertained by her reaction. He was a strong, assertive man, a little too old for her liking, but if he'd been twenty years younger and just a tad less hairy she would have found him quite attractive.

Daniel unlocked the door and pushed it open and she and Hunter entered the office. It didn't look as if Atkins had been in there since the police search. He was obviously lying low. The room was still in a state of disarray, files lying open and messy. Atkins would go mad if he saw it like this; she remembered how neat it had been on their first visit, everything placed precisely in order and in its place.

Hunter went straight to the filing cabinet and started to leaf through the various compartments. Charlie stayed by the door next to Daniel whose bulk was blocking out the light from the corridor. She switched the light on and turned towards him.

'Did Mr Atkins keep all the staff records here too, do you know? We were hoping to find Susan's so we can check back on where she'd worked before?'

'Do you think they might have known each other at a previous school then, before they worked together here?'

'Possibly, but we've got another similar case just come in and we're more interested in finding out if there are any links between them and the new victim.'

'What? Another murder? How awful,' Sophie Pasqual squeaked from behind Daniel. 'Oh my God, Daniel. Do you think Vincent's got something to do with the new one too?'

'Who knows what's been going on? He's always been a bit of a strange character.'

Charlie shook her head. 'Please don't go jumping to conclusions. We're just investigating every possible theory at the moment.' They were both listening intently to what she said. 'On that note, do either of you know which church Susan and her husband went to?'

'I think it was the modern-looking one in Norwood High Street,' Daniel moved to one side as Hunter appeared to have finished. 'I can't remember its name. Susan pointed it out to me one day when we were returning from a conference. She said she helped out at the Union of Catholic Mothers and I'm sure she said that Mickey helped out with the Scout Group that was attached to it. Do you think someone there might be involved?'

'It might be the priest?' Sophie Pasqual piped up excitedly. 'Men of the cloth do lead mysterious lives. There was a priest in my village in France once who was having affairs with five ladies from the parish at the same time. No one knew about it until one of the wives confessed to her husband. The priest was driven from the village by the men, but the church hushed it all up.'

'We are keeping all our options open as DC Stafford just said.' Hunter clearly wasn't going to entertain Sophie Pasqual's notions. 'Now, Mr Roberts, I have taken the files for Mr Atkins and the rest of the staff, as you can see. If you'd care to sign to say I have them, we'll be on our way.'

'Ridiculous woman.' Hunter couldn't keep the irritation from his voice as Charlie drove towards the church.

'Maybe she's got a point though, boss. You know what these Catholic priests are like!' She couldn't stop the grin spreading across her face. 'Didn't you say so yourself not so long ago? The religious fraternity and the educational lot are a bit strange... or something similar.'

'I think you'll find that was Mickey Barton's assessment.' He stopped at the realisation that she was winding him up and frowned good-humouredly. 'But they do have a point, though I'd never have thought the likes of Sophie Pasqual and Mickey Barton would agree on anything. Let's see, shall we?'

She was pulling up in the car park of a brick-built rectangular building. There were no extravagant entrance porches, domes or spires; just two sets of wooden doors and a cross situated at the top of the roof to the right-hand side. A large white sign with the words 'Catholic Church' dominated the wall, but other than these features there was nothing obvious to denote the usual lavishness of the Roman Catholic religion.

'This is refreshingly simple for a church,' Charlie observed.

They got out and headed towards the doors which were all locked, so they walked around the side, realising almost immediately that they had been looking at the rear profile of the building and that the frontage was as large and elaborate as the typical church. A sizeable statue adorned the middle of a central arched window underneath the cross, which stood high on the apex of the roof.

'OK, maybe not. See, boss, it's never as it seems.'

Before Hunter had a chance to answer, they saw the figure of a man approaching. He was olive-skinned, with black hair, neatly trimmed and held in place with what appeared to be a liberal application of hair gel. He looked to be in his late-forties, sporting a cropped beard, little more than designer stubble really, and the outline of a moustache, which added to his carefully tailored appearance. He wore the distinctive everyday clothes of a Catholic priest, a black cassock, tight across his shoulders and upper arms, and a white tab collar. For a priest he seemed remarkably toned. He held his hand out towards them.

'Hello, I'm Father Antonio. Can I help you?'

Charlie held her warrant card out towards him. 'DC Charlotte Stafford and this is DI Geoffrey Hunter. We need to speak to you about Susan Barton.'

'Ah yes, I wondered when you'd come. What a tragedy. Come in. I'll help you in any way I can.'

He led them back towards the car park and unlocked the doors they had first tried, before stepping into the main body of the church. The air was filled with the scent of incense; a dozen candles flickered at a side altar under a statue of Our Lady of Fatima and the main altar was adorned with an embroidered navy cloth. A large silver candelabra containing four candles, each burning brightly, stood at its centre.

Charlie followed behind Hunter feeling suddenly claustrophobic in the heavily perfumed atmosphere. Religious environments always made her uncomfortable. They were taken into the priest's office, which was fitted out with a round wooden table and high-backed wooden chairs. A large golden crucifix hung resolutely against an elaborately decorated backdrop, drawing the eye immediately on entry, with other religious symbols and artefacts dotted around. The walls were adorned with photos of various members of the congregation, along with priests, past and present; several related to visits from bishops to the church. A particularly ornately framed picture even showed a priest kneeling reverently before Pope Benedict. She stared at it for a few seconds, fascinated by the idea that two men could be treated so differently from one another. They were both human after all?

Father Antonio waited for Charlie to finish looking at the photos before sitting down. They chose seats opposite him and he started to speak immediately.

'Susan was a valued member of our congregation here. Her death has been a great shock to us all. She was active on many of our committees and a leading member of the Union of Catholic Mothers. I have been praying for her and her family since I heard the awful news.' He stopped and gave the sign of the cross, bowing his head momentarily. 'God rest her soul. I was hoping that her husband would ask me to preside over her funeral. I know that many people in the congregation would like to say farewell and pay their last respects.'

'Do you know her husband, Mickey, well?' Hunter came straight to the point.

'I knew Susan better.' He smiled fondly at the memory. 'Mickey came to the services occasionally, but I don't think he was interested in fully joining our community. He did run the scout group that is attached to our church though. I know he enjoyed that. He helped coaching the boys in football and other sports and would go to summer camps with them.'

'Do you know much about the breakdown of their relationship?'

'I know that Susan had tried for many years to reconcile herself to the differences between them but she had found it hard. In the last few months I am aware they had separated, but she and Mickey were receiving counselling for their marriage problems. I know Mickey certainly was hoping that they would get back together.'

'And Susan?'

The priest paused, frowning slightly. 'She had a strong faith so I'm sure she would have tried to keep true to her wedding vows.'

'Are you aware of either of them starting a relationship with any other person?'

'As much as I would like to tell you all I know, officer, I am afraid I am bound by my vows of confidentiality. What is said in the confessional, stays within the confessional. All I can say is that I was trying to help them both.'

'Is that a yes then?' Hunter stared at him irritably. Be it legal, diplomatic, medical or religious privilege; anything that hampered an investigation he was running was a source of acute frustration. The priest clearly knew more than he was letting on.

'Is there anyone you can think of that might have wanted to harm Susan?' Charlie took over before Hunter said something they'd regret. She'd seen it before when he was cross.

Father Antonio shook his head. 'I'm sorry, officers. I am honestly trying to help.' Hunter stood and walked to the window. 'Susan was a lovely lady. She helped me an awful lot and I know she helped my predecessors too. I honestly can't think of anyone who would want to see her harmed in any way, but if I think of anyone I'll be sure to let you know.'

'Have you ever heard of someone called Jason Jennings, better known as JJ?'

'Should I have?'

'We don't know. That's what we're trying to establish. Jennings was a forty-two-year-old homosexual man. He lived in this area for most of his childhood and teenage years, before moving away about sixteen years ago. Do you think he could have been known to Susan or Mickey, or anyone else at the church?'

'I'm sure if we had a homosexual man in our midst someone would have known. While I have no problem with his association with the Catholic faith, there are some amongst our congregation that might not have felt the same way.'

'So if he did attend, some people might have had issues with him?'

'Officer, I have only been here for just over four years, although I think I may have heard talk of a man known as JJ. What I'm trying to say is that some members might find his sexuality incompatible with their faith. The Bible clearly says that homosexuality is a sin.'

Now it was Charlie's turn to be annoyed. Father Antonio was not exactly subtle. 'Well it's a shame the church could not be more inclusive and welcoming, then maybe the likes of Jason Jennings would not have had so many problems as an adolescent.'

'This church does try, officer. For years we have worked with youths from all backgrounds. We have close links with the local social services and several of the nearby schools. We have welcomed many disadvantaged children regardless of their ethnicity, faith or sexuality. We have many people within the church, Susan Barton included, who care nothing for the social norms and try their best. At the end of the day everyone here would have tried to provide support and help him to repent.'

He was making things worse, not better. She felt herself repelled by his words the more he spoke. There was something inherently troubling beneath the skin of the outwardly friendly priest. She took a deep breath and composed herself.

'Father Antonio, I think I understand what you are trying to say, though I have to say I don't agree with you. Your attitude encourages hate towards those who may be different and could be seen as the motivation for someone wanting to cause harm. Jason Jennings is dead and for all we know he could have been killed by someone who believes, as you do, that he is a sinner. The next step surely, is to judge that he should be exterminated. Now, is there someone here that might confirm your somewhat vague memory that JJ may have attended and be able to help us?'

Father Antonio nodded. 'I'll get the church secretary, Joan Whitmore, if you'd like. She has a record of everyone who has been in the congregation pretty much over the last century. She's been here almost that long herself, so she might even remember him if he did attend.'

He stood up and went to the door, before turning towards her.

'DC Stafford, just because I have told you what the Scriptures say, it doesn't mean that this man wouldn't have been loved. The Bible says that God so loved the world that he gave his only begotten Son, that whosoever believeth in him should not perish but have everlasting life. John chapter 3, verse 16. I would have loved this man, whatever his persuasions, and I, like many other Catholic priests and bishops, would encourage all the members of our congregation to do the same.'

'Jason Jennings, date of birth 24th August 1974 was a member of this church and the 8th West Norwood scout group affiliated to our parish for about ten years prior to the year 2000. I remember him myself.'

Charlie was immediately excited.

She watched as the old lady folded the large, leather-bound book shut, almost reverently. Had she not done it so carefully Charlie would have expected a cloud of dust to have jettisoned up into the air, so old did it look.

'I've been responsible for the upkeep of records since I was a young girl. There're not many people who have come and gone over the years that I don't remember.'

The secretary pushed her wiry, grey hair behind her ears and adjusted her spectacles. She was a petite lady with a slightly hunched back and reminded Charlie of everybody's favourite granny; she must have been ninety years of age at least, judging by the deep wrinkles in her skin, but she had a kindly disposition and the inquisitive look of a woman half her age.

'I do remember Jason. He wanted to be called JJ; hated his actual name because he said it reminded him of his father. He was a naughty boy, about fifteen or sixteen years old when he first came to us, always getting into trouble. Gradually though, as he got more involved with our scout group and the church, he settled down; in fact he became almost too quiet. I always thought he looked sad but he would never say why. It was a shame when he disappeared. Several people tried to find him, to make sure he was OK. The last thing I heard was that he had moved to the coast and settled down... with a man.'

She slipped the book under her arm and gave Charlie a wink.

'I had a quick chat with Father Antonio before I came in. I gather you've had the lecture! Can I just say, we don't all think the same as our priests. Some women even take the contraceptive pill these days!'

Charlie smiled back at the ageing Catholic lady. It was right what her mother said; you should never judge a book by the cover. Sometimes the most unlikely people were the ones to offer the biggest surprises and Joan Whitmore's attitude was uplifting.

'Oh Joan, before you go. In the next few days could you make us up a list of the other priests who have served here over the years, permanent or temporary, and also anyone connected to the scouting movement that might have helped JJ. Do you think he would have known Mickey Barton?'

'There's absolutely no way he would *not* have known Mickey Barton. Mickey ran that scout group almost single-handedly for twenty years with a rod of iron. JJ was part of the squad during some of that time and after he turned eighteen I believe he helped Mickey to run it. They would have worked together weekly and gone camping together with the other boys most summers.'

Charlie watched as the old lady shuffled away. Her earlier frustration with the priest was waning slightly, replaced instead with relief. They now had the first evidence to link both victims together.

'It's lucky Paul wasn't with you speaking to that priest, instead of me,' Charlie commented as they let themselves out.

'Or Sabira. I wouldn't like to say out of the pair of them who would pack the better punch.'

'True. Thankfully most people are a little more enlightened these days, though with that sort of attitude it's no wonder our unit is still so busy.'

She smiled to herself at the thought of her two colleagues squaring up to Father Antonio, breathing a sigh of relief at leaving the oppressive environment.

'I didn't like that man.' Hunter wound down the window, subconsciously mirroring her sentiment. 'But I can't put my finger on quite what it was about him, aside from his blatant prejudices. Maybe Sophie Pasqual was right about men of the cloth after all. I get the impression he knows more about both JJ and Susan than he's letting on and not just stuff he's heard about in the confessional.' He gave a little shiver and blew on his hands before winding the window back up. Although the sky was bright, it was deceptively cold.

'Me too. He clearly held Susan in high regard but at the same time totally disagreed with JJ's way of life. He gave me the creeps.' Charlie felt a tingle run through her spine.

'Is that your professional opinion?' Hunter laughed.

'Maybe it's more of a gut feeling. One thing I know for sure is that we need to speak to Mickey Barton again, now that we have a positive link between him and both Susan and JJ.'

Hunter nodded, just as his phone rang. He picked it up and Charlie watched his face become more animated as he spoke. When at last he clicked the call off, she could hardly wait for the news he had.

'Well! You may or may not be correct about Father Antonio, but you're quite right about needing to speak to Mickey Barton again. That was the skipper from the Polsa search team that have been going through Barton's flat. They'd decided to do the bathroom last as it appeared quite spartan and clean.' He paused and rubbed his hands up over his face.

'And…'

'Well let's just say, Barton's going to have to come up with a good story for this one. They found Susan's missing engagement ring hidden in the water in the cistern of the toilet.'

25

'We've got the toxicology report back on Susan.'

They'd returned to Lambeth HQ to update the others on their findings.

Hunter perched on a desk and scanned through the report, reading out the relevant points. 'Time of death; estimated to be at around 00.30 to 01.30. Rigor mortis had set in. Liver and rectal temperature checks were carried out and confirmed her death to be within that timeframe.' He stopped and raised his eyebrows. 'So that would put Abrahams' car firmly in the right place at the right time. Her last meal was eaten around 18.30 and consisted of pork, potatoes, carrots and broccoli, followed by apple pie. She was drinking orange juice. This bit's interesting now.' Hunter continued reading, 'Traces of Gamma-Butyrolactone were found in her bloodstream. The lab is unable to give the exact amount she ingested initially, as it disappears from the body fairly rapidly but there is no legitimate reason for it to be there. It is unlikely Susan would have had this sort of substance in her body naturally and it's not present in any known proteins, fats or carbohydrates. Apparently it should never be taken orally.'

'Gamma-Butyrolactone. She was given GBL?' Sabira shook her head. 'It's dangerous stuff, colourless and odourless. It's very similar to GHB, better known as the date rape drug, but it has the same effects. I dealt with a few rape cases where it was used, when I was working on the Sapphire Team. The quantity has to be carefully measured with a pipette or it can kill. Experts are saying that it kills around six people a year but scores more are hospitalised. It's lethal. I read recently that it's being called "coma in a bottle", works out at fifty pence a shot. It's used a lot among gay men, isn't it, Paul?'

Paul nodded. 'It's prolific in the gay community. I'm told it gives users a high which is next to none and aids relaxation, but you're right, Sab, it's got to be treated with care. I'll Google it and read what it says.'

He reached for his phone and began tapping in the name of the substance.

'It would explain how the killer got Susan to the cemetery so easily!' Sabira was animated. 'Do we know how he got her out of the house yet, boss?'

Hunter frowned. 'Not exactly. We know she hadn't planned to go out and we also know now from the download of her phone that after speaking to Emma she didn't get any other calls or texts. House to house enquiries have been negative, but then her road is quiet and it would have been dark after 7 p.m. It was also cold and windy on Sunday evening so most people were probably indoors. If someone she knew had called and invited her out on the spur of the moment, the chances of anyone seeing them would be slim. She was dressed for the cold and had her bag and phone with her, which suggests she went voluntarily.'

Sabira chipped in again. 'So, once he's got her out of the house, he offers her some orange juice which looks like a nice healthy drink, but unbeknown to her it's spiked with GBL. She drinks it quite happily and within a short amount of time he's got her exactly where he wants her, unconscious and under his control.'

Hunter nodded his agreement. 'It sounds extremely plausible. Paul, what does it say on the internet?'

Paul held his phone up. 'Here you go; Gamma-Butyrolactone, GBL, or G is a colourless liquid. It is soluble in water and can be used as a paint thinner, floor stripper or an industrial cleaning solvent. It is derived from GHB, like Sab said, which is illegal, but so far in the UK, because GBL has lawful uses, it hasn't been classified as a Class A or B drug, so it's not illegal to import, supply or possess unless knowingly to be used for human ingestion.'

'Why would anyone want to ingest industrial cleaning solvent? People must be mad,' Hunter addressed Paul.

'Because people will take risks in the search for bigger and better highs. It's only when it's taken in higher doses that it can cause unconsciousness, coma and even death.'

'My point exactly. We'll have to wait for the tox report back on Jennings, but if GBL is linked to the gay community anyway, the chances are it will have been used in his case too?'

'JJ would probably have been familiar with it, but he could easily have been given too much without realising. It really should be banned.'

'There'll always be something else that comes along to replace it,' Bet joined in. 'As soon as one substance is classified, another takes its place. You know as well as I do that legal highs are more popular than cocaine or heroin these days, but they're just as dangerous, if not worse. Whoever thinks, I know, I'll just pop into the local farm shop or garage and buy a few quid's worth of plant fertiliser or metal cleaner to swallow and see what happens?' Bet stopped mid flow and the office stayed silent, everyone taking in what she had just said and processing the information to the same conclusion.

'Mickey Barton.' Charlie said the words that they were all thinking. 'He works in a garage. He'd have access to GBL every day. I've heard it's very good if used to clean the alloy wheels of cars.'

'My brother's not here. He's gone away for a few days. Can't you lot give him a break? His wife's been murdered; he hasn't got a home to call his own at the moment and his daughter doesn't want to know him.'

Mickey Barton's sister was a female version of Mickey. Squat, solid and bad-tempered, she was obviously not going to be told what to do by any copper, never mind ones that had given her brother a hard time. Charlie knew immediately, from the set of the woman's jaw, that anything she said would be ignored, countered and reported straight back to Mickey.

'I'm sure you can understand, we have a job to do and we have *the* most serious crime to investigate.'

'And I'm sure you lot understand that unless you have a warrant, you're not getting in here. My brother needs protection and help, not harassment. He's going through a hell of a time and he needs to be left alone with what family he's got left.'

'Do you know where he is?'

'No I don't. He just said he'd be back when he next needs to sign on bail. He's doing everything you lot asked of him.'

'Well do you have his phone number, so I can at least speak with him. I'm sure he wouldn't disappear without leaving some way his children can contact him if they need to?' That angle always worked well, the good father bit.

'You'll have to ask them then. As far as I know he doesn't want anyone contacting him. He'll phone me or them if he needs to know anything.' She smiled as sweetly as her face would allow and started to close the door. 'Now if that's everything? I'll tell him you called, when he next phones in.'

Charlie stepped back, cursing to herself quietly. The sister was right, in as much as they couldn't just go marching in to look for him without a warrant, unless they knew for certain he was there. Dammit! Maybe they should have sent someone along first to see if they could see him. They'd just presumed he'd be there because that was the address he'd been bailed to. They should have remembered his only real bail conditions were to report to the local police station twice a week and turn up on the date they'd set for bail; not to live and sleep at the address every night.

Just when they thought they were getting somewhere, there was always a hurdle thrown in the way; a door slammed in their faces, metaphorically, or actually in this case.

★

Mickey Barton waited at least ten minutes after hearing the door slam before he stepped out from the wardrobe upstairs and gingerly came down to the kitchen.

'Thanks for that, sis. I owe you.'

'Too right you do. Why do they want to nick you again? From the numbers waiting behind that arrogant bitch, I don't think they'd come for a welfare visit.'

'I have no idea,' he lied. 'You know what Old Bill are like when they think they've got something. Just because Susan was shagging her boss, they think I might want her dead. More like I'd want to see him dead. Bastard. What she saw in him I'll never know.'

He turned and climbed the stairs again, not waiting for an answer, in case his forthright sister said something that might hurt his pride. He'd do what she said he'd already done and disappear. He'd always camped with the scouts and he knew how to survive. He'd take himself off for a few days and enjoy the freedom. Besides, he knew why they wanted to speak to him; he'd watched the news. It could only be two things. Either they'd found the ring or they thought he had something to do with the death of that little faggot.

Well, let them think what they wanted. He had stories that covered both eventualities and the police would have to prove otherwise.

26

Round and round he turned the clear Perspex container in his hands; it was hypnotic. He loved to twist the top on tightly so that he could turn it upside down and stare at each severed finger, each digit bringing back memories, each one a tale of love and betrayal.

He lifted it up towards the bare light bulb in his rented room and rotated it again, savouring the sight, identifying them, remembering each one.

The oldest was small, slightly more discoloured and wrinkled than the others, the fingernail bitten down to the quick. It belonged to his first love, in a different country, so many years before; back when each country in Europe was its own entity, not woven together in one big dysfunctional Union. The girl had been sweet, a worrier who chewed at her nails. They were young, close together in age. She'd doted on him, but had she ever truly loved him? She had been promised to another and, in the isolated village in which he was staying at the time, it was expected they would marry. It wasn't right. When the time had come for her to be betrothed, she had not looked back, betraying his love forever and breaking his heart. It was her destiny and he was no part of it.

Something had snapped within him. The pain had been immense, so it had been easy to kill her. She came willingly when he'd called and when her body was found several days later, ripped open and mutilated, nobody had suspected him. A tragic accidental death, made worse by forest animals feasting on her dead body. Her new husband grieved but moved on. He remained for a time, his grief at her loss tempered only by the knowledge of her betrayal. If he couldn't have her then no one would. No one else had really cared, but he had, and he'd cherished the one part of her that he'd taken, still intact, and still with a nail chewed down to the quick. It would forever remind him of the beautiful girl from the forest.

The next finger was longer, its prints worn down by years of labouring. The nail was short and stubby, worn low rather than bitten. The murder of its owner had been equally as easy, committed in the same foreign country and separated by just a few years. The girl had been older, married previously, but when her husband had died prematurely, he had been her solace, the one she'd turned to for nurture and support. But she wanted him only as a confidante, a friend, while he yearned for more. She moved on, married in due course to a neighbour whose own wife had died in childbirth. It had been a natural progression but he was no part of it and he'd watched her become pregnant with her new husband's child until he could watch no more.

Her murder had been put down to a passing farm labourer, the dullard's mind addled by alcohol, the knife that cut her open planted in his rucksack as he slept. It had been easy, too easy. In those days, there was neither the means nor the will to carry out a full investigation. The farm labourer was convicted and duly hanged from a tree, still protesting his innocence.

He felt no sorrow for either of them. She had betrayed his attentions and the farm labourer deserved no better. The unborn child had caused him some guilt however. The child had done no wrong. It was an innocent, caught up in the sins of its mother. He'd left the child intact within her body, careful not to harm the tiny foetus while removing her heart, his skills at surgery being honed as he did so.

For a second he felt a pang of guilt at the thought. He twisted the jar in his hands in a bid to forget what he had done to the baby and his eyes alighted on the small black finger next to hers. Things had changed by the time he met the youth who was its owner.

Time had moved on. He'd moved on, now twenty-seven years of age. He'd forgotten the baby and met Susan. She was unmarried when they'd met and he had fallen madly in love with her. She was everything he wanted; everything he desired. Twenty-two years old, petite, with long blonde hair and a good Catholic school education. She was clever and pretty and engaging and he wanted her more than anyone he'd ever set eyes on. For a couple of years he made every excuse to be with her; just being near her was enough. Until she too betrayed him and everything changed.

He was once more forgotten, cast to one side, used to help her achieve her goal, but nothing more. Despite her treachery he had loved her, really loved her and even though she'd stuck a dagger through his heart, he couldn't do the same to her. She was too perfect to be damaged in any way. And so it had started in earnest; his self-destruction. He didn't care what he did as long as he got pleasure, like he had never known before. He travelled to Africa on working holidays to help others; building, teaching, labouring, but he had got more out of the visits than he'd given, much more.

He stared at the jar again and remembered the boy whose finger floated in his container; the twelve-year-old boy who had kissed him; who'd been used by the elders of his village. He knew no different. The boy thought he was doing the right thing, but instead of stopping him, explaining what was right and proper, he had allowed the boy to awaken an urge that he had never previously allowed himself to submit to, a passion that he'd always longed for but never experienced with Susan. The boy did everything he wanted; and he wanted everything. He knew it was wrong. He knew it was depraved but he couldn't stop. At last he could be himself, in a country far away where no one would know him, expect anything from him; where he was free to forget his responsibilities and do as he'd always wanted.

He killed the boy two nights before he was due to leave the country, discarding his mutilated body out on scrubland for the vultures and hyenas to gorge on. It had happened after he'd seen his young lover leaving an elder's tent. He knew the older man would have expected sexual favours from him, just as he had. The boy had obviously submitted as bidden but suddenly he didn't want anyone else to have him as he had. The boy was his and he had loved him in his own way. He was doing the boy a favour by killing him really, even though he'd nearly changed his mind at the sight of his innocent, terrified face as he'd held the blade above him. In the end however, the boy needed rescuing from himself and he was the one that could save him.

Afterwards he had returned home, gone back to his day job, this time working more regularly with the down-and-outs, the untamed children, the lost souls whose vulnerability and bodies he could use to satisfy his greed, while maintaining an outwardly normal existence. Nobody knew; nobody would suspect. Not even those close to him, only a few others who traded pictures and stories anonymously. JJ had come to him during that time and he'd loved him just as he'd loved his African boy, transforming him from a naughty child to a man who obeyed his every word. All had gone well until he'd suggested introducing a new boy into their lives to join them, the idea, for some unknown reason, causing JJ distress and triggering his disappearance.

In JJ's absence he'd claimed another, on a trip to Somalia, the child's finger floating with the others. He barely remembered the child's name. He'd loved, he'd lost, he'd killed. He'd come and gone and now he was back and had the fingers of Susan and JJ to bolster his collection.

He stared at the newest additions; in just over a week, Susan's had already taken on a slight yellowy hue in comparison to JJ's. The varnish had faded and the nail appeared tarnished. JJ's was still clean and looked almost alive. He felt the familiar ripple of excitement at the sight. He couldn't wait another week to claim his next victim. He needed to dispatch more on the list before he was up to date. There was a new possibility arriving on the scene already. He loved easily and he lost easily and he recognised the signs building up in his body once again. He was falling in love; he could feel it in the way his words provoked a reaction; in the way he was watched and addressed but he needed to take care. He had a job to do before he could truly love again.

He checked himself in a small cracked mirror above the sink and smiled. The police had no idea of his hidden past. They looked only at the surface, the heres and nows. They worked only on the obvious, the scraps of information he'd allowed them to find. He was too clever for them.

He peered into the container, eagerly counting the fingers. Six now, but room for more.

The tools were ready for action. He'd cleaned them briefly but not so carefully this time. The cops had already pretty much linked the two murders. What did it matter if JJ's DNA was found at the next crime scene; or the next, or the next, as long as his wasn't?

Gently, he placed the container back inside the box on the mantelpiece and closed its lid, locking away his treasures.

He gazed at the photograph of himself, young, good-looking and strong. He looked at his mother, stooped from her labours, and his father, sleeves rolled up ready for work. Would they still be proud of him now? He didn't care if they weren't. It was their fault, anyhow.

He imagined his next killing. The next one would be easy, far too easy. He could almost do it with his eyes closed. He rubbed his hands together with pleasure; one palm against the other, massaging each finger, stroking and caressing, the motion creating heat, warmth, passion. Everything that had been thrown back in his face.

27

When Charlie entered Jamie's graveyard that Wednesday morning something was different. She couldn't work out quite what it was but somehow she felt ill at ease. It was earlier than usual and still dark, but it wasn't that; she was used to sneaking around the backs of shops and estates in the dead of night. It was no use being frightened of the dark in her job.

She made her way through the gate and into the churchyard, conscious of every crunch of her feet on the gravel. Since her last visit, the church trustees and gardeners had been at work. The fallen leaves had been swept and crammed into sacks by the entrance, along with the last grass cuttings of the year. A mountain of fallen foliage lay stacked into a large pile, each branch sawn into manageable lengths for removal by churchgoers, for their open fires and log burners. The graveyard had been made ready for the winter.

Maybe it was that notion that made Charlie uneasy that morning. She hated the fact that winter was almost upon them and the area would stand forgotten and unkempt at least until the Christmas festivities; nearly three months when Jamie would lay in the frozen earth, with only her mother's and her own separate visits, to let him know he was not forgotten. Lucy and Beth never visited. They were more wrapped up in their own lives to think of the half-brother they had never met. Harry, his stepfather, didn't even visit his own daughters, never mind the stepson whose death he had been partly responsible for. As for the man who had fathered Jamie; he probably didn't even know that his child was dead. He'd never cared in Jamie's life; why should he bother now he was gone.

She switched the torch of her phone on, pushing away her thoughts and started suddenly when a twig snapped. Turning quickly, she saw a field mouse scurry into the bushes, its eyes illuminated in the light of the beam. It was gone in a flash and she scolded herself for being so jumpy. But there was something not right.

She made her way over to Jamie's grave and kissed her fingers, passing them slowly in line with the indentation of his name engraved on the headstone as she did on every visit. For a passing moment the action calmed her.

A light gust of wind rattled the weathervane on top of the tower and it squeaked impatiently. She looked up as the clock hands clicked on to seven. Instead of the usual peace, her head filled with thoughts of what needed to be done. They still had a killer at large, who had now murdered in cold blood at least twice and could easily claim more victims. Mickey Barton was their main suspect and needed to be caught. Oscar Abrahams and Vincent Atkins were also both credible suspects, but without further evidence coming to light would remain free, at least for the time being. Abrahams' friend was yet to be identified and the car crucially still had to be found... and of course, Cornell Miller still needed to be detained.

She felt a pang of guilt at the thought of Moses and Claudette still living in fear. She hadn't really spoken to Moses since the arson attack and she needed to. She couldn't let him down any further.

It was still dark when she whispered her goodbyes to Jamie. She would normally wait for dawn to break but this morning she couldn't afford to stay any longer. He would understand she had things to do and she would make up for it on her next visit.

She jogged back to her car and climbed in. Hers was the only car in the car park. It always was. Nothing was different today. It was all in her head. She heard the locks clunk into place and switched the engine on, relaxing as the headlights lit up the trees and shrubs surrounding her.

As she pulled out on to the lane that led to the church, she breathed a sigh of relief and leant forward to select her music. She didn't notice the dark blue Vauxhall Vectra estate parked up, silent and unlit, in the entrance to a field opposite, or the pair of eyes watching her every move.

'For fuck's sake, Mickey Barton cannot just disappear into thin air. Charlie, see if you can speak to Emma, she liked you. Maybe she will have been contacted by her father. We need a location for him and, if we can't get that, we need a phone number. Tell her it's urgent. She's upset that he's been arrested for Susan's murder. Maybe if you tell her that Mickey knew a second victim she'll realise how important it is we get hold of him now. Don't tell her about us finding her mother's ring though. I'd like to keep that little gem for his interview, without giving him the heads-up.'

Hunter's cheeks were ruddy and he looked stressed, and when he looked like that, Charlie worried. During her drive to work, she had been trying to process everything that was going on. Luck was not on their side and they needed a dose of it urgently. She tried to calm his worries.

'Will do, boss. I'm sure he'll come to light quickly. He's got family to think about and anyway he's due back on bail this Thursday. If we don't find him today, we'll get him tomorrow.'

'We could have another bloody victim by tomorrow.'

'Yes, but so far the killer's only struck on a Sunday. If he follows that pattern, we've still got a few more days. We'll just have to keep our fingers crossed.'

'That's hardly a recipe for crime prevention and I can't imagine it going down very well at Coroner's Court either. "Well, Sir or Madam, we did cross our fingers!"'

He sat down heavily as his phone rang and barked his name into the mouthpiece. Charlie wished she'd kept her mouth shut. There was no point trying to reason with him when he was in this mood. He was clearly feeling the pressure, and when his back was against the wall, they all knew about it.

A few minutes later he threw his phone down on to the desk in front of him and leant back in the chair, rolling his eyes. 'That was the traffic department. Oscar Abrahams' car pinged up on the fixed ANPR cameras several times over the weekend on the south coast, mainly around the Hastings area. They didn't think to let us know until now.'

'Not exactly in Brighton, but in the same part of the country.' Charlie was the only one who dared to speak.

'Yes, quite. Fucking wasters. They know how important it is to get that car stopped, but apparently they didn't have any spare units! They must have heard about the Brighton murder on Monday morning and were hoping that it would ping up again later on Monday or yesterday, but it hasn't surfaced since. We've lost our chance.'

He stood up and pulled out a crumpled packet of cigarettes from his pocket, then glared menacingly at Charlie.

'I'm going outside for a fag and don't try and stop me.'

She put her hands up in surrender. Some days she'd get away with telling Hunter off for smoking. She'd promised Mrs H a long time ago that she'd do what she could to preserve what was left of his failing health. It was a standing joke between her and Hunter usually. Today though, she knew better than to even try. It was going to be a long day.

'Woah, what's got into him today?' Paul gave a low whistle after the door had slammed shut.

'F.M.C. Don't you remember. He had it when we were looking for the abductor in the last case?' These days no one mentioned him by name.

'What the fuck's F.M.C.?'

Charlie found Emma's number and picked up the phone. She stopped, prior to keying in the number, and turned towards Paul. Everyone was staring at her.

238

'Frustration Mid Case! It's a well-known condition among detectives. I'm sure we've all suffered from it at one stage or another. And it's very contagious. Now Hunter has it, it's highly likely that we'll all go down with it in due course. So you'd better watch out.'

Bet started laughing and the tension in the office cleared almost immediately. 'I wondered what you were going to say then, Charlie. I'll put the kettle on and make him a fresh brew. We'd better see if we can cure him today, before it's too late for us all.'

Emma Barton answered the phone after its first ring.

'Have you got Mum's killer yet?'

The question caught Charlie by surprise and she regretted her response as soon as it left her mouth. 'We're trying to track down your dad actually. Do you know where he is?'

'You think it's him, don't you?' Her voice had a hard quality about it; as if she'd been through every emotion and this was the only one left that she could muster. 'Husbands often murder their wives when they leave them. I've been researching it. If they can't have them, they don't want anyone else to. Sometimes they even kill their children.'

'Emma, I think you're jumping to all sorts of conclusions here.'

'Why do you want to speak to him again then?'

'Because there's another very similar case just come in and we think your dad knew that victim too. We just need to ask him a few questions to see if he can help.'

There was a long pause before she answered. 'So he's killed two people now?'

'I'm not saying that at all. He may be a very important witness who can shed some light on both cases, but he's gone away and hasn't left a forwarding address or number. We were wondering whether you might be able to help us with where he is or have an up-to-date phone number for him.'

There was another long pause before she spoke again. 'I accused him of killing Mum the other day. Since then he hasn't answered his phone to me and now it's switched off. I think he might have a new number. You can have his old one though.'

She rattled off a number which Charlie wrote down. It was the same as the one they'd previously had, which was now coming up as unobtainable.

'I promise you though, if he does contact me, you'll be the first to know. I want him put in prison for what he's done to Mum.'

Moses Sinkler took a while longer to answer his phone when Charlie rang. When he did, he sounded defeated. His voice still had the same gravelly tone to it but now he spoke more slowly and deliberately.

'Hello, Charlie. Thanks for calling. Any news?'

For a few moments he almost sounded as if he was holding his breath.

'No, nothing yet Moses, but we're doing everything we can,' she lied. She heard his breath release in a long sigh. What was she saying? His case was second best. Priorities dictated that they go all out to catch the serial killer and while Naz and Sabira had made inroads into Miller's case, Charlie had not done the best she could. She should be doing more to help him, like she'd promised.

'It's OK, Charlie. I know you're doing what you can and I've seen the news. I know you're busy.' He was so gracious. 'We've moved out to another address. I couldn't risk putting Claudette in any more danger. She's lost though. Keeps walking round and round in tears, saying she just wants to go home.'

'Moses, I'm so sorry.'

'Don't be. You came when I called. That's all I can ask. I just want my life back. We've lived in that house all our lives. We brought up our children there and apart from the odd holiday we've never stayed anywhere else. It's where we always felt safe...' She heard his voice falter and waited while he composed himself, struggling to control her own emotions. 'Until now. We just need him caught.'

She spoke words of consolation to Moses, knowing that they weren't enough to console him. At the end of the conversation he thanked her for her troubles again. She put the phone down and felt only anger at her inability to help. Whatever happened, tonight she would go out looking for Miller and even if she didn't find him, at least she could say, without lying, that she'd done all she could to help Moses and his wife.

Ben was waiting when Charlie arrived at his place. His arm and hands were still in bandages but he was keen to keep up the training regime. Normality was restored.

'You got Miller yet?'

'Give it a rest Ben, you know I'm trying.'

She couldn't stop herself snapping at him; maybe she too was suffering from a dose of F.M.C. and needed someone to vent at. They ran in silence, longer and faster than they had run before, her body getting a sense of release as she sprinted the last section, back towards his flat. At the gates she sunk down on to the pavement, her breath coming fast and hard; the sweat running from her temples, down her cheeks and neck.

Ben stood leaning on the gatepost, his breath expelled into the air in clouds of condensation. She waited for the adrenalin to settle and the mild euphoria at the conclusion of a good workout to start to take effect. Ben waited with her too, by her side, the trusty protector, with her through rough or smooth.

When she finally felt her pulse rate returning to normal, she got up and leant towards him.

'Thanks Ben,' she said simply, giving him a gentle kiss on the cheek. 'You've cheered me up again. Are you up for another try at getting Miller?'

Ben sat in the passenger seat watching Charlie as she drove around the streets of Lambeth, her face alight with determination. He knew she wouldn't rest until she got Miller. She'd made a promise to an old man and his wife that she needed to keep, and he was determined to help.

He stared out of the window, his eyes focussing on the dark shadows for any sign of movement. He gazed into the walkways and alleys in the depths of the sink estates. He watched for the subtle movement of a wanted man; for that moment of recognition that might indicate that Miller was out and had seen them too.

He tried to look through the crowds in Brixton and Vauxhall and along the South Bank; he tried to concentrate on the manhunt, but all he really wanted to do was take Charlie in his arms.

He could still feel the touch of her lips on his cheek, the murmur of her voice in his ear and he knew he was getting closer; but as near as he was to having what his body had desired for so long, the more his head was beginning to panic.

28

Brixton town centre had retreated under a thin curtain of rain. It wasn't lashing down, but a constant drizzle fell, which penetrated clothing and left any pedestrian without an umbrella cold and sodden. Autumn was living up to its reputation.

Despite this, the dealers were still dealing and the users were still using. Nothing changed. The addicts had to feed their habit whatever the weather and so the business of supply and demand went on, whether in the rain, snow, wind or bright sunshine. He drove slowly, watching as brief liaisons occurred within the shelter of shop doorways. He despised the addicts for their weakness even though he was now one of them; not a user of drugs but a user of the addicts themselves; and the younger and more vulnerable the better. The only difference was he could control his urges; he could plan, develop and execute.

He smiled at the analogy; very soon he would be carrying out his next execution: Tanisha, the young girl he had taken under his wing after JJ had vanished, who he had loved and cherished in his own way, would be dead. Tanisha, who took everything he could offer and then threw it back in his face, giving her body, not only to him, but to every man or woman who was willing to pay. Tanisha, who had turned from his loving arms and rejected him in favour of a violent pimp.

He pulled off the main road and made his way up the hill, through noiseless backstreets, whose inhabitants lived unobtrusive lives, at work during the day and closeted behind the shutters and curtains of their fortress homes at night, away from the evils of the streets. Up, up the hill, avoiding the council's cameras, keeping clear of the areas that the police patrolled; areas where the addicts would queue while awaiting the arrival of their dealer.

He knew the exact spot from where she worked. Hadn't he picked her up from there on countless occasions when his desire for her body had proved almost uncontrollable; rescuing her from the kerb crawlers who would pay for the pleasure, saving her from herself. Yet she had repaid his troubles by causing him more, by opening her mouth and making dirty insinuations, by ruining his life. She deserved everything that was coming to her.

He parked his car up and sat for a few minutes watching vehicles stream past down the main road in front of him. There were cameras in Brixton Hill, so he'd avoid driving on to it, for the time being. He didn't want to make their job too easy.

The clock on the dashboard changed to midnight; the witching hour. It had always been a significant time for him and tonight was no exception. Climbing out of his seat, he hauled his jacket on, drawing his hood high up around his face against the rain. He'd changed his appearance since she'd last seen him, but it wouldn't do to be recognised… yet. The anticipation was better than any drug.

He saw her immediately, standing by thc bus stop in her usual spot. It gave her cover if the cops came round; and it gave her shelter from whatever the sky threw at her. Her attire was all that was needed to make her occupation obvious; that and the way she shimmied out across the pavement if any driver showed her the slightest attention. Most of her regulars recognised her anyway but she was always on the lookout for others.

She'd aged in the last few years, the lifestyle and addiction taking its toll. He still remembered her as a young, slightly chubby, mixed race girl with a broad smile and a larger-than-life personality. He'd been quite shocked when he'd tracked her down, hypnotised by her skeletal body, watching as she worked on several nights to ensure she still maintained the same habits.

Tonight she wore her usual short skirt, T-shirt and ankle-length high-heeled boots but a turquoise leather jacket was pulled across her shoulders. She sat on a seat in the bus stop, her head turned in the direction of the approaching traffic.

He walked through a grassy area adjacent to the road and called her name. She turned immediately and started to approach, her walk stilted and slightly wild. Her legs were bare and red raw from the cold but glistened with moisture. She hugged her arms to her chest, pulling the collar of her jacket further up around her neck. Her long, plaited hair hung lank and wet, with strands that had escaped from the braids plastered across her face and shoulders.

'You call me, love?'

He nodded.

'What d'ya want? Twenty quid for a blow job; twenty five for full sex; thirty quid if you want it without a rubber. But ya don't get nuffin' 'til ya flash the cash.'

He pulled thirty pounds out of his wallet and handed it to her. She stuffed it into the side of her boot and looked towards him, her eyes blank.

'Don't get no ideas. You're my first punter tonight. There ain't no more down there, where I put that.' She looked in the direction of some bushes and a wooden bench. 'You want it here, now?'

He shook his head. 'Come with me. We'll go somewhere a little more private.' He turned and started to walk, hearing the click of her heels next to him as they returned across the pavement. She stumbled as she walked, so he took hold of her arm, guiding her back towards his car.

He pulled a bottle from his pocket and opened the lid. 'Vodka and Red Bull?' He held it out to her and she took it, gulping the contents down greedily. He opened the passenger door and she almost fell into the seat, laughing as she spread her legs to give him a flash of her crotch, naked and enticing. He was tempted to take her then, but as she hadn't recognised him it was clear that it was an invitation that she gave to every man. He felt his anger stirring. If only she'd kept herself for him and her mouth shut, this would not be happening.

He started to drive towards the cemetery he'd chosen, navigating the quiet backstreets again as much as possible.

She was giggling now; the spiked drink taking effect.

'Where you taking me?' Her voice was high and excitable. 'It'll cost ya. You'd better bring me back to where ya found me or my pimp'll have somefin' to say.' She threw her head back and started to laugh again.

He stopped the car, his rage rising further at the mention of her pimp. Roughly he pulled her arms together, binding her wrists with a leather strap. It didn't seem to worry her.

'Ooh, you like it kinky do ya?' she snorted with laughter. 'That'll cost ya more too.'

He'd had enough. The whore needed to be silenced. How he had once loved her was a mystery. She was disgusting now. He pulled a syringe from the side pocket of his door; it was primed ready to go. Forcing her head back against the headrest, he pushed the plunger, shooting the concentrated liquid down her throat. She gagged instantly, choking on the burning fluid and started to struggle. He pulled out a scarf and tied it tightly around her mouth and threw his body weight on top of her, pinning her to the seat. It wasn't long before her eyes turned glassy, her body shuddering and convulsing as she started to lapse into a coma.

He started to drive again, watching her closely as he did so. He was nearly there and he wanted to kill her before she became fully unconscious but he had to admit he was good; he had learnt by now how long it took.

The gates were in view and the street was deserted. Slowly he did one last circuit of the block, checking that the padlock he'd exchanged earlier was still in place. It had been easier to snip the old one off while there was still the noise of evening traffic. He had to be quiet now; this site was situated in residential streets and it wouldn't do to alert a light sleeper with the clunk of metal against metal.

He parked up and stared at Tanisha. She was barely conscious but her eyes were still following his movements. He leant over and checked the tightness of the scarf around her mouth; one scream could be the difference between her living or dying, and he wanted her dead.

Hoisting his bag up on to his shoulder, he half lifted her out of the car, feeling her legs buckle underneath her. Time was of the essence now. He jammed an umbrella between their shoulders, pulling it down over their heads to provide cover in the darkness, and slung his arm around her waist. He started to walk, slowly, slowly at first and then with growing purpose. She moved her legs in time with his but it was his strength that carried her along.

Multicoloured ribbons, notes and floral tributes adorned the gates of the cemetery. In the rain and cold they hung wet and silent, scarcely moving with the lack of breeze. He saw the plaque describing the site as a graveyard for prostitutes, and felt a frisson of excitement throughout his body. He would pin a new message to its gates later, but in the meantime he had a mission to fulfil.

Cross Bones Graveyard was soon to have another victim to add to its number.

29

'There's been another one. Keeping your fingers crossed obviously wasn't enough.'

Charlie closed her eyes, feeling the blood drain from her face. 'When?'

'Last night. A prostitute this time. She was spotted around half eleven by an officer from the vice squad who saw her at her normal spot, at the bus stop in Brixton Hill. He knows her well but he was dealing with something else at the time. He was going to nick her later but she was gone by the time he went back around 1 a.m. I bet he wishes he had now. Anyway, get your stuff. We're required at the crime scene asap.'

Hunter was waiting with his jacket buttoned and tweed cap pulled firmly down on to his head, drumming his foot in time with the vein throbbing on his forehead.

'Just coming.'

She grabbed her usual kit and ran her fingers through her hair. After a late night out fruitlessly searching for Miller she was knackered, but there was no time to even try to find a brush, never mind smarten herself up. Today even Hunter was too preoccupied to care. The shit was going to hit the fan. One body was unexpected; two were unfortunate; three was a bloody disaster; and Hunter was the one that would be taking the flak.

It appeared to be weighing heavily on his mind as they shot through the rush hour traffic. He was offering nothing and she dared not ask. The crime scene was a cemetery in Borough, a short distance from the busy transport hub of London Bridge and within a short walk of Shakespeare's Globe theatre and Southwark Cathedral. They were nearly at the scene when Hunter finally spoke.

'Have you heard about Cross Bones Graveyard, Charlie?' He didn't wait for her to answer. 'I used to patrol that area. I saw the ribbons and tributes on the gates once and looked it up afterwards. It was always known as the outcasts' graveyard. Borough and the surrounding area was one of the poorest and most violent areas of London in the middle ages and for centuries all the paupers and children were buried here. They say sixty per cent of the bodies are children under five.'

He paused, as if allowing her to digest this fact.

'It was also the burial ground for the medieval sex workers who worked in the brothels; they were called the Winchester Geese. Their bodies were buried here until the middle of the nineteenth century. In the end there were believed to be 15,000 bodies buried in the small plot of land and there was no room for any more.'

She didn't know quite what she was supposed to say, so she kept quiet.

'But thanks to our incompetence, there's one more now.'

Redcross Way, SE1, in which the graveyard was situated, was cordoned off completely when they arrived. She parked at the end of the street, switched off the blue lights and waited for Hunter to move. He didn't.

'The latest victim is Tanisha Fleming, a twenty-seven-year-old, mixed race prostitute. She is quite distinctive-looking due to her long plaits and numerous tattoos and piercings. She was found early this morning when a local resident noticed that the padlock was missing and the gates were unlocked. The site is well tended these days and is usually kept secure. The vice squad officer who last saw her was just about to book off when he heard the description on the radio and he has provided a provisional identification.'

He sighed heavily. 'I've dealt with her on a few occasions myself, when she'd been on the receiving end of domestic assaults. I remember thinking she was a bit of a sad case when I got to hear more of her history. Moved around different care homes and went on the game when she was targeted by the dealers and paedos that prey on vulnerable children, like that bastard, Oscar Abrahams. Last I heard she was shacked up with a violent pimp who also controlled a few other girls. Another one who didn't stand a chance. Let down by her parents and society and now let down by us.'

'Like Jason Jennings then?'

Hunter nodded. 'Those two come from the same mould; both victims of the care system. Bet and Paul are checking schools and care homes now to see if there is a common location they both lived or were schooled at. Susan's the odd one out now as far as our victim profile is concerned... and all our fucking suspects were out and about last night.'

He got out and slammed the door a little too hard, striding away towards the crime scene. Charlie followed, running to catch up and apologising to the officer on the cordon, whose request for ID had been summarily dismissed by Hunter with the thrust of his warrant card and a grunt.

When she finally caught up, Hunter was staring down at the mutilated body of Tanisha Fleming. She looked the same as the others except that her skirt had been pulled up, revealing her naked groin and thighs.

'Looks like there might be a sexual element to this one.'

She nodded. Even though Tanisha was a prostitute Charlie still wanted to cover her over; to her mind there was something inherently wrong in leaving her exposed.

They lapsed into silence, stepping round the body carefully, staring down into the young prostitute's thoracic cavity. Instead of the glint of a metal ring as Charlie was expecting, Hunter was pointing towards a small piece of transparent blue plastic, containing a small, creamy crystalline rock.

'Crack cocaine, by the look of it.' He said what she was thinking. 'What the hell is the significance of that?'

'Maybe, the drugs taking over her life? He's shown previously that he's not interested in the monetary value of what he leaves.' Charlie was as perplexed as he. 'The relevance of the objects he's left is important to him, irrespective of how much they're worth; Susan's wedding ring and JJ's commitment ring and now, Tanisha's drugs?'

Hunter turned his own wedding ring on his finger. 'Rings are gifts of love – 'til death do us part and all that – but why remove their hearts and leave the ring in its place? Or in this case a rock of crack?'

'To symbolise something that's replaced their heart? Or his perhaps? He's cast their hearts away in each case, maybe he feels they did the same to him. Maybe he's loved them all in the past?' She was on a roll. 'Each victim has found a replacement for him; in Susan's and JJ's case a partner, in Tanisha's case addiction to drugs? Our man has known and loved them all, that's why it's so personal.'

Hunter was nodding enthusiastically.

'And in Tanisha's case maybe he had a sexual interest too, but we won't know whether sex has taken place or he's just left her naked to humiliate her until the post mortem.'

They moved back carefully and Charlie bent down as she saw a large pool of blood, clotted underneath the prostitute's stiff left hand.

'Boss, her finger is missing too. I doubt she'd be wearing a ring, in her profession. I doubt she even owns one. She's an addict; she'd almost certainly have cashed it in for drugs. So, presuming there's no ring, why cut her finger off?'

'Because he can? Because he wants a trophy from each victim? We haven't found them yet have we, the fingers? Maybe the sick fuck likes a little memento to remember each victim by?' Hunter shook his head in disbelief. 'Doctor Crane has confirmed JJ's finger was removed while he was still alive, like Susan's. It looks like Tanisha's was cut off before she was killed outright too. God knows what the bastard wants with them.'

Charlie shivered, trying hard not to imagine the pain and terror of the woman's last moments. The thought of their killer collecting fingers chilled her to the bone.

'Doctor Crane also thinks the implement used could be similar to rib cutters, which are specialised implements he uses himself when he performs post mortems. Like most things these days you can order them on the internet, apparently on medical websites. If not rib cutters then possibly bolt croppers or something comparable that is sharp enough to cut through bone and ligaments in one snip.'

He stepped back as his phone started to ring and looked at the display, before handing it towards her.

'It's Paul. You answer it. I need time to think.'

Charlie held the phone to her ear, watching as Hunter paced away back towards the gate.

'Hi, Paul. It's me. Hunter's busy.'

'Can you tell him that Emma Barton has just called to say her father will be coming in to sign on as usual, later this morning, so we should be able to speak to him then and, before you ask, she doesn't know where he was last night. I asked her in conversation. Oh, and even more interestingly, Bet has been going through the school records. It appears that Vincent Atkins worked at a St Bart's Junior school in the eighties but then moved to Aspire Academy, a school for problem children in Lambeth, between 1989 and 2004. Guess who else was there?' He didn't wait for her reply. 'Only Jason Jennings. Bet phoned Aspire direct and asked them to check their records. He was definitely there when Atkins first started. He must have taught or at least known JJ.'

'That's brilliant, Paul. I'll let Hunter know. Hopefully it'll be something we can get our teeth into. Do you know if Tanisha Fleming went to any school that Atkins taught at?'

'Bet's just checking that now. I'll get back to you. One more thing, Charlie.'

She caught the hesitation in his voice. 'Yes. What is it?'

'The Chief Inspector is on the warpath. He's getting it in the ear from above and wants to speak to Hunter personally to find out why we've not got any results as yet.'

'For fuck's sake. What does he think we've all been doing? Sitting on our arses writing poetry?! OK, I'll let him know, though he's literally going to burst a blood vessel. That one on his forehead has been beating at twenty to the dozen all morning as it is.'

She put the phone down and looked across at Hunter who was standing by the gate, staring up at the written tributes, flowers and verses of condolence to all the fallen poor. She walked across to join him, watching the concentration on his face turn to excitement.

'Look!' He pointed at a message pinned to the bars of the gate. 'I think our theory might be right.' The paper the message was written on was plain, sodden with the night's rain and its edges curled inwards but it appeared less worn than the rest. The handwriting was elaborate and ornate and the ink had run a little but it was still legible. She peered towards the words and read the message out loud.

'You ripped my heart out! Now I've had yours. Soon I will have another.'

The door was boarded up when they arrived at Tanisha's registered address but it had been forced open again and the catch just about reached the lock on the damaged frame.

Hunter didn't bother to knock. Pushing the door, Charlie watched as it sprang open easily and he stepped into the crack house. She followed in his footsteps and together they walked into the lounge area of the sixth-floor flat. It was as she expected. She'd been to many such dwellings and they were all depressingly similar. Filthy clothing and empty food containers were untidily thrown in piles, amidst a mass of broken furniture. A mattress, stained and dirty, lay in the corner of the room, alongside a large four-seater settee, the cushions of which were piled up at one side to allow its use as a bed. A coffee table, with its glass top covered completely in ashtrays and the remnants of drug use, was positioned directly in front of the sofa.

A young girl, who didn't look much older than eighteen, sat on the settee, her head lolling back; bleached blonde hair spread out against the back of the cushion. Another, only slightly older, stretched out across the mattress, in a state of undress. Both appeared spaced out on drugs.

'Hello? Police,' Charlie called out, shaking the arm of the girl on the settee.

She stirred, opening bloodshot eyes and trying to focus on who had spoken. 'What the fuck are you doing in 'ere?'

She ignored the question. 'What's your name?'

'What's it to you?' Her voice was slurred and loud within the confines of the small room.

'There's nothing to worry about. We just need to speak to you. Do you know Tanisha Fleming?'

'Yeah, I know Tash. She's my mate. Why d'you ask?'

'Because we think we may have found her.'

'What's she been up to this time? If she's bin rippin' off a few punters, then don't ask me for no sympathy 'cause I ain't got none. The dirty bastards deserve everything they get.'

'It's nothing like that. When I say we've found her, I mean we've found her body, at least we're pretty sure it's her.'

The girl suddenly let out a high-pitched wail, like a young child, causing the other girl to stir. Even Charlie jumped slightly in surprise.

The girl turned towards her friend and cried out again. 'Redz, someone's killed Tash. The filth 'ere have found 'er body.' She turned back towards Charlie. 'Sorry, miss, didn't mean to offend ya.'

'You haven't. Anyway we need to know as much as we can about Tanisha. Family, friends, where she's lived, where she went to school, any regular punters, especially any who might have a bit of a thing for her; you know, the weirdos and nutters; who her dealers are; anyone she might owe money to or that might have a grudge. What is your name by the way?'

'I'm Caz; short for Charlene Zara Philips. Sounds quite posh, don't it? Think me mum named me after that royal bird.' She let out a shrill laugh.

'Well, Caz. Can you come with us now? I'll get a colleague to take a statement straightaway.'

She frowned. 'I dunno. I don't wanna get in trouble with me pimp. He'll want me out earnin', ya see. I don't want no beatin', just 'cause I'm talkin' to ya. He hates you lot. Redz, what d'you think?'

Redz had already lain back down on the mattress and was half asleep. The news had clearly not affected her, like it would a normal person. Her reality was a long way from most people's. Charlie wondered briefly what it must be like to live and sleep with the possibility of death with every car they got into; every client they serviced.

Hunter was poking about on the coffee table when Caz turned back.

'Oi, what's he doing?' she pointed towards him.

'Is this yours?' He held out a small blue wrap in his gloved hand.

'It's not mine,' she said automatically. 'You're not gonna nick me for it, are you?'

Hunter shook his head. 'I know it's crack, Caz, and I'm not going to nick you for it, I promise. It's wrapped up exactly like a rock that Tash had on her when we found her. All I want to know is whether it is likely to have belonged to Tanisha, or did it come from the person who killed her?'

'It's 'ers probably. Our dealer wraps them in blue. Says it's so we know that the good gear comes from 'im.'

She got up unsteadily and brushed herself down while Hunter put the rock of crack in a property bag. 'Right lets go. If we're gonna get this done, let's do it quick like, so I can be back before me pimp misses me.'

'Thanks Caz.' Charlie smiled at the young girl. 'We appreciate this, especially as I know it might be difficult for you. I'll make sure you get brought back as soon as we can.' She took hold of Caz's arm and helped her to shuffle towards the front door, stopping for a second to pull out her phone and scrolling through the photos. 'While you're with me, do you know this man?' Cornell Miller's face stared out from the phone screen.

'Yeah, why? He comes in here to score sometimes. Nasty bastard, always boasting 'bout poppin' or burnin' foreigners. We call him Slasher 'cause he always 'as a blade or bottle wiv 'im; waves it through the air like he's slicin' someone.'

'Caz, he's wanted for doing exactly that. He'll kill someone if we don't get him soon. My name's Charlie. If I give you my number, could you ring me if you see him?'

The young prostitute thought for a second and nodded. 'Yeah, I could do that for ya, Charlie; but only if you make sure I get back from the nick, quick, like.'

30

The briefing room was full when Charlie and Hunter returned. She'd phoned ahead and everyone from their office and the Murder Investigation Team was waiting, pens and paper at the ready.

Detective Chief Inspector Declan O'Connor was hunched forward over a desk at the front of the room, glaring at each new arrival through the door and twitching each time it wasn't Hunter. Charlie had gone on ahead with Paul, Bet, Naz and Sabira, while her boss apprised himself of any last minute snippets of information that might appease the DCI. She could feel the tension in every bone of her body and each member of the team looked strained and nervous. The body count was rising and so were the stress levels.

She looked at the Chief Inspector, bushy-haired and windswept, with his trademark crumpled cream linen suit, and remembered with amusement a colleague asking if they were related in any way. They certainly had the same lack of attention to detail when it came to *looking* professional.

She hoped that people were realising that behind the rather scruffy outer persona she actually *was* professional.

At precisely eleven o'clock the door opened and Hunter strode in. Instead of his previous ruddy-cheeked apprehensions, he appeared confident and authoritative. He nodded to the DCI and stood in front of the table to speak.

'Ladies and gentlemen, our suspect has today given us warning that he intends to kill again. We believe he left a handwritten note on the gates of Cross Bones Graveyard in Borough after committing a third murder. The note is being examined by Scenes of Crime as I speak for any possible DNA or fingerprints and by a handwriting expert. The letter says, "You ripped my heart out! Now I've had yours. Soon I will have another."

'We are here to stop him, and stop him we will.

'You know the MO folks. Each victim has been drugged, probably with GBL, bound and gagged and each one taken to a separate cemetery; the first to West Norwood, the second to Downs in Brighton and the third now in Borough. The ring fingers have been severed with a sharp implement, possibly rib cutters or bolt croppers, while the victims are still alive; the heart has then been pierced with a stiletto-type blade, the thoracic area carefully cut open and the ribs pulled apart. Each victim's heart has literally been ripped out, leaving torn parts of the pericardium still attached to the end of the aorta and blood vessels. The heart has been thrown to one side and wedding rings, or in this case a rock of crack, placed in the empty cavity. Each victim, although drugged, would have been in extreme and enduring pain from the amputation, until their heart was pierced. Thankfully it looks like this was done before our man starts to open them up.

'There is virtually no forensic evidence from any of the crime scenes. They are all out in the open, with the weather conditions further hampering the retrieval of samples. Our killer is careful. He leaves nothing and tidies away after each killing. There have been no fingerprints or DNA found on any of the three bodies; or certainly not on the first two. He appears to have used the same tools and we have a few odd fibres that we may be able to match up when we get a suspect, but as yet, nothing to identify him.

'The first victim is Susan Barton, a middle-aged white woman, of good character, who appears to have been an exemplary teacher, churchgoer and mother. Her body was found in West Norwood cemetery. Items of property were left at her side, including her handbag and phone. Her heart was found nearby and her wedding ring was in her chest. We still do not know whether she was wearing her engagement ring at the time of her death; it was not in the house where she kept her jewellery. It has now been found hidden in a toilet cistern at the home of her estranged husband Mickey Barton, who I'll call our first suspect.

'There has been nothing of note found at her home address; there was no forced entry, so she either let someone in voluntarily or left to meet someone independently. Barton had keys to the house. Her phone has been seized and examined and the call record does not show any phone contacts after a call from her daughter Emma at around 7 p.m. A few earlier calls and texts from friends and acquaintances have been checked and ruled out as routine. She had left her husband a few months previously and had recently started an affair with the headteacher of the school she worked at, Vincent Atkins, our second suspect. There were calls from both of these two, among others, but no evidence of what was said during the call.

'There is no CCTV in the area of her house and her car was still on the driveway. A dark blue Vauxhall Vectra estate, registration number LV07JCF, was seen entering the cemetery at 23.19 on the night of her murder and left again at 01.34. It appeared to only have one occupant but we know Susan had been drugged so could have been lying in the back. The car is registered to our third suspect Oscar Abrahams, an extremely unpleasant paedophile with previous convictions for child sexual assault and possession of kiddie porn.'

Charlie watched Hunter as he spoke. It was what she admired the most about him. The way he could recall names, registration numbers, times, methods; details that most people would have had to use notes to refer to. Even at his age and with his eyesight failing, his memory was as sharp as ever. She hoped to be the same as him when she got to his amount of service. He had hardly paused to get his breath before moving on.

'Our second victim is Jason Jennings or JJ, as he was better known. He was a forty-two-year-old homosexual man, in a civil partnership with a slightly older man called Roger Stevenson. Stevenson was away on the night of JJ's murder and has a cast-iron alibi to that effect. JJ was also drugged and killed with the same MO and his ring left in his body cavity. His phone was also left and records show no unusual calls leading up to his death. Stevenson has stated that JJ had a difficult childhood, intimating that he was frightened of someone and had run away at the time they met. He had been reported missing a few times and on one occasion JJ had been anxious that he might be found and asked for the police investigating his disappearance not to divulge where he was staying. As far as we have been able to gather, this report was made by a third party and the details of the person actually reporting him missing were not recorded. His father who had mistreated him as a child has been traced and eliminated from our enquiries.

'Vincent Atkins has been linked to both victims; Susan as a work colleague and mistress and JJ as a pupil in Aspire Academy, a school for difficult children that he worked at from 1989 to 2004.'

Bet's hand shot up into the air. Hunter looked across towards her and nodded.

'Boss, sorry to interrupt. I didn't get a chance to speak to you before the meeting. After Paul's phone call I got Tanisha Fleming's record out and she was also shown as attending Aspire Academy. I phoned the school to confirm the dates and she was there in 2004 for about six months before Atkins moved on. It's only a small school. He will almost certainly know her.'

'Good work, Bet. There you have it then folks. Suspect number two, Vincent Atkins, who we can now say has links to all three victims.'

Charlie gave Bet's arm a squeeze. 'Well done, Bet. That's excellent.'

Bet smiled back, her cheeks glowing red with embarrassment. Hunter got back on track.

'Our third victim is Tanisha Fleming, as we've just mentioned; a twenty-seven-year-old, mixed race female, working as a prostitute on Brixton Hill. She has a similar background to JJ but has stayed local. I've been informed that her flatmate believes she is single and has no partner, other than, if you want to make comparisons, being "married" to crack cocaine or her pimp. I can't think of any other reason why a rock of crack cocaine, which we have identified as almost certainly belonging to her, and not our killer, should be placed in her body otherwise.

'I've also just been told that a quantity of cash has been found in her boot, so the motive is unlikely to be robbery. There may be a sexual element, as her skirt was pulled up, but we are yet to get the full details, we're waiting on her post mortem. She had no phone on her to examine but she was seen in her usual spot by a member of the vice squad earlier in the evening, so it is likely she was picked up from the street there. I need all CCTV cameras from the nearby area scrutinised to see if we can identify a person or vehicle she went off with.

'Her finger was also severed, even though her flatmate has also now confirmed she didn't wear a ring. So we need to find out why. Does our killer have to perform the same rituals? Is there a reason for them? Or does he just like to torture his victim? The pathologist states that with two blood supplies and a whole array of nerves and sensors on each finger, their removal would cause a disproportionate amount of pain. More importantly, does our killer keep the fingers? And if so, where? We haven't found any of them as yet. If one of our suspects is our killer, why haven't we found them? Do they have them hidden in a secret place? A garage, shed, vehicle that we haven't found? We need to find them as a matter of priority, not just for the investigation, but also for the grieving families.'

He paused, allowing his last words to take effect. Each person in the room knew the importance of a murder victim being laid to rest intact. The knowledge that body parts belonging to their loved ones could be hidden away or discarded was untenable to everyone connected to a victim, whether police or family.

'Going back to our suspects; we have three good ones and possibly a fourth as yet unidentified. Two are due in on bail today, the third is due in tomorrow and we're continuing to work on whether there is a fourth and if so, who it might be. The first is Mickey Barton, Susan's estranged husband. He has the motivation to kill her; she had left him and he felt slighted. He didn't want anyone else to have her. He may or may not know about Atkins, he won't say. He also had access to her house at the time. More importantly he has her engagement ring. How did he get it? Why was it in his toilet cistern, if not to try and hide it from us? He also works in a garage so would be likely to have access to GBL. Its legal use is as a paint stripper or alloy wheel cleaner and it is only illegal if it can be proved that it's to be ingested. It causes euphoria if taken in the right quantity, or coma and death if in an overdose and is likely to have been secreted in drinks given to our victims. Now we know what drug has been used, we need to get down to Barton's garage again and find some.

'He still almost single-handedly runs the scout group at his and Susan's local church and is linked to JJ through that. JJ used to attend the group for quite a few years and helped with it until he ran away in 2000. How well were they known to each other and did something happen at the meetings or summer camps to show a possible motivation? Barton is a man's man. Could he have been threatened by JJ's sexuality, or even participated in something that he fears will be made public? Could he be the anonymous person who was trying to track JJ down? And could he also be linked to Tanisha Fleming through the same church? Father Antonio needs another visit; he wasn't saying much when we visited last and I think he knows more than he's letting on.

'Barton went missing after our visit the other night. We firmly believe his sister knew where he was and was lying for him; but why hide if you've done nothing wrong? He's due in to the station to sign on for his bail at midday and his daughter Emma says he intends to come. I need someone waiting for him when he arrives. He needs to be re-interviewed about the engagement ring and his links to JJ and if necessary arrested on suspicion of his murder.'

There was an immediate buzz, with the detectives present all hoping that they would be the one chosen for the next collar. Hunter stood his ground.

'It's good to see you're all raring to go. I need more of you to go out and bring Vincent Atkins in too. He has now been linked with all three victims. We know he was having an affair with Susan, and trying to hide it from his wife, Molly. Did he kill her to stop news of the affair getting out? How well does he know the other two? Did he teach them? Could he have had liaisons with them too? Was there something that they knew that he didn't want coming out so he had to dispatch them? Whatever their relationships, I need to know.'

The buzz grew stronger. Charlie felt herself swept up in a wave of enthusiasm. They had a purpose and even though the chips were down, the squad were eager to get going.

'Lastly,' Hunter raised his voice above the chatter. 'Before your skippers split you up into teams I want Abrahams tracked down and brought in. His car was seen at Susan's murder. It is possible that the killer brought her to the cemetery a different way and the Vectra is a red herring, but the timelines make our scenario the most likely. We need it found. Over the weekend JJ was murdered it was caught on ANPR cameras around the area of Hastings, which is on the south coast, as is Brighton. It hasn't been seen since.

'Abrahams is claiming an unknown acquaintance, who he speaks to on one of those secret chat rooms that paedophiles use, has it, but he doesn't know their name. This so-called "friend" is our fourth suspect, but we know almost nothing about him and have only Abrahams' word that he even exists. Abrahams' computer is in the process of being interrogated by the lab technicians to try to identify any of his associates but it takes time and so far we're not having any joy. There are, however, files and files of porn on it which will be sifted through in due course to see if any illegal material can be found.

'At present we don't know whether Abrahams did have control of the Vectra at the time of Susan's or JJ's murder or if he still does now. We need a positive link between him and both JJ and Tanisha, possibly from their backgrounds. Did he hang around their children's homes, schools or the church scout group that JJ attended? Did he work in any of those places? Were they caught up in a paedophile network that he was involved with? JJ certainly ran away from something or someone and Tanisha was obviously very vulnerable. I'd like to get authority for some surveillance on him; to watch him over the next few days. We've used up more of his custody time clock from when he was last in so I don't want to get him in too soon and waste what time we have left. Justin Latchmere is his solicitor and you know what he's like; if he can spring him, he will, and I don't want that unless we have something more to hold him with.'

About half the detectives in the room immediately started to mutter, beginning stories about their dealings with the crooked solicitor. Hunter clapped his hands and they all became silent in an instant. He glanced towards DCI O'Connor, who nodded his appreciation.

'Our man had only previously killed on Sundays before. Now, with Tanisha being killed on a Wednesday night, he's upping his game, so is he getting impatient? Or fearless? Or getting a thirst for murder? Does he think he can keep killing without us getting close? Or are we too close, and he needs to kill more quickly to fulfil some sort of warped mission? He claims his victims ripped his heart out, but who is he and why does he think this?'

Hunter paused and rubbed his hands together. The room stayed still, silent at his last words. He waited for a few seconds longer before turning to address them finally.

'Right, ladies and gents. Thank you for your time. You know what we need to do, so let's do it!'

31

Father Antonio was taking confession when Charlie arrived at the church. She felt the usual tightening in her chest, the large number of incense sticks making the atmosphere oppressive and claustrophobic. It was as if all the oxygen was being sucked out of the building.

She stood by the outside door breathing in the fresh air for as long as she could while she waited for the confessional door to open. By the time it was released and an old man, stooped and sallow-faced, hobbled out clutching a string of beads, she had acclimatised more to her setting.

Father Antonio stayed seated in his side of the box for what seemed like an eternity, even though no one further was waiting. She was tempted to knock but decided against it. After about ten minutes he appeared, yawning. He clapped his hand over his mouth when he saw her.

'Do excuse me, its DC Stafford if I remember rightly. It can get a bit tiresome sitting in there waiting to hear about others' sins.'

She baulked at his words. He was one sanctimonious, arrogant priest. 'I suppose it is, if you have none yourself?'

She couldn't help herself.

'Well I wouldn't like to say we're free from sin, but we do try our best, DC Stafford. It's what Our Lord expects of us.'

He was moving away towards his office. She followed, not really wanting to be lured into the room by herself with him.

'Father Antonio, do you know a girl by the name of Tanisha Fleming?'

He stopped abruptly at the name. 'Why yes, I do know her. She's a troubled soul, doesn't know wrong from right and will often speak falsehoods. She used to come more regularly, before I arrived at the parish, but will still turn up occasionally if she needs something. I believe she is "on the game" as they say. In the end there was not much we could do for her. She was usually high on drugs and would make a nuisance of herself almost every time she came.'

'So what did you do on those occasions?'

'We would try to placate her then send her away again. She upset the regulars with her language and allegations.'

'What sort of allegations, Father?'

He turned away from her abruptly and stood facing a stained-glass window of the Virgin Mary.

'Oh, this and that. There were too many to elaborate on. Like I said, she was a troubled soul. How strange that I should be standing in front of Our Lady talking about someone who is the exact opposite of her.'

He dipped his head and gave the sign of the cross. Charlie felt her anger stir again. The man had no compassion. In fact she was appalled at his lack of empathy or kindness.

'Why do you ask, anyway?' he ventured, turning back and facing her.

'She was murdered last night. Her mutilated body was left in a prostitutes' graveyard. Fitting, don't you think, considering she was "on the game" as you so quaintly put it?'

She said it how it was, in the hope of provoking a reaction. She got one; but not the one she was expecting.

'Well at least she's at peace now and won't be disturbing anyone else's.'

She stared at him, trying to comprehend his statement. He seemed almost relieved that she'd been killed; as if she was nothing more than an irritating fly that had at last been swatted.

'Nothing like everyone being children of God then?'

'Officer, just as in life you get bad children and good children, so will there be in heaven also. Tanisha will need to learn the way of the truth if she is truly to be accepted into heaven.'

'What is that supposed to mean?'

He shrugged and started to move away from her, clearly finished with their conversation. As he moved towards his office, she turned to see his secretary, Joan Whitmore, bustling into the church with a huge bunch of flowers, no doubt to be strewn about the nave and altar table at the front. She peered out from behind the bouquet and caught Charlie's eye.

'Have you come about that poor, poor girl? It's awful, isn't it? I just heard the news; such a sad, lost soul. It's a shame we weren't able to help her more. I think during the time she was with us we made her worse not better.'

'Hello, Joan, nice to see you again. What do you mean by that?'

'She means nothing, do you, Joan? We tried our hardest. We prayed for Tanisha Fleming's soul and now she has been rescued.' Father Antonio gave the sign of the cross again and moved to where Joan Whitmore stood, chivvying her further away towards the furthest altar.

'Here let me give you a hand with these. I'm sure the officer has more important things to do with her time.'

Charlie knew that was his priestly way of telling her to piss off and she was glad to be going. Father Antonio was keeping something from her, hushed within the church's walls; of that she was sure. The religious establishment was closing ranks. She would phone Joan Whitmore later; her number was on St Matthews' web page. She was about to leave when she realised she'd nearly forgotten what she'd come for.

'Before I go, could you tell me whether Tanisha Fleming would be known to Mickey Barton?'

'Oh, I'm sure she would,' Father Antonio intoned. 'Tanisha Fleming was known to the whole congregation with her antics.' He paused, collecting his thoughts before continuing, 'And some, I'm ashamed to say, more intimately than others.'

Mickey Barton had no alibi for where he'd been on Wednesday night. That much they'd already established. Camping, in the depths of a forest in mid-October? Really?!

Before she'd left for the church Charlie had watched as he was pounced on as he entered the front office of Brixton

Police Station. After the briefing, a small arrest team in plain clothes had been quickly mobilised and were waiting at the doors, blocking off any chance of a possible escape bid. He had come quietly. There had been no point doing otherwise.

Now, he was waiting to be interviewed and he looked nervous, scared even, sitting on the fixed wooden bench in the custody office, anxiously wringing his hands together and peering up and down. It was amazing what a difference even an hour in the cells could make. Not so much the macho man now, the jack-of-all trades; more your average Joe who knows he's deep in the shit.

She gave him a thumbs up as she walked past, noting with amusement the way he moved his hands underneath his legs to sit on them. There was no way he was going to reciprocate the sign, especially not to a woman.

She popped back out to find Hunter deep in conversation with DCI O'Connor in a small interview room. Naz was sitting just outside with Sabira, talking on the phone. When she finished she beckoned Charlie over.

'I've just heard from the guys who've gone to Mickey's garage. They're turning it inside out looking for the missing fingers. Nothing as yet but they've found several containers of GBL at the rear and are seizing some of his tools. There is a set of bolt croppers and various other pliers, blades and saws that they've taken, just in case.'

'Nice one! Let's hope forensics can find some minute traces of blood from one or more of our victims on them. Even the rufty-tufty Mickey Barton would have a job explaining that away. I'm looking forward to hearing what he's got to say.'

Hunter emerged from his meeting as she finished speaking.

'That looked very interesting! Was it a back-slap or a bottom-smack?' Charlie teased, looking up horrified as she realised the DCI was directly in his wake. Why did she always engage mouth before brain?

'It was neither, actually.' The DCI looked stern. 'You're all working extremely hard. You just need a bit of luck to come your way before I decide which course of action I'll take.' She noticed the trace of a smile playing on his lips. 'Or Mickey Barton's confession!'

He strode out of the office, leaving Hunter to shake his head at her.

'Right, come on then, Charlie, see if you can redeem yourself. I've got Bet and Paul on CCTV duty again, seeing if they can find me any suspect or vehicle doing the rounds where Tanisha was picked up. They're the king and queen of CCTV at the moment. They've taken over from you. Naz and Sabira, get yourselves back to the office and see if you can find anything more to link Abrahams and the last two victims. We'll be back soon. Let's go.'

As they made their way into the custody office Charlie filled Hunter in on the find of GBL at Mickey's garage and the fact that he would know Tanisha Fleming. Things were looking up.

Mickey Barton was ready and waiting for them when they got there. The duty solicitor for once seemed quite new and slightly less hostile than most. Charlie hoped Mickey might actually talk.

It started well. Barton confirmed that he had been alone in his flat on Sunday 2nd October 2016, the night Susan died, watching TV. He then stated that on Sunday 9th October, the date of JJ's murder, he had been at his sister's house. He had stayed there all night and he had not gone out at all. Charlie thought back to their last conversation, quickly realising that the woman would verify anything her brother asked, whatever it was. On Wednesday 12th October he had no such alibi. Hunter questioned him about his movements, pressing him to provide details. According to him he had needed some space. The pressure of his wife's murder and his subsequent arrest was taking its toll. His daughter Emma believed he was involved in her mother's murder and even his son, Mickey Junior, was acting cool towards him, probably having his mind poisoned by Susan's parents who had never liked him.

Charlie watched him. He was clearly moved when he spoke about his children; there was no denying he had strong feelings for them. She recalled the way he had showed off the family photo. But could it have been that same passion that had driven him to kill?

Hunter asked him to describe in detail where he was the previous night. Barton said that as a scout leader for many years he knew how to look after himself, how to survive in the open in all weather conditions and in all temperatures. He had access to the scout camping gear which was kept in a lock-up at the rear of St Matthew's Church. He had borrowed a car from the garage where he worked and driven out towards Box Hill in Surrey and stayed overnight in a wooded area at the bottom of the Downs. He could not remember which car he'd taken, possibly a Vauxhall or

Ford, but it was an estate so that he could fit the camping gear into it easier. He'd just picked a set of keys from the safe at the garage and driven on his trade insurance policy without contacting the owners.

While camping he had cooked on an open fire, using wood he had collected from the forest and food he had bought from a small local store, paying cash for the groceries. During the hours between 10 p.m. and 3 a.m. he was alone in his tent, with no one who could verify this. He switched his phone off at the start of the evening and made no attempt to contact anyone, not even his family to let them know where he was or that he was safe. There was no one who cared anyway. He had remained out of contact until this morning when he saw Emma had been trying to ring and, even though they had not spoken for a while, he returned her call. He had just wanted to get away and have some time to himself. He could show the police where it was he had stayed if necessary.

Charlie watched as he talked, noting a slight hesitation as he spoke about the vehicle; the way he rubbed his hands together, as if worried. Maybe he was lying, or maybe he was just nervous for admitting to taking a customer's car out without permission, an admission that could lead to him being charged with several offences.

On the subject of the garage, Hunter mentioned the find of Gamma-Butyrolactone. Yes, he knew they had it; he used it to clean the wheels of cars. Yes, he had been made aware of it being known as GBL or G when they took delivery of it and had been apprised of the effects if taken orally. No, he had never tried it, personally. Why would he? He knew exactly what it did to ground-in dirt and oil. Did he realise that it was widely used in the gay community? Yes, he was aware of that but he wasn't 'one of them'.

Hunter broached the subject of Jason Jennings next. It led on nicely from Barton's last comment. Charlie watched Barton's body language with interest. He was definitely uncomfortable talking about him. He'd read about his death in the newspapers. Yes, he remembered the boy; he knew him as JJ. He was a disruptive influence who had needed calming. The boy had improved over time though, settling down more and becoming useful.

She thought 'useful' was a strange word for Mickey to choose, but Hunter hadn't pressed it. It was a word better suited to describing a thing, an object, rather than a person. Maybe Barton did have a 'use' for JJ that he didn't want anyone to know about? Maybe he had grown fonder of the boy than he should? She watched his mannerisms with renewed concentration as he continued.

He hadn't seen JJ for ages but he had been part of the scout group for some years. He couldn't remember how many, but he did come to several summer camps. They had worked together as JJ had grown older and become a leader but he was always a bit strange and aloof.

Hunter asked Barton if he liked JJ. She saw him almost squirm at the question. He was well and truly out of his comfort zone. Not in that way, Barton assured them. He knew JJ liked men. No, JJ had never made a move on him. The boy wouldn't dare. He didn't care if JJ was a 'poof' as long as he didn't try anything with him. No, he didn't hate gays. Everyone to their own. But not him.

Did he think homosexuality should be a crime? Or banned? Or was it morally wrong. Were gay people sinners?

She had to admire the way Hunter was using Father Antonio's words. They were the words that Barton was likely to have heard during the church services that he would have attended with the scouts on Sunday parade. Did he believe them too?

Barton was struggling. She could see that, as a scout leader he was trying to be politically correct, but underneath his protestations of 'everyone to their own', she could also see that he was fighting with his own conscience.

Hunter moved on, his timing ruthless. Did he know Tanisha Fleming? He did know her. Everybody knew Tash. She turned up at St Matthew's Church fairly regularly and she'd even turned up as the scout group were finishing on several occasions, trying to ply her trade with the young boys; offering to help them lose their virginity for a few quid. The boys had been amused. He had been amused; if only *he'd* had the offer as a fifteen-year-old, but he'd had to put his foot down. He couldn't have it on his doorstep. It was all right on the streets, in the town centre. If girls were happy to sell their bodies, who was he to say they were wrong. There'd always be men who would be willing to pay. He coloured slightly at these words.

Had he ever paid Tash? No, of course not. Had he ever paid another woman? No, of course not; why would a man like him have to pay? However, his voice had a tremor to it. His eyes flicked everywhere but at Hunter. He was lying and Charlie could see it and she knew Hunter could see it too.

Hunter moved on. When had he last seen Tash, spoken to her, conversed with her? He hadn't seen her for ages; he couldn't remember the last time. His voice wavered, his legs became twitchy. He was still hiding something.

Hunter moved in for the kill. 'So, Mickey, tell me how Susan's engagement ring came to be in the cistern of your toilet?'

'I-I don't know.'

'Yes you do. You know exactly how it got there, because you put it there. Didn't you?'

Barton was starting to sweat. Charlie could see the beads of perspiration building up on his forehead even as she watched. He wiped his sleeve across his face in a vain attempt to hide them but he was in too much of a state.

'Yes, you're right. I put it there that morning when you lot came round. I slipped it into the cistern while having a piss. That copper of yours didn't notice.'

She winced at the look on Hunter's face. Paul was going to cop it when they got out. As if he'd read his mind too, Barton perked up.

'And before you bawl him out, it was under my pillow all the time when you two came in and you never noticed either. I slipped it out when I asked if I could use the toilet to get freshened up.'

Hunter looked as if he could explode. It was exactly the reason why she always liked suspects cuffed as soon as possible. You never knew what they were up to, when they were in a place they knew back to front. They were lucky it hadn't been a weapon.

Hunter remained mute and Charlie realised that they were in danger of handing control of the interview to Barton. When at last he spoke, his voice was quiet and icy.

'I don't give a shit how you did it. The fact is you hid your wife's ring in the cistern in an attempt to cover the fact that you had it in your possession. Did you take it off Susan when you murdered her?'

The question was brutal in its simplicity and it swept Barton's feet from underneath him.

'No, no, no. I didn't murder her. I swear I didn't. Why would I? I loved her and would never do anything to hurt her.'

'So how did you come to have her ring?'

'She gave it to me.'

'That's bullshit, Mickey. Why would Susan give you her engagement ring when she'd promised it to Emma all along?'

'I swear she did.'

'You swear a lot, Mickey. You saw Emma's face when she told us it was missing; not in the place where her mother sometimes left it. You saw her crying; you saw her distressed, just like we did, so why didn't you tell her then?'

'I couldn't.'

'Why not, Mickey? Why not at least tell Emma that you had it? Why not show her the ring then? Tell her she could have it as a memory? Give something to your daughter to make her mother's murder even the tiniest bit more bearable?'

'I just couldn't.' Barton was sobbing now.

'You couldn't because you had taken it from Susan's finger when you killed her.'

'No, no, no.'

'She'd left you Mickey and broken your heart but you thought you might still win her back. But then you found out she had started an affair with her boss, Vincent Atkins, and it made your blood boil. He's not half the man you are, is he?'

Charlie watched Barton's reaction. He seemed to have taken it in his stride and clearly knew about the affair.

'So you took your revenge, didn't you?' Hunter continued. 'You went to the house and let yourself in with your key. You offered her a drink laced with a substance that you knew you were allowed to have legally but that would render her unconscious. Then you punished her, didn't you, Mickey, for making you look stupid in front of your mates, for breaking up the home that you had put all your hard-earned cash into, for ripping your heart out and casting it to one side? You tortured her and killed her, didn't you, Mickey? That's why you couldn't tell Emma you had Susan's ring. That's why you tried to hide it from us. That's the real reason, isn't it?'

'No! No! No!' Barton reared up, throwing his head back, his face red with exertion and clapped his hands to his face. 'She gave it to me. It was mine. I paid for it.'

Charlie stood too, ready to restrain Barton if necessary. His solicitor slid his chair to one side, clearly not knowing what to do.

'You're lying, Mickey.'

Hunter remained seated, calm; his voice hushed. He leant back in his chair and stared straight at the man.

'You killed Susan first. What happened then? Did you get a taste for it? Had JJ upset you too all those years ago? Had he made you feel stupid in front of the others? Had he outlived his *usefulness*, come on to you or do you just not like gays? Or do you like them really? I mean, *really* like them?'

Barton slumped back down on his seat and put his head in his hands. Hunter's voice was even quieter now.

'And Tanisha, the prostitute who kept coming round and offering her body? Did you get tempted, Mickey? As you said, who are you to stop her if that's what she wants? You were missing all that night, weren't you? No one knew where you were. Well I think we can guess, can't we? Silencing her, so that she couldn't out you. How awful would that be if people knew that the great Mickey Barton had to pay for sex, as well as losing his wife? You'd be a laughing stock.'

Barton looked around at his solicitor, his eyes bloodshot, his legs visibly trembling. He tried to speak but his voice just came out in a strangulated gurgle.

'Tell him to stop, please. Tell him to stop.'

32

Vincent Atkins seemed to have visibly shrunk in size, not that he'd been huge before. Charlie watched as he stood in front of the custody officer's desk like a child about to receive a lecture from the headteacher. It was ironic really.

He was making hard work of the questions, his voice coming out almost as a whisper, struggling straightaway when having to admit he was still staying with a friend, rather than his own home address. The custody officer was beginning to lose patience.

'Can you please speak up, Mr Atkins. I can barely hear you. Now, have you ever tried to harm yourself?'

'No, sir.'

'Have you ever tried to commit suicide before?'

'No, sir.'

'You don't have to call me sir. Have you got suicidal thoughts now?'

He paused longer than he should, appearing to shrink even further into his skin. His eyes darted around the custody area, moving from officer to officer, prisoner to prisoner, cell to cell before resting finally on the floor. In the end, he didn't answer at all.

'Sorry, guys, he'll be on a constant watch,' the custody officer instructed. His arresting officer, DC George Robertson, mumbled something to his colleague and shook his head. It was not what they wanted to hear. Suicide risks and self-harmers were a daily eventuality, tying police officers' hands; they had to have someone with them at all times and no detective or rookie wanted to have to sit at the cell door keeping an eye on their behaviour hour after hour, when there were so many more interesting or urgent things they could be doing.

'He may even need an appropriate adult, judging by his inability to answer questions. I'll get the doctor. It looks like he might be in the middle of some kind of breakdown.'

DC Robertson groaned out loud. He knew he'd pulled the short straw.

Hunter pulled him to one side. 'Get Atkins booked in and interviewed as soon as you can, George. Ask him to account for his whereabouts last night, then get back to me. I'll make a decision as to what we do with him based on how the interview goes. I don't want you guys tied up too long if it's not necessary. Barton is on the ropes and Abrahams has potential. Atkins is our weakest suspect. Unless something else comes up, I'll kick him back out on bail if he says nothing of interest.'

'Boss, that was a great interview you did with Barton; the way you pulled everything together at the end.'

They were nearly back at the main office. Charlie was genuinely in awe of Hunter. They didn't get to use their interview skills often these days and Hunter was an expert. It was always good when suspects talked, but it was also why most didn't.

'Yeah, well no one's going to make us look like mugs. I'll have a quiet word with Paul about how the ring got to be in the cistern, but other than the three of us, no one else really needs to know at the moment. These things happen; but I don't like them happening right in front of my eyes.'

'What are we going to do with Barton now?'

'We'll keep him banged up for a while and make him sweat and someone can interview him again later. We've great circumstantial evidence for him killing Susan and he has the motive and links with the other two but there's no way the Crown Prosecution Service will run with a charge yet. We may have to bail him out again pending further enquiries. We've no hard evidence and with nothing coming up much on forensics from the crime scenes, we really need to find the missing fingers.'

They lapsed into silence, each mulling over their own thoughts. As they opened the door to the office, they were met with a whoop of excitement.

'Look, boss, I think we've cracked it again. Quick, come over and we'll show you!' Bet beckoned them over to where she and Paul sat in front of several computers. Charlie walked over and stared at the grainy picture, paused ready to be played. Hunter leant in close and squinted towards the screen. Naz and Sabira came over too and peered over their shoulders. Paul was smiling broadly.

'Right, I started by searching the CCTV on Brixton Hill. Here you go. You can see Tanisha by the bus stop.'

He pointed to the first computer. The picture was in colour, although at the time of night the recording was taken, the colours appeared muted. Tanisha's figure, in the same distinctively coloured turquoise leather jacket as when she'd been found at the crime scene, could be seen coming in and out of the bus stop and beckoning towards the drivers of slow-moving cars coming up Brixton Hill.

'The CCTV concentrates more on the road, so you can't see that much of the area on either side of the street. There was nothing much of note on the road; lots of cars but none with Abrahams' registration number.'

'It's a shame we don't have a definite model or index for the car Barton claims to have been driving that night,' Hunter murmured.

'It might not matter. Look, boss.'

Paul pressed the play button on the next computer and it whirred into life. He pointed to a large dark-coloured car, being driven slowly from Arlingford Road, Brixton, into Tulse Hill. It drove up Tulse Hill before quickly turning right into Craignair Road.

'Look, it's a Vauxhall Vectra estate, just like in Susan's murder, and it has a defective rear light.'

'Just like Abrahams' car?' Charlie edged forward. She'd been out driving that night looking for Miller. She wondered if she'd passed it without realising.

'Not the same registration number unfortunately but look.'

He rewound the recording and zoomed in on the rear of the car.

'It's a bit blurry but you can still read the number all right. The index plate reads GN09MHK. When we first see it the time is about 23.37 and it has just one occupier, the driver. I've zoomed in as much as I can but we'll never get a good enough image of the driver to ID. All we can say is he appears to be quite a large guy.

'Now look back at Tanisha.' He started up the Brixton Hill recording again. 'The time is showing just after midnight. She's sitting at the bus stop, then look. She stands up and turns round, as if someone has called her. She then walks off into the grassy area behind. I've tried to follow her but she goes out of shot and we don't see who she meets up with.'

'Dammit,' Hunter pursed his lips.

'Don't worry, look, boss.' Bet pressed the other screen this time. 'Here we go.' They watched as the same dark Vauxhall Vectra estate swung back out from Craignair Road and followed the same path down Tulse Hill and into Arlingford Road. She paused the recording and rewound the tape again, stopping it and zooming in. 'It's the same vehicle. Same registration number, but this time it has two occupants and the passenger is wearing what appears to be a turquoise jacket. The recording will need enhancing but as they go past a street light, it picks the colour up better. It's got to be Tanisha.'

Hunter clapped his hands. 'That's brilliant, guys. It fits the timescale exactly and you can follow the backstreets from Craignair Road and get right to Brixton Hill. It's perfect. Do we have a registered keeper yet?'

'I've done a check, but unfortunately that's where the news is not so good,' Naz chipped in, reading from a piece of paper. 'GN09MHK does come back to a dark blue Vauxhall Vectra registered to an address in the Dulwich area. I got Bill Morley to drive to the keeper's address to see if he could find it.'

'And...'

'It was there. But it was propped up with one wheel on blocks and accident damage to its front nearside wing. Apparently it's old damage and there's no way the car has been driven recently. He didn't knock on the door because he didn't want to show that we have any interest in it.'

The disappointment on Hunter's face was palpable. He threw his head back and raised his eyes upwards, shaking his head at the same time. 'Why the fuck does this always happen to us? Just when we think we're getting somewhere...' A vein throbbed on his forehead. 'Unless... It was Abrahams' car?' He leant forward, staring at the second console which was paused on the rear of the disappearing vehicle. 'And he's put false plates on it. It's strange that after coming to light at the coast last weekend it hasn't been seen again. You'd think his number would have pinged up at least once or twice if it was back in circulation, especially if he'd driven it up to London. Maybe he is more switched on than we thought and has changed the plates over. He's been nicked enough times and he even made that comment about us not finding what we want.'

'He's lucky no one stopped him then if he's on false plates.'

'It is, but then he only needed to be out for a few hours on them and if anyone did a check on it, it would have come back to the right type of car, registered nearby. Who's really going to pull over a middle-aged man in the rain on a Wednesday night? Would you? Unless there was a specific reason, it's hardly likely to be the best stop of the night.'

'I was out looking for Miller that night. If only I'd seen it! I would have recognised Abrahams anytime, whatever car he was driving.'

'If only that vice officer had nicked Tanisha. I'm sure she'd have happily spent a night in the cells if she'd had a choice. But then who's to say it was definitely Tanisha our man was after? He might just have chosen another girl.'

'Right!' Hunter clapped his hands. 'Let's get moving! Rather than "What if's", Bet and Paul, carry on looking at the CCTV and see if the vehicle comes into sight after Tanisha was picked up, in any other locations, or even better, near Cross Bones Graveyard. Naz and Sabira, get a Directed Surveillance Authority written up straightaway. I want Abrahams watched. Charlie, you can brief the DCI on what's happening; he's covering for the Superintendent tonight. Once the DSA is written up you can get it signed off by him and make amends for the last time you saw him. I'll get a surveillance team teed up to join us. I want us following that bastard to his car if it takes us all night. We need that vehicle. Who knows what we'll find in it!'

Charlie took the stairs two at a time and sprinted back along the corridor from the DCI's office. The update had been brief and to the point. She'd be back shortly with the paperwork for him to sign. It wouldn't take long for Naz and Sabira to get the authority typed up and she needed to make a phone call. Time was short. Something in what

Hunter had said had prompted a thought that she needed to check out. He'd said that the murderer might have chosen another girl, but she wasn't so sure. It seemed to her that Tanisha had been targeted, but she didn't know why.

Everyone was busy in the office so she logged on to her computer and quickly found the number. She just hoped it would be answered. It was.

'Hi, is that Joan Whitmore?'

'Yes, it is. What can I do for you?'

'Hello Joan, it's DC Charlie Stafford. It's just a quick enquiry that has been worrying me. You said during the time you knew Tanisha you thought you had made things worse, not better for her?'

'Oh dear. Father Antonio won't be happy.'

'Why? What do you mean?'

'Because he said after you went that it was a period at the church he'd rather not have brought up again and it was better left alone. It was not a happy time.'

'Joan. It might be important. Please tell me what happened?'

The old lady paused, before a long sigh. 'Father Antonio was accused of acting inappropriately by Tanisha. She was a troubled girl, like I said. When we first knew her she was only young but as she got older she became more sexually explicit. I hate to say it, but I think maybe there were a few members of the congregation who did take up her offers, but I don't know any names for sure. Father Antonio, however, was cleared of any wrong doing eventually, but it was a difficult time for him. He was only saved really because she had made similar allegations against our previous priest, Father Michal, four years ago. As those were the first allegations she'd made, some of them stuck and he was required to resign from the post and undergo further assessments and counselling back in Rome. He has never returned and we don't know what happened to him. I wonder now whether he too might have been exonerated in the light of Tanisha's continuing accusations.

'Anyway, it was a sad time for our church and it is probably why Father Antonio adopts a harder line on everything these days. He is a good man, DC Stafford, but he doesn't like to be reminded of that time. He was tainted by the claims and as a God-fearing, hardworking priest it must have been a difficult thing for him to have suffered.'

'I see.' It was an interesting story and if the secretary was right, it might provide a motive for looking further into Father Antonio's activities. His attitude to JJ was questionable; but what reason could he possibly have for harming Susan? Maybe the slurs had made him the unforgiving man he now seemed to be. It certainly didn't make her like Father Antonio any better but whether it was enough to make him a killer? She would speak to Hunter later about it, but for the time being she was needed in the hunt for Abrahams.

'Well thank you for your help, Joan. I knew there was something that Father Antonio was unhappy to talk about and I can see why.'

She put the phone down as the printer stirred into action. Naz was printing off the authority ready for signing. She checked it through and started running towards the stairs again. Once she'd got it signed by the DCI they would be ready to go out and find Abrahams.

33

'Right! Charlie will be our eye on the door. She knows Abrahams and is our super recogniser. She doesn't forget a face.'

Within a couple of hours Hunter had mobilised a squad who were now listening carefully to every word he said. It was always amazing to Charlie how quickly things were provided when the Met's reputation was under fire. They had a serial killer to catch so absolutely everything was to be thrown at it, no trouble. As soon as she thought about this, an image of Moses and Claudette Sinkler came back to her. Hopefully very soon their man would be caught and she would be able to invest more time into catching Miller. She doubted whether she'd get half the resources when that time came though.

'Do you, Charlie?'

She started at the sound of her name, feeling her cheeks redden as she realised that everybody was staring in her direction.

'No, boss, hopefully not.' The pressure was on. She got embarrassed when Hunter complimented her and she hated being the 'eye'. It was great as long as you didn't miss the target, but *the* worst thing ever if you happened to glance away, answer the phone, take a pee; anything that would mean the time and resources of a whole surveillance team would be wasted. She saw a few frowns as she spoke. 'But don't worry. I won't forget his face, ever.'

She just hoped she lived up to her word. She was to be paired up with a member of the surveillance team, Guy, which relieved the pressure a little. He was a good copper and she had worked with him previously on another unit. At least Guy would keep her focussed and be in charge of radio communication. She just had to positively identify their suspect. A member of the team was already in place checking whether Abrahams' flat appeared occupied. It was late afternoon now and the gloomy October day meant most householders already had their lights on.

As soon as they were deployed she was to watch the main entrance to the building through a set of binoculars, from a nearby vehicle. If he left the property she would only have a matter of seconds in which to identify him, and Guy and the team would then take over, by car, by foot, by public transport. Whatever method of transport he used, they had to stay with him or risk Hunter's wrath. If he didn't come out, they were in for a long night.

Hunter was to be in overall charge of the deployment, although would be working in coordination with sergeants from the surveillance team and an arrest squad. It would be his decision as to what action they took if Abrahams was deemed to be arrestable.

After any identification, Charlie was to be picked up by Hunter and his deputies in an unmarked police vehicle, leaving Guy to join the rest of his squad on the surveillance side. What would follow was anyone's guess. Abrahams could stay inside for the night, walk to the nearby shop to pick up a takeaway or lead them on a merry dance, to who knew where.

The atmosphere was electric; everyone hoped it would be the first of the possibilities.

14 Burnet Grove, Camberwell, seemed even more disturbing a location than the last time they had been there. Maybe it was because they personally knew one of its occupiers was a paedophile; maybe it was because the paedophile was now suspected of being a murderer, connected to three grisly murders by vehicle and MO. Whatever it was though, the building seemed to cast longer shadows than before, the tree line seemed to mask even more of its crevices and Charlie could almost feel the evil radiating out from his flat.

The surveillance officer already on scene reported that the first-floor flat was occupied and a light flickered, believed to be from a TV. He had also seen the shape of a figure moving within which was believed to be Abrahams. Now they just had to sit and wait. Hunter would be the one calling the order to stand down as and when he thought fit.

Charlie settled into position. She was in the rear of a van, the normal interior of which had been exchanged in favour of two benches and several gaps in the partition to the rear of the driver's seat, covered over with a net curtain through which to spy. True to the Met's usual form, its inability to provide equipment suited for the job in hand meant that a stool had been thrown in, allowing the occupants the height to see through the netting, the benches being too low to provide a view. In just a few hours she knew from experience that her back and shoulders would be aching and her concentration faltering.

The first half hour was the easiest. She watched, unable to intervene, as a group of teenagers loped past the van totally ignorant of their presence, muttering amongst themselves as they bent down to ignite a firework, sending it skywards. They whooped with laughter as it exploded with a crack, sending a shower of sparks down over the crown of a large oak tree, its uppermost branches snuffing out each bright ember within its wet leaves. The group moved on, stopping intermittently to fire further missiles towards trees, parked cars and into the front gardens of nearby houses. Bonfire night came earlier and earlier each year, as did the menace that came with it.

After an hour the anticipation was waning and the monotony setting in. The interior of the van was cool and musty from the condensation thrown up by their breath and Charlie's hands were beginning to freeze. She rubbed them together to try to fend off the cold.

Several occupants of other flats had entered the building but none had come out. All the inhabitants were most likely tucked up warm and well fed for the night. She was neither. They had little opportunity to chat for fear of missing the miniscule window of opportunity with which to see Abrahams in the light of the entrance. She had to stay alert. Hunter had already intimated that he was looking at around 9 p.m. as a cut-off and as the hour neared she knew they would all be feeling a sense of anticlimax. It was great when there was action, deadly if not.

She checked her watch; there were two minutes to go. Hunter came on the radio indicating they were approaching the time to stand down but then the radio crackled with the muted voice of the officer at the rear of the building.

'Stand by. The lights in the premises have just gone out.'

Charlie pricked up her ears. Abrahams was either going to bed or coming out. She squeezed herself up to the gap with her binoculars, waiting, her adrenalin surging. The hall light came on. She held her breath, then the front door opened and she saw the figure of Oscar Abrahams. There was no mistaking him as he paused, looking up at the night sky, checking the weather.

'It's him, Abrahams.'

'Are you sure?'

'One hundred per cent.'

Guy was peering through a separate gap. He pressed the button and spoke just as a charcoal grey Mitsubishi pulled up outside the building.

'Positive ID, positive ID. Subject is wearing all dark clothing with a red tartan scarf and black beanie hat. Out of venue and towards a grey Mitsubishi, registration number SG12CVB. Subject into the rear now and vehicle off, off, off, heading north.'

She watched until they were out of sight then sat back and waited, relieved to have done her bit. The radio was filling with updates. The surveillance team had the vehicle in sight and under control. They made it sound easy.

After a few minutes, they heard the locks on the side of the van click open and Paul stood by the door grinning. He gave her a thumbs-up and she responded with one of her own. There was no one about, so they scrambled out, taking deep breaths of fresh cold air, glad to be out of the stuffy atmosphere within. The Mitsubishi was heading towards Lewisham. Guy winked and waved and headed off to join his team. They walked around the corner into the entrance to a cul-de-sac and split, Charlie spotting Hunter's car, Paul heading towards another.

'Well done. Get in.' Hunter was seated in the front passenger seat, with the two sergeants from the surveillance and arrest teams in the rear. He nodded towards the empty driver's seat. 'You're driving. We're making the decisions.'

She jumped in and was soon on the move. They needed to be in the vicinity of the subject's vehicle but not within its sight. They had a little distance to make up, but at this time of night the roads were clear and they made good headway.

'Target vehicle at Lewisham BRS. Subject out and speaking to the driver.'

A foot unit was out now, into the train station. They had Abrahams in sight. They would be watching and listening for any clue to his destination. It had been established the car was a mini cab but where the hell was he going now?

'Target has bought a ticket to Hastings.'

The surveillance sergeant quickly entered the information into his phone app and grimaced. 'That'll be the 21.34 via Orpington. Shit, there are quite a few stations to be monitored.' He called up various units on a different channel, delegating members of his team to each station. Although Abrahams had bought a ticket for Hastings it was possible he might get off the train at any station in between to carry out a liaison; they needed to be prepared.

'Target on Platform 2 now. Awaiting train. I'll continue to be the eye.'

'What the hell is he going to Hastings for, at this time of night?' Hunter's eyes were alight.

'Knowing Abrahams, it won't be for a social visit.'

'Knowing Abrahams,' Hunter countered, 'it may well be social, but mixed in with business and a whole load of pleasure. Let's hope he'll lead us to his car. He's heading right towards where it was last spotted. Talking of which...'

'We need to get to Hastings before him?'

'Yes, let's go.'

She pulled the magnetic blue light out from under her seat and slapped it on to the roof, started up the flashing headlights, grille lights and sirens and headed off. The surveillance team would cover the various stations along the route, leapfrogging their way to the prospective destination.

They just had to be there waiting.

Hastings Railway Station was only just over ten years old, built to replace the neo-Georgian one of the 1930s, which in turn had replaced the Victorian station first opened in 1851. The new building was a far cry from the first one, housing not much more than a ticket hall, coffee shop and a small satellite police office, all of which were now closed.

Charlie was tired but exhilarated by the drive which was one of the longest she'd done on blues and twos. Abrahams was not far off, staying seated throughout the whole journey except for the change of train at Orpington. After a quick drive around the station car park to familiarise themselves with what was there, she parked the car in a local service station and nipped in for a quick freshen up and a Red Bull. She needed all the caffeine she could get. They would be waiting just around the corner while the surveillance unit did their stuff.

On the dot of 23.29 the train arrived and the radio sparked into life again. Abrahams was on the move. He summoned a cab and climbed into the rear.

'Now where's he off to?' Charlie followed at a distance.

The cab took him from the station towards the seafront before veering off on to the main road back towards London. It was only a few minutes before they realised where he was heading.

'Target vehicle is turning right, right, right into the Travelodge car park. Standby, I'll drop a footie off.'

She held her breath. For what seemed like ages they had no one watching where he was. After all this, were they now going to lose him if he slipped into a room unnoticed?

'For fuck's sake. What's happening?' Hunter voiced her exact thought.

'Cab is moving out. Target is talking to a white male in his early sixties in the car park at the rear of the block. There's been an exchange. Associate is walking towards a red Focus, part index HR13. Target into stairwell at end of block, furthest away from main hotel area. Up to the first floor. In, in, in to first room away from stairwell, with a key. Door closed.'

'Shit! We need the fucking Vectra,' Hunter mumbled, picking up the radio.

'Any sign of a blue Vectra estate in the car park?'

'Standby. Associate now into the red Focus, full index HR13YGH. Lights on and on the move. Heading out of car park and doing a right, right, right on to Bohemia Road, London bound.'

The surveillance sergeant turned to Hunter.

'I haven't enough troops to pull them off the main subject and do both. It's one or the other, boss.'

'Shit. OK, keep your team on Abrahams. Charlie, follow the Focus.' He turned to the sergeant from the arrest squad.

'Get your lot lined up to go in now. We've got enough to hold Abrahams, just on the fact that his car has pinged up near to the vicinity of JJ's murder and probably Tanisha's too. Once you have him detained, we've got to find the Vectra. If it's in the car park I need to know now.'

The radio exploded into action with both sergeants mobilising their officers. Charlie was already accelerating along Bohemia Road in the direction the Ford was heading, having called in a check on the vehicle while the others were talking. It wasn't shown as stolen but had no current keeper. Hopefully it wouldn't turn off and she'd be with it shortly. She saw the high rear lights of the Focus some way ahead and recognised them immediately, creeping up slowly behind it to confirm she had the right vehicle. It was. She eased back. Better not get the driver spooked until she was told to stop him, if indeed she was to be.

The arrest team were formed up and ready to go. Hunter gave the nod and the sergeant issued the command.

'All units, ready for entry and... go, go, go.'

They waited in the silence that followed, desperate for the words they knew would follow, but wishing they would come sooner.

'Room secured. Abrahams detained.'

She could almost hear the collective sigh of relief at the confirmation.

'Any sign of the Vectra?' Hunter was insistent and she knew why. If what Abrahams had said in interview did turn out to be correct and he had loaned out his car at the time of Susan's murder, then the male they were now following could be their fourth suspect.

'Standby. He has a car key. I'll have a look now.' The voice on the radio was Paul's.

'Boss, the car's here. I pressed the remote from the balcony and the lights flashed on a vehicle parked nearby, behind a van. I've checked and it's definitely our Vectra LV07JCF.'

'Good work, Paul. Don't let anyone touch it. It'll need a full forensic lift. I'll arrange it once we've got this Focus stopped.'

'All received, boss. Don't worry. I'll stay with it myself.'

He sounded happy to hear Hunter's words of praise and Charlie was pleased too. After his faux pas with the engagement ring he wasn't going to make another mistake this time.

'Right, that just leaves our man in the Focus now. Stop him when you can, Charlie.'

'OK boss, will do.'

She accelerated so she was closer to the vehicle, maintaining a safe distance, and put the blue grille lights on, flashing the driver to stop. The Focus carried on going straight ahead, gradually speeding up.

'Great, that's all we need.' Hunter was attempting to change the radio on to a channel which could communicate effectively with the Sussex Force. Any kind of pursuit in the

Met was a nightmare these days, even more so if the pursuit was in a county force out of their jurisdiction.

She flicked the switch, allowing the revolving blue light on the roof to throw its beam across both carriageways and gave the sirens a short burst. There was no mistaking her intention.

The Focus braked sharply and lurched off the main road, catapulting down a service road into a commercial estate and hurtling down the deserted street towards a large supermarket, lit up like a beacon. Night-shift employees milled around at its rear, unpacking pallets of produce from a large articulated lorry.

'At least it can't really go anywhere from here.' She followed it as it weaved back and forth across the road. 'There's only Sainsbury's car park in front and it's a cul-de-sac.'

As if realising the same thing, the Focus slowed suddenly, almost to a stop, before the driver's door opened and its occupant jumped out, running slowly towards a high wall and attempting to climb it. Charlie braked sharply and was out of their car in a shot, closely followed by one of the sergeants; together they had hold of their suspect before he had time to try a second time. He wasn't going any further. He wasn't even going to try. He was old, out of breath and looked almost glad not to have to bother any further. Looking at him, she wondered why he'd even made half an attempt to get away.

'OK, OK. You've got me,' his voice was slightly higher than she expected and with an almost petulant tone to it. 'Ah shit, my car.'

She turned to look where he was staring and saw the Focus had carried on rolling after his early exit and now had a post embedded in it, its front nearside wing wrapped round it and glass from its headlights scattered on the concrete below.

Hunter had only got as far as the crashed car before their suspect had given up. He glanced at the damage briefly before joining them, looking the man up and down with distaste and bending towards Charlie's ear.

'Nick him for murder. He's up to his neck in everything or why try to get away? He's obviously just returned the Vectra to Abrahams. We need to know which one of them had it at the time of all the murders.'

She nodded and turned to face their suspect. She'd expected no less.

34

Arthur Thomas Billingham was saying nothing. The minute he'd been told he was being arrested for murder, he had hardly uttered a word. Now, sat in the rear of a police van, his lips remained sealed. A quick check of his name on the police national computer had thrown up a conviction history that covered almost every crime on the statute book. He was an old lag who knew to keep his mouth shut, and with reports that Oscar Abrahams was now also staying quiet they would have their work cut out.

They stopped off at the Travelodge to see how things were progressing. Abrahams stood sullen and silent on the balcony outside the motel room, his hands behind him in cuffs, his head straining in the direction of each new police officer to arrive, his dead eyes staring and emotionless, save for the odd occasion when they flicked between the room and the Vectra, as if suddenly taking an interest in what was happening.

As Charlie and Hunter climbed the stairs and joined him, he focussed them on her.

'Are you happy now, you bitch?'

'Very happy.' She remembered the young boy's distraught face at the end of the computer recording. 'Very happy indeed.'

He jerked towards her as if to catch her with a head butt but she stepped back easily.

Hunter pushed him back against the wall, his fingers against Abrahams' chin. 'Don't you ever learn? Don't you dare touch one of my officers!'

Abrahams tried to move but Hunter had him pinned. Charlie smiled towards their suspect sweetly, unable to keep the look of pleasure at his predicament off her face. The boss would never let anyone raise a finger to one of his officers, especially not a female one. It was his way, and she appreciated the 'old school' support, rather than worrying about feeling undermined, as the politically correct lobby would have her think. He came from an age where a man was expected to show respect to a woman and would open the door for her, and she was happy to accept his gesture. Abrahams was the polar opposite.

'Worried about something, are we? I thought you said we'd never find anything on you.' She scanned the room, taking in the cardboard boxes and suitcases stacked neatly to one side. 'It looks like we just have!'

'And if you think I'm not going to do everything in my power to get you charged with murder then you've got another think coming.' Hunter released his grip and nodded to the officer standing with him. 'Take him away. The van is in the car park. He's to be taken back up to Lambeth.'

She watched as he was frog marched towards the vehicle, his trousers slipping down over his buttocks as he was escorted away. He grabbed at the back of them with his fingers, just managing to stop them falling further as he was pushed up the steps into the rear. Before he disappeared, he contorted round towards them and shouted, 'Whatever you find isn't mine and you'll never prove it is.'

Half an hour later and they were on their way.

Paul was at the wheel of their car, the two sergeants having headed off with their own squads. Hunter had decided that Charlie deserved a break after the drive down from London and she wasn't going to argue.

Both suspects were also en route and both vehicles had been lifted on to the back of low loaders, to be taken to separate car pounds in South London for full forensic investigations. Met officers were now conducting a thorough search of the hotel room and would be doing so for a good few hours to come. Every single item had to be bagged, documented, exhibited and listed on the respective custody records of their suspects later. Abrahams was right in some respect though. Who would be judged to be in possession of the property: the man physically with it when police swooped or the man who had just passed it over? Hopefully their team would be able to prove one or the other, or better still both.

At least they now had Abrahams' Vectra, although it appeared to have very recently been valeted and repairs carried out. The forensic team would see through that though. New repairs would be obvious in proper lighting, as would evidence of whether its existing registration plate looked to have been changed recently.

No amount of cleaning would remove all the evidence. If Abrahams' car was involved in the murders, the forensic technicians would prove it; everyone knew how detailed the examination would be. If the slightest trace of any of their victims was there, it would be found, minuscule specks of evidence in a fold of the carpet or lining of the boot. It would take time, days, maybe even weeks, but it would be worth it.

'Why don't you try and get a couple of hours' kip on the way back?' Hunter sounded like a concerned parent. 'It's almost four and you'll still have to get Billingham booked into custody once you get there.'

Charlie stifled a yawn but lay down along the back seat. 'What about you? You've been up too.'

'Paul's going to drop me off. We'll be going past my neck of the woods on the way to London, so I spoke to Mrs H just now and she's going to pick me up from a nearby 24-hour service station and take me home for a few hours. Abrahams and Billingham will be entitled to sleep periods too so it's not worth me coming in until later. Mrs H will drive me back in this afternoon.'

'Poor Mrs H! You haven't really just phoned her, have you?' She peered at her watch, which was reading 03.58, but one look back at Hunter confirmed he had. 'She's a saint. I don't know how she puts up with you.'

'I think I said the same about you, to Ben and your mother.' He chuckled to himself at the memory. 'Oh, while I remember, George Robertson phoned while you were driving last night; I didn't want to interrupt your concentration. Vincent Atkins hasn't said anything more of note. He's admitted knowing both JJ and Tanisha through his work at Aspire but hadn't an issue with them then and hasn't seen either for some time. Apparently, he just kept crying, saying he wished he'd never started anything with Susan. I told George to bail him back out again. Atkins was doing his head in and I think he's probably the least of our worries.'

'There's something about him that's shifty though. He gives me the creeps in that hat and waistcoat of his.'

'Most people give you the creeps these days. I think you must be going soft. I had no choice really but to let him go; we've got to make space for our new suspects and I think these two are worthier, plus we get to lock horns with Justin Latchmere again which'll be interesting. I'm also thinking of bailing out Mickey Barton but keeping the surveillance team and re-deploying them to follow him. It worked well with Abrahams; maybe we could strike lucky with Barton too. He might even lead us to where our victims' fingers are hidden.'

'Perhaps we already have them. Maybe they're stashed in the Vectra somewhere, hidden in the boot with a bagful of tools.' She closed her eyes at the thought and she didn't open them again until they were pulling into the yard at Lambeth HQ.

35

'Charlie, Slasher's here.'

The phone went dead as soon as Caz said the words. There was no explanation and no knowing when he'd arrived or was going to leave, but Charlie might not get this chance again.

It was just gone 6.45 a.m. and after a couple of hours' kip in the back of the car she was back at Lambeth HQ, having just finished booking Billingham into custody at Brixton. Both he and Abrahams were now settled into sleep periods. Paul had just left, having dropped the boss off as arranged and booked in the car. She'd been so deeply asleep she hadn't even heard Hunter go. Hopefully a few of the team might be just arriving. Everyone was working twelve-hour shifts at the moment. She sprinted up the stairs to the office. Bet was bustling about, tidying the usual mess that had been left from the day before.

'Where is everybody? Miller's just surfaced.'

As she was speaking Naz and Sabira came in.

'Did I just hear you right? Do we know where he is?' Naz looked almost as excited as she was.

'Yep, I've just had a phone call from Caz, Tanisha's flatmate. He's at their place now. I need someone to come with me. We can't afford to miss this opportunity.'

'Keep your coat on, Sab. Count us in. I want to get him as much as anyone after what he did to Annie and Marcia.'

'Not to mention Moses and Claudette. Thanks, that's three of us then. Bet, could you make some calls and rustle up some more backup. We'll head down there straightaway.'

Within seconds they were on their way, batons, CS spray, handcuffs and radios in hand. It didn't feel like much of a defence against a knife or the sharp edge of a bottle but it was all they had. On their way out, they literally bumped into Bill Morley.

'Well, if it's not Charlie and her angels. Where are you three off to in such a rush?' He started to chuckle but stopped when he saw the look on their faces.

'Bill, we need your help. Cornell Miller has just been sighted going into a crack house on the St Martin's Estate.'

'Say no more. We've all been looking for him. Evil bastard. I'll grab a few guys off parade and make our way.'

'Cheers Bill, see you there.'

'You know he's probably just done another one?'

She stopped in her tracks. 'No, I didn't know. When?'

'Just under two hours ago. Night duty are still dealing. It was by the lido in Brockwell Park. Fits the MO. Lots of blood and unnecessary violence. This time it's an Asian victim. Only enough cash stolen to buy a rock or two of crack.'

'Shit! Well, it sounds like he's bought and is smoking his rock now. Let's hope we can make it his last one.'

Cornell Miller was on a high. A fucking big high. He still had the blood of his last victim smeared down his sleeve and embedded around his fingernails but he didn't give a shit. He had now been on the run for nearly two weeks and the Old Bill had not even come close. Only that soppy bastard who'd followed him and got the edge of his blade for his troubles.

It was too easy. He'd scarcely even had to call in any favours. People knew his face and they knew to give him what he wanted, be it a bed for the night, a place to smoke and socialise or the odd rock, on tick. He would always repay his debts. He just needed to find a better class of victim. All the people out early in the morning worked for a living and had fuck all to show for it. Maybe he should start to target the rich bastards who drove round in expensive motors, showing off their gold.

He laughed to himself at the thought. He should find some black city slicker, who'd taken the job off a white Brit. They would deserve what they got. Maybe he should become a modern-day Robin Hood. He would take from the rich foreigners and give to the poor white. The poor white being him! Then again, the rich and powerful would complain and more would get done, especially if they knew cops in high places. It was who you knew that got people nicked, not what you knew.

Nah, he was happy as he was and it gave him a kick meting out his own form of social and racial justice, unless of course it was advantageous to keep the dirty immigrants on his side. He was his own boss and he was content to dispense whatever punishments befitted his chosen victim. He shifted on the mattress, sitting up and looking around the room at the bunch of losers who inhabited this world. He was better than them. He was clever, devious and in charge of his own destiny. He shifted his weight again and the wad of bank cards in his rear pocket dug into his buttock. It was time to go and cash them in. The Fixer would give him good money for his stash. He was a foreigner but he was also local and convenient. So, until the day he outlived his use he would do. He yawned, stretched and headed for the door. Today was going to be another good day. He knew it.

'Charlie, you've missed him. He's gone to see the Fixer. He's got a load of hooky bank cards on him. He was saying he'd just jacked someone.'

'Shit!' They were still on their way to the flat. 'Who's the Fixer?'

'You don't know the Fixer?'

'For fuck's sake, Caz, if I knew the Fixer I wouldn't ask.' She couldn't stop her frustration coming out, but in the silence that followed, thought better of it. 'Sorry Caz. I really need to get Slasher. Who is the Fixer? I've never heard of him.'

'Apology accepted.' Charlie had to smile at the tone of her words. 'I dunno 'is real name; he's a Polish geezer, big bloke, moves around a lot, I only know 'im as the Fixer. He sorts out all the nicked gear. Will buy anything but especially likes bank cards and ID stuff. The Fixer can make anything up. I dunno how 'e's got away with it for so long but you lot never seem to nick him. Maybe 'e's got a hot line to you too, like I 'ave.'

'Where does he live?'

'I dunno the number of the house but 'e lives in the basement. It's got a red door. It's about 'alf way down Roman Road, on the left if you're walking from the one-way system. You'd better be quick though. The Fixer won't let Slasher stay in 'is place for long.'

'Thanks Caz. I owe you.'

'Yeah you do.'

Roman Road was quiet when they turned into it. It was a residential street, made up of large old Victorian-style semi-detached houses, most of which had been split into flats. A Chinese restaurant, fronting a cannabis café had stood on its corner with the main road for several years until police had got a sniff and closed it down. With that gone, officers didn't really bother to patrol the area because, apart from an alleyway from Caz's estate, it pretty much just led round in a horseshoe. Which was probably why the Fixer was there and why they didn't know about him.

Naz had already phoned Bet to update her and get her doing some checks on the occupants of the street to see if they could identify who the Fixer was and which number he lived at. Bill Morley had called up to say he had just left the station with a car full of eager helpers. All they could do was sit and wait, hoping they hadn't missed him. Charlie parked up and switched the engine off, scanning both pavements for any sign of movement. She had a good view down both sides. It was 07.20 and the sun was just beginning to rise but the street was still bathed in the previous night's shadows. In another hour it would all have changed, with parents wending their way to school, clutching small groups of children intent on escape. They needed Miller to show his face sooner rather than later, while the streets were still quiet.

'Come on. Come out now, you bastard.'

As she uttered the words, she saw him. There was no mistaking his gait. He emerged from the frontage of a house, as Caz had said, about halfway along and right underneath a street light, checked in both directions and started walking casually away. A couple of hundred metres and he would get to the alleyway leading towards several large estates. They needed to stop him before he got there or else he'd be straight into the walkways and lost. Again.

'That's him. I'm sure of it. Damn it. We could have done with him coming out in a few more minutes when Bill and our backup arrive. We're going to have to go for it before he gets to the alleyway. OK?'

Naz and Sabira pulled their equipment to the fore and nodded. Although small in height, Naz could fight like an alley cat and Sabira wasn't afraid to wade into the fray either... but it wasn't going to be easy. Miller had nothing to lose and would no doubt be delighted to take on three police officers Even more so when he recognised Charlie. If they could stall him until the others arrived that might be the best they could do.

'Urgent assistance required, following suspect, Roman Road. It's Cornell Miller, wanted for several GBHs.' She radioed in before speaking direct to Naz and Sabira. 'I'll stop next to him. Let's get him straight down. Be ready.'

The adrenalin was pumping. She accelerated until she was a few feet in front of him and stopped the car abruptly, just having a split second to acknowledge Miller's look of surprise. Naz and Sabira were out in a flash, leaping at him. There was no point in asking him to stop politely. They needed to get him to the ground to gain any sort of control. Charlie ran round the front of the car, just as Miller reared up, bellowing and shaking from side to side, throwing them about as if they were weightless. They clung on like lionesses on a kill. Charlie leapt at Miller too, knocking him several steps backwards against a wall but the structure aided his bid to stay upright. He was bucking and rearing like a wounded animal but because the drugs and adrenalin were giving him extra power, he still wouldn't go down.

She could hear sirens now, getting louder but still some distance off. Miller must've heard them too, seeming to summon a final show of strength to throw Naz and Sabira off. Naz struck the wall, crumpling to the ground, while Sabira too was left floundering on her back. Charlie clung on with Miller dragging her down the pavement. She could feel the skin being rubbed from her knees as she struggled to get to her feet. He was gaining speed and she couldn't hang on for much longer. Then she saw the blade being pulled from his pocket and heard his laugh. Ben had described the moment Miller had rounded on him with his knife and Charlie suddenly felt an unwelcome sense of déjà vu. Miller would have no hesitation in using it. She let go and dropped to the floor, backing away as he waved it towards her.

The sirens were getting even louder. They couldn't lose him now. He started to run towards the alleyway. She gave chase from a safe distance. One copper with CS spray was no match for a drug-crazed knifeman, especially one with his history and motivation, but she'd at least try to keep him in sight for as long as she could. He was into the alleyway now, nearly at the other end and she was keeping pace. The sirens stopped suddenly. Where the hell was their backup? She'd expected to hear the sound of numerous boot steps thundering up behind any second. Miller stopped too and rounded on her, slashing the Stanley blade through the air towards her.

'Aha, DC Stafford. You're on your own. It's just you and me.'

'No it's not.'

A shout came from the other end of the alleyway. Miller turned and Bill Morley unleashed a strong spray of CS towards his head. As he turned away, Charlie pulled hers out too and aimed it directly at his face. He shouted out, throwing his hands up to stop any more and dropped to the ground howling. She ran forward, joined by Naz and Sabira from behind, while Bill pulled Miller's hands behind his back, locking the metal cuffs around his wrists.

'Where did you come from?' She couldn't have been more grateful to see him.

'Local knowledge. You can't beat it. I guessed he might try and leg it through here, so I took a gamble. Thought I'd head him off at the pass. Thankfully I was right.'

'You always turn up just in the nick of time, Bill. Thanks.'

'My pleasure. Glad to have been of assistance.' He grinned at them, dabbing at his eyes carefully, the CS spray having affected him too. 'Ladies, he's all yours.'

Charlie looked down at Cornell Miller. His face was awash with tears and smeared with mucus and saliva from his nose and mouth; every orifice was streaming with the effects of the spray. He didn't look such a big man now as he whimpered and coughed.

'I wish Moses, Claudette and Ben were here to see you now,' she said, pulling him up to a standing position.

'And Annie, and Marcia and all the others whose lives you have ruined,' Naz joined in.

'Yeah, you're lucky, you evil bastard.' She couldn't stop herself. 'The effects of CS are only temporary. They'll be all gone in half an hour. What you've done to your victims will last them a lifetime.'

36

31 Roman Road had a red door to its basement. It was the house they'd seen Miller come from, so it was now the house that they were going to enter and search. If the Fixer, whoever he was, didn't want to answer the door, then it would be put in. With Bill arresting and removing Cornell back to the station, Charlie, Naz and Sabira had a job to do. Miller fitted the description of the suspect for the most recent robbery on an Asian man by the name of Riaz Asim and the MO was his. They had the power to search anywhere he'd just been seen coming from and they were going to use every law in the statute book in the hunt for stolen property and to obtain convictions. If it had been down to the three of them to sentence Cornell Miller, he'd be staying in prison for the rest of his life.

The door was opened by what seemed like a giant with some of the largest muscles Charlie had ever seen. He was barefoot and wore only jeans and a tight white T-shirt cut at the biceps to make room for the muscle mass. His hair was untamed, falling in waves down his neck, and his jawline square, with a strong chin which jutted out, giving the only dimension to his otherwise flat features. He wore a heavy gold chain with a large crucifix and gold rings on all his fingers.

'Yes?'

Charlie showed her warrant card and held her breath. If he didn't want to cooperate they'd be having even more of a fight on their hands than they'd already had. Hopefully the presence of half a dozen uniformed constables behind them would make him more docile. It did.

'Come in, officers,' he held his hand out and she shook it, at once feeling the power in his grip. 'Was that my friend you were with, just now? What had he done?'

His speech was slightly stilted, with an Eastern European accent. He was clearly the Fixer.

'He's suspected of being involved in a recent robbery and was also wanted for several others. As we saw him leaving this flat, we have the power under section 32 of the Police and Criminal Evidence Act to search your premises.'

'Be my guest.' He stepped further back into the entrance hall, positioning himself in front of a closed door and watched as they entered. He was surprising her already with his politeness and eloquence. He was definitely not what she'd expected.

'This is not my flat. It belongs to another friend. I share it with him but he is away abroad at the moment. He lets people leave their property here. Everything inside belongs to others. I just provide, how you say it, a storage area for their things.'

So that was his game. He'd realised that they would soon be knocking on his door, after seeing them with 'his friend'. Now he was seeking to provide an excuse before they'd even found anything. Well it wasn't going to wash with them, though it was clever to get his defence in before anything incriminating was found.

'So who was your "friend" that you saw us with just now?' Charlie started the questions.

'I don't know his name. I just know him from the street.'

'So did he leave some of his belongings with you?'

'Yes, he left the package over there on the side. He gave me ten pounds to look after it for him until he came back.' He pulled a crumpled ten pound note from his pocket and pointed towards a black plastic bag on the hallway table, folded round and round over its contents.

It was a clever story, but it had too many flaws. She reached into her pocket and pulled out a small black pouch containing some blue plastic gloves, slipping them on to her hands. 'So, this ten pound note will also have your friend's fingerprints and DNA on it?' She took it from him and carefully placed it in an exhibit bag from the search kit Naz held. 'And none of the items inside this package will have your DNA or fingerprints on, because it belongs to your friend and you don't know what's in it. You're just looking after it for him?'

The man nodded but she could see that he was immediately nervous. She wanted to get him restrained as soon as possible but she didn't as yet have a reason. Naz had read the signs too and her hand was hovering over her handcuffs.

Charlie took hold of the plastic bag and looked inside at its contents, making sure she didn't touch any herself, to avoid any cross-contamination from the ten pound note. By jiggling the bag slightly she was delighted to see several bank cards, a cheque book and correspondence in the name of Marcia Gordon and Riaz Asim, the name of their latest victim, among others.

'This bag contains stolen property, it's in your possession and you cannot even tell me the name of the person who you say it belongs to.' She nodded to Naz surreptitiously.

Naz moved forward and took hold of one of his arms, slipping a handcuff on to his wrist and telling him she was arresting him for handling stolen goods. For a second he tensed; they all tensed, but then he relaxed and moved his other hand towards his first, allowing her to put the other cuff on.

'Like I said; it is not mine and I know nothing about it.'

'So what is your name?'

'My name is Feliks Makary.'

'I thought most of your friends called you The Fixer? Why do they call you that then? If, as you say you just look after their gear, surely they should call you the Holder, or the Keeper, or something like that? I'm told it's because you can get rid of stolen gear, fix new IDs for people, solve their problems. You've got quite a reputation, so I hear.'

He smiled, the muscles in his face relaxed again now.

'You must be talking about someone else, officer. Maybe you mean my friend who owns this flat. He is the one with the good reputation.'

Feliks 'Fixer' Makary was on his way to custody still protesting his innocence when Charlie, Naz and Sabira realised they had stumbled across a treasure trove of stolen goods and false IDs. The flat was stacked from floor to ceiling. How police had not been aware of its presence was a mystery to her, but then it had happened before.

Two brothers had operated in the same way in an exclusive flat in Waterloo. They'd been careful to always buy the stolen gear away from the flat and had always been polite, well-mannered and as helpful as possible if ever coming into contact with police. Much of the stolen gear from the pick-pockets on the South Bank and the bag thefts in the upmarket bars of the West End and Mayfair had gone straight to them. Nobody had ever suspected them, so they had been able to move around, operating for years. Their demeanour had masked their crimes perfectly. It was much the same with Makary.

His fatal mistake had been to allow his customers to come to him. Once burglars, robbers and crack heads knew the address, it was only ever going to be a matter of time before they turned up on the doorstep, desperate for cash for their drugs, with the Old Bill in tow.

Still, they weren't moaning, in fact they were in their element. They'd been joined by members of Lambeth's burglary and robbery squad and together they were sifting through the bounty.

They'd started in the lounge area first, behind the door that Makary seemed to have been guarding. No wonder he hadn't wanted them to enter. Maybe by admitting to Miller's property he'd been hoping to sweet-talk them out of looking any further. Little did he know that anywhere that Miller had been was of profound interest to Charlie,

Naz and Sabira. Miller was going down and anyone aiding his crimes was going down with him.

The lounge was like Aladdin's Cave. A huge television dominated one wall with a single armchair opposite. Dozens of smart phones in bundles of ten, carefully packaged in bubble wrap, no doubt to be sent abroad to the Asian and Middle Eastern markets, lay ready for dispatch. iPads, iPods and laptops were arranged neatly in piles of new, nearly new and old, alongside a stack of sat navs, sound systems and stereos from many of the cars in the neighbourhood. Every cupboard or sideboard yielded more goods. It would take days to get every item bagged, labelled and exhibited; even longer to try and find owners, many of whom, frustratingly, would never be found. Most of this work would be handed over to the CID officers already on scene but Charlie still wanted a good nose around before they left.

There was only one bedroom but it was in a league of its own. She had never seen anything quite like it before. It had a single bed tucked into the corner, and with no settee in the premises, Makary's claim to be sharing the flat with a friend was patently false; although it would be interesting to imagine how he, never mind another, would fit into a bed that size. Apart from the bed and one wardrobe appearing to contain a few personal belongings and clothes of a size large enough for Makary, the whole room was fitted out with printing equipment, machine presses and a host of identification paperwork. A stack of passports of all nationalities were laid out to one side of a desk and another heap of driving licences awaiting photos were piled haphazardly to the other side. There were also several batches containing National Insurance cards, insurance documents and vehicle registration documents.

In contrast to the lounge, where the property was mostly stacked in organised piles, the bedroom was a mess. The desk was overflowing and a waste paper bin in the corner was spilling over, with screwed-up bits of paper lying on the floor where they had been thrown. Names, addresses, dates of birth and ID numbers lay across the floor for all to see. It was all a bit beyond Charlie's experience. She knew that counterfeit documentation could be produced on a large scale, but with all the measures brought in to try to prevent fraud and identify fake papers, it was incomprehensible to see how one man could do it so easily from an obscure flat in South London. But it appeared it could be done.

She picked a few documents up, staring at them in the light. They appeared almost perfect to the naked eye. Photos of people she'd never met, and was never likely to meet, stared out at her from counterfeit passports. Registration documents covered every kind of vehicle; driving licences included authority to drive cars, buses and heavy goods vehicles. It was horrific to think someone with no licence could be driving around in an articulated lorry or double-decker bus, if the fraudulent licence was not spotted.

She kicked a few pieces of paper into the corner, wondering if every name or number on the floor had been converted into a fake document to be used by criminals in their day-to-day activities. She was about to leave when her attention was caught by a number, scrawled on a piece of paper. She picked it up, her hand shaking suddenly as she read what was on it.

'Naz, Sab, come here and take a look at this,' her voice was shaking too.

There were a couple of letters written at the top of the page. The first was torn slightly, so it was difficult to make out, but it looked like an 'F'. The other looked like an 'M'.

Underneath them there were three numbers. She read the note over and over but she knew she was right.

'Look, LV07JCF, that's Abrahams' registration number, the car that was used in Susan's murder.' She pointed to one of the other numbers. 'And GN09MHK, that was the one Tanisha was seen in. There's another one here, KJ08EDG. I bet if we do a check on this, it will come back to a dark blue Vauxhall Vectra estate and we'll probably spot it near to where JJ was last seen, or around the area of Downs cemetery in Brighton.'

They all stood staring at the paper, letting its significance wash over them.

'Bloody hell, Charlie. What does this mean then?' Sabira said eventually.

'I don't know yet, Sab. But it seems that the Fixer is either our man, or almost certainly knows who is.'

37

Hunter was waiting at Brixton Custody when they arrived back. It was heaving with prisoners, many of whom had been arrested by their team. He took one look at the three of them and shook his head.

'I leave you lot alone for a few minutes and you cause havoc. It sounds and looks like you've been having fun though, while I've been absent!' He grinned at them fondly. 'Good work girls, but now you're all to see the nurse to be checked over; she's here waiting. No arguments either. There's nothing so urgent that it can't wait a few minutes.' He stood up straight and cleared his throat. 'I am responsible for your welfare and I need you all fighting fit. If you need any plasters for your knees, hands or heads, she or Bet is waiting to administer them.'

Charlie opened her mouth to argue but Hunter put his finger to his lips and shook his head.

She looked down at her jeans, noticing for the first time the holes in the knees, edged with dried blood. Naz, too, had a nasty swelling on the side of her forehead, while Sabira had some impressive grazes across both elbows. The adrenalin of the morning had masked what injuries they had. Now, glancing at them, there was no doubt they'd all be sore and aching after a good night's sleep, not that that was likely to happen just yet.

'In a few minutes, we'll nip into the interview room and run through what's been going on.' Hunter looked across to where a stout, middle-aged woman stood in a blue uniform. 'Nurse, do your worst.'

With that, he turned and walked away, chuckling to himself. There was no point in even trying to argue. The injury-on-duty reports were waiting.

'Are we ready?'

Paul and Bet had joined them in an interview room adjacent to the custody suite. Bet was still fussing over them and Paul was running through with Naz and Sabira the events of the night before, but now Hunter wanted to get on.

'Well done for last night, Paul, I'll give you all a quick rundown on how things are progressing this end. Sit down Bet, they'll all live.'

They all did what they were told, Bet smoothing down a last plaster on Charlie's knee.

'Right guys, Abrahams and Billingham are just coming out of their sleep periods and will need interviewing. The Vectra and Focus are yet to be examined and we're still awaiting the arrival of the bagged-up items of property from Hastings. Until that arrives, we can't go through them and so we don't know what exactly those two are up to.

We know either Abrahams or Billingham could have had possession of the Vectra at the time of each of the murders and we know what Abrahams said initially. He can stay as he is. I'll get an extension on his time clock to cover the extra custody, even though Latchmere will probably object.

'I'll also find one of the other detectives to run through an initial interview with Billingham, although I'm not expecting much conversation. They're both well known to police and they both know the score.

'I think I told you this morning that Vincent Atkins was released on bail. He has quite stringent conditions; to live and sleep at his friend's address, to sign on at Croydon Police Station every afternoon and he's had to hand over his passport. He'll be returning in a week or so's time.

'Mickey Barton is still in. Hopefully something will come back forensically from Tanisha's crime scene, but I think I might have to let him go on bail until we know one way or another, but I'll see.

'And now we've got Miller in a cell awaiting further charges. He'll be going straight to court and prison as soon as possible. The sooner he's banged up in a proper prison with medical facilities the better. There's no way I want him going off on another excursion to the local hospital, even if he's gasping his last; and I've made that quite clear to the custody officer.'

'With any luck, he'll do that while he's inside,' Charlie commented, to agreement from Naz and Sabira.

'We'll make sure we get him charged with Marcia's robbery and the GBHs on Annie Mitchell and Ben straightaway so he can be shipped off as soon as possible.' Naz rubbed her head subconsciously. 'Any other robberies and assaults can wait. We'll go into prison and get him charged there if necessary.'

'Good thinking and an excellent job.' Hunter was impressed. He turned to Charlie. 'How did you find out where he was? You've mentioned the registration numbers but I haven't heard the full story yet?'

'Caz, Tanisha's flatmate, gave me a shout. I had a little chat with her about Miller when we went to the flat. She knew him as Slasher. Said she'd let me know if she saw him. He'll never guess she told us where he was either. It could have been anyone. He's so well known around there.'

'Nice! She's a good kid. Shame she is where she is. We'll have to see if there's anything we can do to help her, seeing as she's helped us. Tell me about Feliks Makary? Where does he fit in?'

Charlie had been waiting for the moment. 'Well... Caz said Miller had gone to a guy known as the Fixer, on account of the fact he'll buy in all the nicked gear, and make false IDs. He fixes stuff for everyone, but up until now he's never been on our radar. He's probably used a few false IDs himself. She told us where he lived. We caught Miller coming out of Makary's flat. To cut a long story short, once we'd got Miller detained, we went into Makary's flat. He was very polite and pleasant and gave up the property Miller had just sold on to him, probably in the hope that we'd go away.'

'But obviously you didn't.' Hunter's face was animated. It was just the sort of thing he loved getting involved in.

'No,' Charlie smiled. His enthusiasm was infectious. 'Obviously, he got nicked. You should have seen the place though; more stolen gear than I've ever seen but the most interesting part was his bedroom. It's where he makes all his counterfeit documents. There were fake passports, driving licences, you name it, but then we found this.' She pulled her phone out and scrolled down to the photos. 'I've sealed the original already for the Scenes of Crime to have a look at but I took a picture of it.'

Hunter zoomed in to see better. 'It's got Abrahams' registration number on it.'

'Yes, and look at the other numbers; one of them is the same as the Vectra at Tanisha's murder and there's another index number which also comes back to a dark blue Vauxhall Vectra registered in Sunderland. I've had a message sent to the local force to see if there's one at the registered address. Bearing in mind two of the numbers are linked to two of our murders I wouldn't mind betting we might find that third number is connected to JJ. I'm guessing that Makary has made up some documentation for one or all the numbers. Whether that is for himself – he certainly fits the build of our suspect – or whether it's for someone else we don't know.'

'Possibly Abrahams and Billingham? And the letters at the top? Do we know what they are?'

'The only thing I can think at the moment is "FM" is Makary's initials. Other than that, I have no idea.'

Hunter sat back and frowned. 'OK, that's made up my mind. Paul, can you arrange to get Barton released for the time being. Naz and Sabira, sort out Miller. Charlie, you come with me and we'll speak to Makary. After that you're going home. Two hours' sleep is not enough to survive on, whether you think you can or not.'

*

The interview with Feliks Makary went like so many: 'No comment' to almost every answer. It started promisingly enough as his solicitor passed across a prepared statement, written in Makary's own handwriting.

Charlie read it out as she received it, for the benefit of Hunter, the solicitor and to get it recorded on tape. It said nothing much more than he had already said.

'I, Feliks Makary, am staying at 31 Roman Road. It is not my flat. It is owned by a friend called Radislaw who is out of the country at the moment. I don't know his surname or when he is returning. He allows friends to leave their property at the flat and charges them a small amount to look after it. I have been continuing to do this while he is gone. None of the property is mine and I do not know who it belongs to. To my knowledge the property is not stolen.

'Today police came round after a friend had dropped some property off. I immediately gave these items to police. I do not know the man personally, but I know him from the streets. I had no knowledge of what was in the bag or how he had obtained it. I just look after people's goods for them. I have done nothing wrong.'

Whatever Charlie then asked, he fended off, either by making no comment or repeating sentences from his statement. It was madness. There was no way he did not know that much of the property was likely to be stolen or the names of the people who brought it. There was so much of it and they were all the type of items that were regularly stolen from houses, cars and people.

Likewise, with the printing equipment, he blamed Radislaw for everything. He did not know what it was or what Radislaw used it for. He just sat in front of the TV when he was there and did not get involved.

Charlie was tired, she was frustrated and, more than anything, she wanted proper answers, not bullshit. When it came to asking Feliks about the piece of paper with the index numbers, her patience had almost disappeared. He knew nothing about it. When she told him that two of the registration numbers were believed to belong to vehicles involved in serious assaults, he paused for a split second but then continued to deny any knowledge. He knew nothing. Radislaw must have dealt with it. Ask him. So why did it have his initials on the top of the page? He didn't know. He didn't know what the index numbers referred to. He had nothing to do with it.

She rose to her feet as she felt her anger mounting. She'd had enough. 'Is there anything else you would like to add or alter before I terminate the interview?'

'No.' Makary shook his head.

She leant across and stabbed at the button on the recorder, switching it off.

'Or should I ask Radislaw?'

'Charlie, go home. You've done enough today.' Hunter patted her on the shoulder.

She jumped slightly at his touch and rubbed her eyes. She was exhausted and her body was running on autopilot.

'I'm going to Mum's, she's promised me my favourite lasagne for dinner.'

'In that case, you can take a police car, as long as you bring it back in one piece in the morning. I hope you don't mind but I'm going to ask Paul to ring Ben. If you're heading out that far it'll be better to have him as company, so you don't doze off while driving.'

Charlie nodded, genuinely grateful. Meg would be delighted to cater for Ben, and they'd both be glad to have him there.

'Sorry boss, I nearly lost it in there. I don't care about all the stolen gear; or at least not just now. I don't even mind about Miller getting rid of the property from his robberies there. He's bang to rights anyway. But that bastard holds the key to who is killing and mutilating innocent people and he doesn't give a shit. He also knows all about that note. Did you see the way he paused when I said the vehicles had been involved in serious assaults? He knows. And he knows what the initials on the top stand for. If they're not his, he knows whose they are.'

Hunter nodded his agreement. 'It looks like it's written in his handwriting. I've checked it against his prepared statement. The formation of the letters is very similar.'

'He's lying, boss. There is no Radislaw. There was no other personal property, nowhere for them both to sleep, absolutely nothing to suggest any other person lived or stayed there. There's only one Fixer and that's Feliks.'

'Let's hope a night in the cells will make him more helpful then. We'll show him photos of Abrahams and Billingham tomorrow; see if he recognises their faces, even if he still insists he doesn't know their names.'

'Fingers crossed then?'

'We've tried that once before and it didn't work.'

★

Ben was waiting outside, his tall, lean body propped up against the lamp post. He looked as if he'd run all the way to Lambeth HQ from his flat, as his dark hair was blown back from his forehead and his cheeks were ruddy. He was unshaven but the stubble just made him look more rugged in the fading light. His face creased up into a huge grin as she came into view, his eyes shining in the glow of the street lamp. He looked as alive as she felt dead.

'I came as soon as I was called. I hear you got him then? Well done.' He squinted at her as she approached. 'Wow, you look pooped?'

'What sort of word is that from a rufty-tufty ex-soldier?' she teased.

He picked her up suddenly, spinning her round and round several times before putting her back down and kissing her chastely on the top of the head. 'The sort of word you get from an admirer who is trying to act in a chivalrous manner.'

His actions made her laugh and all her previous exhaustion seemed to melt away. She'd almost forgotten the accomplishment of catching Miller.

'Pick me up then, Sir Ben, our chariot awaits.' She laughed again as he did as he was told, carrying her through the gate into the car park at the rear of the office. 'Though, unless you keep me chatting, the chariot driver might fall asleep at the controls.'

38

The voice that crackled across the phone line was slurred and almost indistinguishable.

'It's too late for me! My life is ruined. It will be better when I'm dead!'

Charlie pressed the receiver to her ear, trying to clear away the fuzziness. The ringtone had woken her starkly from several hours' deep sleep, sandwiched into the corner of the large maroon sofa, her legs propped up on Ben's lap. The words resounding across the line now brought her straight back to reality with a start.

'Who is this?' She recognised the voice but no name had come up on her phone and she couldn't quite put a face to it.

'It's Vincent Atkins.'

He sounded different; volatile, almost excited, the pitch of his voice going up and down in a disconnected way. She remembered the way he'd looked when she'd last seen him in custody, how vacant and distraught he'd seemed; how he'd paused at the question about contemplating suicide. There was definitely something wrong.

'Have you taken something, Vincent?'

'Yes, I believe so.'

'Where are you?'

'I'm in my office, where my life was, before you lot came and destroyed it. But it won't be long now. Come, come and watch me die.'

The phone went dead. Charlie's brain was racing. Atkins sounded desperate. Jumping to her feet, she saved his number and tried to ring back but her call went unanswered. She tried again but it was the same. She couldn't allow him to die. He was one of their suspects, and if he did prove to be their killer, the victims and their families would never get justice. She could never let that happen.

Ben was on his feet too. 'Let me come with you.'

'No, Ben, you can't.' She wasn't going to put him in danger again. 'You're still covered in bandages from last time and I was lucky not to get disciplined for having you with me. If you come this time, they'll want to know why, especially now I'm driving a police car.'

Ben paused, as if about to follow anyway. As an army man she bargained on him understanding the threat of discipline but still he seemed unsure.

'Besides, I'll be back before you know it and I won't be alone.'

She pulled a woolly hat over her head and ran out, leaving Ben standing, crestfallen, at the door. She'd sought his perspective on the case during the journey home, in order to get a balanced view, but for now he'd have to wait.

The clock on the dashboard read half past nine as she started to drive. Her first priority was to get assistance; she was some way off and didn't want to have lied to Ben. Hunter and Paul would still be at work. She put Hunter's number into the hands-free and waited. There was no way she'd be taking this on by herself. Atkins was clearly deranged; he'd been getting more unhinged every time they'd seen him. He could be capable of anything. Hunter answered quickly.

'Guv, I've just had a call from Vincent Atkins. He sounds off his head. He says he's in his office and is threatening to kill himself. I'm heading there now but could use some backup, and it's probably worth getting an ambulance on the way.'

'OK Charlie, I'll get Paul. Naz and Sabira are still here finishing off and they'll probably come too. I can make some calls en route. We'll meet you there.'

He hung up and Charlie suddenly felt uneasy. She'd had a bad feeling about everything since finding that scrap of paper on Feliks Makary's floor, but she didn't know why. The more she thought about it, the more she knew he held the key, but the bastard was looking after his own back. They were missing something.

The grounds of the school were in complete darkness when Charlie arrived. The gate to the main car park was open and a lone vehicle was parked in the far corner. She jotted down the number. It wasn't one she knew. She did a check on the radio set in the car and it came back as registered to Atkins.

She could see a couple of lights shining from within the main block and the odd random light in far-flung classrooms.

Someone was there. She tried Atkins' number again. It rang for what seemed like ages before the line clicked on.

'Vincent, are you there?'

There was no speech, just a mumble, followed by the sound of heavy breathing. Everything about the scene was screaming danger but at the same time Atkins could die if she waited any longer. She tried to get him to speak but there was no more conversation, just the sound of his breaths.

'Shit.'

She ended the call and dialled Hunter's number again.

'How far away are you?'

'We're quite close. Should be there in ten minutes or less. I've called an ambulance but they can't give an ETA.'

'I've just phoned Atkins' number and he answered it but there's just heavy breathing. I can't get anything more out of him.'

'Is anyone else there?'

'Not that I can see. There's only one car in the car park and it's his.'

'You've got to go in then, Charlie. If you don't and he dies, we'll be in the shit. We'll be with you as soon as we can. Give me a situation report when you know what's happening.'

'Will do.'

She rang off and climbed out of the car, her heart pumping, and made her way first to Atkins' car. The vehicle was locked and there looked to be nothing of note inside it, so she headed for the main block. She'd check from the outside quickly first, before going in. His office opened on to the reception but its window looked out across the central square of the school, where he could no doubt keep an eye on the movements and behaviour of all his pupils. It wasn't hard to find.

The window was closed and the blinds pulled down but a light shone out from around the edges. She pushed herself up on to her tiptoes and peered in through a large chink at the corner. Vincent Atkins was sitting in a chair, his body slumped forward on to his desk. In one hand he held his mobile phone, and a fountain pen was balanced in the other, its nib still resting on a pad. Various photographs were arranged around the desk in front of him in a semi-circle and a mug stood to one side.

The door to his office was open and she could see through the reception to what appeared to be the staff room, with a small kitchen area. There was no other movement and no sign of anyone else being present.

She ran round to the main entrance. Luckily he'd left the door unlocked. She pushed it and went in, heading straight through the reception to the headteacher's office.

Atkins was still breathing, though his breath was now fast and shallow. She tried to rouse him but he didn't respond. She ended their call on his phone and removed the pen from his hand. Across the pad was the message, 'I'm so sorry for everything, Molly'. To her alarm it was written in the same ornate, flowery handwriting as on the note pinned to the gate of Cross Bones Graveyard.

She looked at the contents of the mug. Instead of the dregs of a coffee, it contained the last few drops of a transparent liquid. A small glass bottle lay on its side nearby, with a few drops of what appeared to be the same liquid spilt next to it. She picked them up and sniffed them but both were odourless, in Charlie's mind almost certainly GBL.

Vincent Atkins must be their man after all, and he was almost dead. With Hunter and the others not far off and an ambulance on the way, she had to try and keep him breathing until help arrived.

She ran round behind his chair and pulled at his limp body, hoisting him through the air on to the rug below. There was no way he was going to die if she had anything to do with it. His victims and their families needed to see him in the dock. Carefully she turned him on to his side, arranging his body into the recovery position. His pulse was getting weaker; she could barely feel it now. She leant down to listen for the sound of him exhaling and to feel his breath against her cheek. It was at that moment that she felt the hand on her shoulder.

Hunter banged his fist down on to the dashboard. Red brake lights were all that illuminated their path.

'Bloody hell, why can't motorists learn to drive more carefully? Get out of the bloody way, you morons!'

'I don't think they actually can move, guv.' Paul stared in dismay at the line of traffic in front, all of whom were trying and failing to get out of their way. 'And nor can we.'

'Oh my God, you made me jump. Next time give me some warning that you're here.'

Charlie put her hand to her heart, emphasising her alarm.

'Sorry, I presumed you'd heard me. There wasn't much I could do for Vincent while I waited for the ambulance.

I heard you come in as I was making coffee so I took the liberty of making us both one.'

'Thank you, that's very kind.' She stood up, looking down at Vincent Atkins as she took the mug that was offered. 'He's as stable as he can be. Hopefully the ambulance will be here soon.'

He lifted his own mug to his mouth, so she followed suit, sipping the warm, sweet coffee. It tasted different but quite pleasant.

'I put a dash of Krupnik in it. I hope you don't mind. It's a liqueur that comes from Poland. It's made from honey and other herbs. Good for dealing with shocks, and this certainly is shocking. I couldn't believe it when he phoned.'

'He phoned you too?' She took another sip, then another. It felt good to have someone else with her.

'Yes, he was rambling. I told him to come here where we could talk. He arrived a while ago. I said that he should have left Susan alone. That she was mine. That I'd lost her once before and now, because of him, I'd lost her again. He didn't even argue with me. He just did everything I told him to.'

She was confused; but more than that she was light-headed. He was talking in a very matter-of-fact way but he wasn't making sense. She wanted to laugh; the whole situation suddenly seemed ridiculous, but at the same time she was beginning to feel queasy. She tried to focus on his words.

'I thought you were different though. You listened and made time for me. I saw the way you looked at me. You admired me and I admired you. I was even beginning to love you, until I watched you today with that other man swinging you around, carrying you, kissing you.'

He walked across to the side of the room and picked up a bag, setting it on the floor next to her. Charlie was watching but she couldn't talk, her body wouldn't move as she wanted it to. She could hear every little noise and smell the aroma of the coffee as it wafted towards her, but she couldn't walk away, even though she tried to move her legs.

He pulled some cord out of the bag and ran it through his fingers, advancing towards her.

'But you're no different to Susan. Susan never ever really saw me. She liked me, I know that, but she never really loved me, not like I loved her. I was just there as a friend and a confidante all those years ago. Even when I came back she was the same. She would chat, she would pass the time of day, but she looked straight through me. She could have chosen me; she was free from Mickey but instead she started an affair with this excuse for a man. Look at him. He deserves to die. What did he have that I didn't? Neither of us have money but I – I would have given her so much more.'

He laughed then, a deep hollow laugh, edged with bitterness.

'She ripped my heart out and tossed it aside, not once but twice and so I did the same to hers. She didn't even recognise me, not until it was too late.'

Charlie recalled the phrase through the jumble of words in her head. It was the same phrase that had been written on the note left on the graveyard gate and yet it was Vincent's handwriting on the note on his desk? It was Vincent's message to Molly? She looked towards the note, confused.

He saw where she was looking and smiled. 'I just wrote down what he was saying. It fitted nicely.'

'And you... drugged him... just like... you've drugged me?' Her head was becoming muzzy. She threw the mug to one side.

'I didn't need to hide it from Vincent. He drank it neat because he wants to die. You were always going to be harder. But I knew you would come. I could see how Susan's death had affected you; how you so wanted to catch her killer. I wanted you to find Vincent, to see the note, to see the same drug. I knew you'd linked JJ's and Tanisha's murders to Susan's and that you'd found out that Vincent had worked in their school. How sweet that little snippet was, but then the forgotten children all swill around in the same effluent; used, abused, loved and lost. Some stay quiet and disappear with new partners, choosing to hide and reject the love that's offered. Some spread dirty secrets and their talk ruins lives. But I wanted you to work it out, Charlie. I wanted you to get the glory... until you chose to give your affections to another man.'

Her head was spinning now, thoughts and memories of conversations springing to the forefront of her mind, before disappearing again into the fog. She felt him wrapping the cords around her wrists but she was powerless to stop him. She knew the answers but they were just out of her grasp. 'But why? Why you? I don't understand.'

'Because I am not who you think I am.'

He turned towards her, taking off his thick-rimmed glasses, pulling his hair back from his face. She stared at his face, up close now, and her thoughts started to take shape into a man that she had never met, but one she had heard of; a man who would have known all three of the victims and whose career had been tainted by one.

She remembered Joan Whitmore's voice as clear as day. How could she have not seen through the beard, the thick bush of hair that masked his features, the glasses that covered his eyes? How could she have not recognised the clear, clean-shaven face of Father Michal, the young priest kneeling reverently before Pope Benedict in the photo at St Matthew's Church? They say that the eyes are the windows to the soul. As she looked into his now she wondered whether she was peering into the depths of hell.

'Charlie's phone is just ringing out,' Hunter muttered. 'Where the hell is that girl?'

They were on the move again, at last. A few minutes more and they would be there. He saw the blue lights of the ambulance just ahead. It looked as if it was going to the same place as they were. Good, he hated dealing with casualties.

The police car Charlie had taken was in the car park when they drove in and the lights in reception were on. She must be there, so why didn't she answer? He jumped out and headed straight into the building, calling out her name. He tried the number again; this time he could hear it ringing. He followed the sound. It led him to the headteacher's office, its ring tone loud in the quiet school. Vincent Atkins was lying on the floor, unmoving. A paramedic who'd been just behind him took control of Atkins, immediately indicating that he was still alive. Hunter scanned the office but there was no trace of Charlie. She should be with him. He could see her phone now lying on the desk, blinking on and off with his name neatly across the screen. Hunter's mind filled with dread. Something had happened and he didn't know what.

Paul shouted across from the reception. Hunter ran to join him, the adrenalin shooting through his body. Paul was standing directly outside a fire escape, the doors of which had been flung open. A small parking area outside led to the access road, used for deliveries to the kitchens. The gate from the access road also hung wide open and a set of tyre marks criss-crossed the tarmac.

'Look guv.' There was a slight note of panic in Paul's voice. He was pointing at an object lying on the ground. 'It's one of Charlie's hats. I'd recognise it anywhere.'

Hunter ran back to Atkins' office. Maybe her phone would yield a clue to where she was, but it shouldn't be here. It should be with Charlie. She never went anywhere without it. He picked it up and scanned through the call data. Other than calls between the two of them, the only other name shown, within the necessary time frame, was that of Vincent Atkins, and he was still here.

His eyes alighted on the photos, the empty mug and the note. It was in the same handwriting as their killer's and it read as if Vincent had written it. Next to the ornate writing was another style of lettering. It looked to have been written in a hurry, the letters scratched clumsily on the paper, the last letter tailing off as if the writer had been interrupted. He bent down and read it but it made no sense.

He looked back at the phone. His name was still at the top of the call list. Other police units were beginning to arrive, summoned no doubt by Naz or Sabira. Atkins was being lifted onto a stretcher now, still unconscious. He would be saying nothing for a good long time.

Quickly he put the phone and handwritten note into exhibit bags and beckoned to the others to follow him. He'd sent Charlie into this situation. Now he had to get her out of it.

It had been easier than he'd ever thought. Now she was his, to do with as he wanted. He peered round at her sitting in the passenger seat of his dark blue Vauxhall Vectra estate, her hands bound, her mouth gagged, her body kept in place with the seat belts. She was pretty; not too dissimilar to Susan in her younger days, but with more courage and more drive. There was nothing she wouldn't try. He had seen that already, when he'd caught her writing a message. Thirty seconds was all that it had taken to open the fire escape doors ready and ensure the car was unlocked. Thirty seconds shut in the room, with no phone and no way out, and in that time she'd scribbled those letters on to Vincent's suicide note. In the end, he'd decided it was more important for police to find Vincent's message than worry about a few random letters on the same piece of paper that made no sense.

Leaving her phone behind served two purposes; firstly, as confirmation of the call log and secondly to prevent her escape, having caught her earlier trying to surreptitiously remove it from her trouser pocket.

As a witness, he'd been given DC Stafford's work contact mobile to call if necessary. As a suspect, Vincent hadn't. It was a spark of ingenuity getting the headteacher to call from his personal number. He hadn't even had to tell the old fool what words to use; the man was happy to die and he was happy to help him. In fact, it had been fitting. He'd thoroughly enjoyed taking out his love rival. Maybe next time he would do the same again...

This hostage was not as subdued as the others and careful handling would be required. His attempts to get more GBL into her had been futile. She was feisty and strong and had fought him off, spitting out the fluid as she did so. He would enjoy breaking her to his will. It would almost be a shame to kill her, but he knew he'd enjoy the process.

He glanced down at her bindings as he drove, checking that they were still secure. She was twisting her wrists, attempting to loosen them, wriggling and squirming, trying to reach the knot. For a second he was mesmerised by the way her fingers moved, the manner in which each perfectly formed digit bent and pointed and stretched.

He knew exactly where he was heading; he'd been there before. It was remote, undisturbed, inhabited by the dead, and soon it would have another body added to its number. His heart quickened at the knowledge of what was to come; images of blood, flesh, bones firing his imagination.

He looked down at her fingers again and felt the usual twitch of anticipation coursing through his body. He couldn't wait to add this latest trophy to his collection.

39

Feliks Makary was half asleep when Hunter burst into his cell, followed closely by the custody officer, whose keys he'd borrowed on the way through. There was nothing further to be gained at Harris Academy. He strode over to the mattress and thrust the message he'd just retrieved from the school in his face.

'What does this mean?!'

He read out the letters, 'FM is D... Your initials are FM so who or what is D?'

Makary stretched languidly and closed his eyes again. 'I don't know what you're talking about.'

Hunter pulled the blanket off him and hauled him upright. Makary threw his hands up to try to fend him off but Hunter was having none of it. Grabbing him around the top of his T-shirt, he twisted the material so it tightened around his throat, then pushed him up against the wall.

'I don't give a shit about what you or your fictitious mate Radislaw do or don't do at your flat! I'm not interested in what gear you have there or whether you know that it's stolen or not! What I am interested in is what you know about this message with the initials "FM" on it! Your initials! What I'm also interested in is the other note we found at your flat with the three registration numbers on, which has the same initials above them. So... best you start talking!'

Makary shrugged. 'I know nothing.'

A wave of pure rage surged through Hunter and he felt his cheeks burning. The custody officer tapped him on the arm, worried with how the situation was beginning to escalate.

'Leave him, guv. He's not going to speak, and if he does say anything, it won't be admissible in court.'

'I don't give a fuck if it's admissible or not in court, Sergeant, and I don't give a fuck whether he wants to make something of me asking.'

He turned back round to Makary and twisted his clothing tighter still. He didn't give a shit that the man was half his age and twice his size, he had to try.

'Now look, you lying bastard, one of my officers is missing. She was dealing with a suspect for three murders and this note was found at her last known location.' He shoved the message towards him. 'Two of the registration numbers on the other piece of paper found at your flat are linked to two of these murders and your initials are written on both notes, so I suggest you tell me everything you know about them, because if anything happens to my officer, I swear I will hold you personally bloody responsible and I will make it my mission to get you charged with withholding evidence in a murder investigation, not to mention possession of every single item in that flat of yours. By the time I'm done with you, you'll be looking at ten years in a room just like this one and then when they do see fit to release you, I'll make sure you're on the first plane back to Poland.'

He let Makary go and he slumped down on to the bench, with hands held up as if in capitulation.

'If I tell you all I know, will you put in a word for me?'

'It depends on what you have to say.'

'I can tell you that the FM on the notes is not me, but I know who it is.'

'Carry on.'

Makary paused, appearing to weigh up whether he should continue. Hunter took a step towards him. In that moment he knew he wouldn't be able to control himself if the bastard didn't talk. Charlie's life could literally rest on what he said. He had never felt so angry, nor so helpless and neither were emotions he wished to relive.

Makary sighed heavily. 'FM stands for Father Michal.'

'Who the hell's Father Michal and what's he got to do with the registration numbers?' Hunter had never heard the name before.

'Father Michal was a priest. He worked for many years at a church in West Norwood, until a girl who I know as Tash made an allegation against him. The story goes that she was a good kid to start off with but then she changed. She started working the streets and got mixed up with the wrong crowd, kids who did robberies and burglaries, pimps, other prostitutes. Some of them came to me for help, if you know what I mean?'

Hunter nodded. 'Go on.'

'I got to know Father Michal through her and the other kids who got into trouble. He was all mixed up with many of them through his work. We were both Polish so we did business together. After Tash made her allegations there were rumours that others had said similar things but before any of those could be heard properly Father Michal disappeared. The elders at the church said that he'd gone away to continue his ministry elsewhere in Europe.'

'So if he went away, how come he is now linked with the registration numbers?' It was a good story but he didn't see how it was relevant to what was happening now.

'Because he came back. He had changed his appearance. He was wearing glasses and had a thick beard that covered his previous features. He'd always looked so fresh-faced and now he looked old. I didn't recognise him. His speech was different too, as if he had taken elocution lessons. His accent was gone and he sounded posh. He asked me to make new identity papers and some fake CVs and work references for him, so nobody would know it was him. I agreed because he was a friend once and we had known each other for many years. He paid me for my work and I didn't see him again until a few weeks ago when he turned up on my doorstep.

'He asked me to make him up some vehicle registration documents and insurance certificates so he could get some new plates made up. They were all to relate to dark blue Vauxhall Vectra estates, like the one he owns. I did some research with a policeman friend of mine and came up with those three numbers, so I wrote them down on a piece of paper and put his initials on the top. He came back a few days later and collected the documents.

'I have not seen him since that day, although I did hear that Tash was murdered. I do not know what he has done and what he used those documents for but I fear he has taken his revenge.' Makary shook his head. 'Officer, he is not a good priest, or a good man but he paid well. I have heard many things about him through the kids on the street. I hope this helps and that your officer is OK. Is she one of the young ones that came to my house?'

Hunter nodded. He was processing everything that Makary had just said but there was something still missing. 'So who did he become? And who is D?'

'I knew you were going to ask me that and I can't remember. All I can remember is that he said he was working as a teacher. He was teaching Latin. The references had to be from previous school employers in Poland. It would make it difficult for the authorities here to check them. I remember thinking that he should not be working with children again.'

Suddenly it all fitted, the school, the church, the connections, the description, the man in the tweed jacket, with bushy hair and thick glasses. 'Father Michal is Daniel, Daniel Roberts?'

'Yes, yes. That's his name. He said he wanted to be called Daniel because it meant God is my Judge and he wanted Roberts because he'd known someone he loved called Roberts. I remember now. He was very pleased when I said I could do it.'

Hunter closed his eyes. Shit. How could they have missed it? Susan's maiden name was Roberts, Mickey had told them, but it was such a common name. How could they have ever known a respected teacher in a city academy was using a false name?

'Feliks, I'll see what I can do for you, if it's not too late.' He threw the keys towards the custody sergeant and ran out.

'I hope you find your officer.'

He heard the words as they were shouted. He hoped he'd find her too, otherwise he'd be responsible for sending one of his best to her death.

'It's Daniel Roberts. He's a teacher at Harris Academy. He used to be a priest at St Matthew's Church and was known as Father Michal. He left the country in shame a few years ago after allegations that he had abused youngsters but he came back and changed his identity to Roberts. That's who's got Charlie.'

Hunter's cheeks were burning red from the exertion of running as he shouted out his findings. The vein in his forehead was throbbing conspicuously. Paul, Naz and Sabira gathered round him as he sat down, breathing heavily behind a computer. He typed in Roberts' name and waited.

'Oh my God. Father Michal. That's the name of the person who reported JJ missing that last time.' Naz looked horror struck. 'On the initial entry it said he was making the report on behalf of a male anon so I didn't pay much attention to him. I was concentrating on who the unknown informant was, but it must have been him trying to track JJ down.'

'And I remember looking at Daniel Roberts' personal documents among the staff records you brought back from the school. He hadn't been there long. I wondered how on Earth they'd been able to follow up any of his references as they were all from Poland.' Sabira looked equally upset. 'But again, it didn't seem relevant. We were looking at Vincent Atkins, not Daniel Roberts.'

'Well it seems that all of us have missed things then. I've just found his phone number in Charlie's phone, along with other witnesses, but I need to check it against the number shown on his statement to make sure it's the only one that we know of. Right, here we go.' Hunter was peering at a copy of Roberts' statement. He nodded as the number came up. 'Good, it's the same. Paul, I want that phone number cell-sited. Phone the tech guys and tell them we have a missing police officer and to get started immediately. You can do the paperwork they'll need while they're working on it. We must find out where he is now.'

Paul scribbled down the number and picked up a phone straight away.

'Naz, Sab, look into everything we can find on either name. Addresses, associates, vehicles. If we can get an address for Roberts we should be able to get the correct index of his Vectra. Phone up Father Antonio at the church if necessary and tell him we need to know everything about their former priest. That sanctimonious bastard kept this information from us. If he hadn't been so keen to defend his bloody religion we might have realised that Father Michal was a suspect and checked with immigration to make sure of the dates. They would have told us if he'd re-entered the country. He only changed his name after coming back.'

He could feel his anger building again at this realisation.

'He's got twenty minutes on us already. I want this all done in ten minutes maximum. I need to know where Roberts is now and I want us to be on our way. I'll jack up an armed unit. I'm not taking any risks. If we can get to Charlie in time and he gives us the slightest reason, I'll have the bastard taken out.'

40

'He's heading into Surrey.' Hunter was getting a rundown as they headed out.

'Isn't that where Charlie's family lives?' Paul was driving. They had done what they needed in double quick time and were making steady progress with the blue lights and sirens blasting a path. A stream of 'Trojan' armed vehicles, a dog unit, a couple of ambulances and a few other random police cars completed the convoy. 'Do you think we should warn them?'

Hunter pulled out Charlie's phone again. 'Yes, you're right. We don't know what Roberts is planning as yet, but I don't want him taking any more hostages. Meg, Lucy and Beth could be there.'

'And Ben. Don't forget I called him to collect Charlie last night.'

'Ah yes. I'll call Ben. He's a good, strong lad and will make sure the others are safely out of the way.'

Paul smiled to himself. Charlie's mother, Meg, was more than capable of doing the same.

Hunter passed his own phone back to Naz in the rear to keep up with the most up-to-date locations and dialled Ben's number from Paul's phone. It was quickly answered.

'Ben, it's Hunter. Is Charlie there by any chance?' He tried to sound as normal as possible. Maybe she'd somehow got home and they had imagined everything.

'No, she's not.' There was a short pause. 'I thought she'd be with you. What's happened? Where is she?'

He only wished he knew. Of course he'd known she wouldn't be safely with her family but somehow hearing the words made the whole situation more critical. There was no point mincing his words.

'Ben, we think Charlie's been abducted and it looks like she's heading your way. I need you to make sure everyone's out of the house.'

'There's only me and Mrs Stafford here, Lucy and Beth are both away for the weekend and won't be coming back until Sunday. I'll get her out now.' There was another pause. 'Has she been abducted by the mad man who cuts his victims fingers off and rips their hearts out in graveyards?'

'We think so.' There was no time for explanations and Ben had just put into words his worst fears. He put the phone down and took a deep breath. Ben had also provided the final piece of the puzzle. He knew where Daniel Roberts would be heading.

And Ben would work it out too, if he hadn't already.

★

'Where are you taking me, Daniel?' Her head had cleared as she watched the roads streaming through the sat nav on the dashboard.

'You'll see soon enough. We're nearly there now.' He'd taken the gag away so they could speak. And speak he had. It was as if he wanted to bare his soul to her; to tell her everything about his family, his motivations, how his mother and father had named him Michal Nowak, meaning 'who is like God' and how they'd scrimped to pay for his training as a priest, thereby sealing his fate. From the moment they'd watched proudly as he'd sworn his allegiance to God, he'd been trapped. That life was never what he hoped for, longed for, dreamt of, but it was all he'd ever known. He was never allowed to live a normal life, to love, marry, father children. Instead he had to be 'father' to all, loved in his celibacy, admired for the oath he'd taken, but never, ever allowed to be normal.

He'd loved so many times; some before he'd come to this country, some afterwards. He'd fallen in love with Susan years before, but he was just there to conduct the service when what he had really wanted to do was marry her himself. She'd broken his heart; ripped it from his chest, like some before and many afterwards... JJ, Tanisha, others whose names he could not remember, some that would follow.

He'd been tempted many times to give up his calling, his faith, but each time he'd been about to he'd thought of his parents and the look of pride in their eyes as they'd watched him kneel to be blessed by bishops, even the pope. Since their deaths, all that remained of them was a golden box in the shape of an altar, in which he kept his precious memories. It was presented to him on his ordination as a testament to their continuing love for him. It was the only material possession left from his previous life. Otherwise all he had was hatred, loathing and injustice.

'Do you think they'd be proud of you now?'

'I'm not troubled anymore about what they would think. They are dead and their bodies are just dust blown in the wind. I don't care what you think either. I did, but not anymore. I wanted to know all about you, who you really were, your family, where you liked to go...' He tailed off but all the time he drove.

Charlie recognised each road. It was a journey that she could almost do with her eyes closed. At the last junction she saw a sign that gave her hope, but it also served to reinforce where the final destination was to be. It was the place that she visited every Wednesday morning.

Jamie's graveyard was cloaked in darkness when the dark blue Vauxhall Vectra estate pulled into the car park.

She'd only realised exactly where they were heading after he'd taken the left-hand turn at the start of the village. The road led solely to the church and a few remote houses further on towards the end of the track.

'You followed me here the other day, didn't you? I knew something was wrong. I could feel it.'

Roberts nodded. 'I wanted to know everything about you.'

He switched the headlights off and sat in silence, gazing into the shadows as if watching and listening for the slightest sound or movement. None came.

After several minutes he climbed out of the driver's seat, hoisted his bag up on to his shoulder and came round to her side, unclipping the safety belt. She moved her foot out and he pulled her up, taking her by the arm and roughly leading her through the gates. The stillness of the graveyard was overwhelming, the atmosphere taut, but even though she knew what Roberts was intending, somehow, she also knew that whatever happened, it would be all right.

Roberts was obviously not going to replace the gag, they were too far from civilisation to worry about anybody hearing her scream. Just her arms remained bound; he would be relying on his speed and strength. The knowledge that she would be able to talk calmed her further. It was an ability that Hunter had both commended her for and moaned about in equal measures. It might be all that would get her out of this.

She wondered for a second whether her boss had even found the scribbled letters, whether he had worked out who she'd meant, whether he had any idea where she was now. She recalled his instruction to go in to Atkins. If the worst happened, she knew he'd never forgive himself, but he needn't worry, she'd have gone in anyway.

'Come this way.' She indicated the footpath towards her brother's grave and Roberts seemed happy to oblige. She needed to keep her captor talking for as long as she could if she were to stand any chance of survival; but if that failed she wanted to be as close to Jamie as possible if she was going to die.

*

Daniel Roberts felt at home in these sorts of places. He'd spent half his life coming and going from them, seeing lifeless bodies laid out ready for burial, watching as they were embalmed, committing the dead to the soil. The fact that bodies were buried beneath him did not bother him in the slightest. Bodies were just vessels for the soul; they were just the mortal remains, left when the soul went to wherever God saw fit. The souls lived within the heart and carried the essence of the person, their love, their purity, their goodness, or their badness.

Charlie Stafford's heart was bad. She had chosen another over him and now she deserved to die. He had enjoyed the drive with his victim, although he was the real victim in all of this, time and time again. So he'd told her everything, enjoying the fact that she was far less comatose than the others, having fought off his attempt to drug her further.

Now they were at her final resting place she'd become placid, almost accepting. He'd thought she would have more fight, but actually she was just the same as the rest. She knew she'd sinned against him and now she was ready to pay the price and surrender. He held her arm, allowing her to lead the way but he still didn't know if he trusted her.

The small secluded copse was perfect. He watched as she sat down on a gravestone and closed her eyes momentarily. He set down his bag and started to lay out his tools, one by one on a small square of plastic. The sky was dark, clouds blocking any light from the moon. He pulled out a small, powerful lamp and switched it on, bathing the copse in an iridescent glow that captured the greens and browns of the autumn leaves. It was as beautiful a place to die as one could imagine. Her disloyalty would be avenged within the sanctuary of a line of conifers and leafy shrubs. Her deceitful ways ended on the point of a stiletto blade.

There was no one to see them and no one to hear her cry.

Ben lay in the bushes, next to Meg, watching the man's preparations. Charlie looked so serene and beautiful, perched high on the gravestone. Her abductor was unkempt, his hair bushy and wild, his eyes wild too. He had never met the man and yet he wanted to kill him for what he was putting her through, but he was under strict instructions to lie low.

From the moment Hunter had spoken and confirmed the direction that Charlie was heading, he'd known instinctively where the mad man in his sights now would take her. There was only one graveyard important to Charlie. He and Meg had jumped in her car, hoping to get to the church first. Luckily they had and he was now able to report back to Hunter what was happening.

Meg had refused to allow him to act alone. Charlie was her daughter and she would not sit back and wait. She would fight to the death for her, if needed. She'd lost one child; she was not about to lose another. He couldn't argue, he would have done the same.

It had been Meg's idea to leave her old Fiesta at the end of the lane as a sign. It wouldn't do for the man to get spooked at seeing another vehicle by the church and head off into unknown territory, but if Charlie did spot it she would know that help was on its way. Meg was calm and measured, while he was strong and impetuous. They were a good combination.

Meg had led them to within sight of Jamie's grave, instinctively knowing that would be where Charlie would want to be. She was right again. As soon as they'd heard the whine of the engine in the car park, they'd known they were correct and had texted Hunter with an update of exactly where to come and a description of the layout as best as they could. It had taken a while before they'd seen the pair making their way towards Jamie's grave. Ben had been tempted to dive straight in, but Meg had stayed him. They had to be patient and every second they waited meant there was more chance that Hunter would get to them.

His phone light illuminated with another text message. It was hidden underneath an old blanket Meg had pulled from her car. They both squinted at what was written.

2 mins ETA. I have armed police with me. We will stop at end of the road and come to you on foot. Stay down out of the way and watch. Let me know asap if the situation changes.

Will do. Meg texted back. Ben wished with all his heart it could be sooner.

He looked back toward Charlie and the man, lit up as they were in the glow of the lamp. They were just beginning to speak. He could hear the ebb and flow of conversation but couldn't hear exactly what was being said. His hands were shaking with cold and fear. Meg put a hand on his and gave it a squeeze but nothing could reassure him.

Two minutes was two minutes too long. He wanted to rescue her now. He would never forget the look on Charlie's face as she led her kidnapper to the copse; so controlled, so calm and so totally at odds with the memories that were flashing through his brain and the sense of panic that was building.

Charlie could see that Roberts was almost ready. His preparations were coming to an end. It was almost time for him to begin the ritual. Her hands were bound tightly and although her feet were still free it would be hopeless to try to run. It was pitch black away from the copse; she would surely trip and couldn't even reach out to break her fall. He would easily catch her and then who knows what he would do.

His MO was to remove a finger before the knife through the heart. If she provoked him, would he torture her further, remove each finger one by one, perhaps do worse, to teach her a lesson.

No, her only hope was to keep him talking. She'd seen her mother's car, so with any luck... help was on its way. She could only pray that was the case.

'You said you wanted to know all about me, Daniel.'

'I don't care for you now. I did, until I saw you with that man.'

'But that man is my brother.' She was going to take a risk. 'Look. Did you not wonder why I came to this spot? Why I brought you here too?'

She moved her leg slightly, taking care to show only the name etched in the stone. 'This grave belongs to my husband, Jamie Stafford. He was in the forces, fighting; he was killed in action a few years ago. My brother got me through my grief. He has been there for me, persuading me to move on, encouraging me to go out and find someone else. I hadn't seen him for a while so when I heard he was waiting outside my office, I couldn't wait to see him.'

Roberts stopped what he was doing and stared towards her. It was as if he was trying to read her mind, to work out if she was lying.

'I didn't want to think about seeing another man for ages, but my brother has been telling me I can't spend my life pushing any future prospects away. You have to grasp love where you can. I was starting to look.'

'You looked at me. I saw you watching. I could see it in your eyes that you found me attractive.'

'I did, Daniel. I still do.' It was all she could think of to keep him talking. 'Who knows what could have happened if you hadn't jumped to the wrong conclusion. What still could? The police will think Vincent was the killer. He knew all three victims. He had the motivation and he left the note. You could go back to being Father Michal, take me out of the country. Pretend that Daniel Roberts never existed.'

She could hear a distant rumble of vehicles, the sound of a door shutting. Roberts appeared not to notice. He was frozen, concentrating on her every word. For a moment she thought he believed her, but then his face creased.

'Maybe we could have but it's too late now. You know too much.'

He bent down and picked up the stiletto blade, the hunting knife and the rib cutters, carefully placing them on top of a nearby stone, within easy reach.

Lurching forward suddenly, he grabbed her hands, yanking her off the gravestone and forcing her to her knees.

She heard a shout and turned to see Ben running towards them.

'Leave her alone.'

'Who are you?' Roberts' voice was icy and stopped Ben in his tracks. Quickly he reached across and picked up the hunting knife, pressing it to her throat. Charlie held her breath. Ben's voice wavered as he looked towards her, his eyes wide with panic.

'I'm her friend,' he said.

He knew it. He had almost believed her. She had nearly persuaded him. But she had lied. He had seen it in the way this man looked towards her at her office, like a bridegroom setting eyes on his bride for the first time as she walked down the aisle. He'd watched that expression so many times before. He knew what the man was about to say, before he even heard the words. He wasn't her brother; he wasn't even her friend, he was her boyfriend.

Glancing up from where she knelt, he saw the writing on the stone.

JAMIE STAFFORD, AGED TEN YEARS, TAKEN TOO EARLY.

So the grave couldn't have been her husband's.

His anger surged out of control. She was just the same as the others. A lying, scheming bitch who took his words, his trust, everything he'd offered, and cast it aside. How could he even have started to believe that he loved her, that she might have loved him? He saw a woman step into the clearing behind the man.

'Please let her go,' the woman said. She looked older, her eyes filled with fear, her voice trembling as she spoke but he didn't care.

The man took a step forward but then froze, paralysed, his hands held out as if pleading with him to stop. But he wouldn't stop; he couldn't stop.

'You come one step closer and she dies.'

The policewoman was kneeling at his feet and he had to teach her a lesson. He had to have his way.

'Show me your hands now,' he shouted, pulling the knife closer to her neck, nicking the skin as he did so, feeling her wince. She did as instructed, lifting her hands up, still bound together. One false movement and he would kill her. He grabbed her left hand, pulling her fingers out so they were straight.

He saw the man's look of horror as he reached across, swapping the knife for the rib cutters. He aimed them at her hand, screaming at the man as he did so. 'You'll never put a ring on this finger!'

And then all hell let loose.

Hunter was appalled as he saw Charlie's finger flying off into the grass. He heard her cry and saw Ben launch himself towards her, pushing her flat on her face out of Roberts' grasp.

Roberts reared up, silhouetted against the light, grabbing the hunting knife again.

He heard the roar of warning from right beside him and then the shots; two in quick succession sending Daniel Roberts slamming into a tree behind and the knife spinning off out of his grasp.

The armed officer rushed forward still pointing the gun at Roberts but he wasn't going anywhere. Hunter was right behind him. Another officer ran up and patted Roberts down but he had no other weapons. His eyes were still open, wildly scanning the scene. Hunter could see the rise and fall of his chest. Roberts was still breathing but he was no further threat.

Charlie was sitting up now, propped against Jamie's gravestone, her face white with shock, blood pumping from her left hand. Meg was already with her, lifting her arm and tearing her shirt to wrap around her daughter's hand. Her face too was pale with alarm, but her medical training was kicking in and she was taking control of the injuries, dispatching Ben to find the severed finger. It was a cold night and it looked to have been a clean cut; hopefully it could be reattached if they could get her to a hospital quickly.

The screech of ambulance sirens were loud as several sped down the lane into the car park. The beams of torches lit up the whole bloody spectacle, as the paramedics ran across and took over from the armed officers who were keeping Roberts alive.

Hunter made sure Charlie was taken first. She was his priority. She refused to be carried, walking with Ben and Meg on either side. Her finger was transported, carefully wrapped with a sterile dressing, in ice by Paul. He was her closest friend in the office, so he would be accompanying them all in the ambulance. If anyone could put a smile back on her face it was Paul.

A cannula had already been inserted in the back of her right hand and the painkillers were starting to take effect. Some colour was creeping back into her cheeks and she was brightening up.

Hunter waited for her to settle.

'You OK?' The words sounded pathetic. He wanted to say so much more. He wanted to say how sorry he was for sending her in to deal with Vincent Atkins on her own. He wanted to say sorry for not realising who their killer was, and for getting to the churchyard too late for her, but he was never any good with words.

She grinned back at him, her expression returning to the one she usually wore. 'I'll be fine, guv. In a few hours' time the surgeons will have my finger sewn back on and it'll be back fully functioning, as will I, though it might take a little while longer to get my mouth back in full working order. For once it couldn't save me. I had to rely on Jamie sending me some guardian angels.'

Charlie smiled again and waved her bandaged hand, as the paramedic shut the door, taking them all to the hospital.

Hunter swallowed hard at the knot of guilt that was rising up in his throat, threatening to choke him. He felt as far removed from being a guardian angel as it was possible to be.

41

It was almost midday by the time Charlie woke. She tried to open her eyes but her eyelids were still heavy, stuck to her cheeks like glue. She saw the shadow of a hand move across her eye line and a beautifully scented cloth was wiped gently around her face.

'This is like déjà vu,' she recognised her mother's voice through the haze. 'You need to stop getting yourself into trouble. My heart won't cope if it happens again.'

'Thankfully you still have yours, Charlie. I wondered at one stage whether you were going to lose that, as well as your finger.'

She blinked her eyes open at the sound of Ben's voice. It was all coming back to her in a rush. Her hand was covered in bandages, brilliant white and sterile, like her surroundings. It lay by the side of her on the bed, as if it wasn't part of her body, a large unwieldy attachment that was connected but not working as it should.

'It has to stay in bandages for today while it's still swollen and freshly stitched but they'll want you moving it as soon as you're able. Oh, and before you start thinking you can go into training for the Paralympics, you can't. The surgeon who stitched it back on thinks you'll make a full recovery within a few months.'

'So you'll be back making tea for us all before you know it.'

The door had swung open on its hinges and a large bunch of flowers was thrust around the frame, closely followed by Hunter, Bet, Paul, Naz and Sabira clutching an equally large box of chocolates.

'Mrs H would have been here too, but I told her she had to stay at home and have my dinner ready.' Hunter winked and laughed. Gone were the ruddy cheeks and bulging vein on his forehead.

'You've cheered up a bit since we last saw you. There's nothing like a bit of good news to chase away the blues.' Meg shook her head at Hunter. 'If I didn't know you better I'd think you were telling the truth there.'

'He was.' They all answered in unison and laughed, prompting a nurse to pop her head round the door and scold them, which only served to make them laugh more.

The pressure of the last few days was over, like the steam from a boiling cauldron being gradually released, so the jokes flowed in true coppers' style.

'She's pointing the finger at you, boss.' Paul was the first. They all groaned.

'Get your sticky fingers off those chocolates,' Naz joined in, directing her comment at Sabira who was already opening the box she'd just brought in.

Bet shook her head and bustled over to Charlie, bending down to kiss her on the cheek. 'I'm glad it worked this time.'

'What?' Hunter looked quizzical.

'Having our fingers crossed.' She burst out laughing, her cheeks burning red. Comedy wasn't her greatest talent but in the present atmosphere everybody was laughing at everything.

'Oi, that's my phrase,' Charlie grinned at her favourite agony aunt.

'Ooh, Bet, you've just hit the "finger" nail on the head.' Sabira squawked with laughter at her own pun, passing the chocolates round to everyone.

The room quietened as they all popped their chosen flavour in their mouths. Charlie looked round from her hospital bed at each of her colleagues, stood shoulder to shoulder with Ben and Meg. They were all good friends and they'd had a lucky escape... again. This time even Ben and Meg had played their part.

'So, anyway Charlie, you'll be pleased to know it'll be down to me to deal with the Independent Police Complaints Commission investigation when it happens. They might want to discuss our tactics and decisions.' Hunter raised his eyebrows at her with a grin, before suddenly becoming serious. 'But really, we're just glad you're going to be OK and we thought we'd fill you in with what's been happening while you've been in here.'

'Skiving.' Paul couldn't resist.

'Well I was going to say that, but we all know that couldn't be further from the truth. If Charlie hadn't sweet-talked Caz, and you girls hadn't taken your lives in your hands to catch Miller, we would never have found Feliks

Makary. And if we hadn't found him, Charlie here wouldn't have spotted that note with the registration numbers on it, or the mysterious initials FM. Charlie, how did you work out who FM was? I presume you were interrupted when you wrote "F.M. is D" and you were going to write Daniel Roberts?'

Charlie frowned. 'Well, I knew Father Antonio was hiding something when I spoke to him about Tanisha. So I phoned Joan Whitmore and she told me about Tash making allegations against Father Antonio and a Father Michal, who was there before him. To be honest I was more suspicious of Father Antonio and was going to speak to you about him. We hadn't caught up with Makary and seen the note at that stage, so I didn't say anything to you about Father Michal because I thought he'd left the country and it was irrelevant.'

'Well that makes all of us then that have missed something or seen something important and kept it to ourselves. Can we make a point of passing on everything we see, or don't see, next time round? Even if we think it's irrelevant!' Hunter winked at Naz and Sabira. 'Go on.'

'I didn't know what Father Michal looked like but then Roberts made a strange comment in Atkins' office, saying he wasn't who we thought he was. He took his glasses off and pulled his hair back out of his face and I remembered a photo in the church of a clean-cut priest kneeling before the Pope. I suddenly realised it must be Father Michal and he and Daniel Roberts were one and the same person, but he looked so different. I would never have guessed how much hair and glasses could alter someone's appearance. I didn't have time to write Father Michal's full name down and I thought it wouldn't make sense anyway as none of us were really aware of him. And I knew Feliks Makary held the key, so I took a gamble on you getting it out of him and just scribbled FM down. Thankfully you worked it out.'

'With a little persuasion.' Hunter coughed. Charlie grinned and continued.

'Poor Vincent Atkins was just a distraction but one that Roberts could frame. How is he?'

Sabira took over. 'I went to visit him earlier at Mayday Hospital. He's going to make a full recovery. Well at least physically. He said Roberts phoned and told him Molly was at the school and wanted to talk to him, but when he arrived, Roberts said that she didn't want to know him anymore because of his affair with Susan. He didn't want to live without his wife so he just did everything Roberts told him. He was happy to die. Roberts wrote the note for him and left the drugs to try and frame him.'

'Do you think Molly will take him back?' Charlie remembered his voice down the phone, so despairing and desperate.

'Who knows? He's a broken man now. I doubt he'll ever hold down a job, never mind repair a marriage.'

'What about the others? We were sure Mickey Barton was in the frame. He ticked every box. You had him over a barrel in his interview.' Charlie turned towards Hunter but Paul took over.

'Emma phoned this morning. She wanted to speak to you, Charlie. I said you weren't around but I would pass a message on. She told me that her dad had turned up on their doorstep last night, probably when he was bailed out. She wouldn't talk to him at first but then he'd started to cry. Emma was crying too as she spoke. She said that Mickey had confessed that he had taken the engagement ring from her mum. He'd been letting himself in and out of the house, stalking her. He couldn't bear the fact that he'd lost her. He still loved her and had taken the ring a couple of days before she died because it was sentimental to him and made him feel close to her. When he realised that the police thought Susan had been wearing the ring when she was killed, he panicked and tried to hide it.' Paul shook his head. 'Well, he did hide it. He was just unlucky that the search team found it. He told Emma that he was going to give it to her when everything settled down but he couldn't just yet, because we have it.'

'He's a silly man. He shouldn't have tried to conceal the truth from us but he'll get the ring back.' Hunter leant against the wall.

'He won't get his life back though,' Charlie propped herself up on her pillow, wincing as she moved her arm. So much had happened in the last few hours. 'But then perhaps it had been slipping away for a long time. Presumably Emma and Mickey Junior will forgive their father, he's all they've got left. Though I doubt whether he'd ever have been able to patch things up with Susan; they seemed a bit of a mismatched couple anyway.'

'Talking about mismatched couples,' Hunter pushed himself back away from the wall. 'My favourite two have just been charged and kept in custody.'

'What, Oscar Abrahams and Arthur Billingham?'

'Yep. Some of the team that came to Hastings with us got to work on the property that was seized, while we were all otherwise engaged. It seems like they are part of a large paedophile network, working through a secret chat room. The tech guys are still trying to unravel it. Abrahams was actually telling the truth when he said he didn't have the car at the time of Susan's murder. He'd lent it to Billingham while his own car was being repaired. Billingham had travelled across the channel from Dover and driven to Amsterdam. When he returned, he brought back a load of child pornography and they'd met at that Travelodge in Hastings to arrange for it to be sent or collected by other members. The team have checked with the hotel and it appears they've rented rooms there several times. It's a regular trip, the sick fucks. Abrahams thought he was being clever and we'd never catch him, because none of the really bad stuff was at his flat.'

'Except the recording of that young boy.' She thought back to when they'd burst in on him.

'Yes, poor little mite; the child sexual exploitation unit have taken the job on. They're trying to identify the boy and many other kids, and even babies, shown on other recordings. We've got the two of them kept in custody on holding charges while the tapes are gone through properly and graded. Justin Latchmere's face was priceless when I told him his client was not being released. It'll be the start of something big. And all because Abrahams just happened to own a dark blue Vauxhall Vectra estate and some bent copper gave Makary his registration number, to use as one of his fake vehicle IDs.'

'Really?'

'That's what Makary said. I have to say, I usually hate bent coppers, like the rest of us do, but on this occasion, I wouldn't mind shaking their hand. They've done us a favour getting those two off the streets.'

'I wonder if they'd had dealings with Abrahams previously and gave it to Makary on purpose?'

'It's an interesting theory. It might do Makary well to have a little think about whether he might like to talk to us about stuff in a more official way, especially if he knows about corrupt Old Bill. It wouldn't do him any harm at all to get a little assistance when he comes to court. He's already helped solve a triple murder.'

'At least triple.' Charlie lapsed into thought. 'On the subject of our murderer, what about Daniel Roberts, Father Michal, Michal Nowak, whatever he's really called. Will he live?'

'Yes, he will. He was shot in the shoulder and upper arm. He's in surgery as we speak, with an armed guard. Naz and Sabira found an address for him but there's nothing much there, a few belongings in a house he shares with several other teachers. He's not saying anything and it's unlikely he will.'

'He said quite a lot to me.' Charlie's head was buzzing with all the updates, but now she needed to know the job was complete. She started to swing her legs off the bed.

'I need to get out of here.'

'Oh no you don't,' Meg was at her side in a shot. 'You need to stay exactly where the doctors say.'

'And where do you think that is?' The door was pushed open by a man in a white coat. 'Woah, this room's rather full. Off you all go... Now! I need to speak to my patient.'

Charlie couldn't help grinning as they all filed out obediently. What was it about a man in a white coat that stopped any argument dead? It didn't faze her though.

'Guvnor,' she whispered to Hunter, as the room cleared of all except her, Meg and the surgeon. 'Don't disappear. I won't be a minute.'

42

'Now it's your turn to wait. And I mean wait here. I won't be long.'

Hunter wagged his finger at Charlie, before striding into Brixton Custody to collect the sat nav from Daniel Roberts' car for her to check. With the exception of Paul, who was to be their driver, the rest of the team had said their farewells and melted away back to work. Now with her colleagues gone, there was just her, Paul, Meg and Ben sitting in the police minibus. Her arm was held up in a sling and was still sore but the tablets were keeping the worst of the pain at bay.

She decided to do as she was told.

It hadn't taken long to get to the station, after the surgeon had finally capitulated to her nagging and agreed to allow her home, on the strict proviso that Meg took care of her and she was brought back on a daily basis to have the dressings changed and her progress monitored. Meg had been sceptical at first but understood there was no point arguing. Both she and Hunter knew what Charlie was like and it was not so very different from either of them.

Ben was sitting on the rear seat. She'd noticed how quiet he'd been throughout the whole time the others had been with her in the hospital. While they'd all been laughing and joking he'd looked to be deep in thought. She turned to her mother.

'Give us a minute, Mum.'

Meg nodded, gave Paul's arm a tweak and then together they disappeared towards a nearby shop.

Ben turned straight towards her, his voice sounding strangulated. 'It was my fault, wasn't it, the fact he chopped your finger off? If I'd stayed put he might not have done it.'

She climbed into the back and squeezed up to him. She hadn't told anyone what exactly had happened at the graveside for precisely that reason. Ben was not to know that the moment he'd identified himself as her friend, and not her brother, Roberts would have known she was trying to deceive him. Ben would never know because she would never say. Anyway, it was just as much her fault, for allowing Roberts to see Jamie's age etched on the gravestone. Jamie could never have been her husband and Roberts would have been certain that she had lied.

'He looked straight at me Charlie, and said, "You'll never put a ring on this finger." Then he chopped it off.' Ben's voice was little more than a whisper. He looked distraught.

'No Ben, that's not true. He'd already grabbed me. He would have done it anyway. He'd admitted a lot to me on the journey to the church. He couldn't have let me live.'

'But he wouldn't have cut your finger off.'

'Yes he would, because he's cut all his other victims' fingers off. We think he likes to keep them. We haven't found any as yet. I would have been no different. So please Ben, stop it. You pushed me out of the way of his knife. You saved my life.'

She put her arm around him and held him close. His body was rigid, his muscles tightly under control, as was his expression, devoid of any emotion.

'Ben, I wouldn't be here without you. You worked out where Roberts was taking me and got there first. You told Hunter everything he needed to know. Without you, I would probably be dead.'

He relaxed slightly, his shoulders slumping forward.

She looked at his face; the worry lines creased into his forehead, the dark covering of stubble, the haunted look that still flitted across his eyes at intervals, the fatigue from staying at her side through every minute of the night and into the new day. She looked at his hands which still wore the dressings from his attempts to help her catch Miller. He remained staring ahead while she took in his every feature, before leaning across and kissing him tenderly on the cheek.

'You know, you once said that you wanted to be my knight in shining armour? Well, last night you were.'

Ben couldn't even bear to look at Charlie. Just one glance at her arm sent him reeling back to the graveyard, hearing the words, watching as her finger flew through the air to land on the cold grass. He'd picked it up, a small part of the woman he loved, and he'd known that if she was ever to return his love, he'd have to watch his ring slide over the hideous scar that marked where he'd let her down. He didn't know if he could ever do it.

As that thought ran through his mind, so too did the memory of the shots; loud, staccato, startling, stirring up the air all around them. Bang, bang; bullets flying, people screaming, smoke, panic, pain, just like before. Just like the times he was trying to forget.

He could feel her close, her warmth against his body, her hair against his shoulder, but all he could think about was the cold of her severed finger in the grass and the pain in her eyes, as her enemy chopped through her skin.

'That's Miller. Off to court and then prison, for a good long time, thanks to you two.'

Hunter jumped back into the front seat of the minibus and turned to where Charlie and Ben sat, pointing out a large white prison van turning slowly out of the yard, its tiny windows allowing its occupants only a small amount of natural sunlight.

'Hope he rots in there for what he's done.' Charlie watched as the van pulled further away. 'Although, rather ironically, it might be him I have to thank for saving my life, leading us to Makary and his links with Father Michal.'

'More by luck than judgement. He would have quite happily seen you both off himself, if he'd had the chance.'

'I bet Moses is pleased.'

Hunter held the sat nav up and beckoned Charlie up to join him. 'He is, and he wants to speak to you when you get a minute, Charlie. Naz gave him a quick ring while we were interviewing Makary, to tell him that Miller had been caught and he was safe to move back into his house, but she didn't tell him the details. She thought you should.'

'It'll be a pleasure.' She really meant it.

Meg and Paul strolled back to the minibus. Meg climbed into the back, allowing Charlie to clamber up to the front seat between Hunter and Paul.

Hunter passed the sat nav to Charlie. 'Right, what do you want this for?'

She switched it on and waited for it to load.

'I haven't fully debriefed you yet on what Roberts told me on the way to Jamie's graveyard.' She didn't wait for an answer. 'Well, to cut a long story short, his parents wanted him to be a priest from a young age, which meant he could never marry or have a proper relationship. They presented him with an ornamental gold box in the shape of an altar on his ordination and apparently this is the only thing he has left from those days, to keep his precious memories in. I presume it wasn't at the address you searched? You said there was nothing of note found?'

'No, that's right.'

'So he must have the box hidden somewhere else, maybe he has another address, and I'm guessing the "precious memories" he was talking about might be his victims' fingers.'

She shuddered subconsciously, lifting her arm in the sling. The sat nav was fully loaded now so she scrolled through to its history.

'I was hoping this other address might show up in his previous journeys.'

A list of locations appeared on the screen.

'Look,' Hunter pointed to an entry. 'That's Downs cemetery in Brighton, where JJ was murdered.'

'And look at the address shown directly underneath it. Do you recognise that one? Is it the digs that you went to earlier? Or could it be where he stores his tools and trophies?'

Hunter shook his head. 'That's not the one we know about.'

He didn't have to say another word; they were already on the way.

The address shown was a large house, but it didn't take long to track down a resident who had seen Roberts coming and going to his room. He usually carried a large bag and he would turn up in the evening, stay a while and then leave again.

The door to the flat was held shut by a large padlock, but Paul made light work of it with a set of bolt cutters and the enforcer, splintering the wood completely on the first swing of the heavy red lump of metal.

Charlie, Hunter and Paul stepped through into a small room full of old furniture, bedecked with the trappings of a chapel. Burnt out incense sticks still laid in metal holders, the scent of frankincense hanging heavy in the air. Her attention was drawn immediately to the mantelpiece on which a gold ornamental box stood, in between photos of the man who had tried to kill her, and his parents.

Hunter pulled some gloves on and lifted it carefully down off its stand, turning it round in his hands to examine each side. He placed it down on a small table and reached into the back of it, his fingers following each nook and cranny inside. With a slight movement, she heard the sound of a catch being sprung and the top of the altar being lifted out of its position. She knew what was coming but as Hunter lifted the Perspex container from the centre of the altar, the sight still sickened her to the core.

He turned it round in the air in front of them. They had expected to see three, but as they stood mutely counting to seven, they all knew that it was by sheer good luck the number of fingers they were staring at was not eight.

It was another hour before Paul dropped Charlie, Ben and Meg off at the family house in Lingfield. It had been a sombre journey, with all the occupants of the minibus deep in thought.

Hunter had agreed to stay at Roberts' address while awaiting the Scenes of Crime Officer. In addition to the body parts they'd found, the room looked to contain many items of forensic interest that would keep Roberts imprisoned for life. The families of his known victims would be informed of his arrest, and as soon as he was released from hospital he'd be interviewed in an attempt to identify the others. It would be questionable whether Roberts would even remember their names, but Charlie knew the team would try their hardest to find out their identities. If the remains stayed unidentified they would at least be given a Christian burial.

As Charlie walked into the kitchen she knew she was safe at last. No harm could come to her within these walls. She turned to give Meg a hug, as she put the kettle on.

'Thanks for helping Ben out at Jamie's cemetery, Mum. Do you realise it's the first time we've both been there together for years? Maybe the two of us could go on his next anniversary?'

She felt her mother tense slightly and realised sadly that the barrier between them, so recently broken down, had crept back up again.

'Maybe... we'll have to see, love. Now what do you two want? Hot chocolate?'

She watched as her mother busied herself with the drinks. Any hope she had of sharing the pain of her brother's loss was dashed again. She turned away, realising she needed to do one last thing.

'Ben, go and make yourself comfortable. I'll just ring Moses and then I'll be with you.'

The mobile was answered immediately, Moses' soft, gravelly voice purring his thanks down the phone line. It felt so good to know that he was back in his house with Claudette, where all their memories were, where he too could now feel safe. Everybody needed somewhere to hide away from the world.

She ended the call with his gratitude ringing in her ears, when the calm was broken by a scream. She froze at the sound. It was horrifying but she knew instinctively where it had come from.

Running into the lounge she watched helplessly as Ben burrowed further in behind the cushions of the settee. His eyes were closed in sleep, but his body was awake, his brow furrowed in terror, his hands locked over his ears.

She knew with every shake of his body, every whimper of fear, exactly what she was witnessing. She had longed for his recovery, watching with delight each moment of progress, every step towards their shared goal, but now the nightmares had returned. He'd saved her life but forfeited his own, at least for the moment. There was nothing she could say to heal his pain and she didn't try.

They would fight this thing together.

Slowly and with great care, she lowered herself down, moulding her body tenderly against his and held him tight.

Acknowledgements

Thank you to everyone who bought my first book, *Mummy's Favourite*, and have left reviews, good or bad. I have been truly overwhelmed by the comments I have received. The good ones are great to read and very motivating. I have so loved writing the stories myself and it is extremely satisfying to see they have given you pleasure reading them. The bad ones give me food for thought and have made me focus on parts of my writing that need improvement. There is so much to learn. Being a copper for thirty-five years teaches you little more about literature than the format of evidential statements; though hearing a few of the defence stories and mitigation has assisted with the fictional aspects.

Since retiring recently I am enjoying the opportunity to spend more time planning, plotting and composing my characters' next adventures and hope you will follow them in their endeavours.

Many thanks especially to the team at Aria, in particular Caroline Ridding, Sarah Ritherdon, Nia Beynon, Jade

Craddock and Yasemin Turan, whose faith and encouragement got me started. Their motivation and encouragement both for creating the stories, understanding the editing and getting to grips with social media has been inspirational.

My agent, Judith Murdoch, continues to provide a solid base of knowledge and support and for that I'm also very grateful and send my thanks.

My partner, family and friends are owed my biggest debt of gratitude, for their unswerving enthusiasm and ability to put up with my nervous excitement at how my novels and retirement are progressing. It's been a momentous year. Thank you for joining me on my journey.

Hello from Aria

We hope you enjoyed this book! If you did let us know, we'd love to hear from you.

We are Aria, a dynamic digital-first fiction imprint from award-winning independent publishers Head of Zeus. At heart, we're committed to publishing fantastic commercial fiction – from romance and sagas to crime, thrillers and historical fiction. Visit us online and discover a community of like-minded fiction fans!

We're also on the look out for tomorrow's superstar authors. So, if you're a budding writer looking for a publisher, we'd love to hear from you. You can submit your book online at ariafiction.com/ we-want-read-your-book

You can find us at:
Email: aria@headofzeus.com
Website: www.ariafiction.com
Submissions: www.ariafiction.com/ we-want-read-your-book

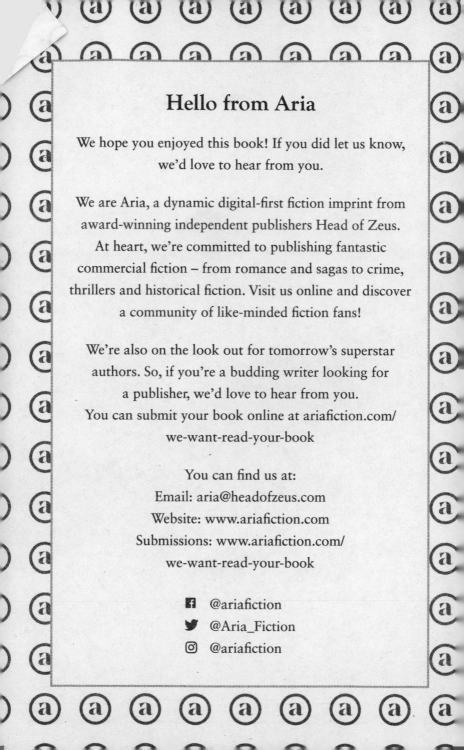 @ariafiction
@Aria_Fiction
@ariafiction